SUMMERLAND

Octobre 16 2001

Happy Birthday Julia

love Keely.

George Ryga (1965)   Photo: Jack Dietrich

SUMMERLAND

George Ryga

Edited by Ann Kujundzic

Talonbooks • Vancouver • 1992

copyright © 1992 George Ryga & Associates Inc.
Introduction copyright © 1992 Ann Kujundzic

published with the assistance of The Canada Council

Talonbooks
201/1019 East Cordova Street
Vancouver, British Columbia
Canada, V6A 1M8

Typeset in Century by Pièce de Résistance Ltée. Printed and bound in
Canada by Hignell Printing.

First printing: November 1992

Canadian Cataloguing in Publication Data

Ryga, George, 1932-1987.
  Summerland

  ISBN 0-88922-313-0

  I. Kujundzic, Ann. II. Title.
PS8585.Y5A6 1992   C818'.5409   C92-091267-2
PR9199.3.R93A6 1992

Notes on Publication

"Theatre in Canada: A Viewpoint on Its Development and Future" was written for the first issue of *Canadian Theatre Review*, #1 (Winter 1974)

"The Need for a Mythology" appeared in *Canadian Theatre Review*, #16 (Fall 1977)

"Memories and Some Lessons Learned" appeared in *Canadian Theatre Review* #36 (Fall 1982)

"Lepa" appeared as "Visit from the Pension Lady" in *The Newcomers*, published by McClelland and Stewart, 1979

"Lepa" is an earlier version of *Letter to My Son*, published by Turnstone Press, 1984

The version of "Village of Melons" appearing in this book is an edited version from the following two sources:
"Village of Melons" originally appeared as an article in *Canadian Literature*, #95 (Winter 1982)

"Village of Melons" was included in *British Columbia: Visions of the Promised Land*. Flight Press, 1986

"Resurrection" was included in *The Moosehead Anthology*, published by DC Books, 1989

Acknowledgements

When I undertook the assignment to edit *Summerland*, I did not know what I was getting into. Recalling the many commitments that George Ryga had undertaken during his Okanagan years brought back some joyous memories, but it also brought many painful ones as I retraced the personal, political, community and work-related events that were part of his life.

At the same time, I also had to become familiar with the vast number of articles, editorials, reviews and other writings that have been published about this remarkable man, and this raised many new questions for me. For example, knowing of his alliance and solidarity with Native peoples, and of the continued success and credibility of his play, *The Ecstasy of Rita Joe*, I would now like to be able to ask him how he would approach the thorny problem of "cultural appropriation." As usual, I'm sure he would have both a thoughtful and a unique response.

In carrying out this assignment, which in the end became a rewarding process of discovery and re-discovery, I am indebted first of all to Norma, George's partner and my good friend, whose memory is sharply incisive, and who generously gave me access to the journal which she kept for five years between 1972 and 1977; and to George and Norma's children, who have been open in their responses to my questions. I am also grateful to the many people who have shared with me their information, observations, experiences and memories of George Ryga. My thanks, in particular, to Roxanne Macneil, Ken Smedley, Jim Belsham, Millie Jenkins, Claire Kujundzic, Linda Charles, Bill McCuaig, Shane Dennison, Judy Kujundzic, John Juliani, Nancy Flight, Renee Paris and Hagan Beggs. There are many more whom I could have talked to, but George's friends and colleagues are outrageously numerous.

This work would have been an impossible task without the support and help of Bill Horne, who encouraged me when the going got tough and sifted through masses of notes and interviews with me. I would also like to thank Mary Schendlinger for sharing her editorial skills; Morgan McGuigan, who read and gave comments; and Robin Rennie, who offered perceptive observations.

Finally, I appreciate having had the opportunity to take on such a rewarding project — a challenge offered me by Karl Siegler and Keith Ledbury.

Ann Kujundzic

CONTENTS

INTRODUCTION

I first met George Ryga in 1964 when he and Norma came to visit our studio-workshop in Kelowna. We had immigrated to Canada only a few years earlier and were still feeling isolated, looking for kindred spirits. Meeting the Rygas was a good omen. From the beginning it was obvious we shared some personal and cultural history: struggling with the philosophy and economics of raising young families on an artist's and writer's precarious income; noticing the influences of Slavic backgrounds in the men, and a Scots and Nova Scotia background in the women. But there were subtle differences, which surfaced more slowly, and these were to have a crucial impact on my life.

In particular I remember an early conversation with George, in which we discussed the relevance of art to peoples' lives. Partnered with an artist for over fifteen years, I was having real difficulty in dealing with what I perceived to be his brand of egocentricity, which placed art at the centre of the universe. Social conditioning had indoctrinated me to accept that my personal needs were somehow of little importance in the grand scheme of things. I was confused over my responsibility to "Art" because of my alliance with the "Artist" — and I was desperately wanting to let go of both. George's straightforward response to my dilemma helped me to choose and, later, break free of this relationship. My life opened up in new ways. He had said that the artist's or writer's work was due no greater elevation than the work of any other person. All honest work was equally worthy. A good plumber deserved acknowledgement, as did a good writer, since the craft of the one echoed the skill of the other. It was simply the integrity of the work which counted.

From that time on, I saw George Ryga first and foremost as a very real and remarkable human being, who happened to have the word "writer" attached to his name. As a young man he had made a living at manual labour. An industrial accident, in which he lost most of the fingers of his right hand when he was seventeen years old, gave him further motivation to develop a love for writing which had been growing within him for several years. However, there is little doubt that his fire and energy of spirit could have been equally directed to whatever work he might otherwise have chosen. His direct, warm nature formed the basis upon which I could truly respect both the man and his work, and that was never to change throughout the many years of friendship we were to share.

Summerland contains a number of selected essays, screen plays and radio plays, short stories and a final poem, all of which were written between 1963 and 1987. The essays, each of which was written for a specific audience, are a unique contribution to the larger body of George Ryga's writing. They speak passionately and eloquently of his concerns as a Canadian and as a writer, and even the earliest of these, "The Temporary Arrangement" (commissioned by the Montreal Star), which dates back to 1967, maintains its relevance. In fact, it is in these addresses and essays that his political convictions reveal themselves most clearly and directly.

His Summerland years straddled three decades: the sixties were a storm of struggles and successes; intensive writing, research, travel and teaching catalysed the seventies; disappointments, declining health and unspoken despair overshadowed the eighties. However, it was never as clear-cut as that; it only seems so in retrospect. There were hard times throughout, but George had an irreverent humour and an unshakeable faith in the human spirit that fuelled his hopes and dreams in the most turbulent of times.

Born in Athabasca, of Ukrainian immigrant parents, George inevitably learned the hard skills of survival at a very early age. He knew how to work the earth, grow a garden, tend animals, and how to build a shelter for himself. These were skills in which he took immense pride. The stoney, unforgiving ground of northern Alberta developed in him the stoic habit of coping with adversity, and, even more profoundly, he carried within him the legacy of a work ethic that was to hound him mercilessly for all the days of his life. As his son Sergei observed: "It was as if he felt like a liability if he was idle. Whatever he did, it was not enough. . . ."

The Athabaska Ryga, a companion volume to this present book, fully documents these early years: his first writings, political influences, visits to Europe, and the influences of other writers, interwoven with manual labour, radio and other work. Yet it is worthwhile to touch briefly on the events which eventually led him to move to Summerland.

George Ryga met Norma Campbell, a native of Nova Scotia, in England in 1955. She already had two daughters, Lesley and Tanya, by a previous marriage. When she returned to Canada she first worked as a clinical photographer in a TB Sanitarium in Hamilton, then, upon moving to Edmonton, she obtained work with the provincial laboratory at the University of Alberta. It was in Edmonton that George and Norma got together and set up house. In Norma, George had found the confidence and stability he had lacked in the freelance years of his twenties. He had learned to respect her values and came eventually to rely on her astute perception of the world as a balance to his fiery spirit. It made sense to share a life together.

In taking this step, however, he had also made a conscious choice: his writing now had to accomodate the commitments of a family. Norma encouraged George to stay at home and write while she provided the main means of income until their second son, Sergei, was born in 1963, two years after their first son, Campbell. By this time economic pressures were taking their toll on their growing family, and they decided to move to Summerland as an alternative to an increasingly expensive life in Edmonton.

This small community in the Okanagan Valley appealed to them because it offered the prospect of growing their own food and of living more cheaply, and at that time older properties were readily available for a reasonable price. But perhaps equally important, as Norma recalls, was that "We always thought that artists are privileged people — they are doing what they choose to do. And being at home with our kids more than compensated for the poverty."[1]

Right from the beginning, their home in Summerland became a haven for artists, musicians, young people and their friends and, later, media people, aspiring writers and political refugees. Their door was always open (they never did, in fact, possess a key to it), and the kitchen table with its ever-present coffee pot welcomed the endless streams of callers. George took on a contract with the CBC to provide scripts for television dramas, of which five are included here. These represent some of his finest pieces for television — in particular, "The Tulip Garden," which speaks with great dignity of the simple request of a country woman to be buried in the soil of the garden she had tended with such love. But the CBC contract required he provide three scheduled drafts for each work. As a consistent two-draft writer, he found this to be a tedious and awkward arrangement. Norma recalls an incident when, with a production deadline to meet in September and the third and final script now overdue, a neighbouring farmer called George to help with the apple harvest. George did not hesitate — he dropped his writing and hurried out the door saying, "the apples won't wait!"

Some of my own children spent their school years in the Ryga household — it was their second home. Like so many children, they knew that this was one place where they might freely search for answers to some of the dilemmas they could not bring up in their own families. Both George and Norma

12

had a great capacity for relating to young people, and they had no trouble coming up with some rather audacious suggestions, many of which were not likely to endear them to other parents. One young woman recalls how they encouraged her to go north to find work — on speculation — in the middle of winter, because a free ride was available. This, after all, was the sixties, when young people were questioning traditional assumptions and authority, and George and Norma felt an affinity with them. I remember George, on one occasion, saying rather wistfully, "I sometimes envy this generation its choices — I wish I'd had some of those freedoms when I was growing up. I often feel I didn't really have a boyhood or a teen-age time."

It was partially George's frustration with what he considered the arbitrary rigours of contract-writing that spurred him to explore the field of stage work, and in 1967 he was catapulted to national attention with the first production of *The Ecstasy of Rita Joe* at the Vancouver Playhouse. In speaking of this play, Leonard George later said: "He came with a different answer. I was into revolting against everything, Indians, government and the city. It didn't dawn on me 'til ten years later that where I was trying to get . . . some brilliant men were already there. They were doing something about the kind of change that should take place and I found it very profound that George Ryga, who, you might say, would be on the opposite end of where an Indian is, would come along and write something so powerful . . . and my father [Chief Dan George] was in there, living it out with the other actors."[2]

This success was followed by a commission from the Playhouse to write another play, *Grass and Wild Strawberries*, for the 1969 season, an even greater box office triumph than *The Ecstasy of Rita Joe*, attracting a new audience of mainly young people. Yet even then, in the midst of these triumphs, George had a sense of how fleeting are the moments of success. During the rehearsals for *Rita Joe*, he would walk from his apartment near English Bay to the Playhouse every day. On one particularly beautiful morning, walking past a newspaper vending machine, he saw the front cover splashed with his name and a favourable announcement of the play. Later, after a long, hard-working rehearsal day, he left the bright lights of the theatre. It had started to rain, and as he walked home, down one of the gutters washed the same newspaper, coming to rest in a grate with other street refuse.[3] A decade later, in the mid-seventies, when he hit the front page of the *WeekEnd Review*, Norma remembers him saying: "It's something to walk along the street and see your face lying on the sidewalk, and people stepping on it!"

Thinking back on those times, I'm struck by how little his spectacular public acclaim affected the household. Everyone was delighted, of course, but life went on just as it normally did. Teenagers in the house were getting into scrapes, Jamie Paul was born, and George spent his hours fixing and extending the house, landscaping the garden and planting new and exotic greenery. Building a goat house was one of his projects at the time. His son, Campbell, has written: "I don't think anyone could fault our parents for not trying the different and bizarre in those days. This was painfully evident given the family experience of owning two goats. . . . I suppose in retrospect the idea was sound, that of supplying the family with goats' milk, and dad creating his version of goats' cheese. But the goats inevitably became far more trouble than we were prepared for. They'd get loose, eat everything and climb up on the roof of the house to the very steepest section, so we had no hope of climbing up to get them down. It seemed like they'd be up there forever, looking down on us and knowing full well what they were putting us through. The goats didn't last much longer, and dad would reflect on that entire experience method-ically, summarizing that if you don't have enough problems, buy a goat."[4]

Campbell goes on to recall: "As children we would often fall asleep at night to the sound of dad's typewriter. I don't believe that sound represented a source of security for any of us in the traditional sense. The sound was a by-product of the medium in which he transcended his emotions and anxie-ties, often well into the night. I remember lying awake in bed and every once in a while there would be pauses of silence coming from that typewriter. I wondered, at that moment, what he must be thinking about or what his emotions might be."[5]

It had always been one of the Rygas' great delights to share folk music, and George rebuilt what had been a very short-lived outdoor swimming pool into an 'Ark' to house regular hootenannies. Folk singers could now come to make music and share songs, and many a budding local musician found inspiration in being part of the vitality generated by the various backgrounds and musical skills that came together on these occasions. Little matter that the fireplace always smoked and that it got freezing cold in winter — everyone just dressed warmly and sang with more gusto.

One friend described the Ryga house as "a social work station where people were rescued, given attention and validation before they moved on." Part of the reality of the Ryga household was that George was always there for the many people who relied on him to write letters of reference or introduction, to pick someone up at a bus depot or airport, to read over a manuscript, to fix a vehicle or give a driving lesson, to run out to the store to pick up groceries — these were the numerous demands he quietly absorbed in a day's schedule, refusing no-one. And the efforts to get away from it, when the summer overload brought wall to wall sleeping-bags, were hopeless. He and Norma would try to escape for a night, thinking to go to the local campground to get away from it all, but the children would demand to come along too!

I marvel to think of the numbers fed at their supper table. Suppertime became a ritual in their household — it was always preceded by the sharing of a pot of coffee — and the table would be set so as to expand easily for unexpected guests. Yet they never considered going on welfare in some of the very lean years they faced. They wouldn't even take money from people staying with them. "What I learned in their home, from the constant heated discussion at their kitchen table, was that the political is personal — which was a twist on the other more commonly expressed adage."[6]

The seventies brought new challenges. George devoted much of his writing time to social issues and, more particularly, to those facing writers and cultural workers. He had a strong sense of pride in being a Canadian. In an interview in the early seventies he said: "To be a Canadian at this time is a great, great privilege. And responsibility. We have to make some crucial decisions right now about our future. And we don't have that much time left. We may not even have two decades before the Americans begin to realize what opportunities they have north of their border."[7] To this Don Rubin commented in 1987: "We're now pushing two decades later and our friendly neighbours are — as George predicted — looking this way with more than just a casual interest. . . . He was preparing for, many years ago, a fight for our cultural survival as a people, a fight for our uniqueness."[8] And Anne Cameron has commented: "He showed us that the colour of Canada did not have to be drab grey, that Canada did not have to mean boring. He told me to write what I knew, and tell the stories of the people I love."[9]

The Playhouse Theatre commissioned Ryga again, for a play for their 1970/71 season. The script he produced for them was *Captives of the Faceless Drummer*, which he described as a morality play, based on the then current October Crisis, when political kidnappings in Quebec and the proclamation of the War Measures Act by the government of Canada resulted in jails crowded with Quebecois and other activists and cultural personalities. "Upset by the politics of the script, the theatre's board refused to produce it, and months of bitter public controversy ensued. For a short time *Captives of the Faceless Drummer* became a *cause célèbre*, but long after the play was forgotten the bitterness lingered and Ryga became increasingly alienated from the mainstream of Canadian theatre."[10]

Within four short years, George Ryga's reputation had shifted from the famous to the infamous. Twenty years later, it is instructive to ask just what were the dangers that George Ryga presented to the establishment? One of his actor friends, Ken Smedley, has said: "George had a capacity to touch the pulse of the realities of the grass roots, because that's where he was from — of the people of the country."[11] And in Norma's words, "He had a hard time with academics. It was a class thing. Academics are middle-class or more, and he didn't have anything in common with those kinds of people . . . who use strong sociological argument in such an objective fashion that they aren't involved. For them it was just a little problem you had to solve — to him it was a matter of life and death. That's why he was so much more at ease with third world people. They saw things the way he saw them — maybe he was in the wrong place. We wanted to go to Cuba, to live in Cuba, but we were never able to arrange it. . . . He was rock solid in his beliefs and although he would always give people their share of the floor, I'm not sure that he could really listen — he had a point of view that he had already cemented within himself. Ideologically, politically, is what I'm referring to — everything else was up for grabs."[12]

But on re-reading *Captives* today, it remains somewhat of a mystery to understand exactly why the powers that were in mainstream theatre felt they had to silence him. His arguments in that play give voice to both conservative and radical positions. His own comment on it being "a dialogue of the deaf, where people have such beautifully framed arguments that neither side hears the other — their views of the world are shaped by their environment and previous history,"[13] is timeless. Nonetheless, as a result of the theatre establishment's reaction to *Captives* and all that this implied, "The potentially greatest playwright in this country was black-listed as carefully and as thoroughly as any one of the 'Hollywood Ten' were under McCarthy . . ."[14] and a major turning point in regional theatre was missed. In the 1971 essay, "Social Responsibilities of Writers," George talks about this with great eloquence.

In the winter of 1971 Norma had emergency surgery on her eyes for a haemorrhage that was affecting her sight. Alarmed by this crisis, George and Norma read George Ohsawa's book, *Zen Macrobiotics*, and decided to adopt this rigorous approach to physical healing. A young friend who was staying with them at the time said, "I couldn't believe it. I came back from the cannery after my late shift and found that George had thrown out almost everything in the kitchen. The cupboards were bare, except for brown rice. And no coffee!!" George experimented with roasting different grains to replace coffee and mixing assorted herbs from the garden for teas, and he tried to make up in enthusiasm and culinary creativity for this drastic change in their lifestyle. It was as hard for their friends as it was for them. They did eventually relax their regime and persisted as best they could with health resolutions, but Norma's eyesight continued to deteriorate.

In October of the following year, they took a trip to Europe — in Norma's words "an odd mixture of pain and pleasure: the pain caused by revisiting, the pleasure found in the new places discovered." George was researching material at the University of Zurich for his play *Paracelsus* and was directed to the medieval village of Einsiedeln, Paracelsus' birthplace. This place had a profound effect on them, and a description of this unsettling experience is recorded in his short story "Mist from the Mountains."

It is very clear that a series of coincidences which literally made George lose his way on a walk through the town and the surrounding countryside blinded him, forced him to confront the image of Paracelsus with a kind of "inner sight," which had about it all the qualities of an epiphany. Deeply troubled by this unsettling and seemingly irrational series of events, George and Norma decided to abandon his work on the Paracelsus papers and leave the town that had taken on a threatening and nightmarish presence in their lives. What was so astonishing about this experience was the uncharacteristic vehemence with which George turned his back on the very research he had set out to accomplish.

What can only be called their "escape" from Einsiedeln led them to London, where they had first met, to find it greatly changed, dirtier and more crowded. Friends had grown older and poorer, their earlier fighting spirit gone, replaced by a rather frightening fatalism that things were going downhill fast, and that both personally and politically, things were beyond help. Increasingly depressed, they fled London quickly and spent a few quiet days in Cornwall.

We climbed a long, winding street leading away from the sea. At the crest, before the road fell away into fields of blue kale, we stopped for breath and one last look at the troubled waters worrying the shoreline with transplanted sun heat of Mexico. "What are you looking for? You are staring as if you expected someone or something to appear," Norma spoke with some anxiety in her voice. "I'm saying farewell. Trying to remember everything as it is. We will never come this way again." When I turned to her, there were tears in her eyes. "Why are you sad?" I asked. "Because life passes. So much of the world to see, and once seen, it changes even if we could return in a short time." "But is it not sufficient to have seen the world once? To see, if not perfection, then at least an attempt at perfection? In our travels we have seen hunger, despair, humiliation — as well as new changes that revealed freedom and exaltation of the spirit. I rejoice because nowhere in the past ten years have I seen men and women functioning as brutalized animals. Everywhere there is hope!" Her eyes clouded and she looked away. "You are too optimistic. Where you see men, I see beasts. The wealthy have never been wealthier. The poor are more numerous. Armies and war machines are mightier than at any other time in history. Our prisons are overpopulated for reasons no one can remember. Parents beat children, and fertile earth is burned with chemicals that force desperate, unnatural growth in simple vegetables . . ." She could say no more. Neither could I. We were both overcome with helplessness, anger, pain. The rising, well-beaten road before us was now pebble-strewn. Pleasant fields misting with soft rain were painful to look at, their serenity at odds with the turmoil we carried in ourselves. "Walk faster!" I commanded harshly, hurrying away from her. "I can't. I have difficulty seeing." Her words were chilling. And the flood of remorse flowing through me suddenly left me wasted, trembling. I stopped and waited for her, my hand extended. What could I know? How dared I to make absolute assessments of the hope and agony of others when I was both blessed and cursed with good sight, hearing, and a body that could absorb almost limitless punishment? I embrace Norma when she reaches me. We forgive in silence more voluble and poignant than any dialogue, and hand in hand walk between fields in the direction of Penzance.[15]

They returned home in November of 1972. "Our excitement over the dramatic sweep of the NDP, and especially the demise of the Socreds, was overshadowed by the surprising results of the national election on October 30th — the country was evenly split between the two 'old' parties giving David Lewis and the NDP a very strong position in controlling the destiny of Canada. The thirty-five NDP members in the House could maintain the Liberal Government or force another election — it creates an interesting situation."[16]

In Summerland, their life resumed its normal hectic pace and George had his usual mountain of mail to sort out. Work was coming in fast and preparations were immediately begun for a family trip to Mexico. Within two weeks they set off in their VW bus (which George outfitted to sleep both their own three boys and a neighbouring young friend) to travel south through Utah, Nevada and Arizona to Lake Chapala in Mexico. There they rented a little adobe house in San Antonio, a community of farm people, and soon acquired six chickens and a cat. In this environment, with the night full of the singing of cocks, dogs, burros and pigs to delight them, time took on a new dimension — it stopped. In days which stretched endlessly, George was able to write for hours at a time without concern for schedule, telephone interruptions or visitors. In Norma's words, "George's *Paracelsus* is a beauty — just pouring out. It seems to come very smoothly — probably because he's so relaxed. . . . I think he'll have very little to rewrite. He figures he'll be able to get the other two plays done as well by the end of March."[17]

In San Antonio they established a close connection with the Sanchez family, a single mother and her daughters, and they invited the eldest daughter to return with them to Canada.

20

"When we talked of bringing Judith home with us, my sister [who was then visiting] remarked: how would our other girls feel about that? It came as a shock to me that they might 'feel' anything other than delight that someone new and very different had joined the family. There has always been a great extended-family way of life about us. But if this were not so, I still couldn't imagine that there would be unhappiness by adding a new love. Love is not a set quantity — it expands — and in fact is richer and deeper when spread around."[18]

The Mexican experience was changing them, and, in Norma's words, they were "reluctant to part with that change, frightened of getting 'like that' again — the pace, the involvement and responsibility we had thrown off for such a little time. And yet, like the material things that we had also forsaken, we questioned whether the re-involvement was worth the price of our new found peace of mind. We tried to convince ourselves that we could salvage some of our better new attitudes, carry them back with us, but I doubt if we believed it. . . . Being back home again is a mixed bag of sweet and sour."[19] George's story, "The Village of Melons," written some time after his return, puts this experience in a haunting perspective.

This period appears to mark a departure in George's writing. An interesting comment on this is made by Karl Siegler: "Having come upon a village square piled high with produce, yet inhabited by obviously malnourished and hungry people, George only sees, and hence records in 'The Village of Melons,' the single possibility that the soil in which this produce has been grown may be depleted, and for this reason, may not be providing the local residents with enough nourishment. Knowing George's politics, it seems almost unthinkable that he does not at least observe in passing the alternate possibility that a system of absentee landlords and/or a cash economy may have created a situation wherein the villagers have grown and are selling the fruits of their labour, but cannot afford to partake of this perfectly healthy produce to satisfy their own hunger."[20]

Following so closely on his abandonment of further research on Paracelsus in Europe only months before, George's omission of his usual and careful socio-economic analysis in "The Village of Melons" seems to confirm a new probing — in his words 'a confrontation of the spirit' — this time evoked by the history and mysticism of the Mexican landscape. It wasn't until several years later, George returned to his experiences in Mexico when he wrote his novel, *In the Shadow of the Vulture*.

On the trip back, George, unable to eat, was in constant pain that could not be alleviated by medication. In Vancouver, six days later, he saw a doctor who diagnosed an acute gall bladder infection and advised him that surgery was in order. It appeared the gall bladder operation had been overdue for some few years.

Back in Summerland, he prepared for surgery. "Your appointment with a surgeon in his operating theatre is not one of the more joyful moments of your life. Even before surgery, there is something cold, impersonal and absurd about blood tests, x-rays, urine-analysis and the myriad of small and large technical idiocies to which your blood vessels, orifices and secretions are subject. Keep a sense of humor and balance about it all. This . . . is an essential nuisance, so don't let it get to your head."[21]

After the surgery, it didn't take long for the very public intensity of their lives to rebuild. Norma wrote in her journal, on May 6th, '73: "The pace is fairly hectic these days and it's great to see George taking it with relish instead of the usual tense exhaustion — he seems actually to enjoy it! . . . We departed last Sunday for Washington D.C. to attend the *Rita Joe* production there, but we were stopped by immigration when George was discovered to be in their big black book . . . we pondered which of his many misdemeanors had caught up with him while we waited for the waiver to come via the State Department, via the Canadian Embassy, via the Washington Theatre. . . . We were finally airborne by nine a.m. the next morning and got to Washington by eight at night, getting to the Undersecretary's house, where a reception was waiting, in time to watch Nixon's efforts to explain to the nation the Watergate affair. It was fascinating to be there, at that time, in the company of U.S. and Canadian diplomats, U.S. pressmen and various other 'responsible' citizens.''[22]

According to a writer friend who lived with them during these years: "When George ran aground or lost direction, as happened from time to time, Norma would act as mentor and go through the process of the work, step by step, to help him put it back on track."[23] His imagination would soar, and her ideas were threads that held the tapestry in shape. She also kept him from being too pious when people set him up as a hero, because people who elevated him as a literary genius didn't acknowledge his wonderful, humanising inconsistencies. Norma had only to say, "That's enough!" when he displayed arrogance, and he'd immediately stop. There's no question that he totally respected her judgment. She has drily commented, "He didn't have a lot of ego — I lived with him for twenty-seven years — I think I'd have noticed!" Another friend called it "a marriage of equals and a battle of Titans," referring to the fact that they could egg one another on in one upmanship in storytelling — each capping the other with an even wilder tale (for Norma, too, has the soul of a storyteller). Underlying this sharing and collaboration, theirs was a truly "open" partnership, a decision which had clearly been reached by both.

Their lives peaked in the seventies in several ways. George had written some seventy scripts for radio and television productions since the rejection of *Captives*, and enough money was finally coming in. They splurged on musical instruments and replaced old vehicles. New and comfortable furniture graced the living-room with an unexpected luxury. George renovated a small shop in the centre of Summerland, and Norma opened and ran the town's first bookstore. George's novel *Night Desk* was published by Talonbooks, and a colleague immediately started work on a dramatized version that could be presented as a one-man show. CTV commissioned him to write "Lepa" for a television drama series, "The Newcomers." This piece was later re-worked as a radio drama entitled *A Letter to My Son* (published by Turnstone Press). Ryga himself regarded this work as some of his best writing for theatre. In fact, he preferred it to *Rita Joe*. The content is — to use a phrase with which he repeatedly encouraged students — "what he knew best," the conflicts of ethnic origins, authenticity and a people's culture.

George had always dreamed of finding ways in which theatre could touch the lives of people in smaller communities. He wanted to discover new ways he could be heard by the people he spoke about, and at this time an opportunity presented itself in their own community. Century House, a handsome, older building (formerly a nurses' residence) was lying vacant in Summerland, and the city council was considering demolition on account of the high cost of repairs and modernization. "Why not develop this into a community arts centre which could provide a year-round theatre with work and studio space for local artists and craftspeople?" was the talk among some in the community. A core group of supporters quickly mobilised, setting wheels in motion to save the building. Petitions, presentations, protests and picketing, even an eventual occupation of the building — supporters mobilised all avenues. Fund-raising in the community exceeded all expectations and support came from many quarters. Nonetheless, the city council, after spending over $8000 on consulting fees, decided to close the building and board up the windows. Damage from the wrecker's ball, which had destroyed part of the roof before demolition was halted by the occupiers, was never repaired.

Despite all the support that "Friends of Century House" mustered, it was a bitter disappointment for George that in his own community it was not possible to develop a grass-roots theatre base. Norma's slant on the meaning of these events was, as always, more practical: "Most people that are committed don't have the option of small-talk. We never ever learned the social graces — we were gradually not invited to places because we would beetle somebody in a corner and talk in agitation and urgency all night, having a wonderful time. But you're not supposed to do that at a party."[24]

Throughout the seventies Norma's eyes were gradually deteriorating. The symptoms were not clearly identifiable and puzzled the medical "experts." George accompanied her on several trips to see specialists and to get treatment in the United States, but there were no effective answers forthcoming. And illness was again costing them money.

The decade of the eighties brought with it a new international mood, as reactions to the popular social movements of the sixties and seventies spanned the globe. Reagan was in the White House, Margaret Thatcher was heading the Conservatives in England, and reactionary years set in on the Canadian political scene as well. At the same time, however, countries in the Third World were continuing to gain freedom from colonialism or dictatorship — Nicaragua being the most notable — while in the Eastern Bloc the working class was gaining power through *Solidarnosc*.

As he was turning fifty and entering a new decade, George thought it was time to take a personal assessment. In talking of his writing and its direction in an interview in 1980, he said: "My head has undergone some changes . . . and lonesome corners. First of all, the obvious struggle for some understanding of why. Why am I here? Why am I reduced or trapped into this particular corner? So when I dealt with the poor white or the person struggling, I was trying to find some type of inner integrity . . . some answers as to the why of this condition. Why had they been either blessed or damned by it. It took a few years of my lifetime to fully understand the implications of all this; the kind of inhumanity that people perpetrate on one another, and also the type of inhumanity that the cosmos perpetrates on us. . . . But there was a point in time when I began to be a bit more preoccupied about the heroism in life. You know, the fact that there was also a kind of divinity to it all. People are capable of rising above themselves."[25]

George took on a teaching assignment at the University of

Ottawa in the Fall Term of 1980. Living in the central hub of Canadian political life, he thought he could become more effective in presenting policy changes on issues of Canadian publishing, copyright law and other matters he saw as crucial to the survival of writers in this country. He had high hopes, since from his home out West he had received no attention to written appeals. However, he was shaken to find that when he knocked on doors in Ottawa, the doors simply wouldn't open. Being there in person didn't get him any better a reponse than his letters had.

But despite the political setbacks, there were joys for George during this trip — connecting with other writers from the East, seeing new work performed by small, innovative theatre groups and connecting with folk musicians. He spent some time in Toronto where he was offered numerous work opportunities. This only confirmed his suspicion that when you live across the mountains in B.C. — just because it's a long distance phone call away — those opportunities don't happen. As Norma said, "The price one pays for being so far from the source is that you don't have much income. We lived fairly well, at times, but we never saved anything. And it was, after all, our choice not to live there."

But as George well knew, we live in an age wherein there are other ways of establishing a connection with the "imperial centre," and this raises the question as to why, given his obvious stature as a writer, he never engaged the services of a high profile agent. I suspect he felt that his strong commitment to the direction of his work might have come into conflict with an agent's more commercial objectives. More important, perhaps, was the fact that George had a strong streak of self-sufficiency in him, personally taking on every challenge that came his way. A man who dug his own septic tank, wired and plumbed his house, who ignored planning authorities and regulations, who raised and milked goats in order to make goat cheese, might not have found it easy to trust a business agent. And he took great delight in all these accomplishments — they meant as much to him as a favourable review of one of his books. Seeing him come into their kitchen, grinning from ear to ear, with feet astride in a cocky stance, spade still in hand — "I've finally planted my huckleberry bush" — it was easy to see where his priorities were firmly rooted. And since his written work was also grounded in the experience of the local, there remained the conviction that writing that comes from *outside* central Canada *should be* as important as writing that comes from inside central Canada.

In 1981 Norma underwent further surgery at U.B.C., and for a brief time she regained her vision. The euphoria this brought on was short-lived, and she returned to living in total darkness. Afterward, she and George spent some months in Vancouver, with the purpose of enabling her to access skills through CNIB services. George had decided to take a break from writing so that he could share more personal time with her, and he took on the role of care-giver. Though noble in intent, this decision proved to be misguided. Norma needed the space and time to learn to function differently, independently and resourcefully, as she had always been known to do so well, and George had shouldered a weight and responsibility in trying to 'fix' something that couldn't be fixed. Norma was blind.

George's misguided decision was also hard on him. It was at this time that he faced his first real experience of writer's block. He would go down to his workplace in the basement and sit, blankly, at his typewriter, shuffling papers around. He quietly despaired for several months, confessing to a writer friend, "I made a terrible mistake, both for Norma and myself, in taking that time off."[26] In remembering this time recently, Norma reflected: "I don't know why we never talked about that. Perhaps, by not talking about it we were trying to give it a place of non-importance." George eventually found a spot in an unfinished area of the basement, close to the furnace, where he crouched on a small stool, with his old manual Underwood on his knees, and started to write again. "If, as a writer, you find the place that feels o.k., you don't mess with it — doesn't matter where it is," he said.[27]

27

Norma also suffered other serious ailments at this time. She had a low grade pneumonia, unidentified for over a year, until a physician familiar with Behçet's syndrome was able to diagnose this condition from her symptoms. This syndrome, which affects the immune system, had also accounted for her loss of vision. But by this time the daily cortisone intake, combined with the other medications required, was wreaking havoc with her energies and emotions and contributing to severe mood swings.

These factors contributed to a fundamental shift in the dynamics of the relationship between Norma and George. A lifestyle which had been creatively but loosely organized now needed to be reorganized around sightlessness. George jumped to Norma's assistance too quickly and took over most of the household duties. He found it impossible to stand by and watch her struggle with physical difficulties — she who had always been a tower of strength, the "rock" in their relationship. Even more devasting was the loss of her ability to read. She had been George's extra pair of eyes on the world, keeping abreast of current literature and journals. This was a further loss for them both. Not surprisingly, George's confidence was shaken.

George's despair in the eighties was further compounded as the B.C. Solidarity Coalition foundered (an unprecedented grass roots movement that gathered the energies of workers, professionals and public employees, the disabled and the unemployed, all of whom had rallied together to oppose the government's 'restraint' program), leaving, in the wake of its failure, an aftermath of apathy and hopelessness about achieving any truly democratic process in government.

During this time, George spent two years writing *In the Shadow of the Vulture* (published by Talonbooks in 1985), planned as the first in a trilogy of novels. Lean years were coming on the Canadian front, but he was now receiving increasing attention on the international scene. Much of his work had been translated for stage and radio in western Europe, and requests were now coming from the Soviet Union. In May of 1983, he and Norma took a trip to Russia, stopping in France to address a Writers' Conference in Bordeaux sponsored by the United Nations. His essay for that international event, "The Place of the Dramatist in Society," is included here. It had been twelve years since the fiasco with *Captives*, and there had been few major stage productions of his work since that time.

As a result of his travels abroad visitors continued to arrive in Summerland. On one occasion I remember him hosting an advisor to the Soviet Ministry of Culture (taking him to a Jazz club where his son Campbell was playing) who asked him, "How do we bring the material prosperity of the West to our people without losing our traditional cultural values? We don't want our country filled with throw-away pop culture and we don't want to use censorship. What is the best material you can offer us in educating our young people around this dilemma?" I remember him being troubled by the question as he went off to prepare a reading list for the advisor that would reflect a broad and rich range of intellectual and artistic material from the West.

Ill health was now plaguing George. He had always taken bouts of ill health in his stride, with a conviction that his strong consitution would surmount the temporary inconvenience, because that was how he treated his own symptoms: as inconveniences rather than as problems or danger signals. There was simply no room for them to get in the way of his writing or other committments. Yet, there must have been a time of doubt, and there must have been anxieties around what would happen to Norma . . . he had not made provision for this. A question I have since asked myself — and it has come up in talking to others who knew him closely — is why did those of us who had been close to both these people keep such a respectful distance from the changes we saw happening? Why did we not challenge the silence around the bouts of ill health and physical deterioration that we noticed? There may have been little we could have done to change the outcome, but there might have been ways in which the process could have been made more tolerable for two people who resisted allowing their own personal struggles to get in the way of what they considered to be "more important" issues. I recall Norma's frustration, later, in having allowed her physical dependency to become a problem, saying: "Why did my friends let me get like this — I would have told *them* what to do."

Meeting and working with writer-performer Cheryl Cashman appeared to give George renewed optimism in '85. He shared her enthusiasm for taking theatre projects into Third World countries and thus developing links with indigenous theatre groups. He had spoken of this potential earlier in his essay "The Artist in Resistance," an address he gave to a workshop of populist theatre companies from Canada and countries of the Third World who met together in Thunder Bay in 1982. This essay talks of the dangers of the destruction, by global technology, of "ancient languages, and with this, the loss of folk memory in a dramatic and irreversible way . . . one which will victimize us all, be we from the industrially advanced, or the poorer regions of the world."[28]

Meantime he was getting disturbing telephone pleas, in the middle of the night, from an actor friend, born in a concentration camp, who was bewildered by the many obstacles besetting the trial proceedings of "war criminals." His "Letter to Yousef" struggles with the enormity of our responsibility to better understand the human psyche and to never allow such monstrosities as the Holocaust to occur again. This, in the year 1987, when combined global military forces had never been more excessively available and ready for use.

The previous year, an opportunity to stage *Paracelsus* had finally been negotiated, thirteen years after it had been written. The Vancouver Playhouse unexpectedly requested it late, as a replacement production, during the Vancouver Expo of 1986. There was insufficient time for the necessary rewriting (it had to be shortened to fit time requirements) and insufficient time for cast selections. But, most damaging of all, there was insufficient time for the "workshopping" required — it had never yet been staged, and it was a play of complexities, textually and visually. Obstacles plagued the project from the start. The Playhouse wanted a "spectacular" production, partly to justify

30

funding received from the Secretary of State and Expo. But technical delays and the desire for an extravagent production obstructed valuable rehearsal time. The artistic director stated publicly that he foresaw "the biggest flop of the season" — a statement which could only subvert the efforts of both the actors and the playwright to surmount the huge problems facing them. George was later to admit: "I was fatigued . . . depressed, drained by the health situation, and by betrayals around the production . . . which I knew would be a failure critically and artistically. . . . I persisted on the advice and suggestions of others to go along with indecisions and bad choices, for they would correct themselves in ample time . . . They did not. And I surrendered to helplessness and hopelessness. I remember sighing uncontrollably and finding a strange comfort in a wish that it all end soon for me — that I was too tired to go on. Yet I kept up a bold front for the benefit of family and friends, despite pain, grief and gathering isolation, spiritually and emotionally."[29]

One might wonder why, given George's previous history with the Playhouse, he was prepared to go ahead with this production under such adverse conditions. One reason was undoubtedly economic — he needed the money — bills kept coming in. Another was that the play had never yet been performed, and as each year went by the chances of it being staged seemed more remote — for one thing, it required a large budget. But perhaps most important, it also presented the hope of an opportunity to mend fences with an old foe.

In the last summer of his life, on June 27, 1987, George wrote in his diary: "This morning, I woke refreshed even though it was daybreak only. No pain or discomfort in stomach regions. Took . . . a strenuous walk which exhilarated me, shirtless in the morning air, birds singing in the trees and dogs barking drowsily in farmhouses and orchards. . . . A feeling of joy and such intense pleasure at being alive, at noticing all and every small and large detail of waterbeads on leaves of grapes, sounds of hissing water systems, odours of someone, somewhere preparing fresh coffee. I am winning the greatest struggle of my life — that I know! That I fully understood and knew this morning — because I want to live — I ache to live with every cell and tissue in my body! There is important work to do, and things to see for the first time, as I did this morning on my walk. . . . I ate well . . . walked with Norma, made plans for construction of a courtyard this coming autumn or next year. . . . All positive, useful plans to further expand our personalities into visible, beautiful things we do with hands and minds.''

July 21 : "I am not spending as much time on writing as I used to, partly because taking care of myself seems to take up a much larger part of my day than I anticipated. However, I somewhat expected this, and will not allow myself any restlessness. Even though at times I am overcome by a peculiar sadness at the way events have gone. . . . Cheryl called in the late afternoon. She was worried and depressed, and wanted to see me to launch some new theatre project to take our minds off these times. She was disturbed by the amnesty Pinochet had given Chilean resistors. . . . It is a calculated and ugly trap.''

July 23: "I am becoming more conscious that the time clock of my life has again moved to that decisive moment when I must return to my study and concern myself less fully with matters of health and recovery and redirect much of this energy into doing the only thing I know how to do well, and without which good health would be impossible anyway. . . . I feel Norma worries about my turning back to work prematurely. We have had four weeks of rich living and intense intimacy as we have passed through the veils of clouds and shadows. She has become increasingly more substantial in understanding my innermost concerns — my feelings — my curiosities and corners of alarms.''

Aug 3: "I know now that the malignancy is more widespread than initially considered to be the case. A long conversation with Norma yesterday evening, reviewing areas of faith over the years, the decades. The commitment and conviction to the great forces changing the social landscape are as intact and joyful as they ever were. 'We can give you nothing, for we have little' she said, in referring to the revolutionary emergence of advanced nations in the Third World — 'We have so little ourselves, but we support and give all we have to make your struggles a victory!' Again we both endorsed this with our hearts and minds as a credo for life and purpose in our troubled, interesting times.''

Aug 28: ''I review . . . my consultations by telephone with Barbara Simpson in Tacoma. She has prodded and poked much in the darker recesses against things which could stand in the way of healing myself. My relationship to parents, early childhood upbringing towards over-responsibility and the deep moral values this implants, which might get in the way of normal living — all these are worth exploring. And I do, in the dead of night, when optimism can be either at its highest, or darkest and lowest.''

The last entry in his diary occurs on August 30: ''I force energy into myself by thinking of the book of short stories I must complete writing. I think of Karl's call yesterday, to tell me Soviet royalties have arrived, and the need for more of these for seasons and years to come, for survival as an artist in my own country is difficult, and likely contributed more than a little to my health breakdown. These pushes against the spirit to force it on are helpful, and I return to the house in stronger condition. . . . I lay down for a short nap. Ten minutes later, I wake rested, and decide to have a tiny cup of coffee with Norma on the balcony. I cannot deny myself the ritual of coffee with her for it has been a pattern with us all the years we have been together, through the best and worst of times.''

The next three months saw a rapid decline in his strength and vigour. He maintained a strict control over diet and exercise. And he made a particular point of being available to his friends and family — many of whom he recognized to have a fear of cancer. I last saw him in early November — little more than a week before his death. I remember his saying, ''It's not so bad'' — but also remarking, when I put my hand on his shoulder — ''that feels like a two-by-four.'' His son,

Campbell, who spent his last moments with him, wrote — "One of the very last things Dad ever said to me was 'Don't let the bastards grind you down.' It was a lesson hard learned by him, and of great importance to me by his example."

A statement he made in the early eighties speaks well as an epitaph to the forces that fired his life and his work. "Because I've been fortunate enough to survive as a writer for the best part of two decades, there's an obligation that I owe back to society. Everything that came to me, or comes to me at this moment, comes on the basis of other people who run machines, grow grain, dig coal; everything that comes out of human labour to which I'm not directly contributing . . . and I think that I have an obligation to make sure that those people who made my life possible are remembered, and are treated with respect and dignity. I owe it to them to defend them because I can speak when others have to be silent. Sometimes I have to speak on behalf of other people who cannot, because of political threat or economic security or whatever the reasons are, they sometimes cannot enunciate an opinion. So yes, I do have to speak up for them."[30]

Until a few weeks before his death, he was still talking of attending the Mirbed Festival of Poetry, an annual celebration of Arab poets, dating back to the Middle Ages, to which a small number of poets from the rest of the world are invited. His last work, "Resurrection," was written for this. Henry Beissel, who read this work at the Festival on his behalf, wrote: "Life and art were of a single piece for Ryga. The struggles of his characters to maintain or recover a measure of human decency were also the struggles of his own life in which he confronted institutions and issues with uncompromising integrity. 'Resurrection' is personal, moving, committed, honest . . . [in it] he spits death in the face as [he] invests his life and his work in the future."[31] Its last lines speak with characteristic vigour, defiance and optimism: "Yes — I am free. Free, free at last! . . . Racing now to meet the dawn — to join the tragedies and triumphs to come."

Endnotes

1. From conversation with Norma Ryga, November 1991
2. Tribute given by Leonard George at wake held in Vancouver, December 1987, organized by John Juliani
3. Incident related by Sergei Ryga from a conversation with his father
4. Letter from Campbell Ryga, May 1992
5. Letter from Campbell Ryga, loc.cit.
6. From conversation with Judy Kujundzic, April 1992
7. CBC radio interview with George Ryga, 1970, quoted by interviewer, Don Rubin
8. Tribute by Don Rubin, Executive Editor, World Encyclopedia of Contemporary Theatre, wake, loc. cit.
9. Tribute by Anne Cameron, wake, loc. cit.
10. Jerry Wasserman, *Modern Canadian Plays*, revised edition, Talonbooks, 1986, p. 25
11. Interview with Ken Smedley, taped March 1992
12. From conversation with Norma Ryga, April 1992
13. C.B.C. interview, circa 1973: excerpt from tape belonging to Norma Ryga
14. Tribute by Richard Ouzounian, Artistic Director, Neptune Theatre, Halifax, Nova Scotia, wake, loc. cit.
15. George Ryga, *Beyond the Crimson Morning*, Doubleday, 1979, p. 157-8
16. Excerpt from Norma Ryga's journal (Sept 1972 - April 1977)
17. Letter from Norma Ryga to Ann Kujundzic, January 1973
18. Excerpt from Norma Ryga's journal loc. cit.
19. Excerpt from Norma Ryga's journal loc. cit.
20. Karl Siegler in conversation with the editor, July 1992
21. George Ryga & D.B. Williams M.D. "Preparing for Surgery" - notes for patients
22. Excerpt from Norma Ryga's journal, loc. cit.
23. Interview with Roxanne Macneil, taped February, 1992
24. From conversation with Norma Ryga, April 1992

25. "An Interview with George Ryga" by Jill Martinez, July 1980
26. Interview with Roxanne Macneil, loc. cit.
27. Interview with Roxanne Macneil, loc. cit.
28. "The Artist in Resistance," *Canadian Theatre Review*, #33, (Winter 1982)
29. George Ryga, personal diary, June 23 - August 30, 1987
30. "An Interview with George Ryga," loc. cit.
31. Henry Beissel, *The Moosehead Anthology*, D.C. Books, 1989 "Spit in the Face of Death: A short Tribute to George Ryga," p. 10-11

THE SIXTIES

George Ryga (1964)   Photo: unknown

BITTER GRASS

Cast:

PETE JOHNSON: farm labourer
MARY RUPTASH: middle-aged widow
NELLIE RUPTASH: Mary's teenaged daughter

Setting:
Farmyard before the home of Mary and Nellie Ruptash. Two steps from door to yard. Washtub on wall beside door. Litter and junk all about. To left of set, broken-down gate to road off-set.

ON CAMERA: PETE is at gate. He is dusty and unshaven, and carries pack on his back. He has difficulty opening the gate and struggles with it. Dog barks. He opens gate and approaches house. Knocks on door, and turns away to dust his clothes. NELLIE opens door and steps out into bright light, which blinds her. She sees PETE, is surprised, and runs back into house. A moment later, MARY comes outside and studies Pete critically.

MARY: Well? What do you want?

PETE: *(Uncomfortable, shuffles his feet and looks away from her)* A drink of water . . . Just a drink of water.

MARY: Yeah . . . sure — you can have a drink of water. Won't be very cold.

PETE: Don't matter. S'long's it's wet an' from a well.

MARY: Sure, it's well water. No dirty dugout water for us. We got a good well on our farm — twenty feet of water, winter an' summer — an' it never boils rust on a teakettle! *(Shouts over her shoulder)* Nellie! Bring this guy a drink of water! *(To PETE)* What's your name?

PETE: Huh?

MARY: Your name? You got a name, ain't you?

PETE: Yeah — Pete . . . Pete Johnson.

MARY: Johnson, hum. That's Swede, no? Don't matter any to me. We've given water to Indians an' hunkies — even a black man once.

PETE: Uh, huh.

MARY: Never knew a Swede before. Sure grow them big an' strong — your folks from these parts?

PETE: Yah — thirty miles back — across the river. Not much of a farm now — we don't even really own it anymore — just live on it. Tax took it when pop got sick.

MARY: *(Laughs bitterly)* Well! Lost it to taxes — some farmer your old man must be! Let me tell you my husband got sick, too — an' he died. But there's no back taxes on our land!

PETE: My father worked hard.

MARY: So who's arguin'? But did he work with his head?

No! He didn't, did he? Went out like all the rest of them, leasing up all the homestead land the government allowed. When the time come to work some farm from the bush, he chickened out — got sick an' died usually, from a heart busted by no hope. It's the women an' kids who stayed behind to suffer! Some farmers!

PETE: You never knew my father.

MARY: It's always the same story, only each tells it different, Swede!

PETE: Pop . . . pop didn't die! He's still out there with mother, workin' as much land as could be plowed an' seeded with two horses! Only our farm ain't as good as yours. Most of it's under rock a foot deep.

MARY: Where you off to? On a holiday?

PETE: No, ma'm. I'm sort of lookin' around.

MARY: For work?

PETE: Yup.

NELLIE appears, carrying tin dipper of water. PETE drinks greedily. Hands dipper back to girl. She studies him quizzically then returns into house.

MARY: *(The bitterness gone from her voice)* Pete Johnson — that's a nice name, even though it's Swede. Like I say, I never met a Swede before. You goin' anyplace particular?

PETE: Just walkin', watchin' the fields. Someone's gonna need a man for stone or root picking. Then there's harvest, an' I'll get a job on stooking or threshing.

MARY: That's usin' your head, kid. There are bigger farms, thirty, forty miles south. They'll be cutting barley soon there. You're a strong boy — should do alright. But you need work first to buy some boots. You start stookin' barley in what you're wearin', an' the stubble will rip the skin clean off your ankles!

PETE: Yes, ma'm.

MARY: How you charge wages? By the day or the job?

PETE: Don't matter. S'long's I get work.

MARY: Well — suppose you was to look around you an' give me your price for puttin' a proper fence around this yard.

PETE: *(Looks around, brows knit)* Rail — just like you got there, or barbwire, ma'm?

MARY: Barbwire, with new posts an' a wooden gate that opens and closes without a fight.

PETE: Take me a week to do it right. You got wire, a stretcher, an' some posts?

MARY: Everything you'll need we got. Posts are heaped in back of the barn. Wire stretcher is in the shed where the binder canvas is kept. Barbwire — well, you can pull down the fence in the west pasture. We ain't got cattle now, so it's only rustin' out there.

PETE: Sounds okay.

MARY: How much you charge?

PETE: It ain't gonna be heavy work. Maybe two dollars a day an' food . . .

MARY: *(Shrewdly)* Hold on, now! You got jobs everywhere waitin' for you? Eh? I'll give you work for a dollar a day — three meals, an' bed in the hayloft of the barn!

PETE: Ma'm — I never hired out that cheap before.

MARY: You got paid anything for walkin' the road today? Or yesterday? Or the day before?

PETE: No.

MARY: You heard my offer. You can start anytime.

PETE: It won't make me rich.

MARY: You're damned right it won't — but you'll eat, and so long's a man eats, he puts hope in his belly. I don't argue, so make up your mind. Then come in for a baloney sandwich an' some coffee. *(Shouts to house)* Nellie! Put the kettle on!

PETE: Ma'm — don't bother about food — it's alright. I et something . . . *(Points vaguely over shoulder with thumb)*

MARY: Don't bother lyin' to me, Pete Johnson. You go into the barn. The ladder's to the right for the hayloft. You drop your gear there. Wash at the pump, then soon's you're finished, come right in an' have lunch. Go on now . . .

Fade.
ON CAMERA: Up on PETE stripped to the waist, dismantling part of rail fence in yard. NELLIE is with him, clawbar in hand, pulling nails from rails he has torn off old post.

PETE: No! I've never heard of no Riley that wrote poems! You ain't got much to do here — so go help your mother . . .

NELLIE: I won't! I got a right to be here or on any other part of the farm.

PETE: Then shut up! I got no time for nonsense!

NELLIE: You ever read a book?

PETE: Maybe I have — maybe I haven't.

NELLIE: That means you don't read!

PETE: I got enough to do without ruinin' my eyes an' time readin'! What's it get you? Does it make Spring come quicker — or your horses fatter?

NELLIE: *(Giggles)* It makes you think!

PETE: Hah! I got enough to think about!

NELLIE: It makes you forget — like sleep with a dream. Time passes quickly, and you begin to ask if maybe someday you can reach a warmer, nicer place than where you been all your life. My daddy didn't go by reading at all. Said it made a soul lazy, an' the price of a book could buy ten pounds of sugar. Isn't that funny?

PETE: Don't see nothin' funny.

NELLIE: You're a blockhead then. A big, silly blockhead Swede!

PETE: *(Hits rail furiously with hammer. Turns on her)* I'll tar your backside good if you don't hush up!

NELLIE: You couldn't run fast enough to catch me!

PETE: I can't, eh? *(Lunges and grabs her)*

NELLIE: Ouch! Let go of me!

PETE: *(Releases her. Looks at his hands with amazement)* I . . . I'm sorry if I grabbed you hard, Nellie . . .

NELLIE: *(Rubs her arm and coughs)* It's alright . . . Nothing to worry about.

PETE: Did I hurt you?

NELLIE: No. Not much. We'd better work a bit more before it gets dark. *(They resume work)* I used to sit up nights in the winter, reading. You ever seen a real orchard, Pete?

PETE: No.

NELLIE: Be kinda nice to see one someday. "And hand in hand we'll wander, down the old path winding yonder — to the orchard where the children used to play" . . . pretty, isn't it? Sad and pretty . . .

PETE: You make that up yourself in your head?

NELLIE: No — that's this guy — Riley!

PETE: An' he was a farmer?

NELLIE: I guess so.

PETE: A farmer wrote them things? What farmer ever wrote a book like that? Hah! What's he say about frost an' drought — an' working twenty years at things that don't pay beans? He ever write about a headache that gives you stars in your eyes, an' you gotta get out an' haul stones in a field so hot you can't breathe? He ever tell about such things? Not a farmer — not a real homestead farmer like you an' me!

45

NELLIE: You ain't no farmer, Swede. You're just *workin'* on a farm — you got no time for dreams.

PETE: Ah! Why talk to you — you're just a kid!

NELLIE: I'm no kid! *(Points to house)* You're like her — an' like what my old man used to be when he was alive! Never any time — too tough, too hard to cry! Then he got old an' mean. Used to fight a horse with his bare fists when he got mad.

PETE: I don't wanna talk — I got work to do!

NELLIE: He ate with his hat on so's he won't have to waste time combing his hair. He'd pray to God before going to bed at night, an' in the morning, he said we had to suffer and hurt so we knew we was alive! I didn't agree with that — I'll never agree!

PETE: You don't have to agree — it don't matter. He was a man, an' you're a kid . . .

NELLIE: You even sound like him — tired an' old all the time — an' blind! I used to say to him, "Daddy, what colour's the sky today?" He didn't know. He'd never troubled to look up, doubled up that way over his lifting or shovelling. He'd get mad when I asked him that . . .

PETE: What's wrong with him feelin' that way? A man's supposed to provide for his family. He done right by you, or you wouldn't be here!

NELLIE: Maybe — maybe it's because here the land is mean an' don't grow crops easy. So we do things the hard way, because it's the cheapest way. Health an' life don't count for much — but a machine costs money, an' we don't have money. So the whole world is crazy an' gray, an' folks make fun of what don't fight back!

PETE: I'm gonna tell your mother on you — the way you talk about your old man!

NELLIE: Go tell her! See if I care! Run — go tell her right now!

PETE: You ought to be ashamed of yourself.

NELLIE: Well I ain't — so there! The way nothing bothers you . . . you remind me of old Andrew Hill, who lived a couple miles down the road from here. Lived to be a very old man, an' when folks asked him how come he'd lived that long, he used to say, "Because I ain't died yet, I guess" . . . He was the colour of earth an' stone an' when he sat in one place, he'd set there all day.

PETE: An old man don't have much strength to move around.

NELLIE: But you do, Swede . . . Can you sing or dance?

PETE: *(Staring at her)* You know somethin'? You're crazy! Yah — you been in the sun too long, an' your head's goin' round an' round, like a lost bird in the sky!

NELLIE: That's it! A bird! Flying lost an' homeless — without a care! Do you dance, Pete?

PETE: Get lost!

NELLIE: I mean it — I want to know!

PETE: *(Turning away)* No. I never been out dancing. Never had the time . . .

NELLIE: Then make time — tomorrow night! There's a

dance at the schoolhouse — the last dance before harvesting. I want you to come with me!

PETE: *(Works angrily)* What silly kind of talk is that? I come to work — make a little money — I don't come here to dance!

NELLIE: You'd have fun, Pete!

PETE: Let them as has nothing better to do with their time go dancin'. Go away now — please, go away!

NELLIE: It's like a dark cloud's come over the countryside. All those that could go to find work somewhere else have gone. Only the old an' very young are left now . . .

PETE: I thought you was happy here. If you ain't happy, then why in hell don't you go with all them that's leavin'?

NELLIE: *(Sits down in front of him and throws her head wildly)* I'm scared, I guess. It's easier waitin' for something to happen than making it happen.

PETE: Why don't you come out an' say what's on your mind, instead of talking in circles?

NELLIE: Alright — I want you to go to the dance with me!

PETE: Hah!

NELLIE: Mamma's giving the farm to me when she gets too old to work it. It's nothin' — just hardship — but what else I got? What good's a girl who can plough an' milk cows in town?

PETE: There's jobs for them that wants work!

NELLIE: Leave this fence then, an' go into town! Find yourself a job, and then find one for me. Write me a letter — or come back an' tell me, an' I'll go with you! I promise I will!

PETE: You're a kid — you're in my way! Go help your mother in the house — you're not doin' anything an' you're keepin' me from work! Go on!

NELLIE: Pete — the big, hard workin' Swede! *(Laughs)*

Fade.
ON CAMERA: Up on kitchen and MARY and NELLIE. Kerosene lamp burns on table. Next to lamp is metal tub filled with sudsy water.

MARY: I don't blame him if he got mad enough to whop you one!

NELLIE: It don't hurt bringing somethin' dead back to life.

MARY: Don't let him hear you say that!

NELLIE: I told him so straight to his face!

MARY: Okay — it's your idea, not mine. But he's a Swede man, an' I never met one of those before. Did you close up his pack just like you found it?

NELLIE: He won't know until he sees his clean shirt tomorrow! I untied his pack an' took out the best shirt in his bundle — an' there wasn't much to choose from, I'll tell you. Then I tied his pack like I found it an' left. Cripes — he's got nothing nice there — he must never dress for Sunday.

MARY: There aren't any Sundays in his life, Nellie. He works well — he'll make out.

NELLIE: Never saw a man for work like him — he's worse than father was. For a man to eat supper, then go out at sundown to pull down barbwire in the pasture . . . He'll be bundling that wire by moonlight, until he gets it all down.

MARY: I know. A body shouldn't work when the sun goes down. That's the time to sit indoors with other humans . . .

NELLIE: But you didn't ask him to stay for another cup of tea.

MARY: Why should I? He's not one of us — we don't even know him. He only came yesterday . . .

NELLIE: But I invited him to the dance already.

MARY: Yes . . . yes! There's times when hours are longer than years . . . I hope he smiles just once. He's such an unhappy boy.

NELLIE: He'll smile at the dance. Wait till he hears the music!

MARY: Don't count on it.

NELLIE: Why not?

MARY: I don't know — I just don't know. He's so strange, an' yet . . . Too bad he hasn't any decent clothes to wear. He's heavier than your father was, else he might have worn the blue suit . . . It hasn't had a proper airing these last three years . . . No! It wouldn't be proper even if it did fit! Folks would recognize the suit, and then tongues would wag.

NELLIE: *(Walks to door)* Call me when you finish washing, mamma. I'll hang the shirt out.

MARY: You can go to hell for that lark! This is your idea, an' you can do both the washin' an' hanging anytime you're ready!

NELLIE: *(Peevishly)* You wanted him to go out.

MARY: I hired the guy to put up a fence for us. If you want him to go dancing an' larking, that's entirely your affair. There's the tub — an' there's the shirt. Anytime you're ready . . .

NELLIE: You're horrible!

MARY: An' if I washed his shirt, I wouldn't be? I'm not courtin' . . . You're such a child, Nellie . . .

NELLIE: Oh, no! Such an unhappy boy . . . too bad he can't fit into daddy's blue suit . . . Did I say that?

MARY: If I wasn't so tired, I'd close you up good for thinkin' such filthy thoughts! You just remember that!

Fade.
Up on late afternoon of following day. PETE, NELLIE and MARY are in front of house. Set is cleaner now. Pile of posts in background, also axe and hammer. MARY is leaning against doorsill, holding stick in her hand. PETE is wearing white shirt, but in same trousers and boots as in previous scenes. NELLIE is wearing a loud, overblown party frock. Her long, dark hair is contained somewhat severely in a heavy pigtail.

NELLIE: *(Studying PETE critically)* Not bad. If you had a cane in your hand an' a cigar in your teeth, you'd look like a cattle buyer.

PETE: I'd smell different. *(Looks to MARY self-consciously)* Thanks for washing my shirt, ma'm.

MARY: *(Moves her stick like fan before her face)* Nellie did the work. Well, don't stand there admirin' yourself like a rooster with a new feather. It's a walk to the schoolhouse — all of four miles. Go in an' eat, so's I can get the dishes done before dark!

PETER: Nellie — I never danced before . . . I don't want to go! I don't feel right — won't know what to do when I get there.

NELLIE: Nobody's learned to dance proper. They just get out on the floor an' stamp their feet to the music an' holler loud. That's a good time.

PETE: I can't do it!

NELLIE: You don't have to dance. You can sit on the bench an' watch if you like. You might as well. You haven't got proper shoes, an' those rundown boots — well . . .

MARY: Your mouth's bigger than a barndoor, Nellie! It ain't important he's never learned to dance. There's no one lookin' now, Swede — so take hold of him, Nellie — go on!

MARY takes down washtub from wall and begins beating a three/four rhythm. NELLIE takes PETE in dance stance and leads him through waltz. On a turn, he stumbles over his feet.

PETE: Oh, to hell with it!

MARY: That's good! You're as good as most. Any other dance is the same, only faster. Anyway, if you're not a dancin' man, then take her there an' bring her back. See what you can see, an' remember you're young an' got only one life ahead of you.

NELLIE: It's his boots, mamma! Aren't there a pair of daddy's Sunday shoes he might fit into?

MARY: *(Hangs up tub and shakes her head sadly)* No — there'll be no fittin' your father's shoes on him. Now come in an' eat . . .

Fade.
ON CAMERA: Same scene only now it is night, moonlit and sounds of frogs croaking. MARY sits on step of front door, irritably scratching her shoulders and waiting. PETE half runs into yard and stops when he sees her. His shirt is torn and bloodied, as are his hands and face.

MARY: *(Rising with alarm)* Swede! Is that you? Where's Nellie?

PETE: Damned if I know — or care!

MARY: What happened to you? What did you do with my girl?

PETE: *(Leans against wall and pants for air)* She's dancin', or comin' home — or doin' something. I don't wanna see her again!

MARY: You got in a fight!

PETE: No — Pete Johnson's never danced an' never been in a fight. You remember that . . .

MARY: Then what happened to Nellie?

PETE: Nothin'. I hardly saw her!

MARY: Thank God!

PETE: So I went — like you wanted me to — like Nellie wanted! An' I'm never gonna go again . . .

MARY: Just cool down an' tell me what you did to yourself. You're bleedin' pretty bad.

PETE: I went through a window — boom! Just like that! They'll say the Swede's head can break glass!

MARY: Why? Who'll say what?

PETE: Everyone — your neighbours! They had a good laugh at me. Some had teeth, an' some never had them no more — laugh at anythin'! Boys four years short of their first shave, too! Stamped their feet an' clapped their hands together. "Swede," they was singin' — "You'd better dance good to dance with our girls!"

MARY: That's nonsense! I know all these people!

PETE: Do you? You don't know them when they're havin' their fun, do you?

MARY: Anyway, they didn't mean to hurt you . . .

PETE: No — not if you got to tear a man's skin open or pound his face to hurt him. But I sat on the bench with my feet under me. The orchestra started playin' fast . . . Nellie was dancin' by herself in the middle of the floor . . . And the musicians came at me with all the people, laughin', shoutin'. I ran through the window behind me. The glass busted so easy I hardly cut my hands. Catch me but don't hold me — who said that? The bearded guy? You? Dammit! *(Strikes wall of house with his fist)*

MARY: They hurt you bad, Swede — they hurt you pretty bad?

PETE: One man I could've trounced with my two hands — even two men! Or one face — I could've talked to one face — told that one face how hard my life had always been — never had time to laugh. Someone might have understood . . . An' said to the others — leave him alone — he is no different than us! But all the faces were the same . . .

MARY: Come into the house. I'll warm some water for you to wash up.

PETE: The plough-horse in a sunny pasture — feed him bitter grass an' watch him vomit . . .

MARY: Don't say anymore, Peter! Come into the house!

PETE: Wait! I must tell you more . . . it will be morning soon, and then there'll be no more to say . . .

MARY: I know enough, Peter.

PETE: No — wait! My father was no big-wheel farmer — you were wrong! He was a nobody. He lived so long with pain he'd come to worship it, like it was religion. He bought his boots at auction sales, an' they never fitted right.

MARY: I know! I know it all!

PETE: When it hailed, he stood outside, watching the barley field die under two inches of ice. ''There'll be a day of reckonin' '' he used to say — the reckonin'! The big pain — the death of all!

MARY: Nothin' ever dies, Peter. It only changes hands!

PETE: I cried much, wantin' my tears to wash away the needs. I lied to you, Missus Ruptash . . . he died, an' mother has a forever headache. Such a little man he seemed then, lyin' on the field, with legs like thin wooden sticks. The stroke had killed him, but he still bit on his wrist . . .

MARY: Sit down — here, beside me.

PETE: *(Moving nearer, but pressing back against the wall)* Last summer, I growed flowers — a little garden this big.

Peonies! I put water on them first thing in the mornin', and last thing at night. They grew green — strong! In the moonlight, they was like candles — beauty an' peace! Never seen anythin' so beautiful! I watered an' weeded them two months. Then a horse ate them down as they were comin' to flower . . .

MARY: Will Nellie be long? I wish she was home now . . .

PETE: My mother laughed from her bed when I told her — she laughed until the tears filled her eyes an' ran down her cheeks . . . She laughed . . . *(Covers his face and laughs)*

MARY: *(Rises and touches him)* Come . . . let me wash your face. You're hurt bad . . .

PETE: No! What is pain here or here? I like the night. It has the taste of wild loganberries, an' the smell of willows in the rain. An' it talks truth!

MARY: The devil take that girl, Swede! If you won't come into the house, then let me wash you at the pump. Poor boy — your eyes are hurt!

PETE: I can see — I'm not hurt!

MARY: Come — first a good wash, an' then I will see you get to bed for a good sleep. Lean on me — you will find me strong — very strong! *(She takes PETE's arm and begins walking away from the house)*

PETE: I will earn enough for taxes an' then go back. She thinks I ran away — I didn't! Even a mother doesn't know her child . . .

MARY: Yes . . . Tomorrow is Sunday. I will wash a shirt for you, an' give you shoes to wear! Then let them laugh, if they dare! I know these people — I have lived here all my life. Don't be afraid to touch me — I will lead you!

PETE: My mother . . . was younger than you. She was fifteen when I was born!

Fade.
ON CAMERA: Up on front of house. NELLIE is wearing same dress as on previous day. Her hair is down, and she holds a book on her lap. She sits on front step. MARY stand behind her. Her face is drawn and tired.

NELLIE: Is he sleeping all day?

MARY: Don't ask me — I don't know.

NELLIE: They sure ribbed me when he went through that window. Old Sammy Ross said it minded him of a cat he owned once . . .

MARY: Shut your mouth! I don't wanna hear about it!

NELLIE: *(Opens her book with disinterest and pretends to read for a moment, then looks up)* What time'd he come home?

MARY: How should I know? Do I sit up waiting for the hired help to come home?

NELLIE: I only asked . . . Mamma, I saw you burnin' daddy's shoes an' suit this morning. The smoke came into my window . . .

MARY: You spyin' on me? Is that what you're doin' — spyin'?

NELLIE: No — I wasn't spying! The smoke woke me, an' I went to the window to see what was burnin'.

MARY: It's the moths! They're all over the house . . . Got to burn all the old clothes lyin' about.

NELLIE: I haven't noticed any moths . . .

MARY: You'll go into the house if you keep arguin' with me!

NELLIE: I wasn't arguing . . . *(Looks up)* There he comes! Our brave Swede! An' about time, too!

PETE: Nellie, you sure dance good! *(Looks up at MARY with shock and disbelief on his face)* Last night . . . last night I dreamed . . .

MARY: Go back in the loft, Swede . . . Pack up your things an' get out!

PETE: But . . .

MARY: Get out! Clear off! Here's your money — now go!

NELLIE: He hasn't had breakfast, mamma — an' the fence!

MARY: You're a child, Nellie — a blind little child! What you waiting for, Swede.

PETE: No — no money — I sold nothin' — you fed me for the fence . . .

MARY: *(Savagely)* Take it! *(Pushes it behind his shirt front and recoils from touching him. He turns and leaves)*

NELLIE: *(Alarmed)* Mamma — what's wrong?

MARY: *(Clumsily lifts NELLIE to her feet and embraces her)* Nothing, my child — hurry, come indoors . . . We have a good farm — it's yours when I get old! You know that, don't you? He's a big, dumb Swede — dangerous to have a man like that around. You're young — there's no heaven nor hell — we gotta hold on to what we got!

NELLIE: Mama! You're hurting me! An' you smell of smoke somethin' awful!

Fade out.

The End

THE TULIP GARDEN

Cast

OLD JAKE
JENNY: daughter of Jake
JOE: a deliveryman
SAM: a blustering neighbour
SADIE: Sam's wife
ANOTHER MAN
ANOTHER WOMAN
Two or three other neighbours for crowd effect

Scene

Up on living room of old and abondoned farm home. Cracked glass in single window. Odd bits of furniture here and there, covered with old blankets for dust covers. Large, round, uncovered oak table in centre of room. Two chairs. An old wood or Quebec heater with stovepipe attached. A few blocks of wood on floor. Door with trace of snow drifted into room through crack under it. Sound of key in door. Door opens and JAKE enters. Removes his hat and rubber overshoes. Walks to window and stares out pensively. Turns, looks about the room and shakes his head sadly. With sleeve of coat, dusts table. Is about to begin lighting stove when he hears truck approach and stop. He goes to door and opens it wide.

JAKE: *(Motions in with his hand)* Okay, boys.

Two deliverymen carry in closed casket.

JAKE: *(Pointing)* Right there — in the centre of the table. That's it — that'll be fine! *(Withdraws billfold from coat pocket)* I'm sorry having to ask you to do this. It was mama's wish. I didn't know any other way of getting her home from the station.

JOE: That's alright, Jake. Glad to help. I took the van in second gear all the way — everything's fine.

JAKE: What do I owe you?

JOE: Nothing — forget it. We don't charge for a job like this — no sirree. It'd be a sin to charge!

JAKE: I insist!

JOE: Oh, no. It's on us. Heck — Roy an' I knew Missus Johnson from the time we was knee-high to grasshoppers — ain't that so, Roy?

ROY: Sure did . . .

JAKE: I'd like to give you something . . . there's gas to pay for, and your time . . .

JOE: Nothin' doing! No sirree! Sure sorry about the missus, Jake. She seemed — well, she seemed so damned healthy when you both come through last summer . . . Guess we never know about these things.

JAKE: Four operations — each one worse than the last. Even I never knew how bad they cut her up.

ROY: They should be stopped doing that when there's no hope!

JAKE: Last time mama went in, she wasn't herself anymore. She reckoned we were back here . . . kept asking if the cow had freshened and what colour was the calf. I told her what she wanted to hear — the calf was brown, with white tips on the ears.

ROY: She couldn't remember you'd retired two years back an' gone into — uh, the home?

JAKE: No.

JOE: Hey! There was a calf the colour you said on this farm. Herb an' I used to feed it chop from the feed-shed. How is Herb?

JAKE: Herb's fine — still in Uranium City. Jenny's coming out, though.

JOE: Herb couldn't make it, eh?

JAKE: He won't know until tomorrow mother's gone . . . Anyway, no sense him coming out all this distance. Those airplane tickets cost a lot you know.

JOE: Yeah — it's a long way. Well, Jake — we're sorry about all the trouble you got.

JAKE: Thanks, Joe. And you, Roy.

JOE: *(Turning at door)* You seen Harding yet?

JAKE: Harding? Who's Harding?

JOE: The undertaker. Nice young fellow. Come into town since you retired. You must've walked past his house coming out from the station. The big new place on the left — biggest darned house in town, I guess. He seen to arrangements when your old man died, didn't he, Roy?

ROY: *(Nodding)* Yeah — did a swell job, too. Looking at him, you'd never think pop was dead . . .

JAKE: No, I won't need him for anything. You remember Swanson, the cabinet-maker? Retired a year before mama and I did?

JOE: The lame guy?

JAKE: That's right.

JOE: Yeah — yeah! How's he keeping?

JAKE: Fine. He got moved next door to us now. Still does the odd job. *(Touches casket)* I asked him to build this last time mama went into hospital. Cost me twenty dollars for the lumber.

JOE: *(Approaches table)* Say — that's not bad! You'd never know it was home-made . . . Look at this, Roy. Would you know it was home-made? *(Is about to lift lid, then steps back)* Is it lined with cushion and velvet inside?

JAKE: *(Bewildered)* Lined? What difference is it going to make if it's lined or not?

JOE: Well . . . aren't you . . . going to open it so folks can see in at the funeral?

JAKE: Why? *(Shakes his head)* Mama was terrible sick before she died, Joe. Terrible sick.

ROY: You *are* planning a proper funeral for her, no?

JAKE: Yes, a simple funeral. She asked for a simple funeral. She wanted to be buried on the south hill, where she had her tulip garden.

ROY: Here? On this rundown old farm — you gonna bury her *here*?

JAKE: I promised her I would.

ROY: You can't do that!

JOE: Sure he can. Come on, Roy.

JAKE: Wait! *(To ROY)* What's wrong? Why can't I? We used to in the old days . . .

ROY: *(Disturbed)* You can't! I don't know why, but you can't!

JAKE: Here . . . Let me pay you. I insist!

JOE: Don't take his money, Roy. We got to go, Jake.

JAKE: Here — take it. If it's not enough, say so . . . *(JOE shakes his head and turns for the door)* I don't want you to take half a day with your van helping me for nothing!

JOE: *(Severely)* We run a van, not a hearse. We done what we done for you. But I think maybe you'd better phone Harding an' let him run the funeral, Jake. It'd be best that way. Well, Roy — we got a bedroom suite to deliver yet. *(They move to the door)*

JAKE: Joe! Roy! If you see someone up town who could spare a few hours to dig the grave for me, I'd be obliged if you'd pass the word around. I've got a grub-hoe and spade in the shed. All I need is a strong man or two. I'll pay for the work. Tell 'em that, okay, Joe? *(JOE nods and both men leave. JAKE slowly and thoughtfully takes matches and two candles out of his pockets. Places the candles at head and foot of casket and lights them. Puts his hand gently on head of casket)* It won't be long now, mama. By night-time . . . maybe tomorrow morning. And then . . . and then — what? Everything's stopping, or running ahead. I can't make out which, mama. I knew everybody once. Now, I know nobody. You won't be touched anymore. I won't let them! *(Walks to stove and picks up bit of wood and kindling. Glances to table, and with pained expression, drops wood back on floor)* I shouldn't of let them! I'm sorry, mama. Nobody should suffer like that . . . It's going to be lonesome at the home now . . . Maybe I won't go back — I don't have to go back! There's enough wood in the shed to keep me warm all winter. After that . . . maybe there won't be another winter. *(Brightens up as if making contact with an old companion)* Everything will be like you wanted! When Jenny comes, I will send her into town to buy some cakes and coffee. I can light the stove then, and help make lunch for all the people who come. They'll remember us again and go home content! *(Sound of car. JAKE goes to window, then hurries to door, which he opens)* Jenny — you've come! I was worried when you didn't call me this morning!

JENNY: *(Enters and shivers)* Hi! I drove to the pension paradise, but your sidekick, Swanson, was the only one around, an' he said you'd taken the train out.

JAKE: You found someone to stay with the kiddies?

JENNY: I didn't look. Jim stayed off work today, an' it's about time. They're his kids, too. Now he'll see what I do with my time.

JAKE: I wanted . . . to be on the train with mama. It's the last trip we'll be taking together.

JENNY: Sure, pop. No need to get spooky about it like that. How come you haven't got the heat on? This place's like a meat locker.

JAKE: Not yet . . . *(Nods in direction of table)* After . . . we'll light the fire and have something hot to drink.

JENNY: You mean . . . *(Stares with disbelief at casket)* You mean she's the way she came out of hospital? *(JAKE nods)* But — that's not legal, pop!

JAKE: I asked the doctor, and he said it was alright.

JENNY: That's ridiculous! If it's the money, you should've said. Herb makes good money — he could've helped. Even Jim and I could've pitched in a little ourselves! Boy, I bet the railway didn't know she wasn't embalmed when they took her!

JAKE: It isn't money, Jenny! Your mama and I are simple people. We never made a big show over anything we did. No need to start now.

JENNY: Listen to me, pop! Let everything go another day. There's a young fellow in town who could do a rush job on preparing her. Then tomorrow . . .

JAKE: You talking about this Harding fellow?

JENNY: Why, yes. You seen him already?

JAKE: You remember the first time mama went in for her operation? You remember how sure the doctors were they'd got the cancer out?

JENNY: Yes . . .

JAKE: Mama wasn't sure. She knew it would only be time. We planned what had to be done — how I would live. I had to promise her I'd make sure to eat hot soup once every day? She figured it'd take the chill away and keep the blood thin. She just kept at me until I promised . . .

JENNY: Have you seen Harding?

JAKE: No — I'm not going to.

JENNY: *(Turns away angrily from him)* I suppose what I feel doesn't matter! Maybe I shouldn't of bothered to come out even!

JAKE: Jenny! Mama had the kind of pain nobody could tell us about — not even she! They kept cutting into her and giving her more and more drugs. Right or wrong, they tried to save her life. But no Harding must touch her now!

JENNY: Why not? She won't feel anything.

JAKE: She's sacred — that's why! Even Christ Himself was left alone once he was dead!

JENNY: Alright, pop — it's your show. Only I wish we didn't have to freeze like this.

JAKE: Let me stay. You go into town and have something warm to eat and drink. And here — take this! *(Gives JENNY some money)*

JENNY: What's this for?

JAKE: Buy a pound of coffee and some biscuits or cake to serve the people after the burial. *(She protests but he shakes*

67

his head firmly) Go on now — no talking back! Take it, and buy the things I told you!

JENNY: I'll bring back something hot for you. A hamburger and a coffee.

JAKE: I couldn't eat — not here. I just want to think.

JENNY: Like heck! I'll bring back a coffee . . . and see you drink it! *(Leaves. Sounds of other cars arriving. Shouts of greeting. Laughter)*

JAKE: *(Musing to himself)* Two men to dig the grave. Someone to say a few words . . . and then . . .   *(Lowers his face into his hands)*

Small crowd enters, becoming subdued when they see him.

SADIE: *(Approaches JAKE and touches his shoulder)* It is a sad day for you to return, Jake. Sam and I are sorry.

JAKE: Mama wanted to come back — among neighbours.

SADIE: Did she — have much pain?

JAKE: Yes.

SAM: *(Taking over)* Alright, everybody — Jake's got to have help! All hands pitch in, an' we'll make short work of the job, as they say. You ladies get the stove going, an' I'll need a man to help dig the grave. Joe Rudyk stopped me on the way from town, asking for a man to help **him** dig. But I'm not waiting on no Joe Rudyk. By the way, Jake — I called Mister Harding to ask where the cemetery plot was, an' he says he knows nothing about it. Doesn't the cluck know what plot you bought?

JAKE: Wait — there is something . . .

SAM: If I ran my farm the way he runs his burial parlour, I'd go broke. Imagine — not knowing which plot a customer owns!

JAKE: I don't own a plot! Mama and I didn't own a cemetery plot. We were happy on this farm — spent most of our lives here. It bloomed and grew everything for us. We wish to be buried here.

SAM: Now wait a minute! Did you say you want her to be buried on this old farm?

JAKE: It was her last wish.

(Murmur of disapproval from crowd)

SADIE: What did Mister Harding have to say to that?

JAKE: I don't know any Mister Harding!

SAM: Then — how come . . . *(Turns and points foolishly to table and casket)*

JAKE: We were simple people, and we want to die the way we lived. Do you understand?

SAM: *(Nods absent-mindedly)* Yeah . . .

JAKE: Mama is dead. Her hurts and worries are over now. If you were to see her you would understand how much she suffered. She is so thin and grey. Her face is bruised from the gas inhalor.

SAM: Hell, Jake. That cluck could fix her up so's she'd look like a million bucks!

JAKE: I don't want her — to look like a million bucks. She didn't ask for that!

ANOTHER WOMAN: Jake — be reasonable like Sam says!

JAKE: Maybe there is a heaven where her soul is going. I hope there is. As I hope God is merciful and will take pity on her wounds and white hair and blackened face!

SADIE: Make her beautiful, then!

JAKE: She **is** beautiful! Don't you understand? Mama wasn't ashamed to show what life had done to her. Does she have to be pinched and shaped by a corpse-washer? What right has he . . . to pump her full of formalin? And pack her mouth with cotton — and paint her cheeks like those of a queen . . . or a whore? What right?

SAM: *(Disturbed)* Now, now Jake! No need to say such things. We know what you've gone through. This has been a bad time for you.

JAKE: I want to bury my wife with dignity!

SAM: Sure, Jake. We understand.

JAKE: *(Looks around him)* I need two men for about an hour. It's soft and sandy on the south hill.

ANOTHER WOMAN: There is a cemetery for our dead. Who ever heard of burying someone on the farm — like a cow or dead chicken! Jake — you're out of your mind.

SAM: Mary's right, Jake. Call Harding. If it's money worries you, then let me tell you there isn't a person here who would mind chipping in to help out. We're all neighbours — known you an' your missus most our lives.

JAKE: No! Darn it, no!

SAM: Jake — relax. *(Glances at others)* We'll take over and see she gets a decent burial. What difference if it takes another day or two. Now just you look at this — *(Walks over and taps casket)* Harding will get an outside box for this. That's the way it's done nowadays. An' he'll touch up her face so we can all see her and remember her at rest.

JAKE: She's not resting! She's dead — you understand? Dead!

SAM: Jake — Jake! We want to do what is right. Times have changed, Jake!

JAKE: What's got into all of you? *(Takes hold of SAM's arm and looks accusingly at him. SAM averts his face)* Will you look at me? When your baby died of diptheria, we buried her in an apple box! You forget that already?

SAM: *(Shaking off JAKE's hold)* Why talk about it . . . times have changed!

JAKE: *(To another woman)* And you, Mary — when your father passed away. It was Swanson built a coffin for him — same's he did that one for mama. Only the one for your father wasn't as fancy. Lumber was expensive. Just a couple of slabs of poplar wood. Old Charlie read a little from the Bible, and those of us who'd dug the grave covered it. You figure we sorrowed less? What had to be done was done — and it was clean and honest! What's got into you since then? Are we so scared we got to show off even in death?

ANOTHER WOMAN: We couldn't do better then. But like Sam says — times have changed.

JAKE: Has death changed?

SADIE: *(With despair)* Yes! Even death has changed!

71

JAKE: *(Angered now)* Well, of all the . . . You've forgotten what death looks like — is that it? Mama won't mind. Come here, I'll show you! *(Moves to casket and attempts to open lid)*

SADIE: No! Don't let him do it! *(SAM steps to JAKE and pulls him back)*

SAM: *(Coaxingly)* Now Jake, please! Haven't we enough troubles in life!

JAKE: Take your hands off me!

SAM: Please, Jake. It's the last thing you'll be able to do for her. Don't hold back now. I know how you feel — my wife going to her final rest would be terrible for me, too. Give her all you can now. There won't be another chance.

JAKE: Give what? What little we've worked all our lives to save?

SAM: We'll help — I said we would, didn't I? What good is it to you — nobody lives forever . . .

JAKE: She isn't a plaster doll. She lived — only three days ago she spoke to me. Told me what she wanted me to do . . . A patch of ground on which she had grown flowers for forty-three years. Just a patch of ground she'd worked once!

SAM: There's a right way an' a wrong way — that's all I say . . .

JAKE: What right? What wrong? "Dust unto dust" — it says in the Bible . . .

SAM: We're above all that! We can afford better things. Forget the cost — just think of what you get for the price — a proper parson, music. And a place people can come to see the departed without freezing and arguing. You can't talk above a whisper in a proper parlor — now that's dignity, if you want dignity!

SADIE: And at the graveside they lay a mat all around that looks like grass. You hardly know that someone has gone, it's that nice and restful!

ANOTHER WOMAN: Almost makes you look forward to the end yourself, it's that nice!

ANOTHER MAN: You gonna deny this for your wife? If you are, you're a cheap old bugger, that's what you are!

JAKE: *(Looks around him helplessly)* What are you saying? I promised her a death-wish. I believe in it! I'm not changing my mind — not now . . .

SAM: Don't make it hard on yourself, Jake. I got nothin' against you — we got along good as neighbours. But — well — you're cheapinin' your property by burying your missus on it. Like you say, maybe we got by alright in the old days. But we got Harding here now. He's been trained to make up nice funerals. This way, you're making a mockery of a funeral, that's what you're doing! If I was you, Jake, I'd be ashamed of even thinking it!

ANOTHER WOMAN: Shame! Shame — Jake!

ANOTHER MAN: Let him go to it by himself, if he wants. He'll learn to get along with neighbours soon enough!

Knock on door, and JOE the deliveryman enters with small wreath of flowers in his hand. Places wreath on casket.

JOE: I come as fast as I could, Jake. Roy took the furniture on himself, so I'm finished work. I been thinkin' what you said when we brought Missus Johnson. Then I looked again at Harding's great big house as we drove by, and I says to myself — what goes on here? How come he makes so much off the dead? So . . . *(Looks at SAM)* you coming to help me dig, Sam?

SAM: *(Avoiding JOE's eye)* I dunno . . .

JOE: I thought you'd be glad to give a hand.

SAM: I would — when I thought Jake was giving his missus a nice, respectable ceremony.

JOE: What the heck — the guy's a phony. I seen him cry for a price. Aw, come on — we all got to die sometime!

SADIE: No, we don't!

ANOTHER WOMAN: We go to sleep — only to wake again!

JOE: *(Startled)* Holy mackerel! What kind of baloney is that?

JENNY slips unobtrusively into room. Stands near door, a bag of groceries on her arm.

WOMAN FROM THE BACK: When Mister Harding fixed up my mother last year, she looked younger than I! Even her fingernails were painted red!

ANOTHER MAN: For twelve hundred dollars, you don't even have to look after the grave! He's got cards with dates on them in his office. Every day he looks at the cards, and if it's an anniversary, he sends someone to put a wreath and clean the weeds off!

JOE: Some deal! I'd do that for five bucks. *(To JAKE)* You want me to go back into town an' get Roy? We can still dig it before night.

SADIE: *(Loudly)* There is no death! Only sleep! Mister Harding makes them sleep!

SAM: Come on, Jake. We'll help you to pay — it's worth it!

JAKE: Stop it! All of you!

SAM: Be reasonable — she can't lie in that condition. It's — unhealthy, if you ask me. Get her embalmed, if you can't make up your mind.

JAKE: I've made up my mind! *(To JOE)* There's a pick and couples of spades in the woodshed. Go ahead and start digging under the big birch in the south garden — go! If there isn't another man in the neighbourhood to help, I'll go and dig myself! And Joe — listen — I'll pay you a hundred — two hundred dollars if you want, so's they'll know it isn't the money! Go now! *(A stunned silence, then hostile murmur from crowd)*

JENNY: *(Angrily)* Wait, Joe! *(JOE stops and stares at her)* We've got so many lies for everything, we forget there's a truth. Even I've forgotten some things are real and ain't ever going to change. Joe — open the coffin. I want to see her.

SADIE: No!

ANOTHER MAN: Don't you do it, Joe!

JENNY: Go ahead, Joe. I've got to see what my mother looks like now — what I'll look like before they plaster and paint until I look dirty and cheap!

ANOTHER WOMAN: Dear God — no!

JAKE: Open it, Joe!

SAM: *(Alarmed)* What is this? What're you trying to do to us?

JENNY: Alright — **I'll** do it! *(Drops parcels and purposefully strides to side of casket. Gently but firmly raises bust lid)* Look! There she is — poor mama . . . poor, hurt mama!

With horror and fascination, crowd draws back then cranes forward for look into casket. Scene has a primitive symbolism to it.

SADIE: Look — she was crying when she died! Why didn't you say she cried, Jake?

JENNY: Who of us wanted to know?

SAM: She's so thin! What did she weigh last time she went in, Jake?

JAKE: Ninety-seven pounds . . .

ANOTHER MAN: She suffered — she really suffered!

Woman begins to whimper in background.

SADIE: At the end of life is this . . . nothing more. Why do we live, if we're only to be cut down? Why?

JOE: I wouldn't be worrying about it yet, Sadie. You're good for another twenty years, or my name ain't Joe! *(Chuckles hollowly)*

SAM: I'm sorry about this, Jake. You know what I mean . . .

JAKE: Sure, Sam. It's alright.

SAM: We get fooled so easy. A guy comes around an' tries to sell you a worn-out army blanket. Tells you it'll keep you warm at twenty below. Tells it to enough people enough times and you start believin' him, like you start believin' all those soap and tooth-paste ads on billboards an' TV. A man's scared to die, Jake. So we've begun to believe all the lies that give death another name an' face. But it's still death. That don't ever change.

JAKE: No. Not ever. *(Goes to JENNY, who is weeping silently on chair at table)* It's alright, child. I cried when my mother left me, and your children will cry for you. But we got to keep living when the dead are buried — think of that, too.

JENNY: *(Through tears)* I didn't know she'd gone through this much. You never told me!

JAKE: It's alright, Jenny . . .

JENNY: Pop, I tried — but sitters were hard to get this last time she went in. Oh, God!

SAM: Come on, Joe. I'll help you. We got to get it over with before night comes.

JOE: You an' me on a couple of spades — be no time at all, eh? *(They leave)*

JAKE: *(Stroking JENNY's hair)* Herb was in school, and you could hardly walk yet when mama planted her tulips around the birch. The newspaper took a picture of her in the tulips, and you in her arms. They sure were some tulips — the best ever raised in these parts!

SADIE: Can I start a fire now, Jake? Sam an' Joe will be finished before the house warms. *(JAKE nods)*

JAKE: Yes, sir! They were the nicest tulips. Mama ordered them from this Ontario seed catalogue. We manured the ground heavy, but all the same we weren't sure they'd grow. It's such a different climate they got in Ontario. But they grew — like I say, the newspaper sent a guy to take a picture!

ON CAMERA: Camera back to take in room, with assembled crowd dividing into twos and threes to converse quietly. JENNY lifts her head to look at JAKE, and through her tears smiles at him.

The End

George Ryga (1964)   Photo: unknown

GOODBYE IS FOR KEEPS

Cast

JOE: 35 years of age. Strong but physically unattractive man.
VERA: His wife. 23 years of age. Thin, tall and meek person.
JENNY: 16 years of age. Cousin of Joe's. Simple, buxom rural girl. Naive but perceptive.
DOCTOR: Middle-aged and heavy, due to excessive drinking. A man fated for a small town practice.
PRIEST: A young, disciplined and cold man.
TWO NUNS
NURSE
TAVERN WAITER

Setting

The kitchen-sitting room of JOE's and VERA's apartment. It is a one-bedroom dwelling, over a grocery store. Door to single bedroom is on the right of stage. On left of stage is gas range and on wall back of it is sink with wall cupboards. Small apartment refrigerator back of this. Left and backstage is door to outside. Centre stage is chrome kitchen table with three or four mismatched chairs. Right and backstage is folding couch and soft chair, behind which is old, upright clothes closet. Window on right backstage wall. A coffee table, floor and reading lamp, broom alongside range completes the furnishings. Cheap curtains, tasteless pictures on walls and garish wallpaper. Bare, overhead light.

Scene 1

ON CAMERA: Open on front room of apartment. JENNY is busy washing and putting away dishes. She is uncertain and goes through the cupboards, as if memorizing the order of the household items there. Door opens and VERA comes in, carrying heavily wrapped baby in her arms. JOE follows behind with suitcase and small bouquet of withered flowers. For a moment, VERA does not see JENNY in the room.

JOE: Well, here we are! Won't want that to happen again soon, eh? Heh! Heh!

VERA: I was scared — when you didn't come to see me . . .

JOE: I got work to do. Can't go racin' to the hospital when I'm workin', can I?

VERA: *(Sees JENNY and steps back with surprise)* Joe! Who's she?

JENNY: Hi!

JOE: That's my cousin — Jenny. I had her come up to take care o' the kid while you was gettin' stronger. Jenny — this here's the wife, Vera . . .

JENNY: I got the crib set up like you asked me to, Joe. An' I got a bottle of milk warmed up for the baby to eat.

VERA: A bottle of milk? I'm going to nurse the baby!

80

JOE: *(Sharply)* No!

VERA: But Joe, I **want** to nurse him, like I done in hospital.

JOE: No. An' there's no more to say about it, Vera. I don't want to . . . Well, I don't think he should be havin' your milk anymore!

VERA: Why not?

JOE: I been hearin' talk around town an' at work, an' it all figures out pretty good. No need takin' chances. So I say no, an' that's the way it's gonna be.

VERA: But . . .

JENNY: I'll take the baby an' put it in the crib. *(Takes baby and pulls off face flap to peer at it)* You sure got a nice little boy, Vera!

JOE: Maybe.

JENNY: What you mean, Joe?

JOE: Nothin'. Take it away. *(JENNY carries baby to bedroom)*

VERA: *(In hushed, nervous voice)* What's she doin' here?

JOE: I told you already. That's Jenny, my cousin out from Long Coulee. She's gonna help out when I'm out workin'. No harm in that . . .

VERA: I don't want her! I don't want anybody meddlin' with me or my baby now!

JOE: Shut up!

VERA: *(Shudders and presses her hands hard together)* I'm sorry, Joe.

JOE: It's alright — forget it.

VERA: It's about my mother they're talkin', an' you're scared — is that it, Joe?

JOE: Never mind what's said or not said.

VERA: I only want to hold him — to look in his face while he feeds on me! He's pretty real, an' at the hospital it was like he wanted to know me better!

JOE: I don't want no more talk about it! Now you be nice to Jenny — she don't know towns or town people. *(JENNY re-enters room)*

JENNY: I put him down an' he's sound asleep. No sense wakin' to feed him, I reckon.

JOE: He'll wake when he's hungry. Now I want you to come down an' meet old man Turney — runs the store downstairs. He owns this whole buildin', an' I know him well.

JENNY: Gee!

JOE: If there's anythin' you need, you just go down an' get it from old Turney. Just say to him — put it on Joe's bill!

VERA: *(Watches them walk to door)* Where you goin'?

JOE: Downstairs. Don't worry yourself none — we'll be right back!

VERA: I wanna go, too!

JOE: You gotta stay behind if the baby wakes. Make some tea — we won't be long. *(They leave room. VERA moves to sink and clutches hard at it. Nods and lowers her head over basin)*

VERA: I wanna nurse him! Dear God, I gotta nurse him! He's my kid — I'll kill him if I can't nurse him!

Fade out.

Scene 2

ON CAMERA: Up on JOE and JENNY on stairs.

JOE: Folks have made Vera what she is now, Jenny, an' I ain't helped much. It's a mean an' busy town. But in case folks is right, we can't take no chances.

JENNY: What you tryin' to say, Joe?

JOE: Well, you'll understand when you get to know Vera better. But she's alright — you just treat her easy, an' she's like a rope in your hands. Get me?

JENNY: I'm a little scared, Joe. We never seen you since you got married.

JOE: No need to be scared. She won't hurt you.

JENNY: Where'd she come from? My folks know her folks?

JOE: Naw — she grew up in an institution . . . one of them Catholic homes for orphans. She's alright — just treat her easy. *(They walk down stairs)*

JENNY: Why can't she nurse the baby, Joe?

JOE: Because — I don't want to take no chances with **her** kind of blood in my kid! Now come on an' meet Turney.

Fade out.

Scene 3

ON CAMERA: Up on front room of apartment. VERA and JENNY are having a cup of coffee and are seated on couch.

JENNY: Old Turney — he reminds me of our neighbour, Tommy By-The-Well . . .

VERA: Tommy By-The-Well?

JENNY: His real name was Tommy Rattan. But anytime you went past his place, he'd be standin' by the well, pullin' up water or lowerin' a milk-can to cool. So folks got to callin' him Tommy By-The-Well.

VERA: *(Laughs)* That's very funny. I'd like to live in the country — people laugh and are happier there . . .

JENNY: He wore a pair of suspenders to hold his pants up, an' the suspenders had clips on them which said "Police." It made Tommy feel important when somebody looked down an' read out the word. Turney reminds me of him — he'd laugh at a rusty nail . . .

VERA: *(Nervously)* People here aren't like that, Jenny. They step out of your way, and then laugh and whisper when you've gone past. Even old Turney does — I know! Did he ask about the baby?

JENNY: No . . . *(Lightly)* When's Joe finish work?

VERA: He's home after four. They got three shifts at the power plant — all day and night there's men workin' there!

JENNY: Must be a good job.

VERA: He'll be a foreman in a couple of years — you just wait and see! My Joe is a good man. He works very hard. He likes me, Jenny.

JENNY: Yes . . .

VERA: He was kind to marry me. People have told me that — and you know it, too — don't you?

JENNY: Yes — I mean, no!

VERA: He was kind to marry me. Nobody wanted to marry me . . . Look how thin I am. A man doesn't want a thin woman!

JENNY: I'm not thin, an' I ain't married yet.

VERA: Well, they got nothing against you. They won't push you around. Did you know I was a Catholic?

JENNY: Joe told me.

VERA: I'll never be a Catholic again. Joe's a Protestant, an' I want to be what my Joe is.

JENNY: All our family's Protestant.

VERA: *(Rises and paces nervously)* Did you answer an ad in the paper? How did you find this place?

JENNY: Find you? I don't know what you're sayin', Vera!

VERA: How did you know we needed a girl?

JENNY: Joe wrote to my father for me when you went into hospital. I'm Joe's cousin, Vera.

VERA: Cousin? Joe never told me . . . *(She goes to window and stares out)* I'm glad you've come. It was so lonely by myself an' Joe at work. Listening to time drive by like a three-ton truck. Feeling my baby growin' and hurting me, an' being happy for it. An' being so afraid . . .

JENNY: Afraid of what?

VERA: Afraid of somethin' happening!

JENNY: Nothing could happen. You don't have to be afraid.

VERA: Joe's a good man. But he gets mad easy, an' then he sounds like all the others have sounded through the years — sayin' the same things in the same voice. I could shout! I could break my head open against a wall! They're wrong, but they'd never believe me! *(Knock on door. JENNY hurries to open, and PRIEST enters)*

PRIEST: Oh, hello! I'm Father Bell. I was driving by and wondered if Vera was home yet . . . *(Sees VERA)* Welcome home! How do you feel?

VERA: *(Moves to couch and sits down)* I'm very well, Father. Thank you for askin'.

PRIEST: And what were you blessed with — a girl, or a boy?

VERA: A boy, Father.

PRIEST: Isn't that wonderful! May I see him?

JENNY: No. He's sleeping now . . .

VERA: He's in there, Father. Go see him — an' tell me . . .

PRIEST: No need to do that now. Like your friend says, he's sleeping so let the little fellow sleep.

VERA: Yes, Father. Let him sleep.

PRIEST: Now — have you considered a name for him yet?

VERA: *(Shakes her head and looks down)* No.

PRIEST: We mustn't expect everything at once, and you're just out of hospital. But you'll want to bring him up in your faith, no doubt. Vera — I'll be happy to christen him when the time comes.

JENNY: What about Joe? He's not going to . . .

VERA: Yes, Father. When the time comes . . .

PRIEST: You look like you could do with a rest. I'll call by in a few days. *(Turns to JENNY)* So happy to meet you — what is your name?

JENNY: Jenny!

PRIEST: Jenny — that's a young and honest name. I like it. Goodbye!

VERA: Goodbye, Father.

JENNY: Goodbye. *(Sees him to door)*

VERA: *(Crosses herself)* Holy Mary, Mother of God — Pray for us sinners!

JENNY: *(Angrily)* What are you tryin' to do? What will Joe say?

VERA: *(Rising, as out of trance)* Don't tell Joe — please, Jenny! Don't ever tell Joe that Father Bell came to visit! Promise me — cross you heart you'll never tell! *(JENNY stares at her in bewilderment)*

Fade out.

Scene 4
Same set as before. Later in the evening. The table is set for supper and JOE takes his place. VERA's place is vacant. JENNY moves to table with pot of soup in her hands.

JOE: *(Pointing to empty chair)* Where's Vera?

JENNY: She's in bed havin' a sleep. Want some soup?

JOE: What's in it?

JENNY: Mushrooms — it's out of a can.

JOE: Sure — sure! Pile it on. Where's the bread an' butter?

JENNY: It's there . . . *(Glances at table then at sideboard)* Oh, I'm sorry! *(Gets bread and butter and puts them before JOE)*

JOE: Think you gonna like it here?

JENNY: I figure so. The traffic noise is sure loud — don't know how I'll sleep.

JOE: You'll sleep when you're tired enough. *(Eats hungrily)* She been givin' you any trouble?

JENNY: Vera? No — we get along good.

JOE: Yeah . . .

JENNY: She must be awful run down. She got a bit shaky an' white toward evenin', so I asked who her doctor was, an' phoned him after she went to bed. I done right, didn't I, Joe?

JOE: What time's he comin'?

JENNY: He said before supper. Did I do right?

JOE: Yeah, kid — you did right. S'long's he doesn't charge the earth for comin' over.

JENNY: He said somethin' about meanin' to see you anyway, an' would you wait for him . . .

JOE: How's that?

JENNY: He said he wanted to talk to you. Can I eat now? I'm real hungry.

JOE: Help yourself — nobody's holding you by the arm. He didn't say what he wanted to see me about?

JENNY: I didn't ask.

JOE rises abruptly and, still munching a piece of bread, goes into bedroom. JENNY doesn't touch her food, but watches bedroom door. JOE returns.

JOE: That kid sure looks like me, don't he?

JENNY: Can't tell. All babies look the same.

JOE: Well, they ain't the same, I'll tell you! *(Leans forward conspiratorially)* She didn't give him none of her breast, did she?

JENNY: He drank milk from a bottle.

JOE: You not lyin' now, eh?

JENNY: I gave him the bottle myself. Vera was hurtin', because she stood over there, tryin' not to watch, an' pressin' her arms tight across her chest . . .

JOE: Anytime she tries anythin' funny, you be sure to tell me. You an' I are kin - you remember that!

JENNY: Yes, Joe. *(They eat silently for a moment)* Joe — you gonna pay me for workin' here?

JOE: Sure, I'm gonna pay you! I don't want you workin' for nothin'. Pay you . . . oh, a buck an' a half a day — with no charge for eats or a place on the couch to sleep! How's that sound?

JENNY: *(Delighted)* Sounds good! I never got money for workin' on the farm. Just money for ice-cream an' drinks when we went to town. But the folks always bought my clothes an' give them to me . . . Joe — Vera's nice. What's she worried about? Is she sick?

JOE: Naw — she ain't sick. Just tired from havin' the baby. She'll be good as gold in a couple weeks.

JENNY: Then I got to go back to the farm?

JOE: Well, if things work out alright, I figure you can stay on an' help Vera — keep her company when I'm workin'.

JENNY: She's so scared . . .

JOE: Don't worry about it.

JENNY: When I finished feedin' the baby, she kept lookin' at it, and sayin' — "somethin' might happen." She said it lots of times, like she was talkin' to herself.

JOE: The kid's alright. There's more me than her in him, ain't there? He's a boy! Just you mind she don't put her milk into the kid, that's all!

JENNY: Why, Joe? *(Knock on door. JENNY rises and lets DOCTOR in)*

JOE: *(Still chewing food and coming clumsily to his feet)* You wanna cup of tea? Give the doc some tea, Jenny.

DOCTOR: No. I haven't the time. What seems to be wrong with Vera?

JENNY: She seemed awful unhappy before she went to bed. I figured you might have something to give her to sleep better . . .

JOE: It's nothin', I tell you. She's tired from havin' the kid, that's all!

DOCTOR: Is she sleeping now?

JOE: She's lyin' there. I didn't look to see if she was sleepin'.

DOCTOR: Well, I'll look in on her, but I don't suppose there is much we can do tonight.

JOE: In there, doc! *(Points with his thumb to bedroom. DOCTOR goes in)*

JENNY: Would you like some pudding?

JOE: Pudding — what kind did you make?

JENNY: Rice pudding.

JOE: Naw — I'm no Hindu. Tell you what — there's a bottle of brandy in the second shelf. Bring it here, an' a couple of glasses.

JENNY: You drink, Joe? Nobody in our family ever drunk.

JOE: It's for the doc. He likes his slug of brandy. Loosens him up after a day of work. Reckon he works hard some nights, too — I've seen him pretty loaded the odd morning . . .

JENNY: *(Finds and brings the brandy and glasses to table)* We never had brandy in our house. You must sure make lots of money, Joe!

JOE: Yeah — yeah, enough. Easy come — easy go. That's the way it is with life. A fellow works hard an' reckons he has the devil by the tail, an' then somethin' happens . . .

JENNY: What happens, Joe? What are you an' Vera talkin' about when you say that?

JOE: *(Angrily)* Nothin'! Nothin's gonna happen! Maybe Vera believes in that kind of nonsense — like all the crazy women in this town — but not me! Now stop your chatterin' an' get on with the dishes. You talk too much!

JENNY: *(Quickly gathering up dishes)* I'm sorry, Joe. Didn't mean to make you sore . . .

JOE: Yeah — well don't worry about it. *(Paces the floor and stops behind JENNY at sink)* I could of done better with my life. I'd bought furniture an' had a steady job. I could of had any of the girls I wanted in this town. What kind of dumpy town is it anyway? Nothin' but pride an' gossip an' hard times. I took Vera because I got a soft heart. Ain't right for a woman to be without a husband, just because she's been brought up in a home, an' because her old lady was the town kook who threw rocks at store windows. Nobody's fault in that . . .

JENNY: Joe — don't say such things!

JOE: Why not? I got a right to say what I think! I made my bed, an' I'm gonna sleep in it. Don't have a kid, they kept tellin' me — an' I got a kid now — nothin' wrong with him, is there?

JENNY: No — I don't think so.

JOE: You didn't know Vera was a mick, did you? Don't matter to me — I got nothin' against micks, so long's they keep their big mouths shut an' their religion to themselves! Maybe there's nothin' to it — but I don't take chances on here puttin' any badness into my kid!

JENNY: You an' Vera sayin' such things — it's like I was dreamin' . . . *(DOCTOR appears from bedroom. Smiles at JENNY and JOE)*

JOE: Well?

DOCTOR: I think she'll live through the night, Joe. And the baby's away like the world had no anxieties. You have a beautiful child in that boy!

JOE: Have yourself a drink, doc.

DOCTOR: *(Hesitates, then goes to table)* What are we drinking?

JOE: Damned if I know what's in it. It says French brandy on the bottle. Go on — fill up!

DOCTOR: One drink won't interfere with my supper, will it?

JENNY: *(Helpfully)* Would you like some hot water with it?

DOCTOR: *(Startled)* Hot water?

JOE: *(Laughs)* Don't mind her, doc. She's fresh off the farms — don't know much about anythin'.

JENNY is flustered and returns to sink where she concentrates on washing dishes.

DOCTOR: This is French brandy, Joe. Haven't tasted any since the New Years' party at the hospital. One of the nurses stole a bottle from her boyfriend . . .

JOE: Maybe she got it some other way, eh? You know what I mean, doc?

DOCTOR: No, I don't know what you mean!

JOE: *(Embarrassed)* I was kiddin' . . .

DOCTOR: Now about Vera.

JOE: Yeah — what about her?

DOCTOR: Your wife had a difficult time with this baby. She's rundown, worried — mind you, this happens more often than you think. *(Swallows drink and pours himself another)*

JOE: She'll be alright. Jenny here can look after things.

DOCTOR: She'll require all the rest she can get . . . Not only that — I would suggest you consider not having any more children for a while.

JOE: No more children! What in hell's a wife for, if not to have kids? It's good for them — fattens them out, an' makes them laugh more.

DOCTOR: I don't think Vera will be laughing much until your little fellow gets on his feet.

JOE: Whatever you say — you're the doc.

DOCTOR: I'll leave these pills for Vera if she should find it difficult to fall asleep again. Well, luck to you and your new family, Joe! *(Drinks and leaves)*

JOE: No more kids! What in hell does he know?

JENNY: If kids makes a woman as tired an' worried as Vera is, than the doc's right, Joe. I brought the crib into this room after lunch today. Vera took the baby to hold after I'd fed it. When I looked next, she'd put the baby in the sink, an' was stackin' dirty dishes in the crib. I got her to go to bed . . .

JOE: *(Slams empty glass on table)* So you been talkin' to him! He told you to say all that, so when he got at me himself, it would be easy for him!

JENNY: Joe! You'll wake her! I never seen the doc before, an' I told you what we spoke on the phone!

JOE: Alright — it's me then! Now don't go talkin' to Vera about what the doc said. No sense disturbin' her more — she'll believe anythin' now, if it sounds bad enough. Don't say nothin'. She's alright — the kid's alright . . .

JENNY: Yes, Joe.

ACT TWO

ONE YEAR LATER

Scene 1
Front room of JOE's apartment. JOE is seated on couch, reading comics. JENNY stands at stove, warming bottle of baby's milk in saucepan over burner. Knock on door.

JOE: Yeah?

VOICE: Phone for you, Joe!

JOE: Okay, Turney. Be right down.

They stare at one another. JENNY wearily takes bottle into bedroom. JOE makes no move to rise. He returns to his reading. JENNY comes back.

JENNY: Ain't you goin' down? There's a phone call for you in the store!

JOE: I know. Nothin's on fire.

JENNY: It'll be from the hospital. You better go down, Joe.

JOE: Alright — so I'm goin'! *(Leaves)*

JENNY: *(Picks up his comic book and begins to browse through it. Hears infant calling from bedroom)* You go to sleep, Jamie! That's a good boy! *(To herself)* Sure hope nothin's the matter with Vera. No need of that foolishness — carryin' another baby, an' her down to ninety-four pounds in weight. Joe's scared, too. Wouldn't even take her in for a check-up. If it was me, I'd have gone in, Joe or no Joe. But not Vera! What's to be scared of? Jamie's a nice, bright boy. But would she stop worryin'? Not Vera . . . . *(JOE enters suddenly. He stares at JENNY in confusion then sits down at kitchen table)* What's wrong, Joe? Anythin' the matter?

JOE: The hospital — Vera's had the baby — a baby girl. They want me to go down right away.

JENNY: Why?

JOE: The girl wouldn't say.

JENNY: Vera must be in trouble. She was so thin an' rundown!

JOE: No, it ain't Vera. They'd have said if it was. It's . . . it's the kid!

JENNY: Now Joe — no sense imaginin' trouble. It's probably nothin' at all.

JOE: It's the kid, I tell you! All the time she was carryin' it, she was puttin' all kinds of worries an' scares into it! Suckin' all the good out of it — an' leavin' behind . . . somethin' that had no right to be!

JENNY: You're workin' yourself up over nothin'. Look at Jamie — he's a fine boy.

JOE: Jamie's all mine! This one ain't. All along, I felt it wasn't all mine — like I knew last time Jamie was gonna be a boy!

JENNY: Well, if you're goin', you'd better get up an' go.

JOE: Who says you're to tell me when to come an' go?

JENNY: *(Looking away from him)* Joe — soon's Vera comes out of hospital, I want to quit workin' here . . .

JOE: Quit? An' go back to the farm? You're crazy!

JENNY: I hate fightin' with you. An' we been fightin' for months now . . .

JOE: Yeah — I know. Maybe I got cause to fight, I don't feel like I felt once. What they got for me at the hospital? What you think they got there?

JENNY: I don't know. It's for you to find out.

JOE: Why always me — Joe? Why I got to eat all the crap an' take all the kicks? Because I got a soft heart — is that why?

JENNY: Yes, Joe . . .

JOE: Sit down, Jenny. I got to talk to you.

JENNY: There's dishes to do, an' laundry to hang out for the night . . .

JOE: There's time for everything. Sit down. *(JENNY settles wearily across table from him)* She's like her mother — I always knowed it, but never let myself believe it. She's funny in the head — you know that! But Joe's got a soft heart an' don't look too close.

JENNY: You've got no right talkin' about Vera that way!

JOE: What about me? What about old Joe — the guy who never had good looks or a break?

JENNY: That kind of talk only busts up life. *(Rises and goes to end of room but watches him uncertainly)*

JOE: Alright — look at me an' tell me I have good looks an' coulda got what I wanted out of life!

JENNY: If you was a kid, I'd tell you what you want to hear — but you ain't a kid, Joe.

JOE: I wanted kids — an' I got Jamie. But that didn't make us a family. Vera was gonna disease him with herself — ruin him — kill him! But I stopped her — so he's okay! But the next one she gives old Joe — she'll make sure it lives up to what she expects — what she even wants!

JENNY: Oh, get out of here — go to the hospital — go anywhere!

JOE: Nobody cares how I feel. Lots of guys feel proud an' good about bein' fathers — but not Joe. What Joe gets, the devil himself wouldn't want!

JENNY: Shut up! I can't stand it!

JOE: You — my own cousin — my kin! You don't wanna know how I feel!

JENNY: Why don't you go on the street — tell everybody you meet how you feel — they never heard your story before! I've had to live it every day . . .

JOE: You see my kid don't cry while I'm out! *(Departs angrily. JENNY resumes housework)*

Scene 2

Hall of small town hospital. NURSE leads JOE to small sitting room.

NURSE: The doctor's waiting inside for you. *(JOE enters room where DOCTOR sits in chair reading newspaper. Sees JOE)*

DOCTOR: I'm glad you've come.

JOE: Yeah — what's happenin'?

DOCTOR: Did I call you away from supper?

JOE: Don't worry about my gut. Is everything alright?

DOCTOR: Well, Joe — a year ago I tried to talk sense into your head . . . *(Avoids looking at JOE)*

JOE: Is it Vera?

DOCTOR: Vera's fine. A bit underweight and tired, but it was an easy birth.

JOE: The kid . . .

DOCTOR: Joe — it's not as bad as you think — she's strong and could have a normal life . . .

JOE: *(Grabbing DOCTOR roughly by the arm)* What you mean — normal life? You'd better tell me, or I'm gonna shake all the free booze outa you!

DOCTOR: *(Alarmed)* Let go — for God's sake! It's not my fault — we didn't even use instruments. The girl has a birthmark — over half of her face!

100

JOE: *(Releases him with shock)* Damn you!

DOCTOR: It's quite frightening to see the first time, but when you get used to her . . . well, just remember she'll be growing up not knowing anything different — you'll understand that after a while. Perhaps in a few years, we can arrange for skin grafts . . . She really can live a normal life, Joe. But you'll have to help her, and so will Vera. It's going to require patience, love and intelligence . . .

JOE: Patience? Love? Shove them words back in your medicine books where you got them! You go put in eight hours a day, six days a week at the lousy power house, an' come home at night to a woman who's gone birdie! Then tell me of patience an' love! You guys are a bunch of preachers who make a church in a sick man's guts!

DOCTOR: Come with me. I want you to see the baby.

JOE: I don't wanna see the damned baby! Get outa my way! *(Pushes DOCTOR aside and heads for door)*

DOCTOR: Wait — Joe! I want you to tell Vera! It's easier than us having to!

JOE: I'll tell her. You done enough already! *(Leaves)*

Fade.

Scene 3

JOE in a rundown bar. He is slouched over table. WAITER approaches.

WAITER: Hey — mac! You can't sleep here!

101

JOE: *(Lifts up head)* Gimme a couple more beers!

WAITER: You've had your load. We're closin' in fifteen minutes.

JOE: Fifteen minutes? What time is it?

WAITER: Time you were home. *(Three boisterous ROW-DIES pass on their way out)*

FIRST MAN: Is he givin' you a hard time, Steve?

WAITER: Naw — he's okay.

JOE: Just a couple more beers, an' I'll go quiet as a mouse.

SECOND MAN: Cheep! Cheep! I'm a mouse. *(Twitches his nose)* Let's go home, fellas!

THIRD MAN: Hey! *(Looks closely at JOE)* Ain't you the guy from the power house? You married the kook's daughter, didn't you? How you gettin' on with her?

JOE: *(Shakes his head)* You got the wrong guy . . .

THIRD MAN: Hell, I know you! Well — wish you luck, buddy!

JOE: I tell you, you got the wrong guy!

Rises and knocks glass to floor. WAITER turns and shouts after him. JOE hurries to door. Looks back, sees the WAITER and Rowdies laughing and waving to him through grotesquely distorted vision. He runs into street.

Fade.

Scene 4

Front room of JOE's apartment. JENNY has made couch into bed and has retired, reading a magazine. She has a small bedside lamp on. A stumbling sound outside and she lowers magazine to listen. JOE enters.

JENNY: Where you been? It's past midnight.

JOE: I been drowning a kid with half a face.

JENNY: You been drinkin'! *(JOE giggles in near hysterical high pitch)* Hush! Or you'll wake Jamie!

JOE: *(Sings)* Jamie, Jamie! I'm half-crazy, over you . . .

JENNY: What's got into you?

JOE: Nothin's got into me, cousin Jenny.

JENNY: How's Vera an' the baby?

JOE: *(Stares down at her and licks his lips)* You sure look comfy an' warm lyin' there like that. But you ain't tucked in too good . . .

JENNY: Joe . . .

JOE: Girl like you should have a boyfriend to tuck you in nights . . . You ain't got no boyfriend. Not quite pretty enough. I'll tuck you in — I ain't very pretty myself . . . *(Pulls back her covers)*

JENNY: What are you doin'? *(He gets knees on bed and begins fondling her shoulders crudely)* You get out of here!

JOE: It's my house . . . You don't want me fightin' you all the time — okay — give me what I want, an' I ain't ever gonna fight you again . . . Please, Jenny!

JENNY: *(Pushes him back)* You're drunk! You don't know what you're doin'!

JOE: *(Angrily)* I know what I'm doin'! I'm paying' you a buck fifty a day — for what? To lie like that when I come in? I don't want Vera! It's you I want . . . cross my heart it's you!

Attempts to get into bed again. JENNY sits up and slaps him. He reels back. She rises after him and continues pummeling him across the floor until he is backed against stove, where he turns his head aside and covers his face with his hands. JENNY goes away to put on her dressing gown. JOE moves to table and slumps heavily into chair.

JENNY: I'll make some coffee to straighten you out. You could get jail for that if I was to tell anybody!

JOE: Don't go makin' trouble, Jenny. I got troubles enough . . .

JENNY: You seen Vera?

JOE: It's got half its face covered over with somethin' — doc said it was a birthmark.

JENNY: Oh, God! How's Vera takin' it?

JOE: She's takin' it alright. The poor thing — half a face — can you imagine! *(Begins to sob. JENNY goes to him and is about to touch his head, but reconsiders and returns to preparing coffee)*

104

JENNY: The doc phoned while you was away. He sounded pretty sore about somethin' . . .

JOE: *(Raises his head)* How long ago was this?

JENNY: About a half hour back. Got old Turney outa bed.

JOE: What'd he say?

JENNY: Said he didn't mind it once, but not to have folks call again at that hour . . .

JOE: Not Turney — the doc!

JENNY: Jus' asked if you'd come in. I said no, and he hung up without sayin' anythin' more.

JOE: It's his own damned fault! He got no right bringin' a thing like that into the world. He coulda given it a needle an' killed it before it knew it was alive!

JENNY: When I first come here, he told you not to have kids again. I was here when he said it, Joe!

JOE: Shut up!

JENNY: *(Turns, holding coffee pot poised)* You holler like that again, an' Jamie's gonna be cryin'. But you holler like that again, an' I'm gonna crack you one with this pot! Now I'm askin' you — did Vera want anythin' sent up to the hospital?

JOE: *(Wrings his hands)* She didn't say.

Knock on door and DOCTOR enters immediately.

DOCTOR: So — you're home at last!

JOE: No need to scare folk, doc. Jenny — pour the doc a drink.

DOCTOR: To hell with your drink. Did you see Vera tonight after you left me?

JOE: *(Shakes his head)* No.

DOCTOR: You mean — you didn't see her at all?

JOE: No.

JENNY: Joe — you said you'd talked to her!

DOCTOR: You damned, stupid fool! Now we're in for it!

JENNY: What happened, doc? What's going on? He don't tell anythin' right no more!

DOCTOR: Simple — the nurse took the baby in to Vera to nurse. She didn't know that Vera hadn't seen the baby yet!

JENNY: And . . . it's face . . .

DOCTOR: She almost went out of her mind — she **is** out of her mind!

JENNY: I'll get dressed an' go back with you to see her!

DOCTOR: No. She's under heavy sedation for the night.

JOE: She's . . . she's pretty rough, eh doc?

DOCTOR: Yes, Joe. She's pretty rough!

JOE: Why blame me? How was I to know a nurse could be so dumb?

DOCTOR: Now you listen to me! She's under heavy sedation, but she isn't sleeping. Her eyes won't stay shut. She keeps saying "It's happened — it's happened!" The nurse found the baby on the floor, and Vera struggling with the window, trying to escape the hospital — or to jump out to the street. It isn't life she's inherited — it's a nightmare — the living death of a sick person trapped by ignorance, deceit and superstition!

JOE: Now you jus' watch what you're sayin', doc! You're pushin' your own blame on me, an' I ain't gonna take it!

DOCTOR: What?

JOE: Nobody would've said anythin' if you'd cut its life short soon's you seen there was half a face . . . yeah — you figure you're savin' the world by savin' every kind of life. You ever reckon on the harm you do — the whole town's made up of folk like me. You wanna sterilize this guy — lock up that guy because we're dumber than you? Or is that why you booze, because you're scared to tell me?

DOCTOR: What right have you to . . .

JOE: I gotta care for that kid 'til I die, an' then what happens? Another Vera?

DOCTOR: That's your problem, buster. I'm a doctor, not God!

JOE: Then stop actin' like God!

JENNY: Joe! The doctor didn't come to argue!

JOE: What else did he come for? He's black as sin with guilt, that's why he's come! Only he'll get tight an' forget by tomorrow. I can't forget. I got a crazy woman on my hands an' a

107

kid that's deformed. I gotta live in a town where I can't raise my head no more . . .

DOCTOR: Look — I understand how you feel. I'm sorry for what happened. We have to plan what to do next.

JOE: I'm not plannin' nothin'.

JENNY: Joe — listen to the doctor!

JOE: *(Turning away)* I've said all I'm gonna say to him. I don't want him hangin' around anymore.

DOCTOR: Joe — as far as I'm concerned, I could wash my hands of you and your family. And I'll have to, if you don't listen to reason! You have a baby girl you haven't seen . . .

JOE: I don't want it! I don't want to see it!

JENNY: Joe!

DOCTOR: What about Vera?

JOE: *(Turns to face DOCTOR)* You want the truth — the honest-to-goodness truth, doc? I don't want her either! I don't care if she never comes outa hospital!

DOCTOR: *(After a shocked silence, during which JENNY has retreated to far corner of room)* I'm warning you, whatever you say, I will have to consider in my own decisions.

JOE: You go to hell!

DOCTOR: Vera is in no condition to return to this home. We'll only get her back in hospital the same day.

JOE: So?

DOCTOR: I'm going to have her commited for further observation, and if I get no co-operation from you, I have no alternative but to recommend she be admitted to a mental institution for treatment.

JOE: Sure — go ahead! You're the doctor!

DOCTOR: Have you no heart, man?

JOE: Lots of heart! That's been my trouble — too much heart
an' not enough in the top story to figure out what to do with it.

DOCTOR: I'll call you when you can take your daughter
home.

JOE: I'm not takin' it! You bring it through that door, an'
I'm throwin' it out after you! I don't want nothin' diseased
like that in my house! I gotta live in this town!

JENNY: I'll take her, doctor!

DOCTOR: I wouldn't do it, Jenny. It's his responsibility.

JENNY: Talk is easy — it's livin' that's hard. Somebody's
got to stay around to take care of Jamie — an' one extra
mouth to feed an' butt to clean ain't gonna make that much
difference.

JOE: Don't be so sure Jamie's stayin'. I'm gonna have my
kid brought up right . . .

JENNY: What you plannin' to do?

JOE: That's Joe's business. Ask the doc. He knows
everythin'.

Walks to bedroom and slams door shut after him. JENNY and DOCTOR look at one another.

Fade.

ACT THREE

THREE MONTHS LATER

Scene I

Front room of JOE's apartment. JOE enters and sits down at table. He stretches and yawns. Scratches his chin, on which a dark growth of beard has begun. His clothes are untidy. Looks about the room.

JOE: Jenny! Jenny — what's to eat?

JENNY: *(Emerges from bedroom, carrying baby's feeding bottle in her hand)* So you finally though of comin' home! An' you're hungry! There's nothin' to eat — not a damned crust except some powdered milk for the baby. Where you been? I phoned the powerhouse, an' they said you hadn't showed up for work all week now.

JOE: What you mean, no food? *(Rises and checks cupboards, then slams them shut irritably)* Why didn't you go downstairs an' get grub from Turney?

JENNY: Turney said if I wanted them on my own bill, I could have what I needed. But he's cut you off — an' no wonder. Four months, an' not a cent paid on your account!

JOE: If he was gonna give you credit, why didn't you take it?

JENNY: I'm not goin' into debt to feed your family!

JOE: My family! I didn't ask for it. I'm real hungry, Jenny. Not even an egg in the place?

JENNY: No eggs — no meat — no bread!

JOE: I quit my job.

JENNY: You what? Joe — you're jokin'!

JOE: When I said I was gonna burn all my bridges I meant it. It all sits on you — you're makin' me do it, Jenny . . .

JENNY: *(Walks away from him)* No! I'm not responsible! You're workin' hard to make me think I'm to blame for everythin' — but I'm not responsible, Joe.

JOE: You still got a chance. After today, it won't matter.

JENNY: What you mean after today?

JOE: What I said. I'm tired of waitin'.

JENNY: You're not our family. They was all good, honest people. But you're mean an' dirty!

JOE: I can't get divorced from Vera now — nobody gets divorced from a wife in an institute. An' she may live another twenty years — who knows? So where's that leave us?

JENNY: Us? I wouldn't have you if you were the last man on earth!

JOE: I'd bring Jamie back . . .

111

JENNY: No!

JOE: You like that thick-faced kid in there? *(Indicates bedroom)*

JENNY: She's human an' good — she deserves a break outa life.

JOE: Give her a break — I'll go along. It's easy, an' nobody'll say a word to you!

JENNY: No! Damn you! No!

JOE: *(Laughs harshly)* You'll never get anywhere, Jenny. You're too honest — same's all our family were. You only got to sit down an' figure out all the angles to see how tough you make it on yourself.

JENNY: Figure out the angles — how about figurin' out how to pay the grocery bill, an' how to make up the back rent owin' to Turney. An' now you quit your job — how you aim to live?

JOE: Like I said, I figured out all the angles, an' it come to me clear as day. I joined the army!

JENNY: *(Drops bottle to floor with surprise)* You . . . joined the army! *(Laughs)*

JOE: Day before yesterday. Had to go out of town to get my medical. An' you know somethin' — I passed with perfect marks!

JENNY: You're leadin' me on — you're not serious, Joe.

JOE: You're lookin' at a new man, Jenny! I figured it out that if the country was gonna keep my wife in an institute, then there's nothin' wrong with them keepin' me alive as well . . .

112

JENNY: But you can work — we've always worked for what we got. You're not like that!

JOE: Joe's gonna be a soldier — good food an' a pension when I get old — no lay-offs or worries! What's wrong with that?

JENNY: You got children, Joe. You got Jamie an' the baby.

JOE: I aim to leave Jamie with the people he's with. I seen them today, an' told them I wasn't gonna make no claim for him, an' Vera couldn't.

JENNY: You got a baby in that room! Don't it mean anythin' at all?

JOE: They were sure happy. They like Jamie, an' had bought him a new suit of blue corduroy. The kid looked like a million bucks — I was proud of him, too. *(Looks at his watch nervously)*

JENNY: If you reckon on me takin' the baby girl back to the farm, you're wrong. They won't allow it at home, an' I can't take a job an' care for her now. Even if I could, this town would get to thinkin' that maybe there was somethin' between us — an' nobody's gonna think that of me!

JOE: Yes sirree, Jamie's gonna be well looked after. Don't reckon I'll be seein' much of the kid after this — won't harm him any if I don't.

JENNY: Her in there *(Points to bedroom)* . . . You're not schemin' to just walk out an' leave her with me?

JOE: *(Savagely)* It was you who brought it here, not me! I told the doc how I felt, but you meddled. So you're gonna stay around an' see them when they come!

JENNY: Who's comin'?

113

JOE: Vera's people. They was always near by, even when I told Vera I wanted no part of them. Now they figure they've won — only they don't know it's me gettin' my own back at 'em!

JENNY: Vera's people? She never told me she had relations living!

JOE: Oh sure — they visit her at the institute every day. Treat her like she never married away from them. *(Knock on door)* Betcha that's them.

He opens door to admit PRIEST and TWO NUNS.

JENNY: *(Bewildered)* Joe — what are they doing here?

JOE: *(To PRIEST)* In there! Take everything . . . blankets, crib, everythin'! *(Indicates bedroom. The PRIEST and NUNS walk to room)*

JENNY: Joe! You can't do this! *(He shrugs her off. She runs after PRIEST and NUNS, but PRIEST bars her way to bedroom. JENNY moves away. JOE lights a cigarette. NUNS emerge — one carrying wrapped baby and the other an armload of bedclothes from crib. They leave without a word)*

JOE: That's it — that's all there's to it! No more family — no more home — no hope — nothin'. Everythin' begins all over again!

JENNY: Does Vera know? Does she understand?

JOE: Who's Vera? When she left, it's as if she'd never been. With a person like Vera, you say goodbye, an' goodbye is for keeps . . .

JENNY: There's no door you close so tight an echo don't come through. You're gonna beg an' plead one day, an' there'll be nobody. *(Goes behind couch and furiously takes out suitcase. Starts packing her belongings)*

JOE: What's the difference? Everybody's happy. Jamie's with folks who want him. I give the micks another soul. Vera — well, she sees things through glass that's bent, so she can't tell the difference. Jenny — there's time to change your mind!

JENNY: Drop dead!

JOE: We can still have a life, Jenny. Out the backdoor an' out into the world somewhere where nobody knows us an' we know nobody an' nothin'. You ain't no Liz Taylor, an' I'm what I am. We can't do much better — you know that!

JENNY: I hate your lousy guts!

JOE: Nothin' in the house to eat . . . Twenty years in the same town, an' a guy could starve to death. An' you still reckon there's justice on earth . . .

JENNY: There'll be justice for the likes of you!

JOE: Where's justice gonna come from? From up there? From here in this town? Why am I to blame? Who wants a wife gone weird — or a kid with that kind of face — maybe even that kind of brain? Livin' on would be payin' for a crime I never done. No sir — people in this town gonna say I done the right thing when they find out. Even old Turney will say that when he gets over bein' sore.

JENNY: The folks in this town stay on to live an' work!

JOE: An' pass judgement on them that are sick an' tired — you remember that. It was they made Vera remember where she come from an' what kind of mother she had. They'll know Vera's kids, an' put them in their place when the time comes. I don't want to be around to see. I took pity on her once . . .

JENNY: Heaven save us from your kind takin' pity! The kind of pity you've been plannin' to give me . . .

JOE: I got a right to live!

JENNY: Sure — same's a skunk or coyote!

JOE: So you're really goin'. Back to the farm again.

JENNY: Maybe. I'll think about it when I get outside.

JOE: I'll help you pack.

JENNY: No need — now stay back!

JOE: *(Reaches into suitcase and takes one mitten of Jenny's)* Gimme this, Jenny.

JENNY: What for?

JOE: Somethin' to remember you by. I don't reckon I'll ever be seein' you again . . .

JENNY: Take it an' don't bother me no more . . . *(Straightens up suddenly and stares at JOE)* Hey! Give it back to me! *(Grabs mitten out of JOE's hand)*

JOE: Why'd you do that, Jenny? It ain't expensive — I'll pay you for it!

JENNY: It don't belong to you. You can't take or give things away that don't belong to you! *(Slams lid shut and looks at JOE)* I got some wages you ain't paid.

116

JOE: *(With hostility)* Stand there 'til your feet grow roots if you aim to get wages!

JENNY: You ain't paid me for two months now . . .

JOE: What you want me to pay you with? I'm broke! An' what you want me to pay you for? Show me what you done that I got to pay you for! Is there anythin' in this room that shows you been here a year? Is there?

JENNY: You better ask yourself that question now. Only there ain't gonna be anybody to answer — nobody's gonna tell you ever again! *(Picks up suitcase and walks out door, slamming it shut after her)*

JOE: *(Walks slowly to window and pulls back curtains. Waves his hand mockingly out)* Goodbye, cousin Jenny! *(Then as if to entire town)* Bye! Bye! *(Stands back to stare at room. Sees the broom standing near the door. Walks briskly to it and picks it up, then makes as if he intended to use it to smash the furniture. But instead, slowly shoulders it as a gun. Starts whistling a marching tune, then falls in step with it and marches back and forth across room)*

Fade out.

The End

BREAD ROUTE

Cast

MISS WOOD: an elderly and retired spinster. At one time a nurse in a general hospital. She is dressed severely and wears a hat indoors.

WILLIE: bread delivery man on a local route. He is thirtyish in age, bare-headed, boyish in nature and pleased with his work and his customers.

MISTER SMOLEK: Elderly and retired farmer. Crippled by an arthritic back. Heavy haired and bewhiskered with a brooding sense of his declining vitality.

Scene One

The kitchen of Miss Wood's home. Sparsely furnished and tidy in an unpredictable way. The kitchen table has linen on it, with salt and pepper set dominant. Behind on back of table, high stack of magazines, piled meticulously, with a small vase and flowers perched on top. Off to one side of room is an end table of contemporary design, again cluttered with publications. This is crowned with a lacy lamp. Kitchen range of older period facing table. On range is coffee pot and large black purse.

Scene Two

Front room of Mister Smolek's home. A barrel wood-heater in centre of room. Blocks of split wood alongside of heater. Pot of water on top. Sack on floor for dog to sleep on. A heavy arm-chair for Mister Smolek to sit on, facing heater. Footstool off to one side. A small pipe-rack table on right-hand side of arm-chair. Same floor as in set one — white plank board.

ON CAMERA: Up on MISS WOOD holding a pocket watch with ribbon tab in her hand. Three raps on the door. She smiles and quickly puts watch into handbag. Takes coffee off hotplate of stove.

WILLIE: *(Voice over)* It's Willie — your breadman!

MISS WOOD: Come in, Willie — the door's unlocked.

WILLIE: *(Enters with bread hamper in hand)* Top of the morning to you, Miss Wood! A nice morning. And how is your rheumatism today?

MISS WOOD: So, so. It hurts if I bend quickly.

WILLIE: And the phlegm on your chest?

MISS WOOD: Phlegm on my chest?

WILLIE: Didn't you have phlegm on your chest last week? Oh, no — that was Mister Smolek — how stupid of me to forget! Now, Miss Wood — what'll we have today? There's white, cracked wheat, light American rye. And a special of the week on coffee cake!

119

MISS WOOD: Special of the week! That's good, is it, Willie?

WILLIE: That's what the man said!

MISS WOOD: Give me one, then.

WILLIE: What about bread?

MISS WOOD: Don't rush me. Sit down — have some coffee.

WILLIE: Am I late or early today?

MISS WOOD: You're early by four minutes! At a quarter to ten, I said to myself — Elma, get the coffee pot on. The man will be here in fifteen minutes. And you came to the door at four minutes to ten. So I see you four minutes longer today! Open the cake — go on! Or would you like some doughnuts?

WILLIE: Say! I haven't had a doughnut for days now!

MISS WOOD: Sell me a package of doughnuts then.

WILLIE: Sugared or plain?

MISS WOOD: What kind do you like?

WILLIE: Sugared . . . but we charge two cents a package more for them . . .

MISS WOOD: So who cares about two cents? Get the sugared ones then!

WILLIE: But two cents is two cents, Miss Wood . . . You've heard the old saying — count your pennies and the dollars count themselves!

MISS WOOD: I want sugared doughnuts, so you sell me sugared doughnuts!

WILLIE: How good you are to a man, Miss Wood!

MISS WOOD: You stop saying that, Willie! Look how red my cheek is turning, and I will pour hot coffee over you for your flattery! Men are all the same . . .

WILLIE: Last week Mister Smolek asked me to say hello to you for him!

MISS WOOD: Mister Smolek! Who cares about Mister Smolek! When I was at the hospital, they brought him in once . . . this was when Missus Smolek was still alive, Lord preserve her memory!

WILLIE: I've heard she was a good woman.

MISS WOOD: They brought him in with the side of his face torn away . . . a terrible thing. He'd been felling trees, and a frozen branch broke off . . . Yes — that's how it happened! A frozen branch broke and whipped back at him. He didn't see it — lucky thing it didn't take his eye out . . .

WILLIE: A terrible thing . . . ah, two spoons of sugar, please, Miss Wood. Thank you!

MISS WOOD: What was I saying?

WILLIE: Mister Smolek was in hospital — the side of his face torn . . .

MISS WOOD: Oh, yes . . . he bellowed like a bull with pain. The windows rattled when he roared, he was that loud! Gave us all a scare, you can be sure . . .

WILLIE: He can be loud — that I know. Two weeks back I tallied up his bill and overcharged him ten cents by mistake. Well! He let out such a roar his dog almost broke the door down trying to get out.

MISS WOOD: A fierce man, yes — a fierce man! Doctor Horton — you remember him? Used to have grey hair . . . He was the one who rode over Maude Turner's mother cat, leaving six kittens orphans . . . a terrible thing . . .

WILLIE: Yes, I remember him. Retired some years back, didn't he?

MISS WOOD: And a shame he did at that. Took to drink out of loneliness and his liver gave out. Can't mess about with the liver at that age . . . no.

WILLIE: Was it Doctor Horton treated Mister Smolek?

MISS WOOD: Yes, and we ladies had to get out of the room. You know how Mister Smolek was given to swearing, even with ladies about. Well he swore like a man who'd lost his soul, and Doctor Horton asked us to leave.

WILLIE: He must have been in bad pain.

MISS WOOD: Pain or no pain, he was no gentleman the way he carried on . . . And the way he talked back to Doctor Horton! I can remember it as clear as if it happened only yesterday. Mister Smolek shouting so he could be heard clear through the hospital — ''Don't worry about my blood or heart — it's my face! Sew up my face, or give me a darning needle and a mirror, an' I'll do it myself!'' Those were his very words. Sent a shiver through a body, it did . . .

WILLIE: I'm sure it would. Would you like a doughnut, Miss Wood — or a cup of coffee with me?

MISS WOOD: No, thank you. I never eat doughnuts. And as for coffee, one cup in the afternoon is my limit for the day. But you have another. You're young and hard-working — everything goes through you like wood through a furnace.

WILLIE: My wife says if I keep stoking like this and ever have to take a month off the bread route, she'll have to have the doors widened to let me out of the house!

MISS WOOD: And how is the good wife?

WILLIE: Great — just great! Children are growing like weeds. Would eat their way through a mountain, miss, if I was to allow it!

MISS WOOD: Children — yes, they eat much, don't they . . .

WILLIE: Is something the matter, Miss Wood?

MISS WOOD: No, nothing . . . *(Looks about and rifles through a few magazines at random)* I had written down everything I saw and heard the past week to tell you when you came. And now I've lost the paper . . . it was here someplace, I'm sure.

WILLIE: Mister Smolek told me they had pills now that a person could take to improve the memory. Had something to do with letting more blood into the head — evidently makes a person very red-faced for a while . . .

MISS WOOD: Did Mister Smolek suggest I should take these pills?

WILLIE: Uh . . . no, I don't think that was what he meant. He was just telling me about them, that's all.

MISS WOOD: Everyone has it in for a poor woman living all by herself!

WILLIE: Miss Wood — you know that isn't so!

MISS WOOD: Yes, that is so! Even you, Willie — what a thing to say to me!

WILLIE: I'm sorry, Miss Wood — that wasn't what I meant.

MISS WOOD: It was so — why try talking your way out with me! Pills! What happens if a person can't remember enough to take the pills? Foolishness, that's all it is! When I was in the hospital, we gave patients nothing stronger than aspirin. If they felt they were improving on sugar and paste pills, then they got those, too. It was their business!

WILLIE: No need to get yourself all worked up. Mister Smolek only said . . .

MISS WOOD: Never mind what he said! When he was in hospital — you just ask him if he took a pill of any sort! Not Mister Smolek — he'd never taken a pill in his life. Only thing I ever heard said he'd swallow that wasn't part of his food was liniment on sugar — and that only when he had a heavy cold. Pills! Everybody is pill crazy, aren't they, Willie?

WILLIE: I don't know much about this . . .

MISS WOOD: They got pills now that can make you eat, and other pills to make you stop eating. Pills to put you to sleep, and pills to wake you up. Pretty soon some politician will come along with a pill to make a soul forget every name but one on the ballot. And then they'll have pills to make a country go to war, and another pill to scare us out of it!

WILLIE: Come now — things will never get that bad!

MISS WOOD: How much do you know that wasn't put into your head by a pill?

WILLIE: Miss Wood . . .

MISS WOOD: Willie — there's something I remember clear as thunder . . . You know Missus Gainer?

WILLIE: Yes. A good customer of mine!

MISS WOOD: And her daughter — whatever was her name? One who married the Polish cobbler?

WILLIE: Elsie! She married a German carpenter not a cobbler, Miss Wood.

MISS WOOD: He was a cobbler, and he was Danish — I know that for sure!

WILLIE: Yes, Miss Wood . . .

MISS WOOD: Now, what was I saying?

WILLIE: If I knew Missus Gainer and her daughter Elsie. Before that we talked about pills.

MISS WOOD: Yes — yes! Some time ago, when Elsie was still a small girl — maybe twelve, I called on Missus Gainer. We were having coffee, and Elsie runs in with a board nailed to her foot. She'd stepped on this piece of board — oh, so long — and didn't see the nail. It went clear through her shoe, her foot, and came out on top!

WILLIE: Oh, for the love of Pete!

MISS WOOD: I wasn't strong enough to pull that nail out. And Missus Gainer, instead of doing what she was supposed to do, she goes over to the cupboard and gets the girl a tranquilizer. One pill for the girl, and one for herself! Well! In five minutes, that girl was sitting at the table with us, drinking a coffee herself and grinning like her brain'd been taken out. Not only that, but she was swinging her leg, dragging this board this way and that across the floor under the table. I'll tell you I never went back to their house again! I was scared!

WILLIE: I don't blame you. Thank God that sort of thing doesn't happen every day!

MISS WOOD: It does — not all at once, but a little at a time. Now where did I put that paper?

WILLIE: You didn't leave it around the stove, thinking when you made the coffee you'd get it . . .

MISS WOOD: That's right! *(Reaches for note on shelf of warming closet back of range)* How clever you are, Willie! What would make you think of that?

WILLIE: My wife uses the kitchen range for filing all our business papers. I was frying an egg before leaving for work this morning, and was reaching up for the pepper when a ten dollar hospital bill for one of the kids comes sailing into the fry-pan!

MISS WOOD: You didn't eat the egg?

WILLIE: Why not? An egg's an egg — sure, I ate it!

MISS WOOD: A hospital bill? Who knows how many hands have been on that paper — what they touched . . .

WILLIE: But that's silly.

MISS WOOD: Never you mind. You can't be too careful! Stationery gets moved — sometimes left in hallways that haven't

126

been cleaned from the night before. Now let's see — yes, on Sunday, Parson Walters came to see me. He asked why I had missed three services in a row, and did I know that Missus Koven was dying and wanted visitors. I was so shamed and frightened, I did not mention my rheumatism to him . . . Willie, why am I told that people are dying, and I failed to visit them? Do you think that perhaps I will die soon?

WILLIE: What a foolish thought! Miss Wood, you're going to be around another twenty years — betcha all the money I make on my bread route today!

MISS WOOD: You're a poor liar, Willie. You overdo it. No — no twenty years for me!

WILLIE: Why not?

MISS WOOD: It's lonely now. In twenty years it'd only be twenty times worse . . . no!

WILLIE: You're happy. You're getting a pension — not much, I admit, but enough to . . . well, give you some security, if few comforts.

MISS WOOD: What about the work I've had — the friends? I might still have managed around the hospital, but no, they insisted I retire. And now, it's been almost eight months since anybody came to see me . . . just a friendly visit and a cup of tea. You're the only one, Willie.

WILLIE: And the parson?

MISS WOOD: Not him! I don't want to see him again! He's preparing me, and I don't want to be prepared, Willie!

WILLIE: Shall I tell Mister Smolek you're lonely for visitors, Miss Wood?

MISS WOOD: No! Heaven forbid — not that!

WILLIE: He's also alone — seldom rising from his chair — thinking about the past and groaning . . .

MISS WOOD: No! I've still got my modesty! What would the neighbours say, me all by myself here and having a man like that visit with no one else around?

WILLIE: I don't see it. He's — well, a few years older than you.

MISS WOOD: That doesn't stop him from thinking, and that's just as bad, isn't it? I know a man like that — what he's thinking when he looks at a lady, especially since Missus Smolek passed away with her cancer!

WILLIE: What happened on Monday?

MISS WOOD: Monday?

WILLIE: Didn't you write it down on your note?

MISS WOOD: Yes — Monday. A farm truck loaded with wheat had a flat in front of my house. I didn't know the farmer, but he had a small boy with him. He cursed the boy all the time he was changing the wheel . . . I felt like going out and telling him how to behave in my neighbourhood — and in front of a child, at that! But he wouldn't have listened to me anyway. So I locked the doors and pulled down the windows. Then I went to bed and waited until I heard him drive away.

WILLIE: Why did you go to bed?

MISS WOOD: Supposing he wanted a drink of water and came knocking at my door? When I'm in bed, I'm not obliged to answer the door for nobody!

WILLIE: And on Tuesday? . . .

MISS WOOD: On Tuesday I woke early. By five o'clock I was dressed. The sun rose and there wasn't a cloud in the sky. The birds were hungry, and already sitting on my window-ledge. I felt very sad, Willie.

WILLIE: I remember Tuesday morning. I had washed my van down, and while I was loading bread for the day, a street-cleaner drove by and dusted the car all over. I'm telling you, that sure loused up my day!

MISS WOOD: So sad . . . so few perfect mornings in life. There were many, when I was a little girl, running to school and picking wild strawberries off the side of the road. Every morning was a perfect morning then . . .

WILLIE: Yes . . . and speaking of time and how it flies, Miss Wood — what can I leave you today?

MISS WOOD: You're not going now? There's lots of day left. Maybe another cup of coffee? Or some cookies — I see you've got cookies in your hamper today . . .

WILLIE: No, Miss Wood — I've got to go, or my day will last until tomorrow. I've still Mister Smolek to call on, and the stores in town — then the other half of the country route.

MISS WOOD: But I haven't read what happened on Wednesday and the rest of the week. Oh, dear!

WILLIE: Tell me next week — I'll be around. Now I've got white, cracked wheat, rye . . .

MISS WOOD: You never stay to hear the end of my week!

WILLIE: Come now, Miss Wood.

MISS WOOD: I'm sorry. The usual, Willie — two loaves of white . . .

WILLIE: Two loaves of white coming up! — Miss Wood, I was wondering — why don't you take another loaf? Two loaves a week isn't much . . . If it's money, than you should know bread is cheaper than any other groceries. Many people on my route who have big families load up on bread — twenty, thirty loaves at a time. Saves them buying meat, and it costs less . . .

MISS WOOD: Two loaves will do, Willie!

WILLIE: Two loaves of white — here you are.

MISS WOOD: Sure — you've got time for another cup of coffee? Maybe I'll forget my afternoon cup and have one with you now!

WILLIE: No, Miss Wood — I can't. Maybe next week. *(Starts to leave and remembers)* I keep forgetting to ask you, but is there anything else you want me to get you from town when I come by next week? Be no trouble for me . . .

MISS WOOD: No, unless . . .

WILLIE: Unless what, Miss Wood?

MISS WOOD: Unless you were to get me a domino set — to keep my hands busy. I can't see so good to knit anymore. But not if it's any trouble for you Willie!

WILLIE: No trouble at all.

MISS WOOD: And I don't want to pay more than a dollar for it. If it's more, then don't buy it . . . here, take some money with you!

WILLIE: No — I'll pay for it and charge you when I bring it. See you next week, Miss Wood!

MISS WOOD: Next week . . . *(WILLIE departs and she carries loaf to open window. Tears it open and takes out chunks of bread which she throws out to birds)* On Wednesday . . . what happened on Wednesday? Two more swallows came to feed . . . no, that was on Thursday. On Wednesday I began reading a book about a mean farmer who mistreated and cursed his son. Oh yes — I remember now — they had a flat tire on their truck and the man threatened to kill the boy . . . It frightened me . . .

Fade out.

ON CAMERA: Up on WILLIE as he enters SMOLEK house and drops bread hamper to the floor.

WILIE: Whew! You've got the heater going again — it must be ninety outside!

SMOLEK: So it's my wood. I paid for it.

WILLIE: I paid for my van, but that doesn't mean I sleep in it. Are you cold?

SMOLEK: No.

WILLIE: Then why the fire?

SMOLEK: To keep spiders from setting in the chimney. Now how about lacing my boots. I got them on, but the back's stiffer than a board this morning.

WILLIE: *(Kneeling down and lacing)* You need a wife, old man. A strong woman who would see you get fed and dressed properly. What do you do with your boots when I'm not around?

SMOLEK: Walk around in socks. When you do them up, I can take a walk — enough to loosen up so's I can untie them myself. Are your loaves getting smaller, or my eyes going bad?

WILLIE: Same loaves, and the price hasn't gone up yet, so don't worry.

SMOLEK: Thought they looked smaller. You sell much of that junk?

WILLIE: Enough to make a living. How's that?

SMOLEK: Don't know. Haven't felt anything in that leg for ten years. Used to be a good leg, that one. When I lifted a sack of wheat to my shoulders, used to put it on that knee first . . . You seen Miss Wood today?

WILLIE: Just left her place.

SMOLEK: She always wears her hat, doesn't she? I wonder why . . . Do you think she goes to bed with her hat on?

WILLIE: I don't know. I never see her off to bed.

SMOLEK: Does she buy your bread, or do you just visit her?

WILLIE: It doesn't matter, does it! Yes, she buys two loaves of bread a week.

SMOLEK: White or brown?

WILLIE: White. Now how does this feel?

SMOLEK: Her stomach must be in rough shape . . . How is she otherwise? She still walks without the help of her hands?

WILLIE: She's fine — she's in great shape. Every week you ask the same questions about her — why don't you visit her?

SMOLEK: Visit her — I've never visited her!

WILLIE: Today — go over and see her today. You've got your boots on.

SMOLEK: Tell me the truth now — did she invite me? Did she ask you to tell me she wants me to visit?

WILLIE: You know Miss Wood. You know she'd never do that. But go and see her anyway. You don't invite me into your house.

SMOLEK: You're young. Pride is the fire in your eye and the bounce in your step. For me, it's different . . . I could never enter her house — she'd be frightened.

WILLIE: Then call her out into the garden. Don't holler at her. Just knock on her door and say you've come over to admire her flowers.

SMOLEK: In her garden — pshaw! Pete would tear up all her cats!

WILLIE: What's wrong with you? Can't you chain the dog at home? Or are you proud that he can chew up fences and kill cats? Is the dog all you've got left of your manhood?

SMOLEK: You see this stick? I can still open your skull with it, so you mind what you say! Pour us some wine.

WILLIE: *(Goes to sideboard cupboard and takes out two glasses and wine jug. Pours drinks for both of them)* It's a shame. You talking to your dog, and she talking to her cats and flowers. It's all a big act. She's the little girl with her dolls, and you're the fire-eater with a club. Like children. Only children share their games!

SMOLEK: Flowers — hell! I don't want to see her flowers! Me, who used to take on three men at a time in a good, clean fight — sniffing flowers in my old age? . . . Drop dead!

WILLIE: Alright — so it's unmanly to do anything but fight. What happens when your fighting ends — when your back gives out?

SMOLEK: That's when the biggest fighting begins — here! *(Points to his head)* I want to find out why I was betrayed, and I'm not dying until I know!

WILLIE: Betrayed?

SMOLEK: Yes, betrayed! Look — God give me these two hands for working, for embracing a woman, and for fighting! The hands of a man. My father had hands as large as these, and in the old country he could work the strongest man to a standstill. He loved many women, and I've seen him tangle with six soldiers who escorted the tax-collector into the village! I can still see him, standing in the village square, his face burning like a lamp, defying the soldiers to enter the village. With his bare hands he fought them for an hour before they beat him senseless with their rifle butts. But the houses of the village were grey with dust and spattered with his blood before the fighting ended!

WILLIE: I see . . .

SMOLEK: You see nothing — you're blinded by your own little world and bent down by that bread hamper! He was a man — and I became a man when I saw him lying there, unconscious, but his teeth bared like those of a wolf! He never humbled himself. He died with dignity and pride.

134

WILLIE: And you were betrayed?

SMOLEK: Yes, betrayed! I've worked as hard as he did, and Miss Wood only remembers I was wild. Even she has forgotten what I did. You never knew. I embraced one woman, but never loved her enough to give me a son. And now with my back, I can't even choose the time and place for my own death. Look at my hands — hooks for a couple of sticks. But I'm telling you, if I don't figure out what went wrong, I'm taking one of these sticks with me when I go, and somebody up on top had better explain or I'm putting this thing to good use!

WILLIE: Would you like another wine?

SMOLEK: Don't mind if I do — have one yourself.

WILLIE: *(Pours SMOLEK's glass full)* No, thanks. I've a lot of driving to do.

SMOLEK: Good wine, eh? A buck thirty a gallon . . .

WILLIE: When Missus Smolek died, why didn't you marry Miss Wood? Everybody expected you would.

SMOLEK: Marry Miss Wood? I though of it, son — lots of times in the first year, and not for the reasons you think. I gave away my furniture bit by bit, because I didn't need it, and couldn't get around to keeping the house looking the same as before. And with each chair I gave away, something of what she left behind went. I thought of Miss Wood then, as one way of keeping together a life. Maybe I was selfish — but not altogether. I knew how lonely she was, and scared as hell of the night and every hungry thing in it . . .

WILLIE: Two lonely people might have found comfort in each other — still could find comfort if they wanted . . .

135

SMOLEK: A glass of red wine full to the brim. I remember a time when a glass was a container for wine, not a measure for how much a man drank. We'd sit in a circle, our belts loosened and our caps pulled tight and low to keep our heads from bursting, and we'd sing the forbidden songs until break of day . . . no, son, it wouldn't have worked . . .

WILLIE: Wouldn't have worked?

SMOLEK: What could hold us together — my selfishness, fear? Or the emptiness outside? What else? Our flesh is too old and tired now for love. And there's no coming together of the spirit. She's modest — a frightened woman who stumbles from looking over her shoulder all the time . . .

WILLIE: And you?

SMOLEK: The space between two mountains is too small for me. Maybe — maybe if I'd been able to shout and trumpet all that burned in me out of myself — then it might have worked. But I failed.

WILLIE: You've lived a busy and eventful life. What have you failed in?

SMOLEK: Failed in living all I was capable of living. Touch me — feel how hot my flesh is! I haven't got a fever — I'm well. It's always been this way. Why do I smoulder like an old haystalk, even when I can't rise to my feet without groaning?

WILLIE: I . . . I don't know . . . Are you certain you feel well, Mister Smolek?

SMOLEK: I feel perfect in my head and heart, and that's the pity of it all.

WILLIE: Yes, I think I understand now!

SMOLEK: How easy it would have been — marriage to Miss Wood! Not courtship, just marriage. Like a business contract — you give me this hen and I will feed it and keep it clean — so it says in the fine print I've never read but understood. In return, it will lay eggs and cluck at five o'clock to wake me. Simple. Even modest, if you like!

WILLIE: There is more to life. I have a family — I know.

SMOLEK: Or the other possibility — I might have surrendered to a nursing home. Been fed three regular meals each day like an old bull who's lost his teeth. Living for each meal, and griping about having to rise and dress, for this would have been all the world left to me. But like you say, there's more to life, so I live on cornmeal, powdered milk and tea — pride doesn't eat much any more. Throw that door open — I'm finding it hot in here!

WILLIE: No wonder . . . I find it hard to breathe even! *(Opens door)*

SMOLEK: What's it like out?

WILLIE: It's a nice day — not a cloud in the sky, and everything just growing like mad in the sun!

SMOLEK: Doggone it, I think I'll go out for a spell. You sit in a dark house long enough and you start to look and feel like a dark house. Leave me a wholewheat before you go! *(WILLIE puts aside a loaf of bread)*

WILLIE: Is there anything else?

SMOLEK: Sure — you'll want to get paid. Why don't you come out and say so, instead of this "is there anything else" nonsense? Here — that's a two-bit piece, isn't it? And I'm gonna have that loaf weighed, you hear — I'm sure it's getting smaller. Pete won't even have a meal out of it . . .

WILLIE: You don't feed your dog bread, do you?

SMOLEK: You don't expect **me** to eat it, do you? Not on your life! There we are — all set to gallop across the moors. Only thing . . . everybody's out working. Nobody to visit, is there . . . oh well, a walk will do me good!

WILLIE: Mister Smolek, there is something I forgot to tell you. Miss Wood asked me to ask you to do a favour for her!

SMOLEK: She what?

WILLIE: She said, "Ask Mister Smolek to get me a domino set," and here I almost forgot to tell you!

SMOLEK: You're not having me on, are you? Because if you are, I can still make you kiss dust — you know that, don't you?

WILLIE: I've told you what she said, it's up to you now.

SMOLEK: A domino set — those little black tiles with dots on them? Where would I get her a set of those?

WILLIE: I can drive you as far as the store, if that would help. They carry dominoes in the children's toys shelf.

SMOLEK: I can walk as far as the store! Alright, I'll get her what she wants.

WILLIE: I'd better give you the money she gave me . . .

SMOLEK: Never mind the money! Old Smolek was never tight with a dollar. Now where's my hat?

WILLIE: It's behind your chair — I'll get it for you. *(Gets hat and puts it on old man's head)*

SMOLEK: I won't go in when I take it to her. I'll holler at her from the road to come out and take it . . .

WILLIE: No! Don't holler — go up and knock on her door.

SMOLEK: Alright — but I'm not going in or staying to look at her silly flowers, you remember that! I'm not going in . . .

WILLIE: No, don't go in.

SMOLEK: You can count on that! Who'd want to be seen jabberin' with a woman who wears her hat to bed! Can you imagine that? Naw — leave the door open . . . if anybody finds anything worth stealing here, they're welcome to it. Yep — never seen her with her hat off her head . . .

Fade out.

The End

George and Norma Ryga (1963)   Photo: unknown

DEPARTURES

Characters:

OLD SAM
TOM OF THE GOSPEL
JOHN: son of old Sam
NURSE
DOCTOR

Sound of hospital buzzer. Voices, footsteps.

NURSE: Mister Homeniuk! There's a gentleman here to see you.

SAM: Old Sam's the name — don't Mister Homeniuk me. What's that you say? A gentleman to see me?

NURSE: That's right.

SAM: Send him home. I don't know no gentleman!

NURSE: He said you know him — that you might want to see him.

SAM: Send him away. Hey — you're not my nurse! You're a new girl.

NURSE: Miss Murphy has a day off today.

SAM: Well, Miss Murphy is pretty, but you're prettier. I like your nose better!

NURSE: Come now . . .

SAM: It's the truth! Look at me — how old you think I am?

NURSE: I couldn't guess. I'd have to look up our records.

SAM: Won't find anything in the records. They only got what I told them, an' I don't know. Ninety — maybe a hundred years old — I don't know. But come closer. I want to tell you something in secret!

NURSE: What is it?

SAM: Don't be afraid — a little closer. There! That's it! Listen — I still like girls!

NURSE: *(Laughs)* Oh — come off it!

SAM: *(Chortling)* Girls with pretty noses turned up like points of a snowshoe!

NURSE: Your visitor is waiting in the hall. What shall I tell him?

SAM: Tell him to turn blue!

NURSE: Now, that's not nice. I'll send him in. *(Footsteps departing)*

141

SAM: You come back here — I'll report you to the doctor for this! Damn you! *(Laughter of NURSE from distance. Heavy footsteps approach)* So it's you, Tom of the Gospel! You, with the low-hanging butt an' the watery eyes. What the devil brings you here?

TOM: Hello, brother.

SAM: What brother am I to you — eh?

TOM: Don't shout. I'm not here to eat you. Just came to see how you are and how you're feeling.

SAM: Lousy. They don't feed me enough, and when I told them I was getting up and cut the grass on their lawns, they took my pants away and hid them! Hospital is a prison — only they talk nice to you. That's the only difference.

TOM: Take it easy, Sam. You're a sick man. You've been through a bad time with that operation.

SAM: Who said so?

TOM: Well . . . everybody says so . . .

SAM: Tom of the Gospel — don't lie to me! Don't you dare lie!

TOM: Look at me — do you think I would tell a lie?

SAM: What for do I have to look at you? What is your face? A pool of water? A flower? A mirror? Can I tell by looking in your face that you half-killed your brother, an' ran your old man into debt to his neck to put you through school? For this? Look at you!

TOM: Now **that's** a lie!

142

SAM: They were going to make a teacher of you, so you could teach little children to read and write. Nobody asked you to pay back all it cost — but you might have. Now look at you — all in black an' your shoulders hunched. Are you in mourning, boy?

TOM: I came . . . to help you.

SAM: Are you in mourning?

TOM: No. I am full of joy.

SAM: I can see that. What do you want? Do you think I'm going to die?

TOM: No — not at all! I came to talk to you — to show you there is hope — that the life hereafter is yours for the asking.

SAM: Tom of the Gospel — you're a fool!

TOM: Please, brother! My name is Tom, not Tom of the Gospel. You gave me that name — to spite me.

SAM: To bring you to your senses, you mean! Who sent you here?

TOM: Nobody. I came because I wanted to.

SAM: Then go away. I don't want to talk to you.

TOM: Alright — your son thought I should see you.

SAM: *(Bedsprings creaking violently)* That does it! Go call the nurse — tell her to bring my clothes in — I'm leaving!

TOM: Now wait a minute, Sam. You can't just get up and leave the hospital!

143

SAM: You won't understand this, but I've a dog at home that's dying of hunger. I've got to feed it — now!

TOM: Is nobody taking care of it while you're away?

SAM: John was supposed to. But if he's seeing you, he's not thinking about my dog — no sirree! Nurse!

TOM: You can't jump out of bed and start hollering "Nurse! Nurse!" because you imagine your dog is being neglected! Not at your age, and at a time like this. Have you no fear?

SAM: Fear of what?

TOM: Fear for your soul. Sam — listen to me — you're an old man!

SAM: Get off my back, you!

TOM: You pretend death doesn't exist. It does, Sam! But it's a blessing — it releases the soul for eternal life!

SAM: Look — your brother was a stone-picker. He grubbed stones with his two hands until his fingers became claws and he could no longer straighten them. He earned four dollars a day, of which he sent three to you to learn wisdom. Then he got polio an' ended on welfare. Go see him — his soul's all he's got left now!

TOM: *(In anguish)* Do you like torturing me? You give me a name I can't lose, and then this! I didn't ask my brother or father to work as they did for me. Are you happier for hurting me?

SAM: Do you know this town?

TOM: Yes.

SAM: How well do you know this town?

TOM: I grew up in it.

SAM: Is it a good town?

TOM: Like others — it has sinned.

SAM: Sin! Sin! *(Laughs)* The Yanks have their atom bombs — the Russians their bad heroes — an' we . . . have you. Come here to the window. I want to show you this town.

TOM: I know it. Nothing to see.

SAM: C'mere like I say! *(Scuffle)*

TOM: Ouch! You're hurting my arm!

SAM: Stand here, and look where I point. Look where I point, idiot — or I'll hang you out this window by your heels!

TOM: I see everything!

SAM: Good. I can't see that far anymore, but do you make out a grey-roofed house, third from the corner, two blocks down?

TOM: I know the place you mean.

SAM: Who lives there?

TOM: Bill lives there — you know that.

SAM: When I die, I want Bill McGee an' my dog to keep vigil over me through the night. I love them both. There is to be a long piece of sausage for my dog, and for Bill a tall bottle of whiskey. I have left instructions with the doctor . . .

TOM: That's childish nonsense!

SAM: And if you try to come in and muck around with me, I swear I will sit up in my coffin an' scare you — whoo!

TOM: Let go my arms!

SAM: Up against the window — right up. Straighten your back like a man! Now, do you see a kid playing in Bill's yard?

TOM: I don't know. But I'm calling for help if you don't let go of me, Sam. John said you were worse than before . . .

SAM: Naw — don't listen to my son, Tom of the Gospel. My brain is fine . . . fine! But my body is weak. I will be dead by tonight. There was so much blood lost. I stood in the corner of the room, watching them cut into me. I saw my life jump out like a red angel before they clamped the arteries. There is nothing to replace the loss now. When I was young, bread and meat turned to blood in my body, and then to a pickaxe breaking stone. Now, it ferments a fever in me, as it does in you. Do you see the child?

TOM: No.

SAM: He is there all the same. What name did you give the child?

TOM: I gave him no name. Bill called him Tony — Antony.

SAM: But you came with fire in your shaky fingers — and you gave the child a new name. You told John and the others — now tell me! Tell me, or I'll break your back!

TOM: *(Gasping)* The child . . . is . . . illegitimate.

SAM: Why? Because his mother was sold for a load of hay

to an old man? Or because she found a boy her age she could love in the pasture by the creek?

TOM: It's none of my concern!

SAM: There was a killing — you were away then, learning to stoke the flames of hell. But I carried the boy in my arms, and Polly followed me, big with child and wailing her soul out. I carried the boy through town. It was a misty morning, not even the milkman's car on the street yet, and the aspens gold from the first frost. Bill McGee, the stone-picker — the dumb brute who kept you in school, built a cross of two-by-fours to mark your kid brother's grave. Then he took Polly by the hand and led her to his home to care for her. And you . . . came home, removed the cross from your own brother's grave — an' branded your nephew a bastard!

TOM: I had to do it — God makes the rules, not man!

SAM: Rules! Damn your rules. Have you ever walked past a bake-shop — no money in your pocket, and seen a raisen loaf for which you lusted?

TOM: Yes, but I denied myself.

SAM: Or had an appetite for a red-haired girl with a turned-up nose?

TOM: Never!

SAM: When I was young and still in the old country, a friend wagered we could create a miracle. On Easter Sunday, we took a razor and slashed the palms of my hands and the tops of my bare beet. We rubbed some of the blood to smear the clothes on my side. Then we drove seven miles to another village, through which I walked.

TOM: **You** did that?

SAM: I did — and you know what happened?

TOM: No.

SAM: The first woman I met fell in a dead faint. Next, a gypsy peddlar turned and gave me a second look. Then the village priest cursed me roundly, and turned me over to the police. I got seven days for public mischief, and a fine of ten zlotys.

TOM: *(Giggles)* That's funny — that's very funny!

SAM: So even now you think that's funny. Get out of here!

TOM: What? I . . . I'm sorry I laughed. Forgive me . . .

SAM: Go away. I'm tired. I'm sleepy . . .

TOM: Sam — please! You don't understand. I though you were joking!

SAM: If I hung a cowbell around your neck, you would be a cow. My hat would cover your face, glasses and all — and you would be a hatrack. That's what you are — a hatrack and a cow. Now get out!

TOM: I'm sorry — it was my fault. Let me leave you something to read.

SAM: You do an' I'll feed it to you, staples and all. Now beat it!

TOM: Goodbye, brother. I will remember you. *(SAM grunts. Footsteps recede out)*

NURSE: *(Laughing)* Well, your friend left on the run. He almost collided into me.

SAM: How long do I have to lie here? I left a dog at home. They haven't fed him . . .

NURSE: I'm sure you're more important than any old dog.

SAM: You — let me tell you something — when you have babies, make sure they all have red hair and turned up noses. Hope for this — pray even — that is all that will save you!

NURSE: You're being rude!

SAM: Then don't speak of my dog. How long do I have to rot away here?

NURSE: I've no idea. The doctor will be in to see you soon. Who knows — you might leave anytime.

SAM: Do you see that pouch on the table?

NURSE: This one?

SAM: Yah — bring it here. I want to show you something.

NURSE: I don't trust you.

SAM: Come on — let's have it. Look! See this? What is it?

NURSE: I don't know. A broken piece of iron, I guess.

SAM: It's a piece of a German grenade. I won't tell you where it was in me, but it kept me from making love four years — imagine! Four years. The widows in the village wept, an' the girls all went to — to men like the one just ran out of here.

And I walked around helpless, cursing a snot-nosed German kid who took his war seriously!

NURSE: Shame on you for talking such talk! *(Walks away)*

SAM: Wait! Get my clothes for me — my dog is hungry! Wait! *(Door slams)* Don't just leave me with four dead walls — four dead walls! Why dead walls? Once the seas were open to me, and I sailed them and spat on the waves. Women smiled, and the roads unfolded like spools of ribbon. Now — the one son I had betrays me, and I am a prisoner of my own tired flesh! Have I arrived? Is this my time of departure? Tell me, God! *(Sound of thunder in distance)* Oh, no! None of your growling or meddling with me — I don't scare easy. Let others run under the wall. If you're taking me, it'll have to be in the fields, where the sun shines and there's plenty of elbow room. They got no right hiding my clothes!

Door opens and footsteps approach.

DOCTOR: How's it going, Sam? Nurse tells me you've been a naughty boy.

NURSE: I told him to stay in bed until you came, doctor!

SAM: Don't listen to her, doc. She's got unborn children clawing the heck out of her.

DOCTOR: It's fine, Miss Jones — you can go. *(Footsteps)* Now Sam, let's have a look at your dressing. Just lie back.

SAM: How many days I been here, doc?

DOCTOR: Eight days — this is the ninth.

SAM: Locked in a house without food or water, a dog couldn't live that long, could he?

DOCTOR: I doubt it. Why do you ask?

SAM: They've killed my dog!

DOCTOR: Who killed your dog?

SAM: My son — his wife — the man in black. Doc — tell me — life is bread, water and sunlight, no?

DOCTOR: As well as housing, medicine, sanitation.

SAM: Hell, you're like them — trying to pepper the raw meat. I didn't ask to be brought here. I took my leave long ago, an' the last attack was the horse I was going to ride home. But you changed all that, and now I've got to fight them all, so the next attack, they won't bring me in again. You know the martyr, the one I call Tom of the Gospel?

DOCTOR: Tom McGee?

SAM: Yeah — him. He had a good thing full of barbs an' spikes growing up in his heart to give him a reason for eating grub. I had to knock that out of him — hard. He fell, an' he's going to fall the rest of his life. Why? Because I'm living an' he's living — an' neither of us got a right to. I'm old, an' he's useless.

DOCTOR: Well, Sam — the blade I used to open your stomach with is the same one that's taken a miner's crushed arm off at the shoulder. It's cut varicose veins, and taken a dead child out of the mother who killed it. That blade is part of my arm — part of my heart and brain. It doesn't condemn. It works.

SAM: You could've done less work with it on me. It feels like you sewed up a bucket of busted glass in there. Can I go home now?

DOCTOR: Your clothes are on the way up. Your son is waiting downstairs. I called him on my way in.

SAM: Ach! The town is small — I can walk home.

DOCTOR: You're in no condition to walk anywhere. *(Fade and up sound on)* Well, here he is — good as new!

JOHN: How you feelin', pop?

SAM: You didn't come to see me!

JOHN: You know how it is . . . I was busy. We had a lot of deliveries at the lumber-yard.

SAM: Sure. The first attack I had, you and Betty brought cigars and flowers. Even a flask of rye — you didn't know, did you, doc. Even Miss Murphy had a swig, an' said it made her feel fifteen again!

JOHN: I told you I was busy!

SAM: First time here, I had a will made up, an' I told you about it. This time, you sent me holy Tom to do a bit of fiddling with my soul. You thought I was gonna die, eh?

JOHN: No, no! Pop — be sensible! No need for a public scene . . .

SAM: Nothing private about what I got to say. How's my dog?

JOHN: Your dog . . . I was meaning to tell you . . .

SAM: He's dead?

JOHN: Yes — Betty and me don't know how it happened. We . . .

SAM: I'll tell you how it happened, you bloodless scoundrel! He starved to death!

JOHN: Aw, come on! I didn't know I was to feed him **every** day. I thought you'd left food, an' today I only had to . . .

SAM: Where was he when you found him?

JOHN: On the floor, in front of the kitchen window.

SAM: I suppose holy Tom went to my house with you.

JOHN: Yeah, yeah — it was he said . . .

SAM: That old Sam was worried about his dog! God, he must've suffered! No food . . . no water.

DOCTOR: I'm sorry about your dog, Sam. Can you come back in three or four days so I can check your dressing?

SAM: The dressing don't matter. Doc, I want you to do something for me — now.

DOCTOR: Sure, Sam. What is it?

SAM: I want you to phone the lawyer — tell him to come down here right away. Tell him old Sam has to see him now.

DOCTOR: As you wish.

SAM: Tell him to hurry — there is no time! *(Footsteps recede)*

JOHN: What's the matter, pop? What you want the lawyer for?

SAM: What do you think I need a lawyer for, eh? You tell me! Come on — tell me. You know!

JOHN: Your will? . . . Because of the dog?

SAM: Hey, that's good! If you live to be a hundred and fifty, you might even be able to tell Tom of the Gospel to go an' find himself another lamplighter! I'm proud of you, son.

JOHN: You're getting revenge — is that it, pop?

SAM: Why revenge — it won't bring my dog back.

JOHN: I'm your son!

SAM: Well, don't spread the news around. How long's that lawyer going to take . . .

JOHN: You can't be serious about this. Look — I'm sorry about the dog. It won't happen again.

SAM: No — it won't . . .

JOHN: It's not that I want your money and house . . . Betty and I don't need it. But what will the town say when they learn you've left everything to . . . Who **are** you leaving everything to anyway?

SAM: Lots of places a man can leave his earnings. The Red Cross — or the municipality — or a home for bad girls. Even Tom — I can leave everything to Tom to help pay his way leading sheep like you! I'll leave it to Tom!

JOHN: That idiot! Pop — you're crazy. That guy is nuts. You think I been swallowing all the baloney he preaches? Nothin' doin'! The wife and I have gone along with him because . . .

well, if we get kids, they got to grow up believing in something. You know . . .

SAM: He's in your car now, isn't he?

JOHN: Yeah, yeah — he came. I didn't want him to come, but he doesn't hear me. Anyway — he's got some things figured out good. But what goes on between him an' me isn't what you think. Look — don't do it. It's not that I need your property — it's the talk that'll go around. *(SAM laughs)* Alright — change your damned will! I'll get even with you! Sure — we was hopin' you'd go this time! Who cares for you anymore!

SAM: That's my boy!

JOHN: Always bellowing, kicking things over — laughing at everyone an' everything — who cares anyway? If Tom with the hanging butt is getting everything from you, Tom can start visiting you to see if you need help. I won't do it anymore. An' the next time you get laid out, he'll kneel over you first before he brings you here — you just remember that! Hell! Why you doing this?

SAM: Go away — get out of here!

JOHN: Sure, pop. I'll go. But I want to tell you — it don't matter anymore. This town won't change one way or another. The same houses will stand — folks will still walk as fast to work — nothing will change because you've gone. **You** think it will, but it won't — because you'll be silent, and pretty soon less and less will be remembered of you, an' even less said.

SAM: I didn't live for nothing, you damned fool!

JOHN: Sure. Maybe you're a couple of men pasted up into one — maybe. You've lived long, drunk and ate lots — loved lots and worked more than your share. Maybe there's even a touch of God to you. Tom reckons now there is. But I don't swallow that. I'm going one way an' you're going the other. The way I see it, you've betrayed me!

SAM: What?

JOHN: Me, or anyone else — what do you want of us? I didn't come into the world with my clothes on an' a pickaxe in my hand. Hell, pop — I'm hungry! I gotta eat up your property like I got to eat up Tom the Gospel. An' you're mad because I forgot to feed your dog. See you . . .

SAM: John — son! Wait!

JOHN: You want me to take you home? I've got to get back to work now.

SAM: No. You go on. I've still some things to do here.

JOHN: Are you sure?

SAM: Sure I'm sure. Don't I know my own mind? Good-bye, son.

JOHN: 'Bye.

SAM: John! Here — I want to shake your hand. Never done that before, eh?

JOHN: You sure you're alright?

SAM: Sure . . . sure. Now take it easy. *(JOHN leaves. Foot-steps approach)*

DOCTOR: Good you're still here. No luck. The lawyer's out of town until tomorrow afternoon. Where's your son?

SAM: He's gone. Doc — you'd better take me back upstairs.

DOCTOR: What's the matter, Sam? Don't you feel well?

SAM: I don't know. Don't matter anymore does it?

DOCTOR: The operation was a success, Sam. You'll be fine — or . . . Sam, is it something else?

SAM: I'm tired, Doc. I want to lie down . . . close my eyes once again . . .

DOCTOR: Sam! Sam — don't you *want* to live? Wait — I'll call your son's house!

SAM: No! Don't call anybody . . . nobody at all, you hear! Doc — for God's sake — take me upstairs. The hallway is dim, Doc — I can't see. Take my hand, Doc. Where the devil are you?

DOCTOR: I'm here, Sam. This way — easy now. *(Shouts)* Miss Jones! Nurse!

SAM: How much suffering my dog have, Doc? Eight days . . . eight hundred years without food and water . . . scratching at the window . . . on the other side was men — an' back of the men was God . . . you believe in God, Doc . . . ? The widows wept, Doc, when I came home from war . . .

The End

COUNTRY BOY

Childhood? No, there was no childhood. For even if there had been, I would not tell of it. Childhood is a bewilderment — a time of accidental enlargements of the known world. Sometimes it can be confused with a time of beauty — and here the danger lies.

My world was small — the size of a homestead settlement — four miles in one direction and three in the other, closed in on three sides by two ravines and a river. Shall I tell you of my life? What is there to tell?

Once, there was a time of questions, when I looked about me and saw but did not understand. Then came the time of answers, when I took the world by the throat and shook it, shouting, "Enough!"

I did not stop the world in doing this, for I am only a country-boy, back bent and two hands to the earth, sifting dust. But I became a man. And in this there is comfort.

There were days and people over which I could not smile. Neighbours of ours, Pete and his wife, were married fifteen years before they had a kid — a girl with one missing arm. The kid learned to walk, and was able to say "ma-ma" and "da-da" when it caught diphtheria and died. Pete had to beat his wife with his fists to take the kid away so he could bury it . . .

The war in Europe — there was a war there, and it took our Joe, the farm-hand, away from us. He walked away into the evening mist and didn't return until the summer after, when he got two weeks furlough.

His hair was cut short, and he looked beautiful in his army uniform and V-cap. His clothes were so clean and pressed, and his back was straight. He might have stood against a tree with his entire length touching it. I ran ahead into the house to tell my mother, and she put water on for tea.

When they were settled in the kitchen and Joe took his cap off and tucked it in his shoulder flap, my father struck the table with his hand in a gesture of pleasure.

"Well, Joe — how's it going? Army treating you good?"

"Sure, Mike. Army treats me good," Joe mumbled.

Dad offered him paper and tobacco, and they both rolled and lit up, while mother stood behind them. I was leaning against the woodbox and wanting to be a soldier, while the water sputtered and warmed on the stove.

"You ain't scared, are you?" My father suddenly asked, looking hard at Joe.

"Scared of what?" Joe seemed surprised.

"Well — fighting — you know, guns pointed at you. Attacks . . . Injury — maybe even death!"

Joe took a deep drag of his cigarette.

"I don't aim to do no fightin'."

"Then what you doing in the army?" Father's voice was getting that angry edge to it. Joe squirmed right out of his military posture and looked like a farm-hand again.

"Why not? Everything's taken care of for a guy. One guy tells you when to get up. Another guy tells you when to sleep. An' they feed you good, Mike — grapefruit juice for breakfast — yeah — a glass this big of the stuff every breakfast! Jesus! I never tasted grapefruit juice before . . . !"

There was hatred in the settlement. The hatred of Timothy Callaghan for his ox, Bernard. Timothy had as many children as a year has months — and these he struggled to clothe and feed on about ten acres of soil, half of which was as stony as a cobbled street. He could never afford a horse or tractor, so the work of cultivating, clearing the land and hauling in wood fell on Bernard.

The ox was wayward, lazy and temperamental. When the work of plowing or seeding was at its most urgent, Bernard would feign illness or a limp. Or worse still, he would lie down in full harnass and, digging his horn into the earth, stretch out rigidly and refuse to rise.

I have seen Timothy beating the brute across the face with his thread-bare cap, kicking him, or hitting him across the flanks with a willow cane. I have heard him curse the ox in the high voice of a woman — and I have seen Timothy down on his knees beside Bernard, weeping as he pleaded with him to rise and help him do the terrible work that had to be done.

"The Devil is in that ox!" Timothy once confided in a dangerous whisper to my father, his face white and fearful. "I have seen the Devil in his eyes — laughing at me — taunting me to kill him. And one day — one day I will kill him!"

But the man and the ox were bound together until the natural death of either. Much as they hated one another, they could not live apart, so great was their dependence on each other. Even today, when both are grey and too feeble to work anymore, they stubbornly persist, waiting with the strong patience of enemies for the end that must come one day . . .

. . . What of love? I don't know. I have never been in love — but I imagine it would be something like becoming lost in the forest in late August, when the trees and foliage one has known all summer suddenly change. You would wander around for hours, even days — lost, and yet not alarmed, for the woods would be delightful, mysterious and warm. All feeling would belong to you — to me, like the scent of our skins under the sun. Love such as this would be heavenly — everlasting — and I imagine I would work hard to make it real.

Love could be a cat's tooth — like the one which bit Clem, the blacksmith. His was a terrible honesty and virtue. Had he been born five hundred years earlier, he would have made it as a saint.

My father and I called on him, carrying between us an iron wagon tire for him to shorten. Clem was in the smoke-stained smithy, his clothes glued to him with perspiration, and his beard and long hair quivering on his enormous head as he worked. He stopped when we entered and grinned a greeting which flashed the whitest and cleanest teeth I have ever seen. When my father explained what he wanted done, Clem nodded and said he would attend to it after breakfast.

"After breakfast? You mean you ain't eaten yet, Clem? It's noon already!" Father said with disbelief.

"I'm all alone, so I eat when I'm hungry," Clem said happily.

Father looked at him and scratched at his chin.

"No need for a man to be alone," he said. "Clem, you been pounding that anvil on to ten years now. When you going to take a break — get out an' meet people? Do a bit of drinking and running around with the girls?"

"Why? I'm happy with what I'm doing. Besides, I haven't seen a girl who really needs me." Clem spoke with some surprise in his voice.

"What you mean — a girl who really needs you? Don't you want a woman for a wife — no give or take?" My father asked, his eyes betraying his argumentative nature.

Clem tossed his head and leaned back against his anvil block.

"I do, yes I do. But a man must give happiness to somebody who needs his help. There is so much unhappiness in the world today."

My father coughed sarcastically.

"Then what sort of woman would you marry?"

"I never thought about it, but now that you ask, I reckon I'd marry any of the world's unfortunates who needed my help." Clem looked at my father with clear, innocent eyes.

"Oh, get off the big words an' tell me what you're saying." My father kept on him.

"Suppose — now just suppose, that I was to see a young woman — a woman about to be a mother, standing on a bridge — wanting to jump over into the river and end it all. I . . . I would run to her and carry her away with me. I would work

161

for her, cheer her! Make her happy and glad to be alive and my companion!'' Now Clem raised his thick arms to us, as in benediction.

My father wasn't listening anymore, but fidgeting and walking out even before Clem finished what he was saying. I followed.

"I'll be back for the tire tomorrow!'' Father snapped over his shoulder.

"Right!'' Clem called after us, and before we reached the road, we could hear his hammer ringing again.

Clem did get married — to a girl from town. No, she wasn't a mother-to-be, nor did she try to jump off a bridge to end her life. She wasn't even particularly young — but then neither was Clem. They met outside the town hotel, where Clem, as a pedestrian, came on her being arrested for insulting the town constable in the most obscene language. Clem sat through her trial, and after she was sentenced, went over and introduced himself. He then paid her fine and took her out to dinner.

A week later, they were married.

Almost from the very beginning, there were battles between them, and for days Clem's smithy stayed shut and abandoned. Horses went unshod — ploughshares were left to rust in the grass, and welding from the settlement accumulated in a heap before his shop. All through this, Clem stayed indoors, repairing the erosions of his marriage. As it was, he had the marriage annulled soon after — but it became community knowledge he was paying her alimony. Even after she remarried . . .

There was a day when my father stomped into his shop to roar at him:

"Look here, Clem! It's none of my business, but you've been shelling everything you earn to that woman! And she's been married to someone else three years now. Just look at you — still wearing the same clothes you bought before your wedding. An' your shop! You haven't even added a new pair of pliers to your supplies — how long you aimin' to go on like this?''

Clem put down his hammer and, smiling sadly, brushed the

grey-streaked, sticky hair back from his temples.

"Let her have what happiness God will allow her," he said softly. "Let her have all this . . . I don't care. I will be an old man soon."

"But you're a fool!" My father's voice was like thunder. "You're not helping her! She still drinks and devils up — on *your* money!"

"I ask you only one favour — stay out of this. You don't understand. It's the way I feel . . . the way I wish it to be . . ." Clem turned his back on us and wearily returned to his labours . . .

So Clem went his way and I went mine. I couldn't ponder too long on him. There was too much to do. There was a cow to buy.

The auction mart was an old abandoned barn, with a plank platform in front, on which the willowy auctioneer stood, surrounded by a mountain of junk — used furniture, old crockery, leaning clothes pillars loaded with second- and third-hand clothing — and bags of meal, salt and overstocks of fertilizer. Many of these goods were stained and damaged by being left out in the rain the previous night.

My father and I pushed our way through the morning crowd of farmers, run-down spectators who came weekly for their entertainment, small boys who piped outlandish bids and fled, disrupting every sale I had been to. A gust of wind blew off the platform to us, and I could smell in it the chemical odour of moistened fertilizer along with the must odour of damp upholstery.

The auctioneer adjusted his glasses, cleared his throat and clapped his hands together twice. This was the signal for the auction to begin, and almost immediately Lame Willy, auction-assistant, led a cow from the barn in back and over to the front of the platform.

"Now what am I bid for this lovely, three-year-old Jersey . . ." His words exploded like fire-crackers over the crowd.

"That's no Jersey! That's a shorthorn!" A big man with

a walrus moustache corrected him rudely, and the crowd roared with laughter.

"Oh!" said the auctioneer and, adjusting his glasses again, bent over for a closer peer at the cow in front and below him.

"Well, so it is! A lovely three-year-old shorthorn — what do I hear, gentlemen? What am I bid? Come on, gentlemen — what offers do I hear?"

My father stabbed his fist into the air as he shouted.

"A hundred dollars!"

"A hundred dollars from the man with the checkered shirt and grey hat!" The auctioneer glanced quickly at us, but did not pause in his explosive patter. "A hundred dollars for this lovely three-year-old shorthorn — do I hear any further offers? Gentlemen — this would be a giveaway — for that price I would have bought the cow myself! A hundred dollars is the bid — what do I hear?"

"A hundred and ten!" The walrus moustache roared, and his heavy shoulders hunched as for battle.

"A hundred and ten! I am bid a hundred and ten . . . who'll bid a hundred and twenty? She's worth every cent on a bargain . . . do I hear a hundred and twenty?" The auctioneer now forgot the embarassment of his earlier mistake. He was burning, leaning forward as if to catch hold of the crowd in his hands and compress it for the excitement it would give him. I saw fine beads of perspiration breaking out on his face.

"A hundred and fifteen!" Father again stabbed the sky with his fist.

The auctioneer smiled ever so faintly.

"A hundred and fifteen — the man with the checkered shirt and grey hat! Gentlemen — let's move this beautiful shorthorn to meadow quickly . . . who'll give me a hundred and twenty? No further bids? Come now! Any further bids? A hundred and fifteen once . . . twice . . . sold! To the man in the checkered shirt and grey hat for a hundred and fifteen dollars!"

The walrus spat a burst oyster into the dust in front of him and, looking at father for a moment with red, vengeful eyes, hurried away, which was not the end of that business. For when my father went up to pay for the cow, he first made a thing of examining its legs, prodding its rump with his thumb — kneading under its neck. Then he took its mouth into his hands and forced it open, while Lame Willy fidgeted behind him with an open ledger, waiting for the money. I watched my father shaking his head sadly and motioning over to Willy. They had a short discussion, and Willy called the auctioneer himself down.

By now, my father was angry, doing all the talking, then opening the cow's mouth again. All three of them looked inside, and the auctioneer caught his head in his hands as if with pain. He said something to my father, who turned as if to walk away. The auctioneer tapped him on the shoulder, and they talked some more, then shook hands. Father paid Lame Willy, then waved me over and we led the cow away.

"What happened? What was all that about?" I asked when we were out of the willow flats and approaching the town.

My father threw back his head and let out a gust of laughter.

"Serves the bugger right!" He said.

"What'd you do?"

Father wiped his eyes with the back of his wrists and blew his nose vigorously to the side of the road.

"I knocked fifteen dollars off the price of the cow, that's what I done!" he replied triumphantly.

"You mean — we got it for a hundred, like you bid the first time?"

"Why not?" he asked. "Remember he didn't know the difference between a Jersey and a shorthorn . . ."

"Well?" I didn't see where all this was leading.

"Well — I was countin' on him not knowing anything else about stock. So I points out to him he was taking me by selling me a bud cow — a cow that didn't have teeth in its top jaw."

"What? This cow got no teeth in its top jaw?" I was wondering what mother would say when she found out. My father grinned.

"No boy. No cow got teeth in its top jaw! Here — you get

behind an' drive her faster. We got to get through town before he finds out . . .''

Such were my schools. I learned nothing of music, history or electricity. But I knew how to buy a cow for less . . .

I could stand by the church, and touch the red bricks of its walls — and know a truth no school books would have taught me — the truth of dedication and despair, such as asthmatic Joe had when he cycled around the countryside at seventy years of age, pleading, arguing, humbling himself like a beggar to find labour and money with which to build his church. Tone-deaf himself, he led a band of women carollers up and down the drifted country roads each winter — singing at each house they passed — arguing with the country people who donated too little, and Joe threatening to sing some more himself if he wasn't given more.

And in summer, when the neighbourhood turned out for the Sunday ball-game, there would be Joe, wheezing like a boiling kettle, canvassing those people the Communists had missed in collections for their newspaper.

Seventeen years it took for Joe to lift his church up from the soil into a tall and magnificent building. And when the time came to dedicate it, a young minister was sent out — a city-bred boy — who took no notice of Joe or his suffering, and made the ceremony notable by insisting he be given title to the building before he would perform the service.

After the ceremony, Joe wept as he stood by the church gate. He turned to the departing congregation and, with his hands and shoulders trembling, spoke to them.

"As God is my witness, I renounce this church and my faith!"

He said nothing more, but turned and, with his back hunched, walked home.

Remaining behind in the churchyard, his children and wife wept and cursed him for the shame he'd brought on them. Then they hurried after Joe, begging him to return and explain to his neighbours it was a mistake — that he spoke out of fool-ishness in his old age. But Joe waved them away and went home to his bed.

He lay there two days without rising or asking for food, and on the third day he died. At Easter of that year, they raffled off his bicycle to help pay for a bell for the church tower . . .

With the first traces of beard on my cheeks, I hired out as a stone-picker in the settlement — heaving boulders out of newly broken fields — slashing away at roots with the small hatchet which was fastened to my belt. My face was bent to the earth now as I worked, and I smelled the sour vigour of the soil. When this work exhausted itself for the summer, I built fences, cut hay and helped to harvest. The seasons and years began to fly — pausing only once when I saw Nancy Burla feeding chickens on her father's farm.

I was working there, repairing their fallen barnyard fence, when she came out to do chores. I saw her and she smiled at me. And I split my thumb with the hammer, for my head was reeling.

I dreamed of her, and the dream was like a hot iron pressed into my flesh. My father knew, but he shook his head sadly.

"Too bad, son, we have no money. If you had a farm of your own, we might think of making a match for you. But you know how difficult it is to make ends meet . . ."

I stayed away from her farm after this. Sometimes I saw her at the country dance, and then I would go home, for I hadn't learned to dance anyway, and only went to look and talk to the other boys.

A year later, I still dreamed of her occasionally, but she was no longer the Nancy Burla I knew. She had become a temptress, with no recognizable face — only a body with an animal scent which swelled until it split her clothes wide open. Such dreams gave me a headache, and in the day I would work like a demon, sucking in my sweat through my wide-open nostrils.

Then, my father died after a long illness which had become so much a routine around our home I had never noticed him declining. The morning my mother told me, I only nodded and continued sipping my coffee. She left, sobbing, to tell the neighbours. I went out into the shed, where I methodically built a casket for him.

Walking to the shed, I felt neither thirst nor hunger — only an emptiness which removed even my thoughts. The fields seemed to fall away, turn to ashes, and the trees parched and wilted, as with some great heat. Then the night came, like a silent mist, without sound or substance. My mother did not return, and by next morning, my nails were broken and my fingers bled, but the casket was polished, glowing like something holy in the dim shed.

I went outside and had to shield my eyes against the red heat of the sun. Turning to the house, I saw it listing and scaly, as if it too had perished and had begun decomposing with the passing of my father. Around me, the countryside was like a desert. Not a soul came over to help or comfort me. I stared at the homes dotting the hillsides, and it seemed as if they were natural growths of the soil — as if no human had ever lived and loved in them. Sheep, cattle and dogs wandered aimlessly over the fields and pastures, but it appeared they had always moved that way, without a master or a purpose. I choked back my tears and, finding a shovel, started walking down the road to the burying grounds. As I walked, my sorrow turned to fear, and I stopped. Laying down my shovel in the dust, I pinched myself and bit my swollen tongue. There was pain — sharp and sweet pain — I was alive!

I dug wide and deep into the solid clay — through the afternoon and into the night, but this time there were no thoughts of Nancy Burla.

"I have killed the animal in me!" I whispered to myself over and over again, drawing contentment from my knowledge. "Now I can bury my father without dishonour!"

Then, there were no thoughts, no struggles. Just the taste of salt in my mouth and the flashing of my big, glistening arms. Suddenly, the truth seared through my brain . . . these arms were all I had and all that anybody wanted — my mother, those who hired stone-pickers and harvest help . . . even Nancy Burla. They were my reason for living! They were my strength and my food and bed — there was no other part of me — never had been.

What I saw, felt and heard all these years were only shadows on the landscape. What I thought was nothing. What price a country-boy's dreams?

I saw the light weaving up the road towards me, and lowering my shovel, stared into it, not being able to understand what it meant. It was as if I had gone into a deep sleep, yet heard the clock ticking and felt the dawn breaking, helpless to rise and shut off the inevitable alarm. The light came closer, washing around me, falling into the pit I was digging, and illuminating my face.

"Are you alright?" my mother asked in a fearful voice, and a strong arm reached down to me.

"Here — I'll pull you up!" Clem, the blacksmith spoke. There were others, murmuring in the background. I let Clem pull me up, and I followed them all home.

I slept with my clothes on, and next morning when I woke, I stepped outdoors and saw to my surprise that the settlement was lively again, and the fields green. Some neighbours were already on the way to our house for their last homage to my father. From the kitchen, I heard my mother giving final instructions to the minister, who was already here, on how she wanted the service conducted. I walked out of range of her voice to do chores, for the cattle were as alive as I was, and as hungry.

Only for them, nothing had changed. Whereas for me, an entire lifetime had heaved and come to rest.

STORY OUTLINE
JOURNALISTIC SERIES

This story occurred in the surroundings of my home two summers ago, when the house was a stopover in the network of Canadian people sheltering illegal U.S. entrants escaping military service in Vietnam.

Two sisters-in-law and their husbands were holidaying here from Boston. They came in an air-conditioned car. Although former Nova Scotian Canadians, they had in the past forty years become part of the granite core of middle-America . . . the conservative element driven through personal fear and paranoia of social change to becoming unthinking supporters of Nixonian policies and morality.

At twilight one evening, a VW bus, beautifully equipped and loaded to the roof with camping supplies, axes, food, etc., pulled into the driveway. There were two couples and a third man in the bus. One of the women had a baby, who was already showing signs of exhaustion and the sort of neglect caused by people not able to cope. They introduced themselves by first names — false names — which was prudent and common. One of the couples mentioned they were from California, the others from Oregon. Again, such information was not solicited by my wife or myself and was not treated as meaningful when offered. There were other visible qualities about these young people that were more telling — they were white, well-educated, well-equipped for entry into another country. In short, they were the children of the privileged American middle-class, who did and do have options when faced with an immoral war.

Over dinner that evening, the two critical factions in American society clashed. Our in-laws were startled and angered by the contempt those youngsters voiced for all things they themselves considered quasi-sacred. Just or not, it was the responsibility of youth to serve in U.S. wars; there were no racial problems — only troublemakers stirring up average people — besides, if the blacks were not happy, they could go back to where they came from; there were no poor or need for poor — look at us — nobody could be poorer than coming from Nova Scotia, and through hard work and keeping clean of trouble, look where it got us? Everybody can do the same! Why, oh why, do you "kids" persist in making trouble and embarassing us, who did so much for you?

The young draft dodgers ranged widely in their responses. One responded with the bitterness of a youth-fascist, damning everything the older Americans said for no other reason than that older people made these statements. Another responded with pseudo-Marxist logic — still another from a highly personal position, which was not very secure. In the meantime, preparations for dinner had turned the kitchen into a shambles, as everyone was co-operatively trying to "help." Milk put on to warm for the infant had searing heat under it, and was burning. Vegetables were being brought in from the bus in fifty-pound containers, and no one remembers where they had been placed, etc.

After dinner, I quizzed the youngsters on their plans. They were going into the mountains of the Interior to buy a farm and set up a permanent base. They had heard small farms were available, and between them they had ten thousand dollars for payment against a land purchase. I asked them about their knowledge of farming, and pointed out that the area into which they were heading was economically backward and offered no employment except for that requiring the most elementary manual skills. They began a long lecture on courses they had taken in southern Oregon and California in horticulture, dairying, cereal farming, etc. I mentioned that what they had studied was sub-tropic agriculture, that, in this country, winter was a powerful economic and cultural obstacle, that all training would have to be adapted to coping with the northern reality, and that there was no room even for one misjudgment. At this point, both the older and younger Americans dismissed this as a backwoods point of view; that with sufficient funds and determination to succeed, there would be no problem.

The draft-dodgers and their dependents left in the morning, after warmer but still cautious farewell wishes from their elder compatriots. As the bus pulled away from the driveway, I noticed they had failed to pack away two axes, a sleeping bag, and the child's collapsible crib. Once they left, the bitterness of our in-laws towards those they felt had betrayed America flowered again. By this time, our family felt somehow on the outside of the argument, for we felt a more urgent disaster was in the making. A few telephone calls to friends along the route the youngsters had taken confirmed our fears — they were losing supplies through carelessness and ignorance at an alarming rate.

In late October, they returned. All of them were threadbare and defeated. Their money was spent. Their bus was now running on only three pistons — the result of a do-it-yourself repair job by the three men while they were stranded half-way up a mountain searching for land to buy. The child was suffering from infections and advanced neglect — its mother by now hardly capable of coping emotionally with the smallest problems. Thin on political or social convictions, softened by the excesses of middle-class American life, badly disciplined and inflexible about personal habits, they had collectively decided they would use the few dollars remaining between them to return home, even if it meant the men having to do military service or suffer punishment for attempting not to.

The story has haunted me as symbolic of a pathetic quality

of self-destruction knit into the make-up of the American conservative, and the impracticality and helplessness of some of its resistors when faced with the most elemental decisions. A cultural crisis in the nuclear age, where both the victim and victimizer have been caught in a web from which they cannot extricate themselves.

THE TEMPORARY ARRANGEMENT
A WESTERN VIEWPOINT

Article for *The Montreal Star*

Thirty years ago, when I was a boy of five, we lived in a corner of northern Alberta where my father still employed oxen to plough the soil and cut down the barley and wheat at harvest. With extraordinary vividness I recall following the oxen over the cool earth, my bare feet sinking into the spongy turf, and the hot acid scent of oxen perspiration that glowed and flecked like stars or crystals of pebbled glass. At that time the earth and everything in and above it was unchanging. I could anticipate the rain; knew the approach of frost by the tingle of evening clouds. I helped slaughter animals that I knew by name and I ate their flesh. Around me, many old men died, leaving their widows, who keened and considered themselves destined for a lonely and desperate old age — until they moved in with their sons and daughters, whose grandchildren were born, and another season passed.

This was life. My parents arrived here from medieval Ukrainian villages, bringing with them patterns of existence that were harsh and simple. Food, shelter and subservience — beyond this, all was dressing on the windows of one's being.

"Most interesting to see the changes in the country," a colleague wrote me, ". . . the growing sense of confidence and security."

In Calgary, Winnipeg, Oshawa — the steel-grey faces of men in the early light, members of trade unions, teaching federations, hospital guilds, sleepily going to work. Driving cars made in other countries or under foreign patent in Canada, radios playing music composed and recorded abroad — men and women smiling at last night's *Red Skelton Show* that not only crossed a sacred border with the ease of a super-statesman but also arrested the attention of a population that could not for that one hour read a Canadian novel, argue a Canadian viewpoint or consider the cost this new life in the shadow of a giant was exacting. The cost is great. The cost is our memory as a people.

We had so little to remember. In the days of my childhood, when I trailed hot oxen in a cold field, I was about to go to school where I would spend some years learning of kings and crusaders, sea-captains, warlords and other useless riff-raff unsuited to any useful pursuit in life. Some came to this continent as empire-builders, traders, officers, priests. Lakes, rivers, landmarks were named after them, yet they contributed almost nothing except a fable. What of the people who came in the holds of ships like cattle to build a country?

"Lord Strathcona drove one spike, all the rest was done by Mike . . ." a labour journalist wrote in one of the many periodicals that reached our home during my boyhood. And of all my education, these twelve words have been the most unforgettable.

Crossing and recrossing the vastness of this country, riding, walking and resting beside fools, poets, students and transients in search of tomorrow, writing words that are so tortuous to collect and imprison, I wondered about the lies I was taught. Louis Riel, my teacher instructed me, was insane and a bandit who deserved hanging. Yet Manitoba, Saskatchewan and Alberta reached provincehood because Riel had been there, and the stamp of his righteous fury still marks the politics and secret

175

thoughts of the prairie-dweller. Where have the untruths led us?

"I am hot," a child once said to me. "Can you hit the sun and kill it?"

No. But I can provide you a shadow in which you may grow for a little while. But after you have grown, what will you do, my child with a clouded heritage? Will you build, as my parents built, structures of wood and paint and asphalt paper that decays and parches as it is being constructed? Twenty years is long enough. After that even the land will be sold.

The Indians were hired, tricked, bribed into slaughtering the buffalo. And then, they were left helpless and hungry.

The Hudson's Bay and the chartered banks built with stone — they knew the footprint of destiny. Around them grew cities, built by common people who thought only in wood.

And fear. For as they cleared away the trees, the landscape widened, and they who widened it became lost in the vastness. They looked up to a stern God to locate and remember them. And lest God was away on the day they called, they painted passages from the Bible on the sides of grain elevators, visible to other men from highways five miles distant even today. The Almighty, with better vision, might see and read from ten times that distance . . .

"The changes in the country" — they are there, yes! We eat and dress well. We are mobile horizontally in a way unknown ten years ago. Farms created by hand tools in the past are now managed by farmers who reside in towns and cities. The industrial worker is freed from excessive labour and is now faced with the strange problems of leisure. Intellectuals are knowledgeable and concerned. Politicians need not be bound to the narrow interests of voters whose prejudices they were compelled to project in debating and writing laws.

But what of the people denied the fruits of this affluence? Who were not there when our parents, and later, we struck the bargain of expediency, the temporary arrangement at the crossroads of our possibilities?

Roy Alphonse Williams, aged twenty-four, was run over by

a train in Lytton, British Columbia, on the 9th of August this centennial year. His parents claim Roy Alphonse Williams had begun to die years earlier when he graduated as a bright technical student but was unable to find employment as a mechanic in a white world that had given him grudging opportunities to train but denied him the right to exercise his skills in making a living. Only occasional work as an Indian labourer was available to him. He rid himself of his frustrations in the beer parlor and, eventually, in death.

Those who will not succeed where the rewards are greatest — what of them? Once, the forests and mines and construction companies used raw manpower. The misfits of today, dropouts from school, some brilliant students at one point, now clutter beaches, highways and campsites. Devoid of the fear of winter, who are they? A new class of the disinherited? Their manpower no longer needed, what will become of them?

The possible answers alarm me, for they deny those who observe a "growing sense of confidence and security."

Short-sightedness has bedevilled our people for so long, as they forced roads and railways through the wilderness and clawed a thousand miles of land from the muskegs and forests of the north. A short-sightedness not entirely of their choice, for the building of the West was accomplished with colonial manipulation, although the word was never used, even when the central government deployed troops to quell Riel's proclamation of self-government. The populations of the Maritimes and central Canada had time to commit themselves to their land, their customs, their lore. The Westerner was to make a temporary arrangement with nature, with the land, with himself and with his children. The consequences are a cultural and historic vacuum whose final resolution is uncertain.

There is no confidence but the confidence of brashness. There is no security. The houses made poorly decay and list. The new cars will not always start on a frigid morning and one man alone will not beat back the winter. The politician from the West who became prime minister of the country is now more concerned with form than content, and his colleagues

177

must leave him behind. The prosperity created by the sale of natural resources is disquieting and unreal, for it does not relate to the productivity of people at work. The hoopla of Stampedes and Klondike Days and the small town fairs has a false ring to it, for it says nothing to the young to confirm that they are of a certain place and time. They drift away. The rural population ages and declines. The faceless, flat cities absorb all but provide no assurances.

Tomorrow may be like today. Tomorrow may be critical in this great basin of food and petroleum resources — this region, for provinces are artificial identities. An upheaval of vision may occur that has nothing to do with comfort or security but would be a hundred times more rewarding, for it would be a blossoming of genuine idealism and pride in country and people.

The region can also slip into a stern Western fascism, self-isolating and eroding, relegating the singers of songs and tellers of tales to the position of curious entertainers, to be paid off by two fresh apples and a fifty-cent piece. Its folk-heroes may never come to birth, leaving a voiceless land, communicating only with its hands.

Which way? West of Winnipeg and east of the Rockies — the place of my birth; the arid, large sweep of country where the sun is hot and the wind cold, even in midsummer. The transient West, the sad country; the many towns with no pavement in their streets except for the chance highway that locates and leaves them.

The country of big-hearted Bill Mitchell, whose laughter was the first to cut the silence, and whose *Jake and The Kid* was slightly off-centre to the soft part of reality. The country of promise and the country of fear; the political Bible-belt where Jehovah still unashamedly takes to the hustings each election year and garners his dividends of frustration and fear from the unmarked prairie grave. Where business is still tied to its recent cousin, the general store; and where the jet-age of the mind is held back by the plodding oxen.

When does the repayment of loans and investments begin? And the start to tending the back gardens of possibilities among our own people? The building of a genuine confidence and security that results from a patriotism and pride more deeply motivated than the hollow exploitation of a field or timber lot? The understanding that we are short-changed, under-developed, culturally deprived — and that there is one hell of a long way to go for such a large portion of Canada before we even begin to arrive at this crossroads in our history.

Left to right: George, Campbell, Tanya, Lesley, Norma, Sergei(1968)
Photo: Jack Dietrich

THE SEVENTIES

George Ryga (1975)   Photo: unknown

DEAR MR. PELLETIER
ADVOCACY LETTER

Summerland, B.C.
12 November, 1970

The Honorable Gerard Pelletier,
Secretary of State
Government of Canada,
Ottawa.

Dear M. Pelletier:

The recent announcement of the sale of Ryerson Press to an American publishing house gives us cause for grave concern, not only for the future of the textbook publications to be used for education of Canadian children, but for the broader implications this has on Canadian culture and identity.

Our history has never been adequately taught, even under conditions which prevailed in the past. This situation is not going to be remedied if control of information for texts falls into hands of people not native to this country. We request federal government intervention in this, as the matter is now of national concern.

Further to this, we urge a study of book publication and marketing in a wider context. We feel that attention to encouraging low-cost publication and distribution of Canadian books of an educational, general and entertainment nature is long overdue. We applaud the initiative of the Canadian Radio and Television Commission and its mandate to establish a Canadian-content factor in radio and television broadcasting. This has already begun to show returns in national self-awareness and a growing sense of Canadian identity. But we also consider this developmental initiative must apply equally to Canadian book publication to balance dissemination of Canadian thought, literature and history. The alternative is a nurtured Canadian culture in radio and television, with a disadvantaged and eventually overwhelmed theatrical, literary and historical tradition. Within this concern, we must also include musical and oral recording.

We, the undersigned — a historical author and magazine editor-publisher of national and international recognition — and a novelist-poet-playwright of equal stature — propose the following recommendations for your consideration:

1. Immediate federal government legislation to forbid outright sale or controlling-interest purchase of Canadian book publishing houses by foreign interests. Also, intervention in any deals of this nature current or pending which would result in further loss of control over our publishing industry.

2. The establishment of a Crown corporation to assist the publishing of low-cost books and periodicals for the widest general distribution through low-interest loans and assistance, patterned after the Canadian Film Development Corporation.

3. Canadian-content legislation safeguarding 50% Canadian-content in production, distribution and sale of newsstand literature, library inventory and educational study materials.

4. Examination of the recording industry in Canada with the
   intent of asserting Canadian ownership, production, content
   and distribution of oral and musical recorded materials.

Sincerely yours,

George Ryga, author   N.L. Barlee, editor-publisher

SOCIAL RESPONSIBILITIES OF WRITERS

It is difficult for me to present my points of view on a writer's social responsibilities without a certain degree of anger. Anger at myself and my peers for not at times being perceptive enough to recognize the degree and speed of social change until the changes have stabilized; and at best our insights becoming defensive or abstracted until they miss the central point of social change and social contradiction.

A writer's responsibilities are first and foremost to the people, of which he is a part. His role is to entertain as a teller of stories — to amuse, to argue — to sift through the sands of the past and the present-day for the paradoxes which throw new light upon the commonplace and elevate the experience of living into humour, pathos and heroism. This undertaking is one of heavy responsibility and distinct danger, even in the most congenial of societies.

Men and women and children who read, who receive their stories and impressions through television and film or through other sensory media, will consume what is offered. Their discrimination is not delicately honed to any appreciable extent — and eventually they forget they can influence what is fed into their minds. I think viewing a few hours of current popular television programming will bear this out.

A writer who consciously panders to this type of entertainment — who shamelessly and without misgivings creates it — betrays not only the sensibilities of people who trust him, but he also betrays himself into a living hell from which it is difficult, often impossible, to extricate himself. For there is no lasting joy in turning a quick dollar in the creation of uselessness. I know a pornographer who assures me each time I have seen him over the past ten years, that he will soon begin writing a good novel. He still has not begun the book. The only thing which has happened is that he has become more frantic discussing it.

Both in his craft and in his integrity as a human being, a writer must be political. Often he is the only conscience functioning within a country. During the gloomy days of the War Measures Act in Canada, many of our finest writers were the only voices of sanity heard in the land — at a time when the so-called "political" people in government either herded together like sheep or protested in whispers, their ears tuned to the artificially created emotionalism of their electorate. Those of us who reacted against the hysteria exposed ourselves to danger — yes — but we slept better for facing the challenge of hard-fisted absolutism. I would like to commend Bob Hunter, particularly, for his unflinching attacks on the stupidity of actions which threatened to fragment our country and its people.

I could dwell for a long while on the special conditions which should preoccupy us in our emergence from an agrarian neo-colonial country into one of the technologically more advanced areas of the world, wedged between two international giants. Or the long, long road we still must travel to evolve a social and cultural maturity in keeping with our resources and future possibilities. There is room for satire, for humour and for bitter condemnation in all these areas. There is also room for dance and song, and the creation of a mythology distinctly our own.

But let us be aware that none of this comes easily. I can speak from personal experience that every inch forward requires social struggle. A writer must struggle for his own sense

187

of honesty, integrity and vision against the ingrained attitudes of publishers, radio, film and television media, theatres — and against the anti-national and anti-heroic attitudes that have conditioned the reactions of many ordinary Canadian people.

Our cultural institutions in Canada are largely staffed by privileged mediocrity. We must learn to make demands for improvement upon them, or ask them to step aside, for the trivia of television soap-opera, or the publisher with an eye to a quick resale to the American pocket-book market, is no longer good enough.

We must, as writers, point out to them that we in Canada also have a civil rights struggle in the making. For in the English-Canadian sector of the country, the Anglo-Saxon rules the cultural media for which all of us, directly or indirectly, pay. This attitude still manipulates our cultural development on the anachronistic precept that the Hudson's Bay Company, the CPR and the Northwest Mounted Police really did build this country, and that the tens of thousands of immigrants who arrived from elsewhere than Britain were a massive social assistance gesture not worthy of official history or a follow-up of its consequences.

When I wrote a television drama for the prestigious Festival series, it had to be cleared through the CBC Board of Governors in Ottawa — because the hero of the story was a man named Duke Radomsky! And although this teleplay was reviewed most favourably both in Canada and abroad, and although I was to be commissioned to complete three subsequent teleplays, they were never produced — for they dealt with people and situations which might upset some special sensibilities. One of these plays dealt with an Indian — it was called *The Ecstasy of Rita Joe*. Need I say more?

In conclusion, I wish to stress that we have proven ourselves capable of creating world art through our writings — not just regional or national art — but world art. This carries with it a grave responsibility to be honest with ourselves for what we are and who we are, and perfect our skills so that we do not falter in the face of challenge — or of greatness.

PROTEST RALLY ADDRESS
BRAZIL INDIAN CRISIS

The most alarming world development to emerge in the past year is the energy crisis developing on the North American continent. For when a shortage of basic requirements faces the technology and culture of the earth's most highly developed continent, the life, culture and choices of all people on the earth will be affected. Treaties governing personal and international conduct become just so many pieces of worthless paper. Painfully developed norms of human dealings that are framed with some understanding and compassion for our fellowman and woman become subversive ideals, and those harbouring them are suspect and harassed. And this process is now rationalized and made expedient through the rise of imperial monopoly capitalism in the form of multinational corporations. At this moment, many of these corporations exercise more political and economic power than most of the countries who were signatories to the Universal Declaration of Human Rights at the United Nations in 1968. That charter guaranteed that human beings on earth could be born FREE and EQUAL IN DIGNITY and RIGHTS, with the hope that they could act towards one another in a spirit of brotherhood. The people of Vietnam . . . the people of Guatamala . . . of Brazil and Chile . . . the people of the Arabian deserts — were soon to learn the charter applied more readily to members of the white race, who, although only a small percentage of the earth's population, devoured most of the earth's food resources — and almost all of the world's mineral and petroleum wealth. If you were of a non-white race, and unfortunate enough to be born in a country with undeveloped resources of tungsten, copper or fossil oils, you were open to invasion, rape of your land and culture — and the imposition of a government you would not have wished on your neighbour's dog — a government perpetuating itself with an endless supply of sophisticated weaponry and paid hooligans to use them.

The examples of North America's inhumanity to the world reads like a catalogue of tragedy spanning the globe — Korea, South Vietnam, Cambodia, Laos, the Bikini Atoll, the thwarted hope of people rising from centuries of oppression in Guatemala, Paraguay, Puerto Rico, Brazil, the Dominican Republic . . . and most recently, the profound heartbreak of Chile. And all in the interest of serving a few American-based multinational conglomerates — notable among these, the mining and petroleum concerns, and the infamous United Fruit Company and the International Telephone and Telegraph Corporation, whose tentacles web this province through the telephone system in operation here. Backed by, and integrated with, the resources and special abilities of the CIA, the grab for resources is aggressive and ruthless — an open declaration of war against genuine human expression for self-fulfilment no matter where it emerges. At this moment, yet another war rages in the Middle East. A war being fought by small, helpless countries who will have little or no influence over the final resolution of the conflict — for the final treaty covering disposition of the Middle East oil reserves will in all likelihood be settled between Washington and Moscow. And because a fuel shortage threatens this continent, the bargaining will be savage — and damn the Arabs and Israelis who died or were maimed shaping the form of events to come!

What is happening in Brazil is particularly bitter to the people of Canada. We, who have been ourselves under colonial rule for so long, find ourselves the colonizers in the Amazon

Basin through our own multinational octopus — Brascan. And our interest in Brazil is not an isolated incident of a wealthy corporation going in and doing God-knows-what . . . Cabinet ministers and former cabinet ministers of our federal government — Robert Winters and Michel Sharp — were on the top-level directorate of this corporation and well informed indeed of Brascan's imperial designs on the Amazon. We now learn that the development, so-called, of the Amazon region of Brazil — an area of great wealth in natural resources — covers an area half the size of Canada! Eighty-three per cent of the dummy companies under Brazilian registry exploiting this region are directly controlled and owned by Brascan. Standing in the way of the wholesale bulldozer rape of this region are 80,000 indigenous Indian peoples — all that is left of a race that once numbered over 3,000,000. Because they resist, protesting the military and political tactics of the present Brazilian military government betraying its own treaties — these Indian people are now victims of a Latin American version of fascism's "final solution" in dealing with its opponents. Arrested persons are tortured and murdered in prisons by the Gestapo-type death squads of paramilitary personnel. To break down resistance and smash the morale of the resistors, children are tortured before their parents and women are violated in view of their families. Low-flying aircraft, often manned by company employees, fly bombing missions over the jungles, bombing Indian villages and machine-gunning fleeing refugees. What resistance takes place is ineffectual and self-destructive, conducted by desperate Indians armed with nothing more than spears and stones — protecting their homes, culture and children. What is taking place in Brazil today is a deliberate program of genocide, with no other consideration than to raise the profits for shareholders of Brascan stocks in Canada. For as long as Indian inhabitants persist in the Amazon, Brascan will not be able to claim full and effective control of the resources of the region. We don't just want most of what we can get — we want all of it!

The *Manchester Guardian*, commenting on the genocide,

torture and poverty of the Amazon Indians in an article dated 16 December 1971 states: ''The smooth financial technocrats are inseperably linked to the generals, the torturers, and the off-duty policemen in the Death Squad, and if one piece is removed, the jigsaw collapses. . .''

And here is how you and I, as average tax-payers in this country, are made to contribute to this outrage: The federal government of Canada has contributed a quarter-million dollars to the new International Centre of Comparative Criminology at the University of Montreal — towards training and research which specifically aids the Brazilian police — a special undertaking of the Centre's program. How this benefits Brascan is obvious in the following facts — two days after the military coup of 1964, Brascan's shares rose from $1.95 to $3.60 per share. Six years later, Brascan, through its subsidiaries, was in control of 50% of Brazil's aluminum smelting and fabricating capacity. Now to entrench themselves even more deeply, and possibly end up in total control of Brazil through military henchmen, Brascan has helped set the stage for the annihilation of the Indian peoples of the Amazon.

They must be stopped, and an accounting given to the Canadian people of events which have darkened our reputation in Latin America. We the Canadian people are not in the business of aggression against other peoples' countrysides and political choices, and we must demand our federal government force Canadian capitalism to behave likewise. Being ourselves locked in a struggle for self-determination, we must demand that our government encourage similar objectives in those countries of Latin America struggling into the twentieth century. Our obscene haste in giving recognition to the junta in Chile was a blow to democratic development throughout South America . . .

THEATRE IN CANADA
A VIEWPOINT ON ITS
DEVELOPMENT AND FUTURE

In Canada, the quality of our lives is largely determined by the amount of snow that falls annually on our landscape. By cutting through it — going over it, creating a lore of seeming indifference about it, and just learning to live with it as a reality for much of our lives — we manage to survive. Until eventually the thought of living without snow of one form or another becomes unthinkable in our mystique. Because of this, the folk-expression ''snow job'' has a particular poignancy when taken off the landscape and applied to such things as the evolution of our national consciousness.

For we are all the victims of a collosal ''snow job'' perpetrated on us by the makers of a history that often borders on being non-history — by definitions of ourselves which have succeeded in making near strangers of each of us to the other — and by so-called resolutions to these problems which are often-times worse than the original problems themselves. It is a process of fragmentation and the creation of systematic chaos within the culture of a people that was never attempted during the hey-day of colonialism in Angola or in Mexico. In Canada it succeeded beyond the wildest expectations of its exploiters. The results are cultural subservience and a feeling of inadequacy that to this day bedevils the dedicated cultural worker in this country. In terms of economic and political manipulation, the cultural disorientation of our people has paid handsome dividends for the dominant economic sector. While the cultural energy of our people was distracted into hollow disputes on the artificial two-nations question, the same forces that have screwed both English- and French-speaking Canadians for a century — the C.P.R. and its handmaiden, the Bank of Montreal — with the co-operation of its American cousins, pulled off the coup of the century in the Columbia River giveaway — an act, which in the words of a Calgary newspaperman and commentator, constituted nothing less than a crime and, possibly, treason, had it been executed by a private and not a corporate citizen. There is more and it is much more frightening. While we debate as to how many angels or dollars can dance on a theatre director's head — the forces that steer us to preoccupy ourselves with smallness are profitably busy elsewhere. In Brazil at this moment, the reputation of our country and people is besmirched by an exercise in imperialism — Canadian imperialism — of which the average Canadian knows nothing. Through the Canadian-based multinational corporation Brascan, racial genocide is reportedly being practised against the Indians of the Amazon Basin, a race of people that once numbered over 3,000,000 and have now been decimated to less than 80,000.

Brascan owns 50 per cent of Brazil's aluminum smelting and fabricating capacity. It now wants the entire Amazon Basin — an area half the size of this country — for full and effective control of that nation's economy. Through the military junta, it already has effective political control in friendly hands. And to make certain it stays that way, you and I, through a federal government grant of a quarter-million dollars to the new International Centre of Comparative Criminology at the University of Montreal, are also reportedly paying for a specific program of counter-insurgency towards training and research which specifically aids the Brazilian police in safeguarding the investments and influence of Brascan!

So what has this to do with theatre in Canada, its development and future? If you have been snowed to the point of indifference, then it has nothing at all to do with anything, and I'm wasting my time. You've already lost your ability to think and speak in the rhythms of your parents. Another decade, and the folk-song collections of Edith Fowke, Barbeau and Dr. Helen Creighton will vanish into oblivion. Our folk dances never did appear in the repertoire of the National or Royal Winnipeg ballet companies, for we were too infatuated with the court exercises of a Europe the Europeans cannot remember and we cannot forget. While the rest of the world, even the most poverty-stricken nations, pride themselves on their folk and cultural attainments, we take Shakespeare to Warsaw and Moscow with the full-muscled support of the Canada Council, External Affairs and God alone knows who else. (I have a recurring nightmare in which the Peking Opera plays the National Arts Centre with a production of *Anne of Green Gables* and *Don Messer's Jubilee* and, mistaking their sarcasm for art, we rise to our feet as one person in the audience and give them a fifteen-minute standing ovation.)

Our theatre is an accurate reflection of our economic and political reality. During the days of British imperial dominance, the English theatrical accent was the passport to all manner of theatre absurdities in this country. It took two courageous men — one a Swede and the other a Jew — to deflate that bladder to size in Canadian radio drama which, in my estimation, was the real beginning of a Canadian theatre. Esse Ljungh and the late Rupert Caplan did more to stimulate good apprenticeship, reorientation and rebellion for new style and content in dramatic craft than all the efforts of funding agencies and professional and amateur so-called theatre prior to, and since, their time. The beginnings of my contribution started with them. I did not know of Canadian theatre when I began writing drama. Fifteen years later, I still know nothing of a Canadian theatre. There is a collection of theatre literature — of which a company here and there periodically produces an item — but there is no Canadian theatre I know of. There is a lot of transplanted English and American theatre of illusion to which a small percentage of our population — notably, those who have never known the biting eloquence of unemployment or enforced welfarism — cling like aging wolves to an arthritic moose.

But a national theatre, a full-bodied, dynamic theatre of people for people, is not going to happen in English-speaking Canada until we clear our heads and move forcefully beyond the outer limits of restriction imposed by the funding agencies through the proliferation of theatrical charlatans and economically-vested boards of directors. We have been trapped forty years behind actual history. A viable national theatre must strive for nothing less than a vanguard position in expression of national ideals and international humanism. In this, we have a long way to go, for we are easy victims of our own lack of confidence in our heritage and quickly dazzled by seeming advances which are no advances at all.

In this latter context, I wish to cite what appears to be an interest in our regional theatres towards encouraging indigenous drama. In actual fact, the picture is grimmer today than it was three years ago, when the issue became a public one as a result of my confrontation with the Playhouse Theatre in Vancouver over *Captives of The Faceless Drummer*, a period when the gloves were off for the first time in a struggle that was to begin a definition of what really was meant by a Canadian theatre — for what end, and for whom. Fighting desperately against imposition of a Canadian-content quota, the regional theatres gave tacit recognition to the need for inclusion of more Canadian works in their programming. In return for this weak retreat, the class-biased structure of theatre control was retained by the same people who had initiated the Playhouse controversy. And, of course, the Canada Council and provincial funding agencies chided the regional theatres, then backed them with continued support on an obscene scale — most of this funding being absorbed into management and operating expenses — and almost none of it trickling into creation of Canadian drama.

What followed was twofold: the beginnings of sabotage

productions of Canadian works — plays designed, interpreted and promoted in ways that would discourage both audiences and champions of Canadian theatre. And the rise of what I call "beggars theatre" — productions of Canadian drama under impossible conditions in garages, church basements, etc. led by dedicated, well-meaning people who failed to see the significance of what they were embarking on — the dangerous possibility that what we might call Canadian theatre might, from its inception, be a crippled, pathetic exercise in futility. I refused, and continue to refuse, to allow my works to be produced under these conditions. For while dinosaurs like the Stratford Festival and the self-indulgent thing at Niagara continue to be lavished with endless resources to produce Molière, Shakespeare and Shaw, I demand the right to equal auspices, for I, too, am an artist of world stature. I refuse to endorse the cheap, diversionary and divisive tactics of the Canada Council and the regional theatres to delight their bookkeepers in announcing vast numbers of productions of Canadian works — when in reality, nothing more than public rehearsals occur.

Because I refuse to divorce theatre from the larger issues of life confronting us, I get punished. My plays are produced less frequently in the regional theatres today than they were five years ago. Words written by me have been bastardized and rearranged beyond recognition, yet my name has been left on the playbills. Last summer I had to endure the agony of witnessing the dedication and talents of many people, as well as my text of a new play — being employed to give credence and dignity to the Banff School of Fine Arts and its hitherto invisible racial and social policies. So the cause of a viable Canadian theatre has reeled under the counter-attack of a social and political system that viciously defends itself against all criticism and examination. Certainly, I've been hurt. And because I've been hurt, so have you. Because I do no more than reflect your experiences, thoughts and possibilities through my art.

But I am not a pessimist. I survive because I refuse to be contained. So will you, and perhaps twenty years from now we can discuss theatre in Canada as a substantial ingredient in our daily lives and not as some abstraction that provides a living for its teachers and administrators, and less than half a living to its practitioners. And as far as the rest of the population is concerned — a thing of no consequence, a private club where working men and women and enquiring youth are neither invited nor made welcome.

Yet we all pay through public funding for this madness. But we have no say over ownership or direction of theatre as it exits. That is in the hands of the interlocked corporate structure that has moved in on public or semi-public institutions by the same means they use to control the means of production — through the boards of directors. They are empowered to hire or fire artistic directors, dictate policy, and even influence what goes onto the stage of a theatre. In other words, the company that pays you wages for your labour indirectly ends up determining what you might be allowed to see in a publicly-subsidized regional theatre. This is in line with a long process of Canadian reflection, beginning with the early vandals who ravaged our landscape for ore, furs and head-counts of Indian dead, writing their own history of these events, thereby destroying truth for all time.

What of the future for theatre? And what can we do about determining that future?

Well, for one thing, we can marvel at the variety and volume of snow that comes our way. Or we can, as part of our theatre experience, begin examining from our community outward just what is it we are doing and for what reason, and whether this energy cannot be used in better ways. I know it can, or I wouldn't be saying these things.

The role of theatre as I see it is to give light, colour and nobility to the quality of our lives. All else is adequately and disastrously covered by television. The history of theatre has few moments of serenity and, as I explained earlier, our times are no exception. Hardship is no problem. Control systems are. And they function only as long as people allow them to. As a result, a priority in future development of theatre in

Canada is for the theatrical artists of this country to insist on direct control of theatre institutions subsidized by the state. From where came this God-given dictum that an artist has to answer to committees of businessmen and management professionals? And if government insists, then I demand parity for artists — that we make board members answerable to us for their enterprises! The entire question is absurd, and the Canada Council is remiss in not coming to grips with it by demanding a total change in the artist-community relationship. A change of this nature would no doubt quickly be followed by a drastic reallocation of funds to creative endeavour towards stimulating creation of an indigenous Canadian theatre that has to take second place to nobody. This is not an abstract suggestion. From personal experience I can assure you that when we manage to take our home-grown theatre product into the outside world, it holds up well indeed!

Herbert Whittaker, in a recent statement, suggests that the Vietnam War was the turning point in our theatre awareness — when we realized we did not want to be identified with the United States or its cultural values. To this, I say, "Bravo, Herb Whittaker!" But to reject, we must understand what we reject, and replace the vacuum of unacceptable values with values based on our own humanity.

I don't know what the future of theatre holds. But it will be exciting and challenging. Learn all you can about theatre crafts, but alongside of that, study this country, its people, traditions, folklore, languages, myths and customs, for this is the stuff of which all good art is made.

Fortified with these qualities, none of us need have an identity crisis.

In closing, I would like to comment on charges made in the past year that I am an anti-classicist bent on destroying traditions, particularly in theatre. To lump my attacks on the Stratford and Shaw festivals with anti-classicism is a deliberate misinterpretation of what I have consistently stated over the past six years. I stated that the Stratford and Shaw festivals are not the national theatres of Canada — they cannot and they must never be — and I oppose those apologists who insult our sense of nation by manoeuvring us for their own advantage into thinking otherwise. I would even predict that unless they retreat from their quaint, elitist and reactionary other-world stance, they may likely go the way of the Dominion Drama Festival — into well-deserved oblivion.

•

L'auteur GEORGE RYGA demande que l'art canadien commence à développer une conscience sociale plus profonde et que les artistes aient plus de control dans les theâtres regionaux.

LETTER TO THE EDITOR

– Summerland Review

For over a week now, I have driven my children to the Summerland schools and watched them cross the maintenance workers' picket lines on the way to their classrooms. For those of us who have done picket duty ourselves at one time or another, this exercise is oppressive and emotionally disgusting. I don't want my children to cross picket lines, for I am also a worker and a union member. It is humiliating and an insult to the dignity of labour. And in a community where people still generally know each other by first names, it is a bitter and socially divisive thing to happen. And we are all responsible to a degree, for it is our tax money and our ballots which have created and maintained the school boards with which the striking union is currently locked in dispute.

Much has been said, depending on which dinosaur one speaks to, about labour unrest being the prime cause of inflation, etc. It would take a longer letter than I am prepared to consider to examine the merits of these arguments. Suffice it to say that neither this municipality, nor this province, nor this country can foreseeably resolve the crisis of diminishing real wages. Today's inflation is a world-wide phenomenon, and a wage-earner who can no longer make ends meet and resorts to withdrawal of his labour to make his needs known is hardly the culprit in the inflationary squeeze. The 300% increase in the price of sugar this past year hardly reflects a similar increase in the wages of sugar-processing workers in Canada or abroad. The 100% increase in profits during the first six months of this year over the *entire profits of the previous year* by some of our more prominent supermarket chains also does not reflect a 200% increase in the wages of checkout clerks or warehouse employees. So why pursue that myth?

For in actual fact, no worker in the world produces equivalent value-for-wages as does the technologically equipped worker in North America and Japan. Pricing in colonized markets for these goods is another matter. For these goods are now largely in the control of multinational corporations, who can and do victimize nations and individuals alike. And their dealings are largely beyond applicable law, which became alarmingly evident when the U.S. government found it impossible to determine whether a real or artificial fuel shortage existed last winter. The government agencies simply could not acquire the necessary data from the major petroleum giants.

Now the problems of the outside world manifest themselves in Summerland, and our school board, along with others in the valley, meets the demands of labour negotiations in a sadly predictable manner. Crippled with anti-union biases and ill-equipped to cope with collective bargaining — which one suspects they scarcely understand — they resort to the primitive frontierism of calling for volunteers to do the work of skilled maintenance workers on strike. As if guided by some notion that by refusing to recognize and face the problem realistically, it will pass away like a bad dream. And this after knowing for at least four months that the problems were coming to a head.

But this is one bad dream that will not pass away. For the economic reality of life in our valley can no longer be brushed aside with backwoods illogic or wishful fancy. For the truth of the matter is that life is no longer simpler or less expensive for the wage-earner here than in other places. The cost of housing is equal to that of metropolitan Vancouver. The cost of food and vital services are in most cases higher, while wages are generally lower — in some instances, deplorably lower. Only a few years ago, a federal government enquiry designated this region as economically depressed. A more recent assessment is not available, but there is little evidence to suggest this situation has changed appreciably.

This strike must be settled at the earliest opportunity, in a manner acceptable to the striking workers to assure them and their families of a decent living wage. There is no indication that any of their demands are either unreasonable or out of line with those of other workers in similar circumstances. In fact, some of the striking workers have been paid wages at or near the official poverty level on their previous contracts.

Certainly, it will mean increased taxation for school support. But that is a choice our civilization made long ago, when we opted for universal education, improved medical and hospital facilities for the infirm, pensions for the aged and helpless, workmen's compensation and unemployment insurance for those of us injured at or out of work, family allowances, etc. The logic then, as now, was that we were no longer jungle animals trapped by industrialization. That socially purchased education, medical care and security from want was preferable to and more human than any previous experience in history. Imperfect as the resulting system is, it works. And like all things, it costs money. And with inflation, it is bound to cost more. There is no avoiding this. But the cost must be borne by all of us equitably, not by maintenance workers on static and inadequate wages, nor by asking our teachers to subsidize education through wage cuts, nor by disregarding the economic needs of medical staff in our hospital and expecting them to provide a social service at private sacrifice. That is not the spirit of progress, and any attempt to define it otherwise is cruel and exploitative.

As is the sight of children and teachers having to cross legitimate picket lines to reach classrooms each morning. As are non-existent labour negotiations that could and should have been concluded during the summer months without the drift to strike action. As are a few well-intentioned misinformed people performing what is referred to in the labour movement as scab labour duty.

Concerned people must ask how the school board intends to justify its misjudgment of the situation should the schools be forced to close due to lack of maintenance — with the resultant waste of public funds on idle facilities, on-going payrolls and depreciation — plus the loss of students' study-time, which may be the costliest liability of all.

THE NEED FOR MYTHOLOGY

Despite the fact that for generations the reasonably culti-
vated Canadian of means purchased his wines from France,
his porcelain and silver from Britain, his woolens from Scotland, his entertainment and hardwood furnishings from the U.S.
— despite the fact that acquisition of a pseudo-English accent
adequately fed a national inferiority-superiority complex for
longer than one cares to remember — despite the fact that
as a nation we appeared to voluntarily submit to a position of
cultural subservience by the cultivation of tastes which depend
entirely on importation of literature, music, drama and dance
— despite all this, all is not as it should be in paradise. Very
late in the day, in an atmosphere of impending crisis, our
leaders — who understand their economic influences better
than they understand their own people, turn to the sources
of their inspiration and are dismayed to find deaf ears. Réne
Lévesque goes to New York to solicit investments for a Quebec
aspiring to independence and is rebuffed. Trudeau, in a startling
display of uncertainity, meets with President Carter in Washington and asks for support on domestic issues in which the Americans should have neither influence nor concern. He fares no
better than Lévesque — yet.

It appears that the culture which we imported and consumed,
much as we import and consume fig bars, is not adequate to

sustain the spirit in times of stress. And it is a crisis of spirit we are experiencing as we slide through the millstones of history. The aspirations of Quebec are not the problem — this question has been with us for over a century. Our inability to cope with the problem is the problem. Our inability to cope with *any* problem is a source of potential satire and humour for generations to come. Faced with the choice of either destroying our Indian people or giving them an opportunity for life, we could do neither. Faced with the problem of defining immigration policies beyond the immediate future, we restricted immigration from the Third World and allotted grants for Canadian-born, middle-class youngsters to publicly practise their Germanness, or Ukrainianess, or Hungarianness!

Sometimes our leaders turn wistfully to the Americans to draw from their experience. But that is a futile exercise, because our neighbours to the south were born out of, and tempered by, a revolution and a civil war. Which involved most, if not all of the people in a wrenching experience which was to shape their character, spirit and relationship to their land in a no-nonsense way. Americans have no crisis of identity or purpose. They know who they are and where they are going, for right or wrong. The language and cadence of their culture reflects this.

In Canada, our learning institutions are proud when they establish something called Canadian literature courses. Apologetically proud, as if what they were nurturing was a mild disease. Do any of us think that in Chinese secondary schools or universities there are tiny, equivalent studies, titled Chinese literature studies? Or that an emerging country like Angola would permit a minor, peripheral status for a study of its heritage? Only in Canada . . .

I recently was called into a school meeting in Summerland, where discussion of educational programs was the main point of the agenda. I noticed the outline paper did not include study of Canadian history — which I felt might be mandatory, at least, for a student born and educated in Canada. The chairman of the meeting became flustered, then called for a motion to include the course on the agenda. The motion was made and seconded. Then began a lengthy and bizarre discussion, during which arguments were raised as to what was more useful — history, or the study of welding techniques. The matter finally came to a vote — thirty people voted for Canadian history to be included in high school studies, six voted against, and two abstained. There would be other, further studies made, and the last word was that the course would be included in the curriculum — sometime in the future.

Among the best-fed, best-dressed, best-housed and best taken care of people in the world, we suffer from an embarassing lack of understanding of ourselves. We live with the myth of the superiority of others and the inadequacy of ourselves. This has hampered our political and economic sensibilities, has made our children increasingly turn to exotic and unworkable philosophies and religions of the Far East, and has caused the pain and exile of our finest and most sensitive artists, who attempt to reflect the reality of our own lives, myths and worth. With the exception of Quebec, where cultural expression has long been integrated into national survival, the rest of Canada, the second richest country in the world, is among the poorest in its cultural deprivation. And because of this, we remain ripe as a dumping ground for the commercial cultural refuse of the world. Even worse, we mimic it, as in the case of a popular composer born and raised in the Maritimes writing a song lamenting the loss of his childhood beside a river in Texas!

The remedy to this problem will not come from a local, provincial or federal level of government granting more funds to undisturbed artists and book publishers who are noted for their caution. It comes only through the awareness of educators, parents, writers, unionists, composers, politicians and others that the key to self-reliance is self-understanding. That it is too late to dally with self-indulgent, elitist experiments . . . that the issue in national survival is the development of a popular, genuine people's culture . . . whether it be literature, theatre, music or film.

And foremost in this is a re-examination of our history and

lore for the discovery of that distinctive mythology which reflects, in our habits and ways, a popularly agreed on interpretation of who we are and how we got that way. Past experiences, climate, the distances of our geography, the role of winter . . . the colour, nature and tone of our storms and sunlight . . . determine the nature of our language, speed of movement and potential of our physical and spiritual appetites. This is at the core of who we are. Nobody can provide us with or sell us a substitute. And we should never accept substitutes, either at discount prices or wrapped in colourful packaging.

It always occurs to me, with surprise, that to be honest in our society is somehow dangerous and not a thing to do. That people with such energy in their language, and mythological resonances in things unsaid, should be so bedevilled by theatre which bears little or no relevance to their lives . . . the same with ballet and concert music . . . the same with much of our literature written by accountants. Where in hell is the home-grown stuff that excites and ignites the imagination? Where are the raging, possessed poets and novelists whose obligation is to become not only writers but the "second government" of a nation, expressing the authentic fears, preoccupations and exaltations of the people? How many writers roared their disapproval at the arrogance and adventurism of the proclamation of the War Measures Act during the October Crisis? Who will remind our governments that opportunism, political juggling, and invitations for foreign influence will not resolve the dynamic problems of a two-nation, two-language, two-culture confederation. That a culture is a living thing, into which the problems of racial inequality, inflation, foreign ownership of resources and unemployment will and must reflect itself. That it pleases and refreshes by amusing, that it pleases and refreshes by isolating problems and proposing resolutions based on a daily contact and examination of people by the artist.

I am not here to beg the cause of Canadian authors or Canadian books. That sort of plea would be humiliating and self-defeating. Rather, I would underscore the sort of complacency which has brought us all to the dangerous brink where the phrase "Canadian literature" gives some of us the vicarious delight of the defeated. Where the word "fuck" (unless appearing in a novel by an American novelist) automatically removes a novel from the reading list, irrespective of the fact that the novel may be of world stature, written out of this country, as has happened to Margaret Laurence. In one effective move, a generation of youth has lost access to a part of themselves and their land. I use this only as an example of the awesome power of the complacent educator in thoughtlessly assuming the posture of censor rather than partisan and advocate of a deepening and more complex cultivation of a people equipped for changing times.

It would probably be a more pleasant world to live in if all things were structured to meet with our biases, approval and aging sense of serenity. But to accomplish this state of dying self-indulgence, we would be required to stop making children. Once we have opted for children, the only promise of immortality left to us, the obligation to history, to a piece of this earth, to the generations to come, begins. We are caught in the business of the spinning earth even beyond the grave. Only madness exempts us from the responsibilities and rewards of changing the landscape and changing ourselves.

There is no time or need for complacency. We do what we have to do — and as long as we don't retreat against our better instincts, that is enough.

Speech - Surrey - 28 February 1977 – Canadian Literature Day

MULTICULTURISM
ADDRESS TO CURRICULUM CONFERENCE

A discussion of multiculturism in Canada is something one approaches carefully and with one eye on the exit door, partly because it can become a dangerous discussion at worst and an uncomfortable one at best. For such a discussion has to puncture some national myths, which in recent years have acquired a halo of federal government recognition. Multiculturism has become institutionalized — respectable, in a narrow, middle-class definition. Yet the term itself is an anachronism. For in actual fact, the history of the entire North-American continent has been remarkable in that the dominant Anglo-Saxon based culture established here has tolerated little cultural diversity.

Whereas there are nations in this world with as many as forty living, functional languages within their borders, we in Canada find it difficult to endure two. For three hundred years, we have defied the classic definition of what constitutes a nation, as it relates to Quebec and the Native peoples of this country. Until the sixties, the very word "multiculturism" would have drawn little more than a disdainful smirk were it mentioned in the corridors of government in Ottawa, as it draws a hail of abuse in many municipalities even today in this province.

It was the populism of John Diefenbaker, with his appeal to the so-called ethnic vote, which caught the attention of the two federal right-wing political parties — and brought with it the dawn of a dazzling new liberalism and the coining of a new intent! Suddenly, money was available to all of us for the development of our ethnicity — providing we were not recent immigrants, in which case it would get in the way of our first duty of assimiliation! Additional monies to promote a workable study of French or Canadian history were not available, but it was possible to acquire a grant to become a little more Ukrainian, or German, or Dutch — for, say, a weekend of folk-dancing or to set up a minor museum on the outskirts of a city. But such grants did not extend, without considerable difficulty, to research of racism on the West Coast or immigrant labour abuse in the mines of the Crowsnest. For, like multiculturism, these practices were also once sanctioned as government policy. And the body politic is not about to examine itself for skin eruptions caused by stress.

For an astute politician with some vigour and imagination, many of the multicultural events staged in this country provided a ready platform and audiences to keep partisan political campaigns going at public cost. An audience of businessmen meeting under an ethnic umbrella could be provided with an entertaining and enticing bombardment of ninteenth-century free-enterprise economic options. Another group, meeting under ethnic religious auspices, could always be conquered with a thundering attack on religious suppression in eastern Europe. It was easy and cheap, as long as the participants were kept from realizing how they had been demeaned.

We are all demeaned by half-truths, by abbreviations of reality from out past, by the corporate and official bias which runs through the core of history taught to our children. And worse still, by the growing tendency among our scholars and researchers to deceive themselves deliberately, within the context of the system, to create false expectations on the basis of a false assessment of history.

At my sceptic worst, I would almost say the multicultural policies of this country were designed to fragment and frustrate the legitimate demands of a two-language, two-nation state.

"If the French can have a nation within Canada, why can't we?" asks a third-generation Ukrainian in Winnipeg. By voicing an illegitimate sentiment, he unconciously has placed himself into the position of diffusing the legitimacy of a historical nation on this continent. He then fortifies himself by deforming his own history in this country by a process of folk-evolution. No, his grandfather was not forced to change his name or go through the humiliating delousing ritual of having his head shaved before stepping ashore as an immigrant to Canada. No, I've never heard the disparaging term "bohunk" applied to anyone in our family. You see, we were different — my father married a woman from Scotland. It's not true what some malcontents say. When the Ukrainians came to Canada, they each brought with them a copy of the Bible and the poems of Taras Shevchenko in their household effects. And so on, and so on . . .

In actual fact, most immigrants allowed into Canada during the waves of immigration were allowed in for their labour capabilities. Their ability to read or write, or carry poems or a Bible on their person, was of no concern to the corporate system bent on rapid railway and mining development using low-cost labour. And if wages could be kept down by promoting competition among immigrant workers on the basis of exploiting traditional religious and language resentments, then why not? As in war, so in the free labour market; the Pole turned against the Russian, the German against the Jew, the Caucasian against the Asiatic, and the governments which fostered immigration turned a blind eye to abuses whose results are with us to this day.

An exploration of the cultural fabric of this country cannot ignore these facts. No more than it can ignore the agonies of separation from early homelands or the aborted expectations which stimulated the finest in a few, a deepening political understanding in many, and criminal recklessness in those who could not adjust.

Coming as I do from a Slavic background, I can speak with some familiarity about this particular ethnic group in our society.

It was never a unified community. It suffered from heritage problems and political developments which likely affect every ethnic community extant in Canada. First, there were the remnants of imperial wars — the separation of provinces and even families in their previous homelands, with each conqueror asserting his religions and language variants willy-nilly. Then the immigrant faced the shortfalls of neo-feudalism and its effect upon language and the mind. Many of the slavic languages brought to Canada were poetic and luxuriant, but there were no words for the internal combustion engine, electrical grids or steam locomotion. Civilizations which revealed the humanism and influence of ancient Greece had not quite made it past the threshold of the industrial revolution. To compound this problem further, most immigrants were of peasant origins, at best villagers or small town dwellers in their previous homelands. Able to cope quickly with the harshness of Canadian geography, they were not as successful in coping with consumerism and the industrial competence of the Anglo-Saxon and the Nordic peoples here. Quickly, a certain cultural erosion happened, which gave rise to labour militancy and a further division between traditionalists and the working class into which the liberal immigrants gravitated. The Russian Revolution had profound effects on both opponents and supporters of the new regime, for a way of life in the nations of their birth vanished, and they were now cut adrift, faced with the choice of raising their children in a hybrid environment at best or in redundant isolation at worst. Thwarted expectations, the reality of self-acknowledgement of a second-rate status — for a British subject automatically became a Canadian citizen — a Slavic immigrant might wait fifteen years with numerous court hearings for the same benefits — and even after a grant of citizenship could be stripped of it and deported for political insolence. These were the realities the parents and grandparents of many of us lived with daily.

Some took the road of ultimate humiliation. They became the hand maidens of forces which even the most mildly liberal member of the dominant culture viewed with misgivings. They turned against their own spiritual, linguistic and cultural heritage, embracing religions, livelihoods and symbols of dominance they neither understood nor executed with dignity, in the fever of opportunism. They even voluntarily changed their names. I remember one such man, who rose through such vacillations to the dizzying height of a municipal road foreman. In his kitchen he hung a paper-flowered portrait of King George the Sixth, to which he bowed each time he entered the room. His children were forbidden to speak Ukrainian. Instead, they spoke a heavily-accented and limited English, a language which hampers them today as middle-aged men and women. The limitations placed on their minds by their desperate father did not die with him.

Takashima refers to a similar incident in her book *A Child In Prison Camp*, where the police employ a Japanese-Canadian veteran of the First World War to control his own people, who are in detention as a race. Each ethnic community in the country can relate its own version of this horror story.

Yet we outlive such turbulent beginnings. But one cannot forget the adage that those who refuse to learn from history are bound to suffer for their ignorance. I find it personally alarming that in recent years an examination of multiculturalism has become such a middle-class indulgence, often not going beyond experimentation with food and wearing apparel. Certainly the first step in absorbing each other's experience begins in masticating and digesting each other's food. But where is the history of the human experience? Where is the courage of our educators in acknowledging that we have never been and are not at this moment free of racism?

Recently some prominent school boards in this province removed a short film on racism from schools on the grounds that the film was political and biased, presenting only one side of an argument. How in hell can such a film serve its purpose without being political and biased? Or is there some way of presenting racism as being something attractive and desirable in the economic development of a country?

For those of us who feel the current generation of youth

214

has progressed beyond this problem, it might be worth a visit to the washrooms of our local high school for a read-out of graffiti from time to time.

So how does one take concepts of multiculturalism to the schools? A starting point might be one of honesty — just plain, uncomplicated honesty. Being able to admit for once that many of our history books are as much myth as they are facts. That the economics of survival in a rich but difficult country took bizarre turns which shaped for all of us a new national personality, possibly a better and more adaptable one than the raw material from which it emerged.

That the militaristic chauvinism of some of our national holidays might take some toning down, or if that is impossible, then tributes to the war dead should be expanded to include all who died in war, including soldiers who served the enemy of the time, for they, too, were ordinary people brutalized in the conquest of markets, as were we, and not demons from nowhere who assumed human dimensions.

Possibly the study of multiculturism should take the form of local or regional examinations and critical evaluations to be most effective, including a re-examination of legends which fortify the negative aspects of our past history. Why are there so few towns and streets named after other than Anglo-Saxon personalities? Why are so many schools, for example, named after a princess or a queen in England who wouldn't know or care they existed? For the child, the disparity of the legend begins the moment they learn the name of the school they first enter. But all the same, the artificial legend leaves no room for an upfront familiarity with Canadian folk heroes.

The work of grinding and reshaping cultures goes on even as we sleep. The music, film, theatre and folk arts we are exposed to play their havoc on, and influence, our sensibilities. An hour of American commercial television displaces an hour of interesting conversation with a neighbour who may have a purple nose. Or whose mother may be a renowned painter — or casino player.

The federal government policy of multiculturism can be

labelled expensive and of obscure intent. Particularly if one examines it alongside current immigration policies. Yet if it helps to excite and stimulate interest in our history — if it helps to redirect our focus towards a reconstruction of the damages of colonialism, then it has merit. And that appears to me the major priority in education for national unity.

George Ryga (1978)   Photo: unknown

MIST FROM THE MOUNTAINS

The train from Zurich to Einsedeln made frequent stops. Only a small group of passengers boarded at the Zurich station. None left at any of the numerous stations of the journey, and only one additional passenger boarded. He was a stout man who took the seat across the aisle from us and promptly fell asleep, his mouth drooping open and a tiny bead of saliva forming on his lower lip. A bead that neither diminished nor grew larger for the remainder of our trip.

The morning had been hectic, and both Norma and I were in a depressive mood. The doctor in the medical archives, an elegant and pleasant woman named Eva Hart, was much on our minds. She was a fully qualified physician and surgeon who could not find work in her profession and had settled to become an archivist. The evening before, when both of us were in the medieval section of the archives, I had commented on the order and serenity of Zurich. She smiled sardonically.

"Nothing is what it appears on the surface," she said. "There is as much darkness and chaos here as there is in the bush camps you have told me about in your country."

"People do not shout at one another. There is not visible violence. The streets and buildings are clean. What and how much can one ask for?"

"Have you been in the alleys by night?" she asked.

217

"Yes," I replied.

"Going from here to there. Following the sausage and beer venders?"

"Yes," I said, feeling humbled, for indeed we had not lingered for any time in any one place.

"Go out tonight and look carefully. We are very skilled at hiding what we wish to hide. I was a student not many years ago when women acquired the right to vote in our canton. I still cannot work at what I was trained to do. You must understand this, and what it implies, if you are to understand that great doctor in our history you have come here to study." She smiled then — a warm, disarming smile, and patted my arm.

That evening, I related this conversation to Norma in our hotel. A soft autumn rain had begun to fall, streaking our tall window and throwing the room into partial darkness. We talked softly and sat close together on the bed, as people in strange places do. And the following day, we had to go to Einsedeln, to the birthplace of Paracelsus, who had preoccupied my thoughts for the past thirteen years.

"Are you nervous? . . . It has taken you a long time to reach the end of your enquiry."

I did not answer. Instead, I remarked, "Eva said we should look at the city again."

In the alleys, with the rain falling more forcefully now, and the gusts of cold wind twisting our coats first from the front, then from behind, we followed the scent of the venders, as we had each night since arriving. The spicy odours from the charcoal briquette burners of the sausage venders; the pungent smell of freshly baked bread under cloth covers of the pushcarts; the sour scent of beer from the warmth of an open doorway. And above all this, the aroma of strong African coffee. It was heady and our hunger became a raw pain. In moments, the two of us were in a darkened doorway, devouring a sausage each in a breadroll, the rain hissing in the street, and rivulets of water falling before us from a roof drain. We ate in silence, scarcely noticing the traffic pulling into the lane and parking willy-nilly over the sidewalks. People emerged from the cars and ran into the light of cafe doorways. There was muted conversation only, and hardly any laughter. Beside us, a tall man in business suit and topcoat appeared, moving into the shelter of the doorway where we stood. I nodded to him, and he silently returned my gesture. He was bareheaded, his iron-gray hair neatly trimmed and severely brushed back over the top of his head. In the pale light from the soggy lane, his eyes were hollow and gloomy.

"Another?" I asked Norma, but she shook her head. We cleaned the crumbs from our hands against the sides of our coats and prepared to hurry from the doorway into a small coffee bar across the lane and a short distance to our left.

"Did you buy the train tickets for tomorrow's trip?" my wife asked as she lifted the collar of her coat over her neck.

"Yes, I did. On the way back from the library," I said.

A young woman, her hat and face streaming with rain water, hurried in to the doorway where we were. She paused in front of us, glancing up and down the lane, as if looking for someone, then stood beside Norma and the man. I remembered her wearing a lemon-scented perfume, elusive one moment, then suddenly strong enough to disrupt a thought. She had strong, youthful features, and lips slightly lifted in a half-smile. A country woman's face. The man spoke to her in soft German, but she gave no indication of noticing. He repeated his comment, this time stammering over his words. Now the girl glanced quickly at him. Lowering her wet hat over her forehead, she moved away, to the coffee bar across the lane. My wife looked at me quizzically.

"Did you understand?" she asked in an undertone.

"I think he was hustling her," I said, and laughed. Then we both stepped out into the rainy alley. The voice behind us spoke in anger now, stopping us.

"America is . . . shit!"

We both turned to face him. We were surprised by his vehemence. But startled even more by the fact that what he said was out of context somehow. He was a sad, conservative man. A man in control of his destiny, of his career and his emotions

— despite the sardonic remark I made to my wife. Such men do not prey on women in alleys — neither in Toronto nor Zurich. Their hungers are satisfied by more orderly, expensive and elaborate arrangements. He stepped out into the full light of the lane now, his eyes somehow out of focus, but his lips quivering in anger. He was swaying.

"He's pissed," I muttered to my wife. But she ignored me and stared at him for a moment.

"Why did you say that?" she asked.

"America is shit," he repeated then furrowed his brows in angry concentration. "People in America . . . are afraid to die! Old people cry a lot and lie in bed at night with lights on. Or watch television waiting for the sun to rise. Afraid to die alone. Nobody cares. An old woman sits for seven hours holding her dog in her hands because she is alone. I could tell you more. I have a friend who went there. He told me everything."

It was a tortured, halting speech, each word lifted out of some deep well of despair. There were tears in his eyes. Then he looked away from us.

"America is a place. But it is also a state of mind," Norma added. He nodded.

"Every place is a state of mind," he said, and walked away unsteadily into the rain. In moments, he seemed to vanish into the greyness of the rain and granite of the ancient buildings.

"Every place is a state of mind . . ." I pondered these words on the train journey to Einsedeln. It struck me that there was a truth somewhere in this thought. In many parts of the world, diets, clothing and means of transportation are almost identical. Despite differences in language, people consume the same artifacts of culture. Even their laws of conduct are interchangeable. If one thinks about it, the jingoism of the Cold War is ridiculous and designed only to aggravate the fears of the ignorant. Protection of life and property, be it private or social, enjoys the same sanctity in the legal interpretations of both super powers. The right to education, medical services and secure retirement in old age also occupies the same importance in the strivings of virtually all organized societies.

Only nations emerging from medievalism, or groping backward for whatever reason into the Dark Ages, would reveal a fundamental departure from these norms of cultural behaviour. It was unthinkable that it could be otherwise, for that was the road to madness and disaster. My lifelong resistance to fascism was founded on these considerations. I believed — I *had* to believe — that humankind was in a state of constant transition from a wild animal beginning to something noble and humane. That it was impossible for human beings to remain for long mired in darkness, ignorance and disease, with all hope banished, and the only rise in spirit possible, a false assurance of dominant bias in colour of skin or a religious faith. And order no longer anchored in human reason, but in the club or the gun, in the hands of those who are themselves brutalized by others above them, who in turn are beaten by still others above themselves — and on and on. Above them all — the source of all authority — is a non-existent presence who neither resides on earth nor among the stars. It is a god without compassion or civility — a monster created in the imagination of monsters to bless their useless existences with pathetic legitimacy. Such is the darkness from which we emerged, and to which we are capable even now of returning, even though the possibility is an outrage to reason and the painful evolution of the species to which we are all participants and equal contributors, be we derelicts, peasants, pipe welders, statesmen or poets of universal renown.

From the train window, we watched the cattle in livid green fields, scarcely raising their heads as we rumbled by. Pale villages were tucked away into tiny mountain valleys, overgrown with woodlands. On a country road, I saw an old woman walking slowly, a basket filled with dark mushrooms hanging from the crook of her arm. In the other, she carried a walking stick. Then we raced through a village and slowed to a stop beyond the village for no visible reason. But the stop was a short one, and the train jerked forward. The mountains now closed around us, and the air felt clammy from the rains of the previous night, even inside the coach.

Einsedeln in the late afternoon of our arrival was a contrast of light and shadows, of green fields and pasture lands and gloomy, brooding old mountains bordering one edge of the town. From my research and studies of maps, I was familiar with the streets of the town, but the Abbey was surprising. Virtually emerging from the mountains with its massive stone structures and walls darkened by time and the elements, it seemed to thrust this darkness into the town. We left the train station on foot and made our way through the streets in search of an inn for the night, in time to the tolling of the bells of the Abbey. The sound was maddening — louder than any bells we had ever heard in our lives and so dreadfully, unbearably gloomy. They were pitched in different tonalities, but there were no happy sounds, even from the lighter bells. We moved into a doorway and stopped, hoping the ringing would be deflected. But there was no escape. Even those long mouldering in their graves must have heard the bells of the Abbey through the earth, for the very cobbles under our feet vibrated. That thought was to recur later in the day.

"On the last day of life on this earth — this will be the final sound that is heard," I shouted to my wife and laughed, not out of merriment, but out of despair, attempting to lighten the atmosphere. Either she did not hear me, or ignored what I said, for she looked past me into some great distance, her eyes shuddering in her skull.

The inn was simple and comfortable, though austere, with a bed, a linen-covered table, and two chairs near the opened window. The walls and ceiling were of mud plaster, with rounded window casements and a deeply recessed closet. We ordered coffee and refreshments into the room. From the street below the window, passing women chattered and laughed. A dog barked in a rich voice, the bark echoing against the masonry walls. Over our light snack and coffee, we discussed plans for the work I had come to do.

The bookstore near the inn, and directly across from the main entrance to the Abbey, was run by two aesthetic, middle-aged women. When I requested any relevant literature that might be available in this, the birthplace of Paracelsus, a very old man was called from the back of the shop. In a quivering, thin voice he explained there had been an active society for the preservation of the medieval doctor's memory, but the members had aged and died out. All that was left of their work was a small bundle of publications, which he presented to me. And then, as if in afterthought, he said he remembered that two tickets had been left for us to view a motion picture on the life of Paracelsus, which was being screened at eight o'clock this evening.

"Who left such tickets? I told no one I was specifically arriving today," I said. He stared at me through pale, dim eyes but made no reply. I took the bundle of literature and the tickets and thanked him. Then we both left. Outside, Norma, who had waited around the corner from the bookstore, was alarmed.

"Is something wrong?" I asked.

"I don't know. Maybe it's Paracelsus . . . There are things happening all around us which I can't see. Or I see them differently."

"In what way?"

"The people in the streets dress like us and do work in the same way as they do at home. But the town — look at it!" she motioned in a sweeping gesture. "Except for the train, electricity and plumbing, nothing has changed in seven hundred years. The crusaders coming down that mountain draw saw the same Abbey . . . the same town that we are now standing in. That cross on the mountain over there dominates the town and surrounding farmlands — Paracelsus must have stared at it every morning of his life here. And the Abbey holds the town in place with its weight and its raging bells . . . Do you think that matters? Can the ghosts of the centuries rest here? Every place is a state of mind, the man in Zurich said . . . My place is in Hamilton, Vancouver — or in our garden. What do I know of a town with a body and mind from the Dark Ages?"

It was a plea for us to leave, but I could not leave.

"I will start working now," I urged. "We will have dinner

after the movie. Right now, I'll walk out to the house where Paracelsus lived and return in time for the show. We can go there and then have food at the inn when it's over.''

She agreed and we returned to the inn, where I packed a camera and a tape recorder into my shoulder bag. Then I left on foot, walking quickly out of town in the direction of the river. The road I walked, and which I knew from old maps I had studied, took an unexpected turn towards the lake. I stopped to consider whether or not to cross the open fields in the general direction of the river. Looking up, I saw even rows of tall, weathered concrete obstructions, bent northward like sickle blades and placed in close proximity to each other. A cow grazed between them and a raven sitting on the tip of one began to crow raucously, his head tilted in my direction. For a long moment I stood perfectly still, trying to recall where I had seen similar devices in photographs. And then it came to me — Panzer tank obstructions, designed to impede a possible invasion from Germany during the last world war! How incongrous it all seemed against the pastoral landscape. The sun broke through the clouds, a low sun skimming the rounded peaks of the western mountains, and the tank traps scarred the green pasture land with long, black shadows. The dragon's teeth of war, decaying ever so slowly, still pointed to the heavens in defiance.

Then the sun vanished. It vanished within a fast moving shadow, racing over the green fields, robbing them of colour and texture. The fields now looked autumnal, cold. A bank of mist had risen over the mountains, blocking out the late afternoon light. The raven rose and flew away in an angry snapping of black wings. The grazing cow threw up its head, then turned and hurried away on the low slope to the north. I followed, leaving the road, convinced I would reach the house of the medieval doctor with no problems, for I was certain of my bearings.

I was wrong, however. I had reached the top of the slope, and was proceeding through open fields, bent over my tape recorder and recording impressions of landscape, vegetation, the thoughts passing through my mind. A cold breeze came down from the mountains, and with it, a solid wall of fog — the mist I had seen earlier, forming on the mountain tops. The light became milky. With the invisible sun setting, darkness began to fall quickly. I continued on, not thinking that I was straying away from the town and might have difficulty returning. Then I stumbled onto a packed earth roadway. There was no visibility left now — only a white, disorienting void such as I have never experienced anywhere before. I shuffled onward, picking out the road carefully with my feet, not knowing in which direction I was going. The clammy cold air was in my clothes and I was shivering.

Then I wandered off the packed road into grass. I tried, but could not find it again. What I knew of the history of Einsedeln came to mind in a rapid sequence of mental images: the dark, fearful forest which once covered these fields had kept people away until the eighth century. The two ravens who attended to the first monk who established the church that was later to become the Abbey, pursuing his murderers into Zurich, where they were apprehended and burned alive. The rebellions of the peasants, forced to battle the nobility who had turned the Abbey into a feudal fortress, with powers of life and death over the very land on which I now stumbled.

I walked into an obstruction — a coarse stone pillar. Exploring it with my hands, I discovered it to be the cross over the gravemound of the crusaders. Crusaders returning from the Holy Land and crazed by disease, starvation and the violence of where they had been and what they had done. Reaching Einsedeln over the mountain pass, they looted and pillaged — devouring all they could slaughter. Then, satiated, they turned their attention to the townspeople and peasants — putting their weapons to use in robbery, rape and devastation of dwellings and storehouses.

Retaliation by the dwellers of Einsedeln took place where I was now leaning against the coarse stone cross, for it was here that the ambush took place. The marauders were killed drunk, as they stopped to rest or sleep: they were simply surrounded and destroyed by the local people armed with clubs, axes and scythes. A great burial pit was dug, into which the bodies of the crusaders were thrown, covered with earth, then other cadavers and more earth, until the devastation ended. The cross I now touched was erected long ago to mark the spot where the remains of the crusaders had been buried in this way.

Shaken, I turned away and began to wander through the dense fog. The grass became deeper and the earth was strewn with stones. My tape recorder and camera, hanging by straps from my shoulders, slapped uselessly against my hips. I understood suddenly what uncertainties drove strong men to prayer and eventual surrender to nature or to fate. Surrounded by reminders of how transitory life is, it would require a supreme act of will to shout back ''I will prevail!'' Men do it through their children, through the fields they till, the buildings they erect, the books they write. But all this became reduced to a lesser dimension of importance in the fog-shrouded fields of Einsedeln. I began to run, even though I was fully aware this was a ridiculous thing to do. Somewhere in front of me, I heard a person cough, and I came to a stop before a peasant with a bucket in his hand. He muttered with surprise, and I quickly began trying to explain to him I was wanting to get to the town but had lost my way. He turned and, with a motion of his head, invited me to follow him. I stayed close to him, aware that only the distance of one step would make him vanish in the mist. As we walked, he asked in a guttural voice what had brought me to his farm. That the ancient road was no longer used and had been overgrown by the fields, I felt, would be too difficult to explain, and so said nothing.

Suddenly, we were out of the fog-bank and standing on the top of the slope which fell away into the meadows where the Panzar tank traps had been embedded. Beyond that, the lights of Einsedeln sparkled in their tracery of streets and thoroughfares. On the mountain overlooking the town, the great cross was also illuminated against the darkness of the forests. We shook hands and parted.

At the inn, the dinner hour had just begun, but my wife was neither in her room nor in the cafe. Checking at the desk, I was told of someone seeing her leave earlier to go for a walk. This confused me, as it was almost time for the screening of the Paracelsus film in the Abbey, and it was out of character for Norma to be late. I left for the Abbey without her.

The screening was in a small theatre off the large square of the massive compound. The square was deserted except for two nuns sweeping before the front door of the main church. When I entered, the room was already filled with people, except for two vacant seats in the second row from the front. The audience was old — half men and half women. The usher at the door was also of similar age, a white haired, bent man dressed in a frayed cardigan and baggy trousers.

"We have been waiting for you," he said.

"I'm sorry, but my wife . . ." I began, but he cut me off in mid-sentence.

"That is fine. Please take your seat."

I asked if I would be able to record the sound track of the film on my tape recorder, and he assured me it would be no problem.

The film ran for just under an hour. It had been made in Czechoslovakia, and was in the German language. There was little of Paracelsus in the presentation, only a haunting examination of a timeless quality of the seasons, of beginnings and endings to things. There was a peculiar religiosity to what was said and presented, but it was unlike any thoughts I had ever entertained around the medieval healer. As if he was totally out of context with *any* historical epoch. Rather, a lone and brilliant star flashing through a long night of the spirit, with healing as his special virtue. This interpretation was troubling, as it placed almost no value on subsequent periods of enlightenment, and yet it was somehow directed to our day and our definition of life and purpose. It was a floodlight with a great field, but a startling low degree of illumination. The film ended abruptly and the lights came on. I was occupied for a moment in collecting and storing my recording tapes. When I looked

227

up, the room was empty. I could not believe such old people could have vacated the premises so quickly and with almost no sound. I rushed to the open doorway, expecting to see members of the audience straggling away across the square of the Abbey. But there was no one there. The square to the main steps, as far as I could see, was vacant. I knew that even a runner could not have reached the stairs in the time since the film had ended. Then a chilling thought came to mind — what if . . . there had been no film? That I had imagined the entire last hour in some gathering dementia?

I heard my heart racing now, as I found the stairwell to the overhead projection booth and hurried up, two steps at a time. The booth was also vacant. I reached out to touch the projector. It was still hot. I sighed with relief. At least there *had* been a projection only moments before. A second thought then struck me and I unpacked a tape nervously and pushed it into the recorder. I had to take a deep breath before I pushed the ''play'' button down. The sound of the commentator on the film crackled through the booth. Assured that there had been a film and that I carried evidence of having seen it, I slowly made my way down the stairs and out into the square, leaving the theatre lit and the door open. I suddenly felt mortally tired, with each step forward becoming a terrible effort. I now sensed there would be nothing left on the banks of the Sihl River, where the home of Paracelsus stood. Nothing but my own memory of his mother throwing herself headlong into the stream far below to end her tormented days, her work done in giving birth to a titan. And his father's endless days of gentleness and bewilderment as he persisted in his work of healing this town and locality, hearing only occasionally the growing legends of his offspring from such far-off places as Africa, England, Poland and China. I already knew, through some intuition, that the home of Paracelsus was now a layer of weed-covered ashes, neglected and forgotten by all except that divine giver of flame whom he served with such austere dedication. My weariness was the end and beginning of all I would ever know of the man — that the truth was not in a bundle of carefully prepared publications or a mouldering set of hand-written books in the dark attic of a medieval medical library — those were essential touchstones and nothing more. The truth was within one's own self, where the darkest questions about human destiny had to be asked. And answered, even if it took a lifetime of sifting and turning the soils of the soul.

And so it was no surprise to me to see my wife waiting at the entrance to the inn, her face betraying anxiety and some anger.

"Where have you been?" she demanded. "We have only three minutes left before the motion picture is screened."

Norma lifted her wrist to me, to show me her watch. I glanced at mine. Somehow it was no longer surprising that our watches were precisely one hour apart, even though we had compared time only some four hours ago when I last saw her.

"I already saw the film. It is now almost nine o'clock," I told her. And then to head off the rush of questions I knew were coming, as well as to dispell her growing despair at being trapped in this place, I said, "We'll talk about it later. Let's go and eat. Then we'll pack and see about transport back to Zurich tonight. There is nothing more for me to see here."

THE VILLAGE OF MELONS

Called on the telephone to write on my thoughts and feelings about life in this province at this time, my first reaction was to sidestep — to move aside in body and spirit from the byway of a temporary madness. Not for reasons of self-preservation, but to save energy by not involving myself in the garish exercise of what has become humiliating daily life. The morning news tells me of a minister of government buying whores on a credit card — another being punched out in a sleazy affair — still another living in subsidized public housing while drawing a ministerial salary of seventy-odd thousand dollars yearly. And all the while, the poor and unemployed grow in numbers, education is reduced, social services and health care are savaged. Veterans of wars and destitute ones are herded like cattle out of skid-road hotels bent on fleecing Expo visitors with a coat of paint and a fumigation against vermin. Another highway to nowhere is being built . . .

In my mind, I return to Mexico, and the village of melons, where something I had once known — and something I might once more be forced to live through, was evident.

It was an arid village, somewhere south of Tepic along the west coast of the country. We drove into it late in the afternoon. We had driven since dawn without food, and were looking forward to a family meal and a rest from the heat and the highway stress of the day. Access to the village was through a narrow lane surrounded by peeling adobe walls enclosing shops and houses. The lane was cool and gloomy, sheltered overhead by palms and banana fronds. Suddenly, the lane ended, and we entered the dazzling light of the village square, crowded with stalls of melons. There were all manner of melons — from vegetable squash to sweet pumpkins, gourds, honeydew, musk and watermelons. On the far end of the square beside the steps of the church, a small cluster of stalls displayed vegetables. But these stalls were dwarfed by the melon stalls in the square. That was my first impression on entering the square.

The second was a fearful one.

For the stalls were run by women and children with distended bellies and blank faces which revealed no animation whatsoever. Despite this cornucopia of melons, the people of this village were starving to death.

I drove quickly out of the village, over the protests of my children, for I was chilled by a spectre I was in no way prepared to face — that of a slow death within an illusion of wealth and abundance.

Over the days following, and over subsequent years, this impression became a disturbing metaphor. It troubled me for a variety of reasons, both personal and sociological. No sooner would I reconcile myself to one face of this image, when another visage, more gaunt and distressing than the first, would turn to confront me with a contradiction of spirit.

Personally, I was distressed by my initial but enduring horror at the seeming inevitability of things and the dawning realization that I on my own could do nothing to alter events taking shape before my eyes. Coming out of a culture whose paramount feature is mobility — the ability to change geographic location easily in pursuit of self-betterment — as well as the ability to flee horizontally from disaster — what I had seen that afternoon was unthinkable. I could not reconcile myself to such fatalism. To the death of will, or so it had seemed.

Yet even in those moments in the village, serious contradictions had begun to bedevil me. I was old enough and travelled enough to realize that a purely mechanistic approach to problems of cultures and traditions was immature and prone to miscalculations. Perhaps I had only half-seen the village and its calamity. Or maybe I had seen more than was really there — and had added details to observations singularly my own. How could I tell?

The fabric of commerce, culture and spiritual values in an ancient landscape is dense and extremely complex. From the standpoint of my own references, which are historically so youthful as to weigh lightly in such matters, the problems in the village of melons appeared quickly evident and easily resolvable.

They were simply this: the agricultural soil from which the village survived was either nutritionally depleted or seriously contaminated and, therefore, no longer capable of providing nourishing food. Therefore the village should, for reasons of survival, abandon the fields and houses and migrate elsewhere to re-establish another village and farmlands from which people could produce health-giving vegetables, cereals and fruit. It was a simple and practical solution, evident to anyone coming from a nation of people to the north, where each individual can change geographic and provincial residence twice in one year in pursuit of career, education, or satisfaction of restless whims. Where it is not unusual to meet people daily who have bought and sold homes four or five times in their lifetimes — and who, when asked, would define "home" as a dimly remembered address on a dimly remembered street of a city to which, often as not, they had only the vaguest stirrings of affection or belonging.

The village of melons had likely existed on its present site for five hundred or a thousand years. In all probability it was built on the ruins of one or more previous ancient villages of which there is no longer memory or record. The cobbled streets over which I had driven so quickly would hold some memory of my passing, as they harboured the mute echoes and minute imprints of ten million footfalls of people and animals relentlessly coming and going through the nights and days of a hundred and a thousand years. And in antiquity prior to that. Here people had loved, laboured, murdered, fled pestilence and returned, died and been reborn in a baffling panorama of time and history which I could only guess at. The stones and fields were hallowed by the endless procession of people, shaping and reshaping the earth to survive. All this I could only guess at, from evidence no more substantial than the silent echoes of the walls.

So the simple resolution was meaningless. Even measured against the horror I had seen, the death of history would be far more profound than the possible extinction of a hundred villagers through starvation. It would be an outrage to suggest these villagers had arrived at this decision through considered personal choice. Had there been a choice, the village might have been abandoned when we found it.

So I hurried out of the village of melons, while the villagers remained, numbed and bloated, victims of vague and complicated emotional and spiritual interactions of which I knew nothing. I parked on the outskirts, listening to the complaints of my children and watching a bent young woman approaching on the dusty road, leading a burro laden with dried corn husks.

And as I watched her approach and move past our vehicle, the nature of my visit to Mexico changed. I was a writer, but this time I was not researching or writing. I had come for the sun and a rest, leaving behind me all my notes on pending work. My family and I had already swum in the warm waters of Mazatlan, had seen our first shark, had tasted our first fresh coconut, which had fallen overnight beside our van in the campgrounds. But actively writing or not, I was still busy harvesting impressions. On the outskirts of the village of melons, I was confronted with a dilemma which required all the resources I had honed over the years as an author before I could go anywhere ever again.

Confronting me was a conditioned reaction rising out of my own culture, which is so centred on the maintenance of physical comforts. Posed against my welling emotions was a different cast of mind and spirit — one which appeared to willingly

233

accommodate the frailty, aging, and eventual death of people and things as inevitable and necessary. With the village smouldering behind me in the heat of late afternoon, I struggled against the deepening sensations of moral helplessness and pain.

In my mind I scrambled into my own early country upbringing — knowing that a village must have a well for water and surrounding fields for an economical supply of food. That would suffice in Canada. Our Prairies are dotted with such hamlets.

But in Mexico the village square and the church are equally essential, for this civilization is more gregarious than mine. Man and God live in close proximity here, in a natural relationship which northerners find disturbing, but somehow reassuring. People walk in this hot desert country, covering distances slowly. They carry burdens on their heads and shoulders. The aged and very young share much in common — know of each other's existence and shortcomings. The old person lifts the infant to its feet for the first time. The infant in time leads the old person through the streets by the hand, conscious of the elder's faltering footsteps and declining days of life.

Despite this reduced alienation of people from people, life is far from benign. Only a fool or an insensitive brute would fail to notice drudgery, minimal schooling, inadequate health care and other social shortcomings as highly visible components of the landscape. I marvel to this day at how a well-fed, indulged northerner in good health can sit in a cantina and stare into the street through the open archway and see virtually nothing, except that here his money buys more than at home. This indifference and detachment separating us from them has entered all too easily into popular myth.

It is not the role of the writer to deepen such divisions created by ignorance and calcified personal traits. The world is better served through facing and carefully exploring the reasons for such differences, even if such an exploration creates personal cultural or moral distress. Again, one does not choose the time or place for such decisions. One is thrust upon them willy-nilly and seldom in the best of circumstances. To flee from such turmoil and confrontation of the spirit is not admirable, unless one has already opted for a gloomy and cynical withdrawal from faith in human potential.

Responding to my own cultural conditioning, my first impulse was to flee from the village of melons. But pausing on the outskirts of the village, I could not escape the metaphor of this chance encounter with devastation and what it implied. It was not something as isolated and alien to me as I would have wished it to be. There were many parts of the scenario I already knew of, yet dared not assemble, concentrating instead on better craftsmanship in my work.

From my craftsmanship I had learned long ago that studying another language strengthens the understanding of one's own language. Extending that truism further, it should be possible to comprehend one's own culture in a new way by entering another. Particularly an ancient culture, so close to us geographically. Yet as I write these lines, I am deluged by recollections of acquaintances who went to Mexico over the years, and the surprisingly narrow focus of their observations, their tastes and preferences. They spoke highly of the whorehouses in the border towns, the spicy food, the beggars, the availability and low cost of textiles and leather goods.

Even Malcolm Lowry can be faulted for a consumer fascination with this ancient world, though his consumerism was tortured and burdened with heavy demons of the heart and mind. Unlike Lowry, my friend the bee-keeper settled for one good dinner and getting himself laid. Hardly a seasonal accomplishment, yet complete in its own dimension. So what is left to do then? Turn the car around and head for the American border and the familiarity of the Western Hotel chain? And on return home, add to the restless myth dividing peoples by dwelling in conversations on the other's poverty — making that the total distinction between ourselves and them on racial, economic, social — and, eventually, human values?

It is such a simple and unfulfilling tack to take. Repeated over the years and generations, it must invariably lead to a deepening gulf between civilizations. An indifference and a faltering of curiousity which enters into the very language that we use. The designation "banana republic" is not so much derisive as it is cynical. For it implies that some people are capable only of producing bananas. Their language, songs, what they think and feel, count for nothing. Such a dismissal of human worth may have little effect on the peoples against whom it is directed, for human worth matters little in economic exploitation — either for its architects or its victims. But it is a disastrous reflection on the culture from which it originates, for it tarnishes it with decadence and raises the spectre of another kind of eventual decline and death.

An artist in our time can turn and flee from all this — rush away to some patch of earth reasonably insulated from the drumbeats of ongoing history. Here you can, if you wish, select the birds you wish to have sing in your trees by shooting down those whose songs you do not wish to hear. You can build a house with irregular walls if you wish, and spray-paint your lawn some different colour from the universal green. All it takes is money and an extra burst of energy, both of which we have in abundance compared with the villagers in the tropics. You can create, with modern technology and some electrical current, your own environment of sound and light to mirror the growing madness festering in your skull. Yes, you can turn and flee. Flee from the village of dreadful illusions . . . Flee from what in time you yourself might become.

But that is not the only choice. There is another method of approaching this uncompromising dilemma. And that is to continue on into the desert, accepting what is there as a distressing fact of life and losing garments of personal culture in the process — memories and attitudes — all the real and cosmetic dressings of what I and you once were — approaching nearer and nearer to the abyss of revelation about what it is to be human in a universal sense. It is not a journey for the timorous. One must brace for anguish and self-denial. One must be free to receive — to allow new language and metaphor to filter into oneself through osmosis of food, climate, pacing, humour, fear. Even the theft or loss of personal possessions and surface trimmings on the vehicle you drive are inconsequential. They were only surplus acquisitions to begin with. And they will be replaced by late-night rituals and processions of worship as alien to the national catholic church as they would be to any foreign influence attempting to penetrate and redirect one of the world's oldest civilizations. You will hear folk songs whose language and nuances reveal a new dimension of dramatic and emotional expression. You will discover explosive humour and profound introspection. You will experience legends, such as those incorporated by the folk writer Azuela, that transcend death by moving the human personality into the nether world populated by the spirits of those departed and those to come in a complex and dynamic relationship, struggling out of the morass into something more just and moral than the life of streets and fields in the endless procession of nights and days.

You may, if you are fortunate, stumble into a primordial darkness of spirit. And engage in spiritual and physical slavery, wrestling with yearnings for fascism, socialism, a craving for vengeance against the oppressors who came with Cortes. And left only yesterday morning in a Toyota camper, its compartments loaded with crafted Tasco silverware, which they acquired for less than the market value of the metal.

You will bear witness to the darkness and the light, the skies crackling and exploding as faceless horsemen and their women appear racing from near shadows into distant gloom, the horses trailing sparks beneath their pounding hooves. Celebrations of simple food and passionate discussions, laced with timeless hatred for the mendacity of those who rise from among the people only to betray their trust, race, memory and history.

And through this fierce vortex will pass the men with rifles — the robbers, the corrupt police and militia — the warriors cut loose from command or personal discipline, surviving on the fear they generate. Through this fierce vortex will pass the revolutionaries, bandoliers across their shoulders and guitars in hand, linked to the people more through emotion than political concensus. Brilliant, God-like, tragically foolish — all grouped into a common body of fatal heroism from which the legends and folksongs of the future will erupt.

Through it all I recall how the light pales and darkens. In the fields, the corn matures and is gathered by the shawled, black-clad women. In a small town where I lived a while, the most beautiful woman I had ever seen was scandalized by her husband, her children taken from her, and was driven out to survive in the streets as a scavenger and a whore. It was all a brutal joke. The entire town became smaller for it. While in the fields, the corn aged and was gathered.

And in the mountains, young boys wearing large sombreros — my sons among them — poached wood, returning home under cover of darkness. I sat in a doorway with my friend and watched them pass in silence, their slight shoulders burdened with bundles of twigs and branches. They vanished in the darkness and my friend and I spoke of Emiliano Zapata, who could not read or write — and Hidalgo, who could. And my friend sang two fragments of songs he remembered of the time.

I have not returned to the village of melons. But in a way, I have never left it. My seasons in Mexico altered me, more profoundly than any comparative event in my entire life. I abandoned my intent at a holiday and began writing again, feverishly and late into the night. Around me in the darkness, the restless animals in the hamlet called to each other. Children cried fitfully in their sleep. Drunkards sang raucously and off-key, and rang the churchbells in the square.

And as I wrote and listened in my pauses to the sounds of the dusty streets around me, the village of melons took its place in a deepening mosaic of observations which defied the sequences of time and chronology. Pressing new questions began to concern me: since life and human destiny were so uneven and full of surprises, what validity should I give to the traditional demands of order and progression in my work? Was not life itself a revolutionary process, with its own fluid and ever-changing disciplines? Did I not learn this from the folk procedures of Azuela, when he took my imagination into places with the authority and ease of someone documenting a commonplace event?

On our return to British Columbia, I was startled by the

austere visions I had somehow acquired during my time away. And reminded in a different way of the village of melons. For here food was overabundant, housing sumptuous and airtight. Our own home was suffocating with the clutter of needless accumulations gathered by a family over the years. These illusions of plenty baffled even my children, and for days we wandered as though lost through the rooms and over the grounds of our garden. We missed adversity, and the fine edge of despair which made all the seconds and minutes of life so precious and memorable. We had everything we needed once again, and yet we collectively experienced the haunting realization that we had nothing of consequence. All that surrounded us was transient, destructible and a purely material and cosmetic assurance of security against a savage climate and the loneliness of a young culture barely finding its own feet.

We had yet to rediscover the medical and social security systems of our country — those great and reasoned achievements of our society that commit us to help one another in times of hardship.

Some days later, I was called by Judy LaMarsh to appear on her radio talk show in Vancouver to speak of my impressions from my visit to the south. She was a representative of the Canadian establishment — authoritative, confident, glacial in spiritual inflexibility. I have my problems with establishment, not unlike problems I have with God: namely — with such credentials, why are they so prone to mistakes? She questioned me, and I recalled with rising animation what I had seen and confided my conviction that despite all the problems of poverty, armaments and the oppression of peoples, the human will to live and perfect itself would prevail. Even as I spoke, I was aware she had become distant and dull-eyed . . .

And in the parking lot of the radio studio that morning, I again remembered the village of melons and the venders I had seen, starved of will, staring uncomprehending at something distant and visible only to themselves.

Rider On A Galloping Horse
Impressions And Notes On China

June 20, Canton

Always thoughtful, Mr. Lien has again tried to locate a grocer who will sell us dates from the thorny date shrub. He has tried unsuccessfully for over a week, as have I. The fruit is almost identical in shape and taste to dates grown on the tropical date palm. I want a handful of seeds to introduce the shrub to Canada. In Linhsien County in Honan Province, to which it is indigenous, the climate and desert conditions are almost identical to the southern Okanagan Valley of British Columbia, where I live. Catalpa, amur cork trees, ailanthus and Chinese chestnuts grow in Honan desert country. They thrive in my garden. I wish to introduce the date to Canada. Mr. Lien cannot distinguish a willow from a hawthorn. But he is a man of generous spirit.

"You shall have dates," he tells me daily. But none have materialized. It is too late in the season for last year's crop, and too early for this year's, the local grocery clerks tell us . . .

For hundreds of kilometres he and I have been seat companions over the rear wheels of a bus. Through agricultural communes at harvest, peopled to the far horizon with harvesters bent in toil, sickling each precious stem of wheat — through villages crumbling slowly into ruins — through the streets of

240

teeming cities where the outcries of commerce are strangely silent . . .

Lin Piao is dead now. So is Confucius. Yet the civilized but stern condemnations of the Cultural Revolution are most consistently directed at these two personalities. Dead men make easy targets. Burdened and agonized by her past, China is cautious about the future. The oldest civilization in the world is going through renewal. Renewal of the landscape and the very souls of men, women and children. But the culture is peasant-based, and most advances are rooted in peasant logic. Chairman Mao is of peasant origin; the poet-philosopher loading one-fourth of humanity towards a new threshold of dignity. Always the concern is with food, the expansion of agricultural lands, the realignment of rivers.

Mr. Lien tells me China now has food reserves to last three years, buried in mountain caves. I tell him this is a unique achievement. He only half-hears me. There is no completion of intent — only a progression. Obviously a three-year surplus of grain is not enough. It is only a start . . .

Society is chaste, the mores conservative. One is struck by the cleanliness and good health of the population. All physical movement is vigorous and purposeful. The basic blue dress of the people is deceptive. The mirror of personality is in the faces — candid, curious, easily amused, shy. Country people . . .

Smoking is prevalent, particularly by those over thirty years of age. But drinking of alcohol is not visibly practised. An elegant woman my age who travels with us has wine on our urging after dinner on an overnight train. She sips it very slowly, and develops hiccoughs . . .

''Serve the people!'' is the motto on the lips and minds of everyone: children, factory workers, soldiers, teachers, doctors. It is not an idle slogan. It is a commandment. It is the basis of self-criticism, that remarkable process of evaluation beginning with each individual person, wherein individual egocentricity is dislodged and replaced by a conscious fusion into a family of eight hundred million other members. I notice

241

no diminishing of personality in all this. My travels are marked by surprising displays of individual initiative, wit and provocative debates with our Chinese companions . . .

"What will you do for a living?" I ask a hauntingly beautiful apprentice guide who came from near the Korean border.

"I will do what the masses ask me to do," she replies.

"What would you *like* to do for a living?" I rephrase my question. She smiles broadly.

"I would like to teach school. I am very good with children," she tells me. She is eighteen years of age . . .

"Self reliance" is another motto governing daily life. Self-reliance of the neighborhood, the village, the commune. All leadership must rise from work. The person with strong initiative and an innovative approach to labour qualifies for cadre training and party membership. Because of this, the landscape is in turmoil. Ancient methods of cultivation and production are fortified by technology. Factories producing machinery, chemicals, textiles and building materials arise in grainfields and remote villages. No position in life is inherited now. It must come from labour and a loss of personal self-interest. There is no other source of strength. To an outsider it appears as a massive drive towards purity and virtue — a first step towards some ideal of social responsibility which I find difficult to isolate in my mind. As an artist, I have many questions to ask, but little opportunity to request explanations . . .

The Maoists in our group are irritated. What readings from Marxist literatures are most frequently studied? Which of Mao's writings are discussed? They press cadres and ordinary workers for answers, but the replies are vague and noncommital. We have not been in China long enough to learn that all things are a progression from what has been to what is possible. We are an instant civilization from the abundant West, with instant resolutions to all problems. The realization that our methods are a trap has not yet occurred to us. One thing, however, has settled on my sensibilities — coming from the land, I am aware China can out-produce us acre for acre in wheat farming . . .

In the caves of Kwielin, a guide takes us on a fantasy journey through an illuminated world of dragons, virtuous warriors, poets singing songs without end from high towers . . . cities glowing on the edges of eternity. I am washed by her voice and easily drift into her luxuriant world thirty metres below the mountain surface. When we emerge, the sun and green rice fields hurt my eyes.

"Do you write poetry?" I ask the guide, who is now pals and tired.

"Yes," she replies. She nods quickly and leaves us. We are outside now, on the bridge connecting the roadway with the cave entrance.

"What kind of shit was that?" asks a young woman in our group. Her voice is louder than it need be. "I thought we were to see some caves, not listen to her bullshit! . . ."

Nobody responds to her indignation.

City lagoons are stocked with carp. Each evening, the carp are fed scrapings from hotel restaurants. The fish are farmed. They know when feeding time approaches, and they congregate in an agitated mass of flesh beside the lagoon walls. When the food is dumped into the water from metal tubs, the water turns to froth as the fish thrash and struggle over scraps. A moment later, the schools separate and swim slowly to other sections of the ancient water system . . .

"Good news! Tonight, we will go to the theatre!"

Mr. Lien is excited as he holds up a fistful of theatre tickets. We have talked often about art and the revolution. The meaning and implications of the slogan "Art Serves The Masses." On one occasion I expressed a sentiment that just possibly art had no role in China at this particular time. That since the role of revolutionary art was to inspire and ignite new potential in the people — to open new dimensions to the human spirit — that perhaps revolutionary idealism itself had assumed this role. Mr. Lien considers my thoughts very carefully, but witholds comment . . .

China is the only truly classless society on this earth today. Communist Party membership carries no privileges. It is a severe and exhausting obligation. Museums and history are carefully preserved, but all remnants of class oppression, of pomp, of pride of possessions, of arrogance of manners, have vanished from everyday life. Yet nowhere on earth is there such a dedication to class struggle — a struggle without end. It is more than a struggle against classes no longer extant in the country. It is a struggle against a state of mind and personality which creates separations and advantages. On more than one occasion I have wondered if it is not a struggle against nature itself . . .

"My small brother went to sleep last night
And he dreamed of Chairman Mao . . ."

The singer of this song is six years old. In a playschool concert, Mr. Lien translates the lyrics to a melody which is gentle and evocative. There is not more to the song . . . only this.

Two thousand years of slavery, followed by another two thousand of feudalism . . . On a June morning, the Great Wall has the glow of aged bone in the sunlight. It is heavy and awesome in its death. It was not designed to protect an enormous nation against invaders. It was designed to protect feudalism within that nation long after its natural and overdue demise. I am startled at realizing how basic masonry can sustain an emperor . . .

The Great Northern Plain and the wheatfields of Saskatchewan are identical. Miles and hours of waving grain rippling golden to a puff, clouded horizon . . .

We sit five rows back from the stage at the Sun Yat Sen Auditorium. The night is hot. Three thousand people have crowded the theatre. The Canton Symphony opens the concert with *The Yalu River Symphony* — a fine pastoral work with echoes of Mendelssohn. It is difficult to hear the performance. The audience will not be silent. Conversations which began before curtain time continue.

The feature item of the evening is a ballet, *Sons And Daughters of The Grasslands*. Design and lighting are superb. The performers are acrobatic and highly competent. But they have difficulty with form. Stylized elements of movement from

244

the Peking Opera are blended with dance taken from the dynamics of working people in motion. The hybrid seems unnecessary and is not effective. The ballet-story is a morality play: a corrupted party official arrives on a commune to take her daughter back to a self-indulgent life in the city. The daughter refuses to go. A wicked landlord and a blizzard throw obstacles in her way and in the way of the lives of her Red Guard companions and workmates. They struggle and exhaust themselves. The People's Liberation Army arrives in time to save them. The wicked landlord is banished. The party mother sees the error of her life and repents. The blizzard passes, spring arrives and the people dance the finale through a meadow of bursting flowers. All the political elements prevalent are knit into this professional production — the struggle against party revisionism, the extended metaphor of the threatening landlord, the purifying idealism of the Mao-inspired young Red Guards, and the final unity of the people in a setting which always includes a benevolent nature.

But the third member of the people's unity was missing — the proletariat, the industrial worker. In this particular ballet, only the peasant and soldier had definition.

The conversation in the auditorium during the performance was only interrupted when the landlord appeared on stage. The audience hissed and booed him. At the conclusion of the performance, the curtain rises and the weary dancers applaud us in the audience. There is no reciprocal response from the auditorium. I turn to see three thousand people blocked in lineups at the seven exits of the building.

The performing artists applaud the backs of the Cantonese citizens of the classless new society . . .

At the hotel, Mr. Lien and I debate the evening at the theatre.

"Serious art in the People's Republic is as outflanked by tradition and expediency as it is in Canada," I argue. "If art cannot lead, then it must follow. What I saw tonight was a politicized version of the American western, which is an extension of the medieval morality play. It is not enough!"

245

"It is not the same at all," he argues quietly. "In China, art serves the masses. It leads them by defining issues. The problems are many, but the verdict of the people is correct . . ."

"The same wall, the same foundation remains," I continue. "The audience tonight behaved like a new bourgoisie. They turned their backs on fellow workers . . . And what of the emerging industrial worker? He will have no fields to till, no changing seasons, no ancestral pathways on which to walk. He will be as alienated from his labour as all industrial workers have become. For his loss of peasant stability he will make demands — for leisure times, better wages, art that will inspire, give meaning and energize the purpose of his or her existence! Today in Canada and in China, the concerned artist leads — *must* lead the masses . . . with a very long rope!"

A smile plays on Mr. Lien's lips and he removes and cleans his glasses.

"That, my friend, was an astute observation . . . coming, as it were, from one who is seeing China from the back of a galloping horse!"

He nods thoughtfully, then adds, "We must think on this matter and discuss it further. Otherwise, how can we learn from each other?"

The tension passes. We clasp hands and part for the night into our separate worlds under one heaven.

THE OVERLANDERS

Episode ". . . Their Names Were Mark and Colin . . ."

Setting
Northern valley of Alberta badlands near Drumheller.

Music reference
The Book of Common Praise (hymn book of the Church of England in Canada)

Theme song - G. Ryga (music to be scored)

Scene One
ON CAMERA: Wide angle. Evening. Long shadows. Exterior. Mark and Franklin.

A long chase sequence. MARK is running desperately through the badlands, broken chain manacles hanging from his wrists. He is in panic, scrambling from rock to rock, clawing his way up to higher ground over crumbling stone ledges.

FRANKLIN is in distance behind him, rifle in hand, running. He stops only to raise his rifle and attempt to get an unobstructed shot at MARK. For two or three pauses he is unsuccessful. Then

MARK begins running in a straight course across an opening of level ground. FRANKLIN shoots. The shot echoes harshly through the badlands valley, sounding like a volley of shots. MARK is spun by the impact of the shot and thrown to the ground.

FRANKLIN hurries towards MARK, reloading his rifle. MARK struggles to his feet. He has been hit in the right arm. He pulls the arm close against his abdomen with his good arm and continues to flee. But his running is now erratic.

FRANKLIN sees that MARK is attempting to reach high ground through a cleft in the overhanging badlands walls. He runs in an arc up a shallow incline to a position which will intercept MARK at closer range. MARK is not aware of the manoeuvre. Looks back and sees FRANKLIN no longer pursuing him. He coughs and continues climbing.

A difficult climb up some loose shale and soil. MARK is gasping for breath.

FRANKLIN appears off to one side from behind a hoodoo. His chest is also heaving with exhaustion. MARK does not see him. FRANKLIN raises the rifle slowly. The kill is leisurely, precise. The shot is fired, echoing and re-echoing among the hills. MARK falls headlong, as if undercut.

FRANKLIN approaches him, the gun cradled in his arm. He is not reloading, knowing he has killed MARK. Placing his boot-toe under MARK's shoulder, he rolls him over on his back, as if the man were just another dead animal he killed in the woods.

FRANKLIN clears his throat, removes his hat and, staring down into the valley, sighs. Then placing his hat firmly on his head again, he begins his way down the steep slope to the bottom of the valley.

ON CAMERA: Camera lingers on the stark, unearthly land-scape. The two men in the foreground, the distance between them widening as FRANKLIN retreats.

The entire sequence has an animal savagery to it. The only sounds are the gunshots, and the gasping breathing of the hunter and the hunted.

Fade out.

Act One

ON CAMERA: Wide-angle shot — PATTERSON's group on overland trek. A few days earlier. Squealing and creaking of crude carts and wagons. Shouting of people as the procession works its way through a field of mud.

There is a sense of disorganization and disarray, bordering on hopelessness, about the group. FRANKLIN, gun always on arm, bearing upright, is admonishing the driver of the lead wagon.

FRANKLIN: If you'd gone over left, the wagons would have remained on hard ground!

DRIVER: *(Shouts, ignoring FRANKLIN)* Blake! . . . Anderson! . . . Get around to the other side . . . Keep it going, men! Keep it going! Hah!

He lashes at the horses who veer sharply to the right. Cry of pain.

CUT IN TO: Close on right side of wagon.
COLIN had been walking alongside the lead team. The horses, turning suddenly, knock him down. He lies helpless, shouting. The front wheel of the wagon rides over the toes of his foot before the wagon stops.

MARK is instantly beside COLIN, lifting him and pulling him back. COLIN continues shouting. MARK soothes and calms him.

MARK: *(Leading him from wagon)* Easy Colin . . . it's alright. We'll be stopping soon . . . can you walk?

COLIN: A little bit . . .

MARK: We'll stop soon . . . I'll make soup and rub your feet . . . On Sunday you can sit wrapped in a blanket all day . . . don't worry.

CUT IN TO: Medium wide shot on front of wagon train. FRANKLIN and PATTERSON. PATTERSON is a short distance ahead of wagon. He is waving frantically to driver to bear right.

PATTERSON: This way! . . . Don't stop again — keep moving! This way!

This is contrary to FRANKLIN's instructions. As the driver turns sharply right, he rolls the wheels against wagon box and there is danger of tipping the wagon. Driver now attempts to turn left slightly. More confusion, shouting.

FRANKLIN waves his arm with derision at both PATTERSON and the driver.

CUT TO: Long shot from some elevation. In foreground of shot are the two blacksmiths, the lead wagon and its entourage in background of shot.

The two blacksmiths are pulling a small cart, two-wheeled and covered with all their tools and possessions inside. They pull it by a pole, two ropes attached to the end of the pole and the rope-ends over their shoulders. They are their own draft animals. Their cart is above the mud below. They stop and watch the commotion lower down.

FIRST BLACKSMITH: The fool!

SECOND BLACKSMITH: They're **all** fools! . . . More than half of them have been to college . . . yet none of them know where they are, where they're going, or how they'll get there!

FIRST BLACKSMITH: *(Spits)* The sons of the rich . . . out to rule the world!

INTERCUT: Scenes of the wagon train's progress: the train stretched out a long distance in hot sun, squealing sound, a cloud of dust over them. Wash up at a river. Horses are driven into the water. They drink — the trekkers drink beside them, some from cups, some from the cups of their hands, others with their faces against the water.

MARK scoops us water in his hat and carries it to COLIN, who stands staring distantly on the dry beach. MARK holds the hat and COLIN drinks a few sips. The blacksmiths drink leisurely then, removing their shirts, splash water on themselves.

FRANKLIN: *(Angrily)* Hey! If you're going to bathe, go downstream! We're drinking your wash water here!

FIRST BLACKSMITH: *(Laughing)* It's as far downstream for me as it's upstream for you, friend!

Some of the young men start a playful water fight in the river. A team of horses become startled and bolt, turning sharply, dumping their driver into the water. A pursuit of the runaway wagon begins, to laughter, shouted instructions, hubbub.

The train moves on, with blacksmiths last in line, pulling their cart with ropes over their shirtless bodies. The first blacksmith sings raucously, almost defiantly.

BLACKSMITH: *(Sings)*
> Hey, all you young dandies
> From Boston to Ottawa
> There's incredible fortune out here to be made . . .
> Just put down your money
> Say goodbye to your mummy
> An' eat bread and honey
> On the overlander's brigade!
> O'er hills and flat prairie the miles we are countin'
> Until we're in sight of the land of the mountains
> Until we're in sight of the lands of he mountain
> And then it's hoorah! The journey's been made . . .

Evening stop. Wagons are circled on open land.
An argument starts between a few young men trying to light a campfire.

ONE YOUTH: No, I'm not . . . the wood I've got is my own!

ANOTHER YOUTH: Then what will we do?

ONE YOUTH: I'm not leader of this group . . . If I was there'd be wood and water when we need it!

The other youth reaches out to reason with him, but the first youth brusquely pushes him aside. A pushing match starts between them and another two young men.

ON CAMERA: Segue to a short but spirited fight between MARK and COLIN some distance from the wagon train. COLIN is knocked down. They are not recognizable at this distance. The fight is watched from forground of shot by FRANKLIN and another man.

Wagon train on the move. The blacksmiths are some distance in front of the group now. A cold wind is blowing. All the group

252

*are dressed and wrapped heavily. MARK follows the smiths, but
he is alone now.*

FIRST BLACKSMITH: *(Singing)*
    They promised us roads
    And they promised us transport
    They promised us lodging and dinners with wine
    They promised us cities of civilized splendour
    If to dancing and theatre we were inclined . . .

Over Song:
*ON CAMERA: Cuts of FRANKLIN and PATTERSON argu-
ing as they ride PATTERSON's wagon. FRANKLIN keeps
motioning back as he talks, referring to some incident that occured
earlier. PATTERSON is angry with him and indicating he does
not share FRANKLIN's opinions.*

ON CAMERA: Shot of the wagon train entering the badlands.

*Close studies of the faces of the trekkers at first sight of the awe-
some, ancient landscape. There are traces of fear in some faces.*

FRANKLIN: Where, in your infinite wisdom, did you bring
us to, Patterson?

PATTERSON: I don't know . . . but there's shelter down
there and tomorrow's a day of rest. Let's make camp in the
hollow.

He motions to the wagon train to go downward.

*ON CAMERA: Cut to an Indian man and woman watching
the train from a knoll.*
*A couple of the trekkers see the Indians and seem undecided what
to do. One of them raises his hand tentatively in greeting. The
Indian man responds.*

YOUTH: Let's go and talk to them . . . They're not armed . . . they might tell us where we are . . .

CUT TO: Camp. Night. A huge bonfire of sage wood. Laughter. A banjo being plucked in the night.

CUT TO: Medium shot on youths offering stew to the Indians, who squat and share the meal. The Indians eye the tethered horses. Off to one side, FRANKLIN eyes the Indians. He eats standing up, his rifle resting against his hip.

YOUTH: *(To FRANKLIN)* They speak no English at all . . .

FRANKLIN: I suggest you send them packing soon's they're finished with dinner. Or we'll be missing a couple of horses by daybreak . . .

YOUTH: They're fine, simple people, Franklin!

FRANKLIN snorts.

YOUTH: They are . . . and smart, too. I'd sure like a jacket like the one he's wearing.

FRANKLIN: Then take it off him and boot him out of camp. That's a language every savage understands!

CUT TO: MARK — food in his hands, but he does not eat. Voices of conversation carry to him, but he does not hear.

FRANKLIN: *(Voice over)* If you want to live through this journey you learn to live lawfully but firmly.

YOUTH: *(Voice over)* We can't rob him of his clothes!

FRANKLIN: *(Voice over)* Why not . . . ? He means to rob you of your horses . . . that's called upside-down justice.

(Laughs)

MARK smiles, but at some inner memory. The voices fade out.

DISSOLVE TO: Passage of time over super of COLIN's face. It is morning now. Sudden boom of voices singing. MARK looks around, startled, the food still in his hands.

CUT TO: MARK's p.o.v. Wide-angle shot of camp in daylight. Sunny. It is Sunday. The tethered horses are standing, satiated. The Blacksmiths have set up a smithy on the far edge of camp and are working over repairs to wagons and gear. Most of the other trekkers are seated in a wide cirlce around a low burning fire. They sit on barrels, on the ground, and on short blocks of wood.

Most of the trekkers are dressed incongruously against the stark landscape — young men wearing the Sunday attire of city dwellers of the time. At the head of the circle PATTERSON stands with a Bible in his hand, conducting the hymn with his other hand.

HYMN:
> O God, our help in ages past
> Our hope for years to come,
> Our shelter from the stormy blast
> And our eternal home!
>
> Beneath the shadow of thy throne
> Thy saints have dwelt secure;
> Sufficient in thine arm alone,
> And our defence is sure . . .

CUT TO: Close shot on three youths and Indians behind a wagon. One of the youths is trying to swap his drab work jacket for the Indian man's jacket. The Indian smiles but does not respond.

SECOND YOUTH: *(Over hymn)* It won't work, Jess . . . he won't play cards, he won't take a trade . . . maybe we should consider what Franklin said . . . who would know?

FIRST YOUTH: *(Over hymn)* I would . . . there must be another way . . .

CUT TO: PATTERSON beginning the Sunday sermon.

PATTERSON: This Sunday is two months to the day of our departure to whatever awaits us in the Cariboo country in the western mountains. Despite misfortunes and privation, the guiding hand of the Lord has sheltered us . . .

His sermon is interrupted by clanking of hammer on anvil at the smithy.

The two blacksmiths are not part of the service. They are dressed in leather smith's aprons and are hammering a glowing horse-shoe into shape.

CUT TO: Close on blacksmiths.

SECOND BLACKSMITH: Do you suppose he killed him?

FIRST BLACKSMITH: Nothing this group would do would surprise me . . .

CUT TO: Wide shot on Sunday sermon.

PATTERSON: *(Over clanking of smiths)* . . . He has sheltered us from hunger and serious disease . . . He has sheltered us from death . . . for all this, let us give praise and thanks on this day of rest . . .

CUT TO: Trio of youth with Indians.

The young men are flat on their stomachs, playing a crude version of "pick-up sticks." The game is designed to attract the participation of the Indian man.
Voice of Patterson in sermon is heard in b.g.

CUT TO: PATTERSON preaching.

PATTERSON: Let us also give thanks to the Lord for providing us with this opportunity to observe the vastness and grandeur of the country through which He has led us in His providence . . .

CUT TO: Close shot of hammer blow on horseshoe. Loud clang. The horseshoe breaks.

BLACKSMITH: *(Voice over)* Godammit!

CUT TO: Wide shot of congregation, now rising to its feet to sing:

HYMN:
> From all that dwell below the skies
> Let the Creator's praise arise;
> Let the Redeemer's name be sung
> Through every land, by every tongue.
>
> Eternal are thy mercies, Lord,
> Eternal truth attends thy Word;
> Thy praise shall sound from shore to shore
> Till suns shall rise and set no more.

DURING HYMN CUT TO: Close study on MARK's face. He does not sing, but towards end of hymn, tears trickle down his cheeks.

DISSOLVE TO: COLIN and MARK riding on back of wagon. MARK is talking. COLIN is excited. Hymn in b.g.

MARK: . . . And with the money we earn from our claims, we'll open a general store.

COLIN: Just you and I, Mark?

MARK: Just you and I . . .

COLIN: An' a bell on the door that rings when people come in?

MARK: Yes . . . and a big sign over the porch reading "Colin and Mark's General Store". . .

COLIN: I wonder if we'll get a bell like the one at home?

MARK presses COLIN's arm reassuringly. But MARK is troubled.

DISSOLVE TO: Wide shot on congregation.
The hymn has ended. The group settles down on their seats again. The preacher opens his Bible and prepares his text. The hammering at the smithy continues, but more softly now.
Sounds of crows in distance. The atmosphere is not that of a church. Members of the group relax and begin small conversations.
FRANKLIN, an overpowering young man who already has the markings of becoming a lawman at a future date, breaks from the congregation and approaches the preacher, PATTERSON.

CLOSE ON: FRANKLIN and PATTERSON.

FRANKLIN: *(In a quiet voice)* I don't like the way you're leading this group! We have no guide . . . our supplies are low . . . a man disappears and not a word is said . . .

PATTERSON: This is not the time, Franklin! This is a day for giving praise and thanks for our surviving this long.

FRANKLIN: There is a suspicion of murder, Mister Patterson!

PATTERSON: We have a long way to go . . . let it wait until we reach a town with duly commissioned law officers and a recognized court!

FRANKLIN: He'll be gone by then . . .

CUT TO: Close on Indian man's face, now intense.
WIDEN SHOT TO: Include the three youths and Indian woman seated on ground in b.g.

The Indian is stripped to the waist, as are all the young trekkers involved in the game of chance. The clothes are on one side of them, neatly stacked. The Indian is silent as he carefully works to unravel the cluster of sticks without upsetting any of the pile.

FIRST YOUTH: Who's keeping score?

SECOND YOUTH: We're tied . . . he's won three . . . you've won three.

THIRD YOUTH: Suppose he gets us?

FIRST YOUTH: Don't worry . . . we can always change the rules if he gets ahead.

SECOND YOUTH: You know what you're doing . . . but that's the only good shirt I've got . . .

CUT TO: Close on PATTERSON and FRANKLIN in congregation.

PATTERSON: You're certain he killed him?

FRANKLIN: **I'm** certain, but he's entitled to the benefit of a trial. And unless he's tried **now**, Mister Patterson, this wagon train will go nowhere for the fear and suspicion surrounding us!

PATTERSON: Very well, but if he's guilty, what do you propose we do then?

FRANKLIN stares at PATTERSON, not understanding.

PATTERSON: *(Smiles bitterly)* Not many will remember us or care what happens to us. The other groups are weeks ahead of this group — we may never catch up to them. Only God sees us now, Franklin, and He will forgive us many things. He has to . . . or we will never reach our destination . . .

FRANKLIN moves away. Looks at MARK, who stares back at him.

DISSOLVE TO: FRANKLIN and MARK in almost identical stances to scene above. Only now MARK is repairing a canvas sheet. FRANKLIN is in front of him, gun in hand, holding a grouse he has just killed.

FRANKLIN: In Maryland I shot wild turkeys. All I can sight here are magpies and these . . . I swear the Indians are keeping the bigger game moving away from us.

MARK: I used a gun once, but I wasn't very good at it.

FRANKLIN: Where are you and your brother from?

MARK: *(Evasively)* A small town in Ontario. You would not have heard of it . . .

FRANKLIN: I've been to many places in my time.

MARK: It was only a small town . . . I've been told you're a good marksman.

FRANKLIN: Anything larger than this I can hit through the eye. It keeps the meat from bruising . . .

MARK: I only used a gun once . . .

FRANKLIN: You should learn how it's done and soon. With all the Indians we've seen so far it may make the difference between saving and losing your scalp!

He laughs at MARK's startled expression. Moves away.

Fade out.

Act Two

ON CAMERA: Medium shot MARK and COLIN. Day.

MARK is cutting through deadfall in front of wagon train. But the sounds of his axe on the wood are the sounds of the blacksmith's hammer on the anvil. COLIN is holding the log steady. MARK stops chopping, looks around and leans towards COLIN.

MARK: It's important you understand what I'm saying to you . . . you are not to talk to anyone about where we came from . . . do you understand?

COLIN nods vaguely.

MARK: And our names are Mark and Colin Anderson . . . we will be Andersons for the rest of our lives!

COLIN nods again.

MARK: And never . . . **never** . . . are you to tell anyone about what happened . . . Never!

COLIN: I didn't mean to do it, Mark . . . I didn't mean to do it . . .

MARK: I know . . . don't worry. We'll build a store soon . . . with a rocking chair on the front porch and a bell on the door . . . just like it used to be.

COLIN: *(Cheerfully)* An' we'll write to papa to come and see us selling flour an' tobacco and things . . .

COLIN drifts off, a helpless expression on his face.

COLIN: But mama won't come . . . she's dead . . .

MARK: *(Angry)* We have a lot of work to do!

MARK begins cutting at the tree again.

COLIN: Will you fix my boot tonight, Mark? There's a nail sticking in my foot an' it's bleeding. My sock is all dirty with blood . . .

CUT TO: PATTERSON and congregation. Sudden loud sound of hymn being sung.

HYMN:
> Before the hills in order stood,
> Or earth received her frame,
> From everlasting thou art God,
> To endless years the same . . .

Hymn ends. There is sudden stillness.

PATTERSON: The Lord is my shepherd, I shall not want . . . Consider the wisdom of the scriptures . . .

CUT TO: Medium close shot on Indian and trio of gamblers behind wagon. Franklin is with them, standing over them, watching.

PATTERSON: *(Voice over)* . . . The Lord is my shepherd . . . We are in a strange land surrounded by hostile winds and geography. The only people who watch us passing through are Indians who appear savage and unpredictable to our understandings. They could turn against us on the slightest whim, or they could provide us with food and guidance should we falter. The Lord is our Father, watching over us like a shepherd over his flocks . . .

During above sermon, FRANKLIN begins laughing as he watches the players in their game.

FRANKLIN: What in hell are you up to? You'll be lucky if you come out of this with your underclothes!

FIRST YOUTH: *(Fevered with gambling)* Go away, Franklin . . . just go away!

FRANKLIN continues laughing as he turns away.

CUT TO: PATTERSON preaching.

PATTERSON: We are filled with fear . . . the road ahead and the days to come are ones of anxiety. The other groups in the overlanders trek are larger than we . . . there are some among you who feel they were better led, more organized, better supplied with provisions.

FRANKLIN wanders back into congregation at this point.

FRANKLIN: *(Still smiling from previous scene)* Amen to that!

PATTERSON ignores him, continues with his sermon.

PATTERSON: But the same Divine Providence watches over them as over us. In the end I feel we shall all be re-united at our destination . . . life will stabilize . . . we shall prosper if we maintain the faith and conviction in the ultimate wisdom of God . . .
Looking about me at the strange formations of geology, I cannot help but feel how transitory is our life . . . how fragile our destiny. Around us is a landscape frozen for eons in an expression which startles and terrifies, for we are men who wear clothes, have grown up in the shelter of homes . . . have known gentleness and love . . . Perhaps we must learn to live with the savage face of a land we face for the first time . . . perhaps that face must become part of our face if we are to become more than strangers passing through the wilderness . . .

DURING SERMON CUT TO CLOSE ON: Blacksmiths, half listening with some amusement.
CUT TO: Close on MARK's face.
DISSOLVE: With MARK's face in faint superimposition to exterior of General store of past century. The legend on the false storefront reading "Johnson's General Store."

WALTER JOHNSON, MARK's father, is talking to a neighbour on porch of store on which stands a rocking chair. JOHNSON is a strong, athletic man. PATTERSON's sermon in faint b.g.

JOHNSON: I would not repeat it to a soul, Melvyn . . . I say this to you because you are a man of integrity . . . let the word go no further than your ears!

NEIGHBOUR: The woman is poor and widowed. I find it difficult to believe she would steal . . .

JOHNSON: Then who did? My sons were with me in the shop . . . there was nobody else but her!

NEIGHBOUR: Still . . .

JOHNSON: She stood near the cashbox . . . undecided, as if making up her mind about her purchases . . . when I returned, the cashbox drawer was on the floor and some of the money gone.

NEIGHBOUR: Were your sons in front of the shop?

JOHNSON: Mark was with me and Colin had gone out to play . . .

MARK: *(In superimposition, softly)* It was Colin who took the money, father . . .

JOHNSON: It was her, Melvyn . . .

The neighbour leaves. JOHNSON stands in thought.

MARK: *(In superimposition)* I found Colin near the river . . . throwing those coins into the water and laughing . . .

DISSOLVE TO: PATTERSON preaching to congregation.

PATTERSON: . . . I shall not want . . . With the Lord watching over us, our wants are few . . .

CUT TO: Medium shot on Indians and gamblers.
The second youthful trekker is nervously down on the ground on his elbows, his seat in the air, trying to remove the pile of sticks. His hand shakes and the pile topples. With aloof dignity, the Indian picks up the pile of clothes and carries them to place them in the lap of his wife.

SECOND YOUTH: That sonofabitch got me . . . *(To third youth)* You take over!

PATTERSON: *(Voice over)* We have food, water and shelter at the end of day. What comfort is denied us is only fitting . . .

CUT TO: Close on PATTERSON.

PATTERSON: . . . when we remember the rewards which await us at the end of the journey . . .

Sound of Blacksmith's hammer.

CUT TO: Close on MARK's face, intense and preoccupied.

PATTERSON: *(Voice over)* It is the fate of man to struggle for his attainment of happiness. If the reward is gold or fame, he must endure discomfort and long hours of toil, or the rewards would be undeserved and sinful . . .

HYMN: *(Sung voice over)*
A thousand ages in thy sight
Are like an evening gone;
Short as the watch that ends the night
Before the rising sun . . .

Over preacher's sermon and hymn, which sustains in b.g.

DISSOLVE TO: Medium shot on backs of children in school. Interior. Day.

A female teacher faces the class.

TEACHER: If I had seven apples and gave you four apples, how many apples would I have left? Colin Johnson?

CLOSE SHOT: Over shoulders of boy, twisting his hands and rumpling paper with distress.

TEACHER: *(Voice over)* I have seven apples and I gave you four . . . I would then have how many apples, Colin?

SUPER: Face of MARK on shot.

MARK: I know the answer — please, let me answer for Colin!

TEACHER: *(Voice over)* In a moment, Mark . . . I want your brother to give me the answer to this question. He can count. He has ten fingers on his hands!

Laughter of children. Boy becomes agitated.

MARK: You would have three apples, Miss Harrison!

TEACHER: *(Voice over)* Yes, I would have three apples left. Now why are you so stupid, Colin? . . . . Why can you not use your brain as your brother does? And to reward him for thinking and doing your schoolwork for you, I will give him this apple to keep for his lunch . . .

CUT TO: Two shot over shoulders of small boys on a grassy knoll. Exterior. Day.

One boy is holding apple, offering it to the other. The other boy refuses.

BOY: I don't want it . . . I'm dumb! . . . Dumb! . . . Stupid!

Fade out.

Act Three

Sound of hammers on anvil. Rattle of steel chain.

Zoom shot on congregation. PATTERSON is staring, startled.

CUT TO: PATTERSON's p.o.v. — FRANKLIN approaching from his wagon, carrying handcuffs and chain in his hand. As he nears PATTERSON, he stops. Drops the chain on the ground. Watches PATTERSON for a reaction.

CUT TO: Medium shot on blacksmiths, watching the proceedings from their distance.

FIRST BLACKSMITH: When the Almighty gets men like Franklin on His side, somebody's bound to get hurt.

SECOND BLACKSMITH: They aim to kill the poor devil . . .

CUT TO: Close on face of Indian, shaking his head.

PULL TO: Medium shot on Indian and gambling youth.

The Indian stands over them, shaking his head. He will not continue the game except on his conditions.
The young men stare at their clothes, held by the Indian women. The Indian points to his footwear — indicates he will play for their shoes against all the clothes.
The young men begin undoing their boots and footwear.

CUT TO: Two shot — FRANKLIN and PATTERSON. PATTERSON is resolute.

PATTERSON: Permit me to continue with my service in the name of our Lord!

FRANKLIN: I am impatient to see justice done — so are many of the others.

CUT TO: Wide shot on congregation.
There is a substantial murmur of agreement. MARK lowers his head and draws into himself.

PATTERSON: Laws are made by man . . . only God can judge us in what we do . . .

VOICE OF GROUP: We don't know where we are! We have no firewood!

ANOTHER VOICE: We have short provisions and no containers for water!

PATTERSON: *(Opening his Bible)* I will read to you . . . a passage which may not meet with your approval . . . hopefully it may temper your anger and impatience . . . *(Reads)* And Lot went up out of Zoar and dwelt in the mountain, and his two daughters with him . . . for he feared to dwell in Zoar . . . and he dwelt in a cave, he and his two daughters. And the firstborn said unto the younger — our father is old and there is not a man on the earth to come in unto us after the manner of all the earth . . . come, let us make our father drink wine and we will lie with him that we may preserve the seed of our father. And they made their father drink wine that night, and the firstborn went in and lay with her father, and he perceived not when she lay down, nor when she arose . . .

MOVING SHOT: Over faces of the group. Many are disturbed. Some begin to understand.
Hold shot on blacksmiths. As they hear the sermon, they stop with hammers poised in midstroke, glance at each other. The first blacksmith shrugs at the other, as if to say that some strange things take place on this earth. They resume hammering over PATTERSON's reading.

269

PATTERSON: *(Voice over — with growing intensity)* . . . and they made their father drink wine that night also, and the younger arose and lay with him, and he perceived not when she lay down, nor when she arose . . . Thus were both the daughters of Lot with child by their father . . .

CUT TO: Close on MARK's face on above speech.
DISSOLVE TO: MARK's face at an earlier time. Only now he is alarmed.

PATTERSON: *(Voice over)* And his firstborn bare a son, and called his name Moab, the same is the father of the Moabites unto this day. And the younger she also bare a son, and called his name Benami, the same is the father of the children of Ammon unto this day . . .

MARK: I don't believe it! . . . Colin, you're lying!

WIDEN SHOT TO: Two shot MARK and COLIN.
Colin is pleased, arrogant, defiant in a childish way.

COLIN: Nobody saw me . . . she was alone.

MARK: You were told to leave the groceries on her front porch and come directly back to the store!

COLIN: She was pretty . . . I was going to kiss her like papa kisses mama when he's been to Ottawa . . .

MARK: She sold eggs to us . . . there were chickens in that coop . . .

COLIN: Two of them got out . . .

MARK: The others burned to death, Colin!

COLIN: Two of them . . . their feathers smoking . . . I chased them . . . one died . . . the other ran into the raspberry bush an' I couldn't find him!

DISSOLVE TO: PATTERSON and congregation.

(With finalty) Sometimes . . . the ways of men are difficult to understand . . . They become the ways of the land into which they have strayed. But when there is a threat to our species . . . when we are in danger of faltering and dying . . . unusual things are sometimes done . . . as in the days of Lot . . . I want to leave you with this thought . . .

He closes his Bible. The group sings.

HYMN:
    Come, thou long-expected Jesus,
    Born to set thy people free;
    From our sins and fears release us,
    Let us find our rest in thee.

    Israel's strength and consolation,
    Hope of all the earth thou art;
    Dear desire of every nation,
    Joy of every longing heart.

    Born thy people to deliver,
    Born a child and yet a King;
    Born to reign in us for ever,
    Now thy gracious kingdom bring.

    By thine own eternal spirit
    Rule in all our hearts alone;
    By thine all-sufficient merit
    Raise us to thy glorious throne.

DURING ABOVE SERMON AND HYMN — DISSOLVE TO: Close on MARK. He is worried, afraid.

RHYTHMIC DISSOLVES TO: FRANKLIN and PATTER-SON to MARK.

Hymn in b.g. Argument between FRANKLIN and PATTER-SON through dissolves — some on camera, some voiced over:

FRANKLIN: Our affairs for the day are not at an end, Mister Patterson! You are the leader of our group . . . I charge this man with murder!

PATTERSON: I was to preach the sermon this Sunday. I will not sit as judge in trial!

GROUP MEMBER: *(Off camera)* I disagree. It was you who said men must abide by new standards of conduct when they are threatened in the wilderness!

Rattle of handcuff chains . . . hammer sounds on anvil, now loud over hymn.

PATTERSON: As you wish . . . but any trial we hold here can only be provisional. If he is guilty, we must regard this only as the judgement of his peers. He must be entitled to another trial and the passing of sentence by another court!

FRANKLIN: If he's guilty, he will be punished.

PATTERSON: Henry Wilson . . . will you write a record of this event? . . . I will name twelve of you to step forward and assume the duties of a jury . . .

CUT TO: Sudden silence.
Another court. Interior. Day.

MARK is seated together with his father and mother, facing trial judge. COLIN is in prisoner's dock.

COLIN is oblivious to his surroundings.

JUDGE: There is little doubt in my mind that Colin Johnson approached Missus Valliere on the afternoon of May 6th . . . ostensibly to deliver groceries from his father's shop. Suffice it to say an unprovoked act, indecent perhaps, took place on the person of Missus Valliere. Colin Johnson was repelled by Missus Valliere, at which time she secured her home against him. He then set fire to her chicken house and its contents, namely fifty-four laying hens and an undetermined inventory of supplies and feed for the hens. Despite the representations of Colin Johnson's family, this court must consider the suggestion in passing sentence that the accused is not of sound mind and should therefore be committed to . . .

JOHNSON: *(Father. Rising in anger)* My son is not mad! What are you saying?

JUDGE: *(Placating)* You are a well-known and respected merchant in this town . . . I value your judgement. But this is no longer a child . . . you cannot account for his actions.

MOTHER: *(Rising to stand beside her husband)* We can and we will . . . Our son will not be placed into a madhouse . . . Please let him go!

PROSECUTING ATTORNEY: Your worship, I object!

MOTHER: We have money to care for him. He will never be asked to help outside the store again!

PROSECUTING ATTORNEY: Your worship . . .

The judge is troubled. Turns to the lawyer.

JUDGE: Young man, I respect your knowledge of the law, but I am older than you and I've learned through age to temper my learning with an understanding of life. All of us in this courtroom know each other . . . we've all raised children . . . we can appreciate the agony of seeing a child given to us with a crippling disease . . .

WIDEN SHOT TO: Include MRS. VALLIERE, on her feet now.

MRS. VALLIERE: *(Addressing the judge)* I did not ask that he be put away for the rest of his life into . . . a place for madmen . . .

FATHER: *(Turning to her)* We'll make restitution for your hens and building if you'll . . .

Prosecuting attorney throws up his hands in disgust.

JUDGE: This court has heard the offer of payment for damages incurred by the accused . . . if I can be satisfied that Colin will henceforth be confined to his home and guarded with due care, then perhaps it will be in the best interest of all concerned that . . .

CUT TO: Hymn in b.g.
RHYTHMIC DISSOLVES: on MARK, FRANKLIN and PATTERSON in congregation, Blacksmiths watching the proceedings stonily.

PATTERSON: *(Off camera)* Were you a witness to the murder?

FRANKLIN: *(Off camera)* I saw the two of them fighting. Howie Smith was with me . . . we watched them together.

PATTERSON: *(Tight on camera)* Is this true?

Close on MARK, struggling for words.

SMITH: *(Voice over)* Yes, it's true.

PATTERSON: *(Voice over)* When did this fight occur?

FRANKLIN: *(On camera)* Three days ago . . . He was help-less . . . A wagon had run over his foot . . . he fought back with his hands, but he didn't have a chance . . . He was being beaten with a wooden club!

PATTERSON: *(Voice over)* Was there no attempt made to break them apart?

FRANKLIN: When we approached, they stopped fight-ing . . . they watched us . . . like two animals . . . it was frightening.

PATTERSON: *(Voice over)* Was there any other wit-ness . . . to the murder?

DISSOLVE ON: RONALD, a member of the group, volunteer-ing information.

PATTERSON: *(Voice over)* Yes, Ronald . . .

RONALD: It was still daylight when Franklin and Howie saw the fight . . . they told me about it when we set up camp. Mine was the last wagon in that evening. I was outside, repacking my supplies because they had become wet with the rain . . . The accused came into camp much later . . . almost at dusk. His shirt was torn and bloodstained . . . he said something about falling and cutting himself. Then . . . he asked me for loan of my shovel.

PATTERSON: Which you gave him?

RONALD: Yes . . . he returned it a couple of hours later . . . it had been well-used . . . all the rust was scraped off the blade.

PATTERSON: What did the accused look like?

RONALD: He was tired when he returned . . . the sweat was showing through his clothes . . . He didn't appear to know me . . . He just propped the shovel up against my wagon . . . The light was faint . . . but it seemed to me like he was in tears . . .

DISSOLVE TO: Close on MARK's face. His eyes are shut, his expression haunted.

PATTERSON: *(Voice over)* Mark . . . do you want to say something to add to what these gentlemen have told us?

OVER MARK's FACE, DISSOLVE TO: Flames. Sound of fire crackling. A shrill shriek of a woman, over and over.

QUICK MONTAGE OF SHOTS: Reflections of fire over MARK's father's face. The rocking chair on store porch, beginning to ignite from heat.
On shrieking of woman, father attempts to throw himself into flames, but is restrained by neighbours.
Woodshed, MARK and COLIN — MARK has his hands around COLIN's throat. He is beating COLIN's head against a wall. COLIN is terrified, sobbing, not resisting.

MARK: She was in the store taking inventory! . . . You killed her, you sonofabitch!

COLIN: He asked me to burn . . . the torn sugar sacks . . . wind blew a sack under the store . . .

276

PATTERSON: *(Voice over)* Mark . . . have you anything to say?

MARK releases COLIN. The shrieks die away. MARK steps back on dissolve.

CUT TO WIDE SHOT: Campsite.
The hymn has ended. The group all stare at him in silence. MARK speaks in a dead voice as he faces his accusers, his hands now chained together.

MARK: I killed my brother Colin three days ago . . .

Fade out.

Act Four

ON CAMERA: Commotion of voices on:
Wide medium shot of Indian man and woman and three gamblers.

The three youths are barefoot and stripped of their upper cloth-ing. The Indian man wears his leather jacket. He and his wife each have a bundle of clothing under their arms. They walk away from the camp . . . rather quickly . . . up a hillside.

FIRST YOUTH: Hurry . . . go call Franklin to stop them! I have no other boots! . . . He's taken my boots! *(Turns to his companions)* That Indian took my boots!

SECOND YOUTH: It's no use. Franklin wouldn't do it now. He'd only laugh.

CUT TO: Medium shot: MARK and blacksmiths.

MARK is chained to the blacksmith's anvil. Voices of group in b.g. It is turning darker now, evening is coming. The first black-smith sits near MARK, writing a letter for MARK. The second blacksmith is working the bellows to restart the smithy.

PATTERSON: *(Voice over)* Quiet, everybody . . . let us have order!

MARK: Write to him, "Dear father; I am nineteen years old today. I do not know where I am or what will become of me . . ."

FRANKLIN: *(Voice over)* Hang him, I say! He confessed!

MARK: "Colin was twenty-three years old this year. Before I tell you what I must say . . ." *(Shakes his head, uncertain how to begin)*

PATTERSON: *(Voice over)* Besides escorting him under guard to the nearest authorities, I am at a loss as to what to say . . .

FRANKLIN: *(Voice over)* Hanging's too good for him! *(Some approval from group)*

MARK: *(Over b.g. commotion)* "Colin began school three years before I did . . . he was still in school when I left. If you had been a drayman instead of a merchant, Colin would never have been allowed inside a school . . . we were not the same, father! . . . He learned to tie his shoelaces, but he often put his shoes on the wrong feet . . . he knew up and down, but he didn't know left from right . . ."

PATTERSON: *(Voice over)* We shall do no such thing!

MARK: "He rocked at songs our mother sang . . . he cried at things that made me happy . . . I knew what hurt him . . .

278

He was stronger than I . . . bigger . . . but he held the paper on which I drew . . . and he held the boards I cut . . . he pulled the grocery cart from which I counted meal and eggs . . .''

FRANKLIN: *(Voice over)* The law says an eye for an eye! Until a better law comes along, I live with that!

PATTERSON: *(Voice over)* You're a fool, Franklin!

ANOTHER VOICE: *(Voice over)* So are you!

MARK: ''He who walked with difficulty had to run, because all others he resembled ran . . . he who could never learn to read was told he had to spell, because all others he resembled spelled . . .''

SUPERIMPOSE: A field of wild horses, clustered. A child runs towards them. The horses scatter, galloping off in all directions. The child watches them run, his face reflecting his confusion.

MARK: *(Voice over)* ''He who learned the directions but not the names of streets and lanes in our town was considered capable of knowing the nations and oceans of the world, because others he resembled knew . . . As a cat is not aware of Holy Scriptures, father, or the births and deaths of kings, so it was with Colin . . .''

ON CAMERA: Lose super. Close on MARK's face. He is in tears.

FRANKLIN: *(Voice over)* Why are we on this journey then? . . . This is no place for fools and their guardians!

MARK: ''What choice was there? He was a man, of age to be tried in a court of law when he burned a widow's building in a fit of anger . . . His sentence would have been the madhouse, chained to the walls and floors like a dog . . . fed in a bowl kicked towards him at indifferent times of the day . . . wallowing in his own manure . . . forgetting speech and instinct . . . trapped by the deep night of incompleteness.''

WIDEN SHOT: On MARK and first blacksmith. MARK continues dictating, not aware the blacksmith is watching him, deeply moved, no longer writing his words.

MARK: ''We watched over him . . . night and day . . . keeping him prisoner . . . *(His speech quickening with emotion)* without his knowledge he could no longer wander to the river or the lane behind the shop. There . . . was some sacking to be burned . . . some cord from wrappings in the store . . . he was to watch the fire . . . I had an errand to deliver . . . you had gone into the house to close the days' account books . . . mother was in the store . . . in the basement storeroom . . . a gust of wind blew a burning sack beneath the store porch . . . He did not know the dangers . . . or the consequences . . .''

OVER LAST LINES OF DIALOGUE: Faint scream (of mother).
SUPER: Opening fury of a storm — lightening, wind, deluge of rain. Screaming increases, scream on scream.

CLOSE ON: MARK's face, mirroring horror.

WIDEN SHOT: On MARK and first blacksmith. MARK has forgotten he is dictating a letter. Now relates the story directly to the one person who will hear it.

FRANKLIN: *(Voice over)* We need to set an example! . . . We need firm, decisive leadership!

MARK: The roof had dropped . . . the burning walls had fallen . . . and still we heard her screams from the tomb beneath the building . . . In the few moments of the holocaust, my father's hair turned from black to white . . . the flesh of his cheeks disappeared . . . he was staring at the embers, his lips shrivelled . . . his teeth fixed in the grin of the dead . . .

PATTERSON: *(Voice over)* Your kind of law is lawlessness!

MARK: They searched the countryside with dogs, guns and ropes. I hid him in a cave by the river . . . Father . . . gave me two thousand dollars when he recovered . . . a printer whom he knew changed our documents of birth from the name Johnson to Anderson . . . we slept by day and walked at night . . . a hundred and sixty miles . . . to join this trek . . .

FRANKLIN: *(Voice over)* Is there a goldfield where we're going? . . . Is there anything there? *(Laughs harshly)*

PATTERSON: *(Voice over)* Only God has the answer, Franklin . . . I haven't.

MARK: I promised him anything he wanted once we reached our destination . . . mended his clothes, prepared his food, removed slivers from his palms . . . I sang to him and played whatever games amused him . . . but the journey was too long and he became homesick. Three days ago he started back on foot . . . . I pleaded, wrestled with him, but he was stronger than I . . . I had to club him down . . . .

PATTERSON: *(Voice over)* And then . . . .

CUT TO: Wide shot congregation. MARK stands before PATTERSON, in the earlier trial.

MARK: Franklin and Howie saw us . . . I tried to bring him back. But when they left, he struggled again . . .

DISSOLVE TO: Scene of murder in slow motion in silhouette against darkening, stark horizon.

MARK: *(Voice over)* He threw me down and began to run . . . I caught and tripped him . . . struck him on the head with a rock . . . and then . . . he looked at me, and we were equals at last . . . he knew everything in that moment . . .

COLIN: *(Distant voice over)* Kill me, Mark! Please help me . . . Kill me, or I'll kill you!

MARK: *(Voice over)* I stared at him, and he reached for my throat with his hands, pressing and twisting . . . I had to hit him again to live!

ON CAMERA: MARK rises in slow motion over prone body of his brother, picking up shovel as he rises. Slowly he digs a grave. Rolls his brother into it and covers it with spadefuls of earth. Then he leans, kneeling over the grave, and strikes his head against the earth in a rocking gesture.

Ringing sound of metal being hammered.

CUT TO: Wide shot of encampment. Evening, as in opening scene of story.

The blacksmiths are busy. MARK is chained to the anvil, his head lowered as he sits. Near him is FRANKLIN, seated on a barrel, his hat low over his eyes, the rifle in his lap. He will maintain a vigil over the prisoner. In the background, a scene of tension. PATTERSON is brooding beside his wagon. People with food in their hands are standing around, much as they stood during congregation service, their eyes seldom away from the prisoner at the smithy and FRANKLIN. HOWIE brings FRANKLIN a bowl of food. FRANKLIN begins eating, but eyeing MARK. HOWIE goes back.

FRANKLIN: You want some of this? *(Holds out bowl to MARK)*

MARK looks up, startled. Stares at the bowl, his face expressionless.

FRANKLIN: Well, when you're ready, you say so. The concensus is you shall be turned over, living and healthy, to the hangman!

The blacksmiths continue with their work, but are attentive to what goes on around them.

FRANKLIN: You had two thousand dollars when you started?

MARK: *(Head lowered)* Yes. We spent some on provisions. Most of it is left.

FRANKLIN: Have you thought who you'd leave it to? Because you're going to die, you know . . .

MARK: If you want it, it's in a wallet in my back pocket.

FRANKLIN: *(Laughing)* I'm like this country . . . flat, thin, hard . . . but honest!

FIRST BLACKSMITH: Why are you on this trek, Franklin? . . . You're not after gold . . .

FRANKLIN: No, I'm not . . . I've no problems I'm running away from, and I'm not greedy. When I get where I'm going, I'll become a lawman. God may worry about us, according to Patterson . . . but heaven's a long way off, as I see it. In the meantime, somebody's got to protect us from ourselves!

SECOND BLACKSMITH: Everything's sure cut and dried for you, eh?

FRANKLIN: You won't build a country by listening to every

opinion. Whatever the Indian has to say, for instance, is going to cost me some land and wealth I'm entitled to for going out there and sacrificing myself to get it. In the end, it's more important to have pickaxes and railways than to keep criminals alive or to teach grown men to read and write . . .

FIRST BLACKSMITH: I'm just plain greedy . . . but I'll listen to a man who isn't . . . My mother wasn't greedy, an' I can't get over it!

FRANKLIN laughs and rises to his feet to return his empty supper bowl to his wagon. The blacksmiths quickly move to the anvil near MARK and pretend to busy themselves.

FIRST BLACKSMITH: *(To MARK)* He'll kill you before we reach the next settlement!

MARK: I know . . . Promise me that letter reaches my father?

SECOND BLACKSMITH: Don't let him kill you!

MARK: *(Smiles bitterly)* I haven't any choice, have I?

First blacksmith withdraws a packet of food from behind his shirt and slips it into Mark's shirt front.

FIRST BLACKSMITH: Here . . . take this! . . . It's all I could carry out without being seen. He's got the key, so we can only cut the chain apart . . .

MARK: But . . .

FIRST BLACKSMITH: You run . . . keep running . . . don't stop or look back . . . Find the Indians . . . find anybody. They'll help you or **kill** you . . . but at least you'll have a chance! . . . Ready!

284

The second blacksmith begins a rhythmic hammering on the empty anvil.
The first blacksmith pulls MARK up by the handchains until he has them over corner of anvil. The second smith continues hammering, placing a chisel over the hand chains.
Now the hammering becomes powerful, heavy, as the chisel bites through the steel of the handcuffs.

In the background, FRANKLIN approaches leisurely from his wagon, not aware of what is taking place.

TIGHTEN SHOT: On handcuffs over anvil. The chisel cuts through the last link. Mark's hands are free.

FIRST BLACKSMITH: *(Harshly, voice over)* Go! . . . Run! . . . RUN!

WIDEN SHOT: To include FRANKLIN.
He sees MARK bolting away. The lengths of chain attached to his hands tinkling.
FRANKLIN runs for the gun beside his barrel.

MARK scrambles away, running with the panic of a man whose every moment might be his last.

FRANKLIN reaches the gun and is about to cock and raise it. The first blacksmith jumps in front of him.

FRANKLIN: Goddamn you!

FIRST BLACKSMITH: Let him go, you fanatic! . . . He's only nineteen . . . where will he go! . . . If he lives, how will he live?

FRANKLIN tries to get past. The blacksmith grabs him by the arm and holds him.

FIRST BLACKSMITH: If he doesn't live, let him choose the time and place of his death . . . every man has that right!

FRANKLIN: *(Furious)* You fool! . . . I'll have you tried and imprisoned for this!

FIRST BLACKSMITH: No doubt you will . . . but we're the only blacksmiths you have . . . a wagon train needs a blacksmith more than it needs a lawman or a preacher . . . or are you still that certain of yourself?

FRANKLIN draws his gun back and strikes the blacksmith over the side of the head. The blacksmith staggers back, but remains on his feet. FRANKLIN breaks free and runs in pursuit of MARK.

FIRST BLACKSMITH: *(Shouting a taunt)* Never mind! . . . You'll all die! . . . And I'll sit on your graves and laugh!

CUT TO: Wide shot on encampment.
PATTERSON is stunned. The other members of the group are on the verge of exploding with tension. A long silence. Suddenly HOWIE turns and sees the barefoot, shirtless trio of gamblers beside him. He laughs — a nervous, girlish, high-pitched whinny. PATTERSON starts to sing, the others joining in at once.

HYMN:
    Time, like an ever-rolling stream,
    Bears all its sons away;
    They fly, forgotten as a dream
    Dies at the opening day.

    O God, our help in ages past,
    Our hope for years to come;
    Be thou our guard while troubles last,
    And our eternal home!

Sound of first shot in the hills silences them. The sound echoes and re-echoes. They all stand frozen, listening. Another long moment.
Second shot rings out. There is a finalty about it. The congregation wilts.

Loud hammering noise.

CUT TO: Blacksmiths.
The first blacksmith pounds a tempo on the empty anvil. He breaks into a raucous song, stamping his foot, angrily spitting out his own emotions and feelings at the group.

FIRST BLACKSMITH: *(sings)*
 Old Joe Clark's a rough old man
 Mean as he can be,
 He knocked me down with his right hand,
 And walked all over me.

   Git out of the way for Old Joe Clark!
   Hide that jug of wine,
   Git out of the way for Old Joe Clark!
   He's no friend of mine.

 Old Joe Clark he used to be
 The biggest bum in town
 Til Andrew Johnson appointed him
 The marshall of the town.
 He's pull out the wine, he's pull out the breeze,
 And you oughta hear him brag,
 But all good rebels know that he's
 A lowdown scalawag.

  chorus:

When Old Joe Clark comes to my door
He treats me like a pup.

287

He runs my bear dogs under the floor,
And drinks my whiskey up.
He puts his banjo in my hands
And tells me what to play;
Dances with my pretty little girl
Until the break of day.

    chorus:

OVER CREDITS:

WIDE SHOT: on camp.
At first a few, then others of the young men join in the song.
Some start a dance around the fire, delighted for the angry release
the blacksmith has given them.
Others join in handclapping.

Only PATTERSON stands brooding.

The camp begins to resume normal life.

OVER SONG AND CREDITS:

DISSOLVE TO: FRANKLIN against badlands, returning to
camp. The sound of the singing diminishes and dies into silence.

FRANKLIN walks rigidly, a man apart from other men. His
mission accomplished, his hat rigidly and squarely set on his
head, the rifle cradled on his arm.

For a moment he falters, stops, looks back, then continues on.

Fade out.

The End

LEPA

1 FADE IN: Ext. Country Church — Day

Filling foreground, distinctly Slavic in architecture. Sound of an approaching car. Camera pans from the church to show us that it is situated beside a highway. A late model compact car passes the church. Camera follows.

2 CUT TO: Int. Car — Day

NANCY DEAN, attractive, mid-twenties, is driving. On the seat beside her are her handbag and a briefcase which bears the inscription: Government of Canada. Nancy glances at her watch, then returns her attention to the road.

3 CUT TO: Ext. Highway — Day — Travelling p.o.v.

A crossroads with a signpost. As camera moves in on the signpost, we see that some of the place-names are Slavic.

4 CUT TO: Ext. Highway — Day

Nancy's car makes a turn at the crossroads.

5 CUT TO: Ext. LEPA's Farm — Day

Small but well-tended, with a fenced barnyard and a few aging outbuildings. Some old farm implements and machinery are visible near trees at the edge of a field. There are a few clusters of flowers in front of the house. Sound of a car approaching. The front door of the farmhouse opens and IVAN LEPA *steps out, scowling as he shades his eyes against the bright sunlight, peering curiously towards the sound of the car. He is 65, dressed in rough work clothes, powerfully built, with strong Slavic features suggesting the face of the classic peasant one sees in medieval paintings.*

Another angle to include NANCY's car as it stops and she gets out. Lepa steps off the porch. They meet.

NANCY: *(pleasantly)* Mr. Ivan Lepa?

LEPA: *(not truculent but also not friendly)* Yes . . .

NANCY: My name's Nancy Dean. I'm with the Department of Health and Welfare. I'm here about your application for an old-age pension.

LEPA: How come they don't send a man?

NANCY: *(evenly)* Your case was assigned to me.

LEPA: I filled out papers in the spring. It's summer.

NANCY: *(sympathetically)* I know. I'm afraid we've run into a few problems.

LEPA: *(suspiciously)* What kind of problems?

NANCY: *(uncertain)* I'm not quite sure how to . . . *(opens briefcase, takes out yellowed clipping)* One of the people you

290

named as a reference sent us this. It's dated August 24, 1934. *(reads)* "Timmins, Ontario. A shaft collapse at the 600-foot level of the Prettygirl mine late yesterday was responsible for the death of two men. . . ."

LEPA: One! One man. Vladko Olynk.

NANCY: The story mentions Olnyk. It also names you. Ivan Lepa.

LEPA: Let me see. *(takes clipping, looks at it, then quietly)* I was right behind him. We started into that shaft. I heard . . . *(stops)*

NANCY: Mr. Lepa?

LEPA: You watch a thing like that happen . . .

His manner changes. He hands the clipping back to NANCY.

LEPA: *(briskly)* Well, I says, to hell with it. I just turned around and got out of that mine. Didn't punch out or nothing. Walked seventeen miles. Got on a train and left Ontario. So they think I'm dead. *(laughs)* That's pretty funny, eh?

NANCY: *(smiling)* As long as we can prove you're alive.

LEPA: *(smile vanishes)* What you mean, prove? Look at me! I'm here!

NANCY: Do you have any documents we could —

She doesn't finish. LEPA has turned and is stomping angrily towards the house. NANCY hesitates, then follows.

6 CUT TO: Int. LEPA's Kitchen — Day

291

Comfortable, relatively neat, but certainly not luxurious. LEPA enters, furious, crosses to the stove, rattles a pot. There is a knock. LEPA turns. NANCY stands outside the screen door.

NANCY: Can I come in?

LEPA doesn't answer. NANCY opens the screen door, enters the kitchen. They look at each other. NANCY is young and not too experienced. She's not sure how to proceed.

NANCY: Mr. Lepa . . .

LEPA: Mr. Lepa. Maybe because my name's Lepa you think you can cheat me out of my pension, eh? What's your name again?

NANCY: Dean. Nancy Dean.

LEPA: That's not a Jewish name.

NANCY: *(coldly)* Who said I was Jewish?

LEPA: *(short laugh, insinuating)* What's your real name?

NANCY goes rigid with anger. For an instant it appears that she will storm out of the house. LEPA watches her. After a long, cold beat:

NANCY: My grandfather was a Russian Jew. His name was Odinsky.

LEPA: *(softly, vindicated)* Aha.

NANCY: He came to Canada in 1912. The first ten years he was a pushcart peddler in Winnipeg.

LEPA: *(softly)* Your grandfather the pushcart peddler, what kind of man, eh? Was he ashamed of his name?

NANCY: *(evenly)* When he landed in Halifax, the immigration officer didn't know how to spell Odinsky. Or didn't want to. The landing documents were made out in the name of Dean.

LEPA looks at her for a second longer, then fills two mugs with coffee, hands one to NANCY. She nods her thanks, then:

NANCY: You want your pension?

LEPA: I'm sixty-five years old. I got a right to it.

NANCY nods curtly, takes a notebook out of her handbag, jots notes during:

NANCY: What year did you arrive in Canada?

LEPA: 1927.

NANCY: You remember the name of the ship?

LEPA: You think I could ever forget? The *Gdynia*. Polish tub. It sank. I can still smell that stuff they cleaned the floors with. We had to get our heads shaved before they let us go ashore in Canada. Did you know that?

NANCY: *(looks at him for beat, then)* Do you have your landing card?

LEPA: I always used to carry it around in my shirt pocket.

NANCY: Where is it now?

LEPA: In 1929 I put my shirts into a laundry in Winnipeg. My landing card got boiled, washed, hung in the wind and ironed.

He is looking at her, deadpan but barely containing the laughter. It's a test. They can go on formally, with a slight edge of

293

hostility. Or . . . NANCY smiles. LEPA grins. They relax a little.

NANCY: OK, the ship's a start. I should be able to find a record of your entry that way. Now this farm. It's yours?

LEPA: You're damn right it's mine.

NANCY: Then you must have signed some documents after you were supposed to have died. After 1934. Your deed for example?

As NANCY speaks, LEPA's eyes begin to loose attentiveness.

LEPA: *(repeating absently)* The deed . . .

NANCY: Mr. Lepa . . .

7 CUT TO: Int. Barn — Day (1930)

HANYA, about 18, is milking a cow. Her head is close to the animal's flank, so her view is pretty much restricted to the udder. She's intent on her work. Suddenly two hands appear across from hers, grasp the cow's other two teats and begin to milk. HANYA, startled, lets go the teats and almost falls backward off the milking stool. The other pair of hands continues to milk the cow. Apprehensive but curious, HANYA bends down. And finds herself looking directly into the devilish smile of LEPA (as a YOUNG MAN).

HANYA: Ivan?

LEPA: *(mocking, but meaning it)* Yes, my cherry blossom?

She pulls herself together. She's bananas about him, but it will never do to let him know.

HANYA: *(sternly)* You're supposed to be working.

LEPA: I **am** working.

HANYA: Mr. Swystun won't like it if he finds you gone from the fields.

LEPA: He won't care. I told him I was coming to ask you to marry me.

HANYA: You didn't!

LEPA: I thought about it.

HANYA: Please, Ivan, let me do my work. I have to finish here and help Mrs. Swystun get supper.

LEPA: You like cucumbers?

HANYA: *(puzzled)* Yes? . . .

LEPA: Marry me and I'll grow a whole field of cucumbers for you.

HANYA: Don't joke about marriage.

LEPA: Marriage I joke about. Cucumbers I don't.

He comes around the cow towards her, his smile fading. She watches him, torn between uneasiness and wanting him to take her in his arms.

LEPA: *(dead serious now)* Hanya,I want you. I want you for my wife.

HANYA looks at him meltingly, wavering. Then suddenly her glance slides past him. She gasps.

HANYA: Mr. Swystun!

LEPA turns, disconcerted. There is no one. HANYA giggles, darts around LEPA, grabs the pail of milk and runs from the barn. LEPA remains, a slow smile growing.

8 DISSOLVE TO: Ext. Prairie Wheatfield — Day (1930)

Harvest time. Bright hot sun, vistas of ripe grain. LEPA is part of a threshing gang, sweating, specks of chaff glued to his face.

LEPA'S VOICE: We worked on the same farm. About a hundred miles north of Saskatoon. 1930. Some ways it was just like now. Some ways different.

9 DISSOLVE TO: Ext. Saskatchewan Farmhouse — Sunset (1930)

The men are coming in from the fields, trooping across the barnyard on their way to the pump. HANYA and another girl are standing on the back porch of the farmhouse. Just before LEPA takes his turn at the pump, his eyes meet HANYA's. She looks steadily at him, finally smiles. LEPA smiles back, and ducks his head towards the trough. As he does:

HANYA'S VOICE: No!

LEPA'S VOICE: Why not? Hanya . . .

10 CUT TO: Ext. Barnyard — Night (1930)

LEPA and HANYA arguing in the shadows beneath some trees.

LEPA: Why not?

HANYA: Because this is no time to get married.

LEPA: *(manner changes, reflecting)* You know, Hanya, you're right.

HANYA: *(sadly)* I know I am, Ivan.

LEPA: This **is** not time to get married. *(suddenly brisk, urgent)* Not tonight. Marry me tomorrow!

HANYA: *(laughing)* Ivan . . .

Laughing too, he grabs her. She struggles briefly and not too hard, then allows him to kiss her. He holds her close, whispers in her ear.

LEPA: I got the land.

HANYA: You . . . got it?

LEPA: Last week. I went to the land office and picked out the homestead. We build our house, grow the crops, raise kids . . .

HANYA: *(breaking away)* No!

LEPA: *(angry)* What's wrong with you? You don't want to marry me, you just say so. Once. Serious. And then I leave you alone.

HANYA: I . . . don't want to go away from here.

LEPA: And what's so fine about Mr. Swystun's farm?

HANYA: (quietly, pleading) I get wages here. Not much, but I get paid. I have all I want to eat. So do you. Ivan, we could —

LEPA: No! I'm not working for somebody else the rest of my life. Hanya, trees grow on that land I picked out. Trees! In the old country my father had to buy firewood from the "pan." Here we can **sell** it. Our own house, Hanya. Tomatoes we grow ourselves. Milk from our own cow . . . Hanya?

HANYA: *(slowly)* I'm afraid, Ivan.

He reaches for her. She starts into the embrace, then wrenches away and runs from him. LEPA's expression is bereft.

11 DISSOLVE TO: Ext. Wheatfield — Noon (1930)

The threshing gang, LEPA among them, working. LEPA glances up.

From his p.c.v.: HANYA. She is carrying lunch for the men wrapped in a bright-coloured tablecloth. She sees LEPA looking at her and averts her eyes. The other men see her and crowd around her, laughing and joking, helping her unwrap the tablecloth and lay out the food. LEPA walks a little away and stands with his back to the laughing group. We stay in tight on him.

HANYA: *(o.s.) (softly)* Ivan . . .

Angle widens as he turns. HANYA is standing facing him.

HANYA: *(softly)* Yes.

It takes LEPA a couple of seconds to realize what she means. When he does, his face lights up.

12 CUT TO: Int. LEPA's Kitchen — Day (Present)

LEPA, his 65-year-old face glum and withdrawn, in contrast to the elated young man we've just seen. NANCY watches him. After a beat:

NANCY: This farm . . . is this where you homesteaded?

LEPA becomes aware of NANCY's presence.

LEPA: Don't you want your coffee?

NANCY: *(sips coffee)* Do you have the deed?

LEPA: *(flat)* It was in her name. She signed the papers when I was away. It's here somewhere.

NANCY: *(sighs)* Okay. We'll have to think of something else.

LEPA: *(edgy)* What's the matter with you? You drink coffee like it was made of tears.

NANCY: *(patiently)* I'm trying to help you, Mr. Lepa. If you want your pension, there's a certain amount of verification the department requires, and we —

LEPA: *(sudden anger)* You tell your department to go to hell! Like always, the government lies!

NANCY: *(losing patience)* And what else do you want me to tell them? Look, its not that complicated, Mr. Lepa, but we have to prove you're you — a birth certificate, your wedding license, even a voter's lists.

LEPA: I was wrong.

NANCY: What?

LEPA: Jews . . .

NANCY: Now you look here —

LEPA: You're not Jewish.

NANCY: What?!!

LEPA: You're not Jewish. You're one of **them.**

NANCY: All I'm trying to do —

LEPA: You're trying to push me around!

NANCY: *(gets up, angry)* I don't think you know how to live without being pushed around. You're — you —!!!

She clamps her mouth shut and strides out of the room.

13 CUT TO: Int. Home for Aged — Day — Close on DEAN

He is in his late eighties, seated in a wheelchair in the lounge of the home. He carefully bites a chunk off a lump of sugar, holds it in his mouth as he takes a sip of tea. Then he smiles — radiantly, beatifically.

DEAN: So what's troubling you?

Another angle to include NANCY. In the far corner of the room a NURSE is visible, busy with some duty.

NANCY: I didn't say anything was troubling me.

DEAN: Not a holiday. Not even **shabat**. But you're here.

NANCY: *(smiles)* I know, grandpa. I should visit you more often, but —

DEAN: Sha, sha, not a word. One of the benefits of being very old is the ability to accept things for what they are. You come to visit me. A pleasure. Should there be anything else?

NANCY: *(smiling)* Well . . . no.

DEAN: Ah, but there is.

NANCY: *(puzzled)* What?

DEAN: A question. So what's troubling you?

NANCY: I really didn't come here to talk about it.

DEAN: *(softly)* Didn't you?

NANCY: *(burst of exasperation)* This — this boneheaded Ukrainian peasant. This . . . this **muzhik!**

DEAN: In your office?

NANCY: No, a client. I should say an ex-client. I turned his case over to another worker.

DEAN: You couldn't deal with a Ukrainian?

NANCY: He's stupid. And stubborn. And . . . he's anti-Semitic.

DEAN: *(softly)* Ah.

NANCY: I saw him standing there with that flat peasant face, disliking me, maybe even hating me, and I started thinking about you and every other Jew and all the things he and his kind have done to us and, well, all of a sudden I just thought — who needs it?

DEAN: *(almost musing)* You couldn't deal with him.

NANCY: *(surprised, confused)* You're . . . you're disappointed in me.

DEAN: *(shakes head: no)* How could you know?

NANCY: Know what?

DEAN: In the old country . . . yes . . . the distrust, the

antagonism, sometimes even the hatred. But when we got here . . . everything so strange . . . so strange for us both . . .

He bites off a piece of sugar, raises his glass of tea to his lips, takes a sip. His eyes close.

NANCY: You're tired.

DEAN: *(eyes open)* You'll come soon again?

NANCY: Of course.

She kisses him and leaves. The NURSE comes over to DEAN.

NURSE: We'll go upstairs for our nap now, eh, Mr. Dean?

DEAN: *(beatific smile)* So new . . . so strange . . .

The NURSE smiles back, condescending to what she thinks is his senility, and wheels him towards the door.

14 CUT TO: Int. NANCY's Office — Night

In the Health and Welfare Building. Two desks, front-ended together. NANCY is working at one of them. She closes a folder, squinches her eyes wearily. When she opens them, they are looking across at the other desk, drawn to a stack of folders. She gets up, moves around her desk to the folders, looks down.

P.O.V. CLOSE: A folder, reading: LEPA, IVAN.

NANCY reaches out slowly, as if to pick up the folder, then quickly draws her hand back.

NANCY: No, dammit! I'm right!

She returns to her desk, makes brisk preparations to leave.

15 CUT TO: Ext. Truck Cafe — Night

On the edge of town. The parking lot. Trucks, cars, neon. Faint sound of the jukebox inside the cafe. NANCY's compact parked prominently in the foreground.

16 CUT TO: Int. Truck Cafe — Night

Truckers, a sprinkling of ordinary townspeople, not crowded but busy enough to create an impression of liveliness. The jukebox full-blast now, blaring. NANCY is seated in a booth, finishing a cup of coffee. She gets up, picks up her check and starts towards the counter. She stops.

What she sees is LEPA sitting at a table, a cup of coffee in front of him.

NANCY turns away abruptly, starts to leave, stops.

There is something vulnerable, pathetic almost, about the hunch of LEPA's shoulders.

NANCY hesitates a second longer, then makes up her mind, walks over to him, stops. He doesn't glance up. Beside him is a bag of groceries.

NANCY: Mr. Lepa . . . *(jukebox record finishes)* Mr. Lepa . . .

His eyes come up to meet hers. There is torment in them.

NANCY: I . . . I want to apologize for the way I acted the other day.

LEPA: *(abstracted)* What way?

303

NANCY: Mind you, I think you asked for some of it, a lot of it, but there was no excuse for me losing my temper.

LEPA: *(glances sharply at her)* Somebody tell you off?

NANCY: *(smiles)* My grandfather.

LEPA: A good man. I know him well.

NANCY: You . . . know my grandfather? *(confused when LEPA nods)* But . . . when did you meet him?

LEPA: We spoke the same language. I wanted land and he wanted a store. He knew how to get around in the city, so I always went to talk to him . . .

NANCY: **My** grandfather?

LEPA: *(sudden edge)* What the hell difference whose grandfather? He was a Jew, I was a Galician. That's all that matters.

NANCY: *(beat, then)* Yes, well . . .

LEPA: Don't go. I'll buy you a cup of coffee.

NANCY: I just finished one, thanks. *(looks at groceries)* Been shopping?

LEPA nods, his expression pinched and pained. When he sees NANCY looking at him, he turns quickly away.

NANCY: I'll give you a ride home.

LEPA: I already bought the bus ticket.

NANCY: Save it for next time.

LEPA: *(turning to her quiet anguish)* This business . . . alive or dead . . .

17 CUT TO: Int. Mine Tunnel (1934)

A rock-face glistening with moisture, the light erratic, flickering. Water drip-dripping from some unseen source. A little distance away, growing rapidly louder, a man's voice singing a Ukrainian song. The singer comes into frame. He is VLADKO OLNYK, a miner. The lamp on his cap shines directly into the lens, so that it takes a moment to distinguish his features. He is carrying a pneumatic drill.

As OLNYK passes camera, LEPA comes into view, following, carrying two pickaxes.

Another angle. The blackness of the entrance to a drift, and as we see it, the singing stops. Again the silence, the dripping water, the crunch of the men's footsteps.

OLNYK disappears into the blackness. For a moment we are able to see the darting beam of his lamp. Then nothing.

LEPA starts into the black tunnel. But as he does, we hear the first creaking, groaning, grinding as the earth begins to shift and the tunnel caves in in front of LEPA. Debris showers over him. A huge piece of shoring timber fells him. As he goes down:

LEPA: *(shouts)* Vladko!

The roar, rumble and crash as the tunnel completes its collapse. We should have the feeling that anyone in the tunnel is dead, but that LEPA is safe. We remain in the midst of the chaos for a moment, then

18 CUT TO: Int. Truck Cafe — Night

LEPA is sitting, staring into the past. Faintly, a desperate cry:

LEPA'S VOICE: Vladko!

The jukebox starts again.

NANCY: *(gently)* Come on, let's go.

LEPA is drawn back to the present. He smiles uncertainly, diffidently, and gets to his feet.

19 CUT TO: Ext. Highway — Night

NANCY's car in a runby.

LEPA'S VOICE: War. All the time I was a kid, seemed there was a war. I seen two soldiers . . . *(stops)*

20 CUT TO: Int. NANCY's Car — Night

NANCY driving, LEPA beside her.

NANCY: Yes?

LEPA: *(after beat)* When I was about six or seven, I seen two soldiers, they were drunk, they came up to a kid I knew, he was about the same age as me and he was standing on the street eating chestnuts. They took the bag away from him and when he yelled one of them put a bayonet in his back and they just walked away, eating the chestnuts. *(beat, then softly)* I came to Canada because I wanted something here, but I was running away from war, too.

NANCY: *(pause, then an idea suddenly occurs)* You have any family here, Mr. Lepa?

LEPA: I got a sister who goes to church and her husband

who builds expensive houses. I haven't seen them for years. I got a son, Stefan.

NANCY: Oh? Does he live here?

LEPA: Regina. He's principal of a high school. *(smiles)* Principal. Not bad for the kid of a Hutzul, eh?

NANCY: Hutzul?

LEPA: *(smiles)* Ask your grandfather.

NANCY: Your wife . . . has she been dead a long time?

21 CUT TO: Int. Rural Hall — Night (1931)

LEPA's and HANYA's wedding celebration, total Ukrainian flavour. Trimbita (dulcimer) and violin music. Dancing. The feast table, laid out with special wedding cakes and bread, a groaning board of delicacies. Everyone is dressed in his best, but no one wears traditional costume.

We discover LEPA and HANYA dancing, whirling among the guests. In tight on them. HANYA is happy. LEPA looks troubled. HANYA notices.

HANYA: Aren't you?

LEPA: What?

HANYA: Happy on your wedding night?

LEPA kisses her hand. HANYA is embarrassed.

HANYA: Ivan . . .

LEPA: Aren't you?

HANYA: What?

LEPA: My wife. Let's go.

HANYA: Ivan, we can't. Not yet. The gifts . . .

LEPA: Just outside. *(troubled again)* I got to talk.

She glances at him, then stops dancing. They start towards the door.

22 CUT TO: Ext. Hall — Summer Night (1931)

LEPA and HANYA emerge. The music continues, muffled, in b.g. LEPA doesn't know how to begin.

HANYA: Well?

LEPA: The land. I got the land.

HANYA: Ivan, you told me that last year . . .

LEPA: I got enough money to start the house and buy some seed.

It takes HANYA a second. Slowly she turns to him.

HANYA: **Start** the house?

LEPA: I'll earn enough for us to finish it.

HANYA: Where?

LEPA: On the railroad. Cutting wood. I'll earn it.

HANYA: You mean you'll have to go away.

LEPA: Not for a while. Not till we get the house started. Then only for a few months.

HANYA: A few months . . . Times are hard. People out of work. How do you know you can get a job?

LEPA: I'll get one.

HANYA: *(distressed)* You made us quit our jobs here. Mr. Swystun's already hired people in our place.

LEPA: If we stay here, we won't have our farm.

HANYA: Why didn't you tell me before?

LEPA: I . . .

HANYA: You tricked me!

LEPA: I thought I'd have enough money. I though I could get credit. When they told me I couldn't . . . I was afraid you wouldn't marry me.

HANYA begins to weep, silently, the tears running down her cheeks. LEPA, very disturbed, puts his hand under her chin, gently makes her look up at him.

LEPA: Hanya . . . there are only two things I want. My own land, and you on it with me.

HANYA smothers a convulsive sob, abruptly turns and runs back into the hall.

23 CUT TO: Int. Hall — Night

The musicians, beginning to play one of the traditional songs accompanying the giving of gifts. We move from the musicians

to the happy faces of the guests (but **not** to LEPA and HANYA),
then

24 CUT TO: Ext. Prairie — Summer Day (1931)

LEPA and HANYA, seated on a wagon pulled by a somewhat
spavined horse. Behind the couple are heaped their possessions:
clothes, a smattering of furniture, pots, pans, some farm tools.

Silence. And HANYA's stony expression as she stares straight
ahead. The squeak of the wagon wheels, an occasional snort
from the horse. Insects. LEPA glances at HANYA. Nothing.
Again. Still no reaction.

LEPA gets an idea. He doesn't know if it'll work, but it's worth
a try. Anything rather than this plague of silence. He begins to
sing — the song we heard last at the wedding. First softly, then
louder, almost forgetting why he began, beginning to lose himself in the joy of the music.

HANYA gives him a quick glance. She does, after all, love him.
A gesture — resignation, acceptance. A fleeting smile. And then
she is also singing. Softly, so softly that at first LEPA doesn't
hear her. Then he does. They're looking at each other now, their
voices rising.

25 CUT TO: Int. NANCY's Car — Night

NANCY driving, LEPA beside her. A silent beat, then:

NANCY: How much of the house did you get built before
winter?

LEPA: Not enough.

NANCY: You found work?

LEPA: I found it.

NANCY: Where?

LEPA turns to look at her.

26 CUT TO: Ext. Northern Woodlot — Winter Day (1931)

Deep snow. Long rows of stacked cordwood. LEPA and three other men are cutting wood on piecework, using axes and hand-saws. One of the men, the MAZUR, is in his sixties. He finds the going rough, has fallen behind the others, looks disoriented and exhausted. LEPA notices, goes back to him.

LEPA: Come on, Stash. They'll take your wood and charge you rent for the ground you stand on.

MAZUR: I don't feel so good, Hutzul.

LEPA: *(concerned, peering at Mazur but keeping it light)* How many times I got to tell you I'm no Hutzul. Galicia's where I'm from.

MAZUR: *(trying to go back to work)* You call me Mazur. You think I'm from Mazovia?

LEPA: What's wrong, Mazur?

MAZUR: I don't know . . . I . . . I get dizzy when I bend over.

LEPA: Don't make me laugh. The only thing a Mazur likes better than bending over is laying down.

MAZUR: One day, Hutzul, you go too far.

Meanwhile LEPA is looking around, covertly motioning for the other two men to come help him. Even before they get there LEPA pitches in, stacking the wood the MAZUR has cut.

LEPA: What you do then, call in the Polish army?

MAZUR: You think I need them to take care of a Hutzul?

LEPA: You bet, the whole Polish army. They take a look at one Galician standing there and they turn around and run a thousand miles past Krakow.

The old man takes a vicious swipe at a log with his axe. LEPA, stacking wood, grins unnoticed at the furious MAZUR.

27 DISSOLVE TO: Ext. Mine Pithead — Winter Day (1931)

Activity of some sort, preferably a shift change.

LEPA'S VOICE: The cordwood was cut and they laid us off. I had to go further away from home to find work. We stuck together, me and the old man.

28 CUT TO: Int. Crude Bunkhouse — Winter Dawn (1931)

LEPA sets out tea he has brewed, eggs he has cooked over a wood-burning stove, hacks hunks of bread off an enormous loaf. He glances towards a double-tiered bunk. The MAZUR is lying on the lower section, asleep. LEPA advances on him, shakes him.

LEPA: Wake up, Mazur! The bolsheviks have taken Warsaw!

The MAZUR begins to wake up, terrified. LEPA laughs. As he realizes what's happening, the MAZUR becomes livid.

MAZUR: One day you go too far!

LEPA: I could've said the Pope died, but you got a weak heart.

MAZUR: Try to talk to a Hutzul.

LEPA: Galician. Breakfast is ready.

The MAZUR gets out of the bunk and goes over to the crude wooden table where the food is laid out. LEPA follows, taking a letter out of his shirt pocket.

LEPA: Stash . . . I got a letter from my wife. She . . . I want to go see her.

MAZUR: I got four days holiday coming. Go home.

LEPA: You'll take my shift?

MAZUR: Did you have to wake me to ask that?

LEPA: *(moved, covering)* Try to talk to a Mazur.

They look at each other for a second, both close to tears, then embrace warmly and we

29 CUT TO: Ext. Prairie Highway — Winter Day (1931)

LEPA gets off a bus and strikes out across a barren, snow-covered field.

30 DISSOLVE TO: Ext. LEPA's House — Winter Day (1931)

Amid lightly wooded surroundings — a partly finished, crudely constructed cabin and, a little distance away, a "barn": little more than a leanto sheltering a single cow. Smoke is coming out of the cabin stovepipe. LEPA enters frame, walking out of the woods, stops, then starts to run towards the house.

31 CUT TO: Int. LEPA's House — Winter Day (1931)

Unfinished, the roofless portion covered only by a sheet of badly secured tarpaulin which flaps in the gusts of wind. HANYA is busy plastering chinks in the log wall with a gooey mud mixture. She is wearing heavy clothes against the cold. LEPA bursts into the room and stops, looking at HANYA. She turns to him, shock submerging the joy she wants to show. LEPA closes the door and starts towards her. Halfway across the room he lunges towards her. Passion bludgeons the gentleness out of him. He seizes her, begins to tear at her clothes.

HANYA: *(half-responding, half-frightened)* Ivan . . .

32 CUT TO: Ext. LEPA's House — Winter Night (1931)

A crisp, windless night. Smoke climbs from the stovepipe, vaporizes and hangs immobile against the cold, dark sky.

33 CUT TO: Int. LEPA's House — Winter Night (1931)

HANYA is peeling potatoes. LEPA is inspecting the plastered walls, appraising what must be done.

HANYA: *(very evenly)* When do you have to go away again?

LEPA: *(not looking at her)* Tomorrow. *(beat)* Next month I think I get work on the railroad. I hear they want to build a spur line.

HANYA: I wish . . .

She turns back to her potatoes.

LEPA: You know how tough things are. I can't stay.

HANYA: I know that. I wish . . . I had some neighbours.

LEPA: *(studying the walls)* There's a lot to do here. And the cow's going to have a calf.

HANYA: *(wheels angrily)* You're not listening to me!

LEPA: *(turns towards her, equally angry)* What can I do? There's no place for you where I work! I can't **make** a neighbour for you like I make a table or chair! *(anguished, frustrated)* What you want from me? We get sent to jobs nobody else will work at. We get land that's too dry or too cold or too rocky to farm. And we're supposed to get down on our knees and thank them.

HANYA: Keep talking like that and they'll send you back to the old country.

LEPA: Let them try. I'm not a horse they can beat or a wheelbarrow they can shove around. I'm a man!

HANYA: *(hard, angry)* Some man! Your sister doesn't cut trees and mix mud plaster to keep from freezing.

LEPA: My sister. You want me to be like **her** husband? Dmitro falls down in front of them and licks their shoes and says please sir I can cut a board straight sir, please can I build a house for you sir? He joins a church and prays for kids he'll never have. What kind of life is that?

HANYA: *(flaring)* It's better than —

She bites her tongue and turns back to the potatoes, close to tears. LEPA, disturbed, moves to her side, strokes her hair clumsily.

LEPA: We'll have a roof soon. *(HANYA nods)* It won't be long.

HANYA: I don't mind we don't have a roof. I —

She breaks off. LEPA looks at her for a second, then goes to a rough wooden chest, opens it and takes out a battered mandolin. He strums a chord or two, then begins to sing the wedding song we've heard before — looking at HANYA, hoping to draw her in, start her singing, raise her spirits. A few bars, and he stops. It's not working. In the silence:

HANYA: Ivan . . . I can't take being alone.

34 CUT TO: Int. NANCY's Car — Night

NANCY driving, LEPA beside her, lost in thought, expression tortured with memory. NANCY flashes him a compassionate glance.

NANCY: Mr. Lepa . . .

LEPA: *(savagely)* What do **you** know?

NANCY: *(rocked)* What? . . .

LEPA: *(angrily)* Like the Queen of England. You sit. You look. You don't see nothing. I asked for a pension. I'm not selling no confession.

NANCY: *(responding to his anger)* And I'm not buying one!

LEPA: Then give me my pension and get off my back!

NANCY: Mr. Lepa if you have family living in Canada, you'll get your pension . . .

LEPA: You're damn right I'll get it . . .

NANCY: **I'm** talking! *(beat)* I've turned your case over to another worker. For a little while I . . . *(stops)*

LEPA: What?

NANCY: *(cold)* The worker's name is Telford. He'll be contacting you in due course.

LEPA: *(sneering)* Telford. What did **his** name used to be? Telinsky?

NANCY sets her expression and drives, stony gaze ahead. LEPA, knowing he has gone too far, glances at her, embarrassed, ashamed.

LEPA: Stop. Please. I am getting out.

NANCY jams on the brakes.

35 CUT TO: Ext. Highway — Night

NANCY's car stops. LEPA gets out, reaches back in for his bag of groceries. For a moment it seems that he will say something. Then he closes the car door and begins to walk. NANCY looks after him for a moment, then makes a U-turn and drives away in the opposite direction.

36 DISSOLVE TO: Int. LEPA's Kitchen — Night

Darkness, the lonely sound of a cheap alarm clock ticking. The screen door opens. LEPA's figure is silhouetted. He crosses to the table and deposits the bag of groceries without turning on a light.

Far in the distance a diesel locomotive whistle sounds. LEPA turns slowly in the direction of the sound.

37 CUT TO: Ext. Field — Winter Day (1931)

Trudging through the snow towards camera: the STRANGER,

317

bearded, carrying a crude wooden cross over his shoulder, the fixity of his eyes fanatical yet childlike.

38 CUT TO: Int. LEPA's Kitchen — Night

Again the mournful sound of the diesel. A beat. Then:

LEPA: Hanya, I—

39 CUT TO: Ext. LEPA's House — Winter Day (1931)

Silence. HANYA, bundled up in a cumbersome, heavy coat, is carrying hay and water to the lean-to barn. On the way she glances across the field and stops, looking.

What she sees is the STRANGER, carrying his cross, advancing towards her.

HANYA watches, torn between curiosity and a vague apprehension.

The STRANGER reaches her. Or almost. While he is still fifteen or twenty feet away, he stops, smiling vacantly, and calls across the distance between them as if it were a quarter-mile.

STRANGER: Praise be to God, sister. Is your man home?

HANYA: No.

The STRANGER stares at her. His unflinching gaze annoys and frightens her.

HANYA: What do you want?

STRANGER: I serve the Lord.

HANYA: Yes?

STRANGER: You have wood to split . . . work . . . something . . .

HANYA: Nothing while my man's away.

STRANGER: I serve the Lord.

HANYA: Nothing.

STRANGER: Shelter . . . I . . .

He trails off. HANYA remains silent, adamant. The STRANGER shrugs confusedly and turns away. He starts to retrace his steps across the field, carrying the cross awkwardly, ridiculously, under his arm.

HANYA stares after him, remorse nibbling at her adamancy.

The STRANGER continues to walk away. His figure grows smaller, beginning to blend with the steely horizon, the dark patches of frozen trees, and the deepening gloom of a winter afternoon.

HANYA puts down her water bucket and starts after the STRANGER.

HANYA: Wait!

The STRANGER hears her, turns. When she sees that he has heard and is returning, HANYA waits.

40 DISSOLVE TO: Int. LEPA's House — Winter Day (1931)

The STRANGER is plastering the log walks. HANYA is preparing food. The atmosphere is one of companionable silence. There is the sound of foot-stamping outside. HANYA looks up, startled. The STRANGER, oblivious in some world of his own, notices nothing. HANYA moves towards the door.

HANYA: *(softly)* Ivan?

The door is flung open and LEPA strides in, a hopsack bag of groceries slung over his shoulder. HANYA reaches out to him happily. He is about to take her in his arms when he sees the STRANGER. LEPA pushes HANYA away and drops the bag. Groceries spill out unheeded across the floor. LEPA stares at the STRANGER.

HANYA: I didn't expect you home till the end of the month.

LEPA: *(harshly)* Yeah. Looks like it. *(to STRANGER, shouting)* Who the hell are you? What are you doing here?

The STRANGER is frightened. He reaches for his jacket, then scurries for the water bucket, picks it up and starts towards the door as if he intends to fetch water.

LEPA: Put that pail down! *(STRANGER does so)* Get out of my house!

HANYA: *(frightened)* Ivan, it's not what you think! He came looking for work. He doesn't sleep in the house, he stays in the barn . . .

STRANGER: I serve the Lord.

LEPA looks at him for a second longer, then turns slowly, deliberately, to HANYA. The STRANGER, paralyzed now, watches.

LEPA: You take what belongs to you and go to hell with him.

HANYA: *(desperate)* It's not that way . . .

LEPA: You're not my wife!

HANYA: Ivan . . .

LEPA slams his clenched fist down on the kitchen table, making the dishes and pots jump.

LEPA: Get out!!

HANYA: But I'm telling you —

LEPA: Out!!

The STRANGER hurries through the door, buttoning his jacket as he goes. He's so frightened that he neglects to close the door behind him. HANYA picks up her jacket. She is weeping.

HANYA: I don't want to go . . .

LEPA remains furiously silent. HANYA comes to him, embraces him. He's a block of stone. She slides down his body, arms encircling him, until she is crumpled on the floor.

HANYA: *(weeping)* Please, Ivan . . . Let me stay . . . please!

Another stony beat. LEPA disengages himself from HANYA's clutching hands, crosses to the door, kicks it shut. He stares at HANYA for a moment, then goes to the table, sits down, covers his face with both hands.

41 DISSOLVE TO: Ext. Scrub Brush — Winter Dusk (1931)

The STRANGER trudges through deep snow. He stumbles over a hidden branch, almost falls, then regains his balance.

42 DISSOLVE TO: Ext. Railway Embankment — Winter Night (1931)

The STRANGER emerges from woods to the edge of a steep bank, at the bottom of which is the railroad track, plowed clean of snow. The STRANGER slides down the snow-covered bank to the tracks and begins walking between the rails, clapping his hands together in rhythmic action to keep them warm. It is snowing.

Sound of an approaching steam locomotive. The whistle blows.

The STRANGER stops, confused, not sure where the sound is coming from. Realizing he is in danger, he crosses himself and beings running down the tracks. Another blast of the train whistle, now nearer, and the STRANGER turns in total confusion now and runs in the opposite direction. The yellow light of the locomotive, blurred by snow and darkness, becomes visible, bearing down on the STRANGER. He begins to scramble frantically up the steep bank beside the track.

Another angle, close on the bank, to show the STRANGER scrambling, soft snow giving way under him. The train, o.s., rumbling closer. The STRANGER seems to be making progress. Suddenly, in a swirling white avalanche, he disappears from frame with a soft despairing cry which is immediately lost in the roar of the passing train.

As the sound of the train dwindles, camera pans down to the tracks. The body of the STRANGER lies like a shapeless bundle of rags next to the track, snow from the wake of the train eddying about him.

43 DISSOLVE TO: Int. LEPA's Kitchen — Night

LEPA stands where we saw him last, remembering. The distant ournful sound of the diesel is repeated. LEPA closes his eyes.

44 *CUT TO: Ext. Home for Aged — Day*

NANCY is pushing DEAN in his wheelchair across a broad lawn. DEAN holds a photo album on his lap, and though we're aware of it, our attention should not yet be especially focused on it. They reach a pleasant glade with a bench.

NANCY: Here?

DEAN: Why not?

She stops the wheelchair, sits down on the bench. DEAN is watching her.

DEAN: So what does it mean?

NANCY: So what does what mean?

DEAN: So never once since you were a little girl have you asked so many questions. And suddenly now . . .

He waits and watches her shrewdly while she gathers her thoughts.

NANCY: I don't know. I . . . my boyfriend, his family came from Scotland.

DEAN: Why do I think they're Icelanders?

NANCY: *(smiling)* That was Carl. Two years ago, grandpa. **Bob's** people are from Scotland.

DEAN makes a bemused gesture, accepting.

NANCY: You're not going to ask me why I don't find a nice Jewish boy?

323

DEAN: No . . . Who can legislate romance?

NANCY: My mother, for one.

DEAN: Your mother . . . and if you ever say a word to her I'll deny everything . . . your mother went with a Frenchman from St. Boniface before she met your father. So what's your Scotchman got to do with your sudden curiosity?

NANCY: Scot, Grandpa, they prefer to be called Scots.

DEAN: Listen, when I was a pushcart peddlar in Winnipeg I was called a lot of things I didn't prefer. *(beat)* Your "Scot"?

NANCY: His family came to Canada in the 1820s. They were in Ontario for a long while, then they moved out here. He knows stories about them from a hundred years ago. Oh, I know where we came from, and when, and why, but . . . nobody ever told me stories about us.

DEAN: *(dry)* Nobody ever asked.

Rueful smile from NANCY. DEAN gives her a small smile in return and opens the photo album.

DEAN: My brother loved pictures. Your uncle David's father. He took some of these himself. Some he collected. When he passed away he left this book to me.

45 CUT TO: Insert — Photo Closeups

As album pages are turned, we see a series of Eastern European Jewish immigrant photos from the early 1900s: shipboard, arrival, someone beside a pushcart, someone beside a larger, horse-drawn wagon, a tiny store, etc. — poverty tempered by upward mobility.

DEAN: *(o.s.)* The **stetls** we came from, poor, you wouldn't believe the poverty. We were cold all winter, we were hungry all the time. So when we were finally able to scrape together enough money for passage on one of those crowded, dirty ships, terrible as they were, for us it was like walking through the gate to the kingdom of heaven. And here, this tough, hard land with a climate even more vicious than the old country, the people staring at us like we were some kind of freaks, making fun of the way . . . Listen, do you know what it's like to be the only one on a whole street of people wearing a long black coat and your hair curling down around your ears in a funny way? Have you any idea what it's like to try to get directions or ask for something you need when you can't speak more than a word or two of the language? We made up our minds then that our children would never have to endure what we did, and from the pushcart and the little store we sent them to university to become lawyers, doctors . . .

46 CUT TO: Resume Two Shot — DEAN and NANCY

DEAN looks up from the album with a slight smile at NANCY.

DEAN: . . . Fancy government workers.

NANCY: *(smiling)* Not so fancy.

DEAN: A car to drive. White bread to eat. You know, the memories that particular kind of dark bread brings back . . . All the years I've lived in this country, I could never bear to eat it again. *(sighs, motions to album)* Want to take this along?

NANCY: Could I?

DEAN: Look at it, we'll talk some more soon. *(beat)* How's your Ukrainian friend?

NANCY: *(knows what he means but plays puzzled)* Ukrainian friend?

DEAN: The one you told me about the other day. The old farmer.

NANCY: What made you ask about **him**?

DEAN: You were angry. I thought he might be part of the reason you're getting interested in who you are.

NANCY: That stubborn, bad-tempered old man, he— *(shakes head angrily)* I don't want to talk about him.

DEAN: He's been here a long time?

NANCY: 1927.

DEAN: *(nods)* It was hard enough in the city. The ones who lived on the farms . . . the loneliness, the memories . . . Don't judge him too harshly, child.

NANCY: How can you be so tolerant?

DEAN: What's your friend's name?

NANCY: Stop calling him my friend . . . Lepa. He doesn't like Jews.

DEAN: No, so can I say with any honesty that all my best friends are Ukrainian?

NANCY: You know what I mean. The anti-Semitism, it's, well, it's inbred in people like Lepa.

DEAN: You think Mr. Lepa ever took part in a pogrom? You think he ever hurt a Jew?

NANCY: That's not the point.

DEAN: *(softly)* What is the point?

47 CUT TO: Int. Historical Museum — Day

P.O.V. TRAVELLING: Rows of everyday objects from the past: clothes, tools, furniture, etc., with emphasis on objects from the 1930s.

NANCY walks among the artifacts, stops in front of a photographic display.

P.O.V. PAN: over the photographs. Immigrants at manual work, families in front of sod houses, the hardship of their lives indelible in their faces.

48 CUT TO: Ext. LEPA's House — Day

LEPA emerges from the house carrying a sheet of glass. He pauses as he hears the sound of a car.

NANCY's car stops. The driver's door opens.

LEPA takes the glass to a rickety wooden table. In tight on him as he begins to cut a piece for a window pane. The legs of the table are wobbly, and LEPA is having trouble holding the glass steady and cutting it. A pair of hands enter frame, help hold the glass steady. Angle widens to show NANCY. LEPA finishes cutting the glass, then looks up.

NANCY: Did you use a walking plow when you first farmed this land, or were they from earlier?

LEPA: What do you know about walking plows?

NANCY: I saw one in the museum.

LEPA: Museums. I bought a harrow in 1932 for seven dollars. Last year they pay me fifty, take it away from me and put it in a museum. Fifty dollars!

NANCY: We've got to find some way to prove you were alive after 1934.

LEPA: I thought you gave up on me.

NANCY: So did I.

LEPA: Want some coffee?

NANCY: *(shakes head: no)* What year did your wife die?

LEPA: 1933. Right after my son was born.

NANCY: Did you raise the boy yourself?

LEPA turns abruptly and walks several paces away, stands with his back to her. Nancy follows.

NANCY: Mr. Lepa . . . if I said something . . .

LEPA: *(turning to her, tortured)* I couldn't raise him, I couldn't! This goddam place in the middle of the depression, this place — it killed her and it would've killed me if I'd stayed.

NANCY: *(softly)* Your son? . . .

LEPA: The railroad. I got my job on the railroad.

49 CUT TO: Ext. Railroad Section — Summer Day (1934)

In the bush, a group of section hands laying track through a cleared right of way. Establish, then find LEPA and the

MAZUR. LEPA is driving spikes, the MAZUR holding. LEPA miscalculates. His sledge glances off the spike.

MAZUR: Hey watch out! You try to drive me into the ground?

LEPA: You think I don't know the difference? The spike ain't wearing a hat.

MAZUR: One day, Hutzul . . .

LEPA laughs and raises his sledge. As it descends,

50 CUT TO: Ext. Railroad Junction — Late Summer Afternoon (1934)

Little more than a switch point, with a crude shack, a cement platform, a few freight cars on a siding together with a caboose containing the kitchen for the section gang.

A large handcar enters shot and stops. The section hands we saw earlier get off the handcar. The MAZUR and one or two others walk off. LEPA's attention is caught by something out of frame, as is the attention of a couple of other SECTION HANDS.

What they see is a frightened group of East European IMMIGRANTS, huddled together and peering confusedly around from the cement platform, their belongings heaped at their feet.

LEPA and the two SECTION HANDS continue to look at the Immigrants.

HAND ONE: *(contemptuous snort)* Look at them. Fresh off the boat. Somebody ought to tell them we got a depression here.

HAND TWO: They'll find out soon enough.

HAND ONE: Hey, you think they've been brought in to take our jobs?

HAND TWO: Na. They're off for homesteads.

LEPA slips away quietly and hurries towards the caboose.

The immigrant group. Young children are crying, frightened and confused mothers trying to soothe them, the men standing about unhappily, powerless to assert themselves in this alien new world.

LEPA emerges from the caboose carrying bowls and spoons, followed by the COOK carrying a pot of stew.

The immigrants are hungry. The children spring forward gleefully as the COOK begins to ladle out stew. The women are effusive, the men quietly grateful. LEPA laughs and jokes with them in Ukrainian. Suddenly he sobers, puzzled, looking towards the shack.

Just outside the door the MAZUR is standing disconsolately, looking towards LEPA, who strides over to him.

LEPA: Hey Mazur, what's wrong? You forget the words to the Polish national anthem?

MAZUR: Don't joke, Lepa.

LEPA: Lepa? Three years he don't remember I'm a Galician. Now he can't even call me Hutzul.

MAZUR: *(puts out hand)* Goodbye, Lepa.

LEPA: *(apprehensive but clowning to cover)* You're going to the outhouse? *(shakes MAZUR's hand)* I wish you a good trip, a happy stay, and —

MAZUR: I'm going to Kenora.

LEPA: *(dropping his hand)* Kenora?

MAZUR: The foreman just told me. They need an extra hand.
I . . . I told him I didn't want to go . . .

LEPA: I'll talk to him. He'll send me, too. I'll tell him you
and me been working together a long time. Kenora, hell,
Mazur, we'll bust Kenora wide open. *(turning)* I'll go talk to
him.

MAZUR: Lepa! *(LEPA turns back)* They only need one hand.

LEPA: *(returns slowly, then)* When you going?

MAZUR: Right away. There's a highball coming through in
ten minutes.

*A beat. Then they embrace quickly, roughly. Then the MAZUR
turns and walks away.*

LEPA: *(calls after him)* Hey Mazur! *(MAZUR turns)* Write
me a letter sometime.

MAZUR: *(calls)* You know I can't write.

*He turns and continues away. LEPA watches him go, the sense
of loss heavy in his expression.*

51 CUT TO: Ext. High School — Day

Nancy's car pulls into the parking lot.

52 CUT TO: Int. Principal's Office — Day

Close on STEFAN, smiling, standing beside his desk. He is in his mid-forties, a high school principal.

STEFAN: Dead? You must be joking.

Another angle to include NANCY, seated, smiling.

NANCY: Fortunately I am.

STEFAN: *(shakes head, bemused)* My father. You might know something like this would happen to him. And of course he wouldn't come to me for help.

NANCY: He didn't know he needed help until a few days ago.

STEFAN: He still wouldn't have come. Imagine that. Officially dead since 1934. Not funny — but it is, you know? *(shaking head again)* Well, what can I do?

NANCY: Your birth certificate for a start. And then what would really help is one recorded detail after 1934. Anything documented that proves he didn't die.

STEFAN: You see the trouble is I didn't see much of him for a long time after I went to live with my aunt and uncle. What about the national registration during the war?

NANCY: He says not. He says he was on the move too much.

STEFAN: Figures. He was on the move all right. And the kind of jobs he had, nobody asked any questions. For years, trying to get enough cash together to go back to that beloved farm of his. I . . .

He stops. The LEPA reveries. Oblivious.

NANCY: Mr. Lepa?

STEFAN: *(out of it, quick smile)* Sorry. I was just thinking about the day he left the farm. I should say, the day **we** left. I don't actually remember it, of course, I was just an infant, but I've heard my aunt tell the story so many times . . .

53 DISSOLVE TO: Ext. LEPA's Cabin — Winter Day (1933)

LEPA at the door, holding a padlock. He hesitates a moment, then hooks the lock through the hasp, clicks it shut. He walks away from the cabin, stops, turns.

Wider view. The windows are boarded up.

LEPA takes a final look, turns and trudges through the snow. Past him we can see MARINA, LEPA's elder sister, late twenties, and her husband DMITRO, a little older. MARINA is holding a baby. Behind them is a 1933 sedan.

54 DISSOLVE TO: Int. DMITRO's Car — Winter Day (1933)

DMITRO driving, MARINA on the front seat beside him, holding the baby. LEPA is sitting in the back seat.

DMITRO: Ivan . . . you're sure you don't want to come with us?

LEPA: How would I live?

MARINA: In our house.

LEPA: Times are getting worse. Who's gonna give me a job? *(to DMITRO)* You?

There is an uncomfortable silence. Then:

LEPA: Anyhow, I don't like to live in a city.

MARINA: Not even to be close to your son?

LEPA: *(sudden flare)* Just don't sell him to the priests, you hear?

MARINA: And just what do you mean by that?

LEPA: You wait till he's old enough to make up his own mind.

MARINA: If **you** spent a little more time in church, maybe you wouldn't be as bad off as you are now.

DMITRO: *(gently)* Marina . . .

MARINA: Godless!

DMITRO: Marina!

LEPA: *(pause, then)* Could I . . . hold him?

MARINA's harsh expression softens. She glances down at the baby, then at LEPA, then hands the baby into the back seat. LEPA clasps the baby to him. A moment later DMITRO puts on the brakes.

55 CUT TO: Ext. Small Prairie Town Railroad Station — Winter Day (1933)

DMITRO's car comes to a stop.

56 CUT TO: Int. DMITRO's Car

LEPA is still holding the baby, oblivious.

DMITRO: *(quietly)* Ivan . . .

LEPA nods slowly. He hands the baby back to MARINA. DMITRO twists around, reaches over the back seat, holds out his hand. LEPA takes it.

MARINA is hunched over the baby. She chokes back a sob, and now we see she's crying.

MARINA: You . . . take care of yourself, Ivan.

LEPA: Yeah.

Clumsily, swiftly, he presses his cheek against the shawl covering her hair, then opens the car door.

57 CUT TO: Ext. Railroad Station (1933)

LEPA gets out of the car and closes the door. The car pulls away. LEPA looks after it. Camera moves in on him until he is framed in a close-up.

58 MATCH DISSOLVE TO: Ext. LEPA's Farm — Day — Close on LEPA

The old man, glowering, quietly angry.

LEPA: You went to see my son.

Angle widens slowly to include NANCY. LEPA is holding a pitchfork. They are standing near a compost heap. LEPA has been filling a wheelbarrow.

LEPA: **My** son. Without my permission.

NANCY: *(quietly)* I didn't know I needed it.

LEPA: You asked him questions.

NANCY: Yes.

LEPA digs the pitchfork angrily into the compost heap, transfers a forkful to the wheelbarrow, then holds the fork pointed vaguely in NANCY's direction.

LEPA: *(furious)* Why?

NANCY: *(also angry)* Because I damn well had to!

This seems to satisfy LEPA. He nods, lowers the pitchfork.

LEPA: How did he look?

NANCY: Very well.

LEPA: He's a good-looking boy. You can see that, can't you? He don't look like no Hutzul bohunk greenhorn. Dresses good.

NANCY: Yes.

LEPA: I don't see him a whole lot these days.

NANCY: I know. He wishes he could get over more often.

LEPA: *(shrugs)* I could go to Regina whenever I want.

59 CUT TO: Int. MARINA and DMITRO Kitchen — Summer Day (1940)

As much Ukrainian ambience as possible without becoming ludicrous: embroidery, calendar, pictures on the wall, etc. MARINA, wearing an apron over her Sunday best dress, is taking some luscious-looking bread out of the oven. As she carries it to the table we see LEPA, now almost thirty, sitting at the table, shirtsleeves, no tie.

LEPA: Looks good.

MARINA permits herself a tiny smile — as always affection and disapproval warring in her whenever she is with her brother. She continues to prepare breakfast.

LEPA: Maybe I should go wake him.

MARINA: He gets up by himself.

LEPA: I was hoping he'd still be awake when I got here last night.

MARINA: It was late. He needs his sleep.

LEPA: Marina . . . you think he'll know me?

MARINA: *(beat, then)* It's been a long time, Ivan.

LEPA: I couldn't get here any more often.

MARINA: *(sympathetically)* I know. *(smiles)* Wait till you hear him talk Ukrainian.

LEPA: *(slight frown)* You sent him to language school.

MARINA: Sure I did.

LEPA: With the priests?

MARINA: That's where a child goes to learn Ukrainian.

LEPA: It's not the only place to learn.

MARINA: *(quietly, adamantly)* It's the only place **I** want him to learn.

LEPA: *(rising anger)* I told you not to —

337

MARINA: *(sudden warning)* Ivan!

LEPA follows the direction of her glance. STEFAN, aged 7, is coming into the kitchen, dressed in little-boy best. He stops, looking at LEPA, shyly.

MARINA: Go kiss your father, Stefan.

STEFAN advances hesitantly towards LEPA, who sweeps the boy into a bear hug, raises him in the air.

MARINA: Ivan, be careful.

LEPA: He likes it. He likes the old man to give him a ride.

And indeed, STEFAN is grinning. He is after all seven, and the only reason he wouldn't like what's happening is the potential indignity. In this case, that's no problem. LEPA circles, still holding Stefan aloft, humming a Ukrainian tune, performing a mock dance.

MARINA: Ivan!

LEPA: *(dancing, ignoring her)* You know what I got for you?

STEFAN: What?

LEPA: A present. Something special.

STEFAN: Where?

LEPA: When we finish dancing. Never break a dance in the middle. *(teasing flash at Marina)* Old Ukrainian proverb.

MARINA opens her mouth to protest, decides against it. LEPA hums to a climax, laughing, whirling STEFAN in the air, then sets him down, leads him by the hand to a cardboard box, not wrapped, in the corner.

STEFAN: This my present?

LEPA: Open it.

STEFAN begins to open the box. LEPA can't wait. He helps STEFAN remove the cover. Inside is a toy train.

LEPA: Like it?

STEFAN: Oh yes.

LEPA: Look at it good. Learn all the parts. Maybe one day you work with your old man on a section gang.

STEFAN: Can I run it?

LEPA: Sure. You think the railroad wants its trains sitting around the station?

MARINA: Not now, Stefan. You have to eat your breakfast and get ready. You too, Ivan. You better put on your tie and jacket.

LEPA: What for?

MARINA: It's almost time for church.

LEPA: *(swelling up)* Church?!!

MARINA: *(sweetly)* Church.

LEPA: If you think I'm going into that —

MARINA: *(sharply)* Just a minute! *(to STEFAN, normal)* Stefan, would you go tell your Uncle Dmitro breakfast is ready.

STEFAN: Okay.

MARINA: *(when he has gone)* I know how you feel about the church. You've told me often enough, so you don't have to say it again.

LEPA: Bunch of phony, no good, thieving —

MARINA: Shut up! *(beat, then)* What you do when you're not here is your own business. But you gave us your son to take care of, and we're taking care of him the best way we know how. In this house we go to church on Sunday. We **all** go to church.

MARINA's expression is totally adamant.

60 CUT TO: Ext. DMITRO's House — Summer Day (1940)

The front door opens and LEPA appears, tied, jacketed, and glum. Camera pans him towards a 1939 car in the driveway. MARINA, DMITRO and STEFAN are waiting. LEPA looks at MARINA, starts to say something, smothers it disgustedly, gets in the car.

61 CUT TO: Ext. Ukrainian Church — Summer Day (1940)

We see the church in full shot, and also hear the sound of an Orthodox hymn. Camera moves in slowly on the church, narrowing angle towards the door. Just as the door is closely framed, it bursts open and LEPA emerges. He is fed up. He starts to slam the door behind him, reluctantly reconsiders at the last moment and, laboriously controlling his temper, closes it with exaggerated care. He lights a cigarette, takes a deep drag, then turns and happily, contemptuously, defiantly, blows the smoke at the closed church door.

*62 DISSOLVE TO: Int. MARINA and DMITRO kitchen —
Summer Day (1940)*

The door from the living room opens. MARINA enters, stops short.

What she sees is LEPA at the kitchen table, once again in shirt-sleeves, a glass and a pint of whiskey on the table in front of him. The bottle is about a quarter empty.

MARINA: Your son will be coming in here.

LEPA: So?

MARINA: He'll see you drinking.

LEPA: Men drink.

MARINA: **Men** don't get drunk.

LEPA: I'm not drunk.

MARINA: You will be. Haven't you caused enough trouble today? Now you get drunk in my kitchen in front of your son.

LEPA: I'm not —

He stops. It's no use. He gets up, drains his glass, slips the bottle into his pocket.

LEPA: Marina, what is it? We had the same mother. We were kids in the same house. We speak the same language and I can't make out a word you say. I —

He stops. Her face is expressionless. He makes a helpless, inchoate gesture and stalks out of the kitchen.

63 CUT TO: Ext. DMITRO's House — Summer Day (1940)

DMITRO is washing his car, with care and pride. LEPA bears down on him.

LEPA: You do that on Sunday?

DMITRO: Only day I have time.

LEPA: *(spiteful)* The Lord's Day?

DMITRO: *(glances at him, smiles)* It's not that bad, Ivan.

LEPA: Marina —

DMITRO: Marina has her beliefs.

LEPA: She believes I'm a bolshevik.

DMITRO: You shouldn't have walked out of church like that.

LEPA: I couldn't breathe in there. *(looks at car)* Nice.

DMITRO: Uh-huh.

LEPA: *(brings out bottle)* Little gasoline for the engine?

DMITRO: Not now.

LEPA: Afraid people talk about drunken bohunks?

DMITRO doesn't answer. LEPA uncaps the bottle, takes a long, ostentatious belt. Another.

DMITRO: Put it away now, Ivan.

LEPA: Aha. Ashamed of being a Ukrainian.

DMITRO: Being Ukrainian doesn't mean getting stupid drunk in front of your neighbours. I'm not ashamed. Everybody knows who I am.

LEPA: Because you go to the folk dances? Because you got a Ukrainian tablecloth and a Ukrainian calendar in your house?

DMITRO: *(simply)* Ivan . . . we're proud of who we are, Marina and me.

LEPA: Some proud. I seen the hopak danced in Winnipeg like it was a bunch of sweet Frenchmen doing a waltz. I know a jeweller in Drumheller. Talks all the time about how Ukrainian he is and names his kids Godfrey and Charlotte. You call that proud? You call it honest?

DMITRO: And you, Ivan? How are you so honest?

LEPA looks at DMITRO, then shoves the whiskey bottle back into his pocket.

LEPA: I got things I want, really want. Once there was my wife. Now there's just my land. That land . . . it means . . . I fought for it. I had to leave it. But I'll go back. That's what makes me proud. I want. I can hold my head up to any man and know what's inside my guts. What do **you** want?

DMITRO: I **don't** want to dig ditches, Ivan. I don't want to work on a railroad or in a mine. I don't want to walk behind a plow. Is that so terrible?

LEPA: Painting Easter eggs, giving money to the national

hall, wearing fancy Ukrainian shirts. And saying sweet yessir to every Anglo you see, kissing his — aagh!

DMITRO: If **you** don't care enough about the old things, the stories, the dances, the church, if you don't care enough to keep them alive, that's your business. I do. But I also believe in getting along with the people I live with. This is my country, too. I want to be part of it, get somewhere, be somebody. Is that so terrible?

They look each other in the eye for a long moment. Then:

LEPA: My son . . . I feel like my son, he's . . . I don't know, slipped away from me.

DMITRO: *(softly)* If we hadn't been able to raise him . . .

LEPA: *(softly)* Sure. *(pats DMITRO on shoulder)* But . . . you understand . . . I want to take him back on the land with me as soon as I can.

64 CUT TO: Ext. LEPA's Farm — Summer Day (1949)

LEPA and STEFAN (now aged 16) are working in the fields. STEFAN is happy. He likes the work, likes being with his father. We see it in the grin they exchange unexpectedly in the middle of the work.

LEPA'S VOICE: "As soon as I could" turned out to be longer than I wanted. Stefan was sixteen by the time I got enough money together to start the farm up again.

65 DISSOLVE TO: Ext. LEPA's Farm — Summer Sunset (1949) — Long Shot

LEPA and STEFAN walking home across the fields. STEFAN is a little distance ahead of his father. LEPA stops. We hear the faint sound of his voice as he calls his son. STEFAN turns and walks back towards him.

344

66 CUT TO: Ext. LEPA's Farm — Closer

On STEFAN and LEPA as they meet.

STEFAN: Father?

LEPA: You like it here?

STEFAN: Yes.

LEPA: The work. You like that, too?

STEFAN: Yes.

LEPA: Smell the air. Sweet, clean, eh?

STEFAN: *(smiles)* It's one of the things I like best.

LEPA: I'm going to build you a bedroom in the house. Curtains, varnish on the floor. Just like the one you got with them.

STEFAN: Father . . .

LEPA: *(gestures towards woods)* This winter we'll start clearing over there. Ten acres, maybe fifteen if we're lucky. Pull stumps soon as it thaws and next year we'll take a crop of winter wheat off it.

STEFAN: Father, I've registered for the fall term in teacher's college.

LEPA: *(after beat)* You're not going to stay here with me? *(STEFAN shakes head: no)* But I thought . . . I was sure . . .

STEFAN: I like it here, dad. I . . . you know I do, I told you and I meant it. But . . .

LEPA: You want to be a teacher.

STEFAN: *(quietly)* Yes.

A spasm of pain flickers across LEPA's face. He turns away from STEFAN until it's gone.

LEPA: *(heartily)* It's a good thing. You had a great-uncle, Mikita. He was a teacher in the old country. So I guess it runs in the family. You need money, son?

STEFAN: I don't think so. I saved some working with Uncle Dmitro last summer, and I got a scholarship.

LEPA: *(pleased)* A scholarship, eh? You need money, you let me know. I can borrow, or maybe take a job at the elevator couple nights a week. But you listen now, Stefan.

STEFAN: Yes, father?

LEPA: Don't go running through life hanging onto a priest's skirt.

STEFAN: *(simply)* I believe in God.

LEPA: *(slight beat, then)* Yeah. Sure you do. And you keep on believing. Think you can still come out here and help me during the summer?

STEFAN: Sure.

LEPA: Good. Let's go fix some supper.

He claps STEFAN on the back. STEFAN starts walking ahead. LEPA follows. Only now do we see the full extent of his disappointment.

67 DISSOLVE TO: Int. NANCY's Office — Day

The phone is ringing. The door opens. NANCY enters and answers the phone.

NANCY: Nancy Dean . . . Oh, hello! . . . No kidding. Can you give me any details? . . . It might. It just might. Thanks a lot.

68 CUT TO: Ext. LEPA's Farm — Day — Close: LEPA

Scowling . . . this time because he's embarrassed.

LEPA: Arrested? Me?

Angle widens to include NANCY, carrying her briefcase. They're standing near the porch.

NANCY: You. In 1937. Three years after you were supposed to be dead. Why didn't you tell me?

LEPA: *(evasive)* Must've slipped my mind.

He turns and goes to sit on the porch steps. NANCY follows.

NANCY: How could a thing like that slip your mind?

LEPA: How'd you find out?

NANCY: Your son rememberd.

LEPA: *(quickly)* He doesn't know why, does he?

NANCY: He doesn't even know where. *(sits on steps)* Where?

LEPA: Don't sit there. You'll get dirty.

NANCY: Mr. Lepa . . .

LEPA: *(without feeling)* To hell with the pension.

NANCY: Where?

LEPA: *(sighs)* Vancouver.

NANCY: What happened?

LEPA: You have to know?

NANCY: Not necessarily from you. I'll check with the Vancouver Police Department.

LEPA: Will they say why I was arrested?

NANCY: Probably.

LEPA: I never told Dmitro and Marina. They lent me the money to pay the fine, but I never said what . . . You really have to call them?

NANCY nods. LEPA sighs.

LEPA: Then I better tell you. In case you get the wrong idea.

69 DISSOLVE TO: Ext. Vancouver Square — Summer Day (1937)

A protest SPEAKER is haranguing a group of unemployed LISTENERS. (This speech will continue as o.s. dialogue over succeeding sequences.)

SPEAKER: What are we asking for? Diamonds? Caviar? Gold? No, brothers, all we want is **work**. W-O-R-K. Work. And we're entitled to it. We've got a right to a paycheck. We want to feed our wives and kids and put clothes on their backs and make sure they've got a roof over their heads. That's our **right**! And we are damn well going to take it. Why should the bosses ride around in Cadillacs and have a hundred suits in their closets and throw away food while we have to fight each other for a crust of bread? Well, brothers, we're not going to fight each other any more. We're damn well going to **unite**! We're going to join together and fight the bosses. We're going to tell them we damn well need jobs and if they refuse us again we're damn well going to **make** them give us work. You hear me, brothers? **Make** them. And if it takes force to do it, **we are damn well going to use force!** They've kicked us around too long. They're not going to kick us around any more. We're going to win, brothers, we're going to —

70 CUT TO: Ext. Vancouver Square — Another Angle

LEPA, walking idly along the edge of the square, hears the voice of the SPEAKER, a portion of the dialogue above. He drifts towards the group of LISTENERS, obviously not involved, passing time.

71 CUT TO: Ext. Vancouver Square, Alleyway

A small cordon of uniformed POLICE grouping, preparing to charge. The o.s. voice of the SPEAKER continues.

72 CUT TO: Ext. Square — Speaker and Listeners

Including LEPA at one of the most distant fringes. No one is aware of the impending police charge. It hits them. One POLICEMAN grabs the SPEAKER, who goes on with his speech until the very instant the POLICEMAN knocks him senseless with his billy club at the point of cut-off indicated in the speech.

Meanwhile, the LISTENERS are fleeing, scattering before the police onslaught.

LEPA, directly in the police path, takes the initial brunt of the charge. Two burly POLICE OFFICERS grab him. LEPA struggles.

LEPA: Hey, let go, I didn't do nothin'!

POLICE OFFICER: Shut up, hunkie.

The epithet enrages LEPA. He struggles in earnest now, and is very nearly a match for the two officers. He knees one in the groin.

POLICE OFFICER: *(in pain)* You . . . hunkie . . . bastard! Grab him, Pete!

PETE tries, but LEPA breaks loose. The officer he kneed trips him as he starts away. LEPA sprawls onto the pavement, gets to his hands and knees and begins to scramble away. He almost makes it, but PETE gets hold of his pantsleg. LEPA's belt breaks as he continues to struggle. PETE keeps pulling on LEPA's trousers and they come down, bunching around his ankles, revealing long johns. LEPA manages to get to his feet but is hobbled by his trousers. Nonetheless he tries to run. The POLICE OFFICER hurtles at him, seizes him from behind by the waistband of his long johns.

73 CUT TO: Ext. Square — Close Angle LEPA

There is the sound of ripping material. LEPA's eyes widen in consternation.

74 CUT TO: Ext. LEPA's Farmhouse — Day

The older LEPA sitting on the porch steps, twisted away from

NANCY so she won't see his expression, which is the same embarrassment we have just seen on the young man's face.

NANCY: They put you in jail?

LEPA: For a couple of weeks. 'Til I could get the fine money from Dmitro. That's why I never want Stefan to know. He shouldn't be ashamed of his old man.

NANCY: Ashamed? Because you got arrested for — what, disturbing the peace?

LEPA: That's not what they say. They call it showoff.

NANCY: What?

LEPA: That's what they say. Indecent showoff.

NANCY: *(getting it)* Indecent exposure.

LEPA: That's it.

NANCY: Well . . . I guess it was.

LEPA: It was.

NANCY smiles. LEPA grins. NANCY laughs. LEPA roars. For a moment the laughter rises. Then NANCY's fades. She stares at LEPA, then suddenly turns away. LEPA's laughter subsides.

LEPA: So?

NANCY: *(flat)* I've got some papers in my briefcase for you to sign. It will take a little time, but I'm sure everything's in order. You'll get your pension.

LEPA: We go inside and sign. I got a little rye somewhere. You take a drink with me to celebrate?

NANCY: Sure.

LEPA: *(looking at her)* You mad at me?

NANCY: Oh no!

LEPA: *(quietly)* What is it, child?

NANCY: I . . . All of a sudden, I just, well, I understood.

LEPA: Understood what?

NANCY: Mr. Lepa . . .

LEPA: Say . . . Say!

NANCY: *(reluctantly)* How . . . sad your life has been.

LEPA looks at her for a moment. There is great empathy between them now, very nearly affection. Finally:

LEPA: *(quietly)* No. Not sad. Never sad. Just . . . hard.

They walk up onto the porch. LEPA holds the screen door open for NANCY. They enter the house. The door swings shut behind them.

75 DISSOLVE TO: CU Photos

Ones we have already seen: Ukrainian work gangs, farmers, families in front of sod huts, etc. And over these:

NEUTRAL VOICE: As early as 1801, a few Ukrainians arrived in Canada, part of an English military unit. But it was not until 1892 that they came in appreciable numbers. Between then and the turn of the century, 25,000 Ukrainians poured into the country. At approximately the same time, others from Eastern Europe — Russia, Poland, the Balkans — also made the long journey. They tilled the land, they turned forests into lumber, they drove railroads through virgin wilderness, they hacked minerals out of the earth. They performed the most menial tasks. They were industrious and persistent. Today there are more than 580,000 people of East European origin living in all the provinces of Canada. They are active in every facet of the national existence: industry, culture, science, politics, sports, education. It was a long transition from the earliest days. It was often painful. But it has been accomplished.

76 CUT TO: Ext. Highway — Day — Travelling p.o.v.

Approaching a crossroad signpost — the Slavic place-names we saw earlier in the film.

77 CUT TO: Int. NANCY's Car — Day

NANCY driving, briefcase and handbag on the seat beside her.

78 CUT TO: Ext. Highway — Day

As NANCY's car passes camera

79 PAN TO: Ext. Country Church — Day

From the initial shot, Slavic architecture, filling frame at the end of the pan. Hold on it briefly, then

Fade out.

The End

THE EIGHTIES

George Ryga (1984)   Photo: unknown

MEMORIES AND SOME LESSONS LEARNED

By its very nature, radio is a moment of life instantly committed to memory. Visceral and bold-stroked to arrest attention at all, radio drama has its own conventions and unities. We were becoming, in a relatively short time, masters of this art form when two events combined to divert this development — the advent of television, and the numbing paranoia of the Cold War. The rest, too, is now memory. In time one would hope this ground will be thoroughly examined by scholars and researchers to determine just how profoundly radio drama was to foster the rise of our theatre as a reflection of post-colonial national maturity.

Radio drama was a dominant influence in my early development as a dramatist, and it continues to shape many of my perceptions of theatre to this day.

Reduced to its essentials, radio drama strays very little from the dominant role of the spoken word as both a motivator and poetic interpreter of the human odyssey of spirit and body. And despite many and varied attempts at introducing the magic and bounty of technology, such as stereo, kunstkopft, frequency modulation and non-hiss reproduction, radio drama profits little from such innovations if productions lack sensitivity and intelligence. A radio director simply cannot cheat or take shortcuts behind the screen of technology. It is too honest and austere an art form to tolerate excesses. After working in radio drama for over twenty years now, I would even suggest that radio technology might better serve the creator and the audience with more sophisticated and longer range transmission of simply produced materials rather than invading the production studios and intruding on the passion of the spoken word locked in a process of action and revelation.

Although I have written more for radio than for any other forum of dramatic expression, this work, as far as it applies to Canada, was influenced by only two radio drama directors. In some ways, I must credit them for shaping much of what I subsequently have done in theatre, film, television and in musical collaborations. They most directly taught me discipline, and both the limitations and the almost endless possibilities of spinning out the dramatic moment in theatre. Providing it didn't cost too much to produce, and that it ran a half-hour or hour in duration, with no more than a cut of a minor line of dialogue to come in on time!

I never personally met Rupert Kaplan, who directed a series called *Shoestring Theatre* out of Montreal. A shoestring theatre it was — arid, stripped-down radio drama of half-hour length, overseen by a master craftsman. To this day, a hallmark of my work in radio was his production of *Indian*, with the soaring rages of Percy Rodriquez in the title role.

Kaplan and I never corresponded. He proposed his commissions by telephone, and his notes were given the same way. His notes were gruff, never off the point, and absolutely understandable. I would be asked for corrections only once, and they were to be in the mail the following morning. In addition to his other values, he taught me the discipline of writing through the night.

Then in 1962 or 1963, he called me for a longer conversation that was typical of him. In this call he explained that his program was running out of money. And then he asked if I might consider writing new works with fewer characters — four or three if necessary, two if possible. Peculiar and even artistically repressive as this suggestion might appear later, I was earning barely enough to keep some optimism alive, and welcomed what I considered his concern for my welfare and his ability to provide me with further commissions. So I began reaching outward by turning inward — grasping for the techniques of allegory, the compressions of irony, the possibility of the multi-level line of dialogue, the heightening of reality and dimensions of character by finer selections of place, time and spiritual context, which also made external reality necessary only as a reference point. Released from the restrictions of the traditional unity of time, the will could stray and people a landscape with itself, providing that in the end it returned to alter something in the creator and his audience.

Esse Ljungh was in many respects an opposite to Rupert Kaplan — and this I say with reservations, for Esse was a friend I saw many times while working with him. Flexible and gentle, he stimulated what was already within the dramatist. His concern for originality from within a specific Canadian setting sharpened my appreciation for the regional nature of our culture. He had love for the languages of the country and supported their evolution. He encouraged drama from other sources and classes of society than those abundantly represented in bourgeois culture. And he possessed that rare love of poetry in theatre, without which there is no ignition of wonder.

Deprived of live theatre in my generation by geographic and social location, radio drama became my theatre. Nothing else could have filled that void, for what passed for theatre was not relevant to those such as I. Our experiences were too gaunt. And largely severed by circumstances from heritage which others seemed to have in abundance, one looked more to structure and repetitious variants of folk-songs than one looked to the formal stage. So the human voice became all — ranging over the spectrum of loneliness, alienation, crisis and salvation.

In retrospect, this was not much, for the period of my intense radio drama activity was hardly long enough to be an apprenticeship. The golden age of Canadian radio was at an end, a victim of administrative indifference and the CBC's fascination with television, whose primary impact was to flood our lives with commercial American cultural reflections to the point of suffocation of national expression. Rupert Kaplan departed from us, and Esse Ljungh moved to Victoria to teach.

Esse and I worked together one more time after years of professional separation. He was commissioned to direct a twelve-part series of folk dramas I authored on the early Canadian West. The series evoked strong public support and was to spawn my stage play *Ploughmen of the Glacier*. But it came to life on the eve of a theatre arts conference convened by the CBC in the early seventies, at which the dynamics of radio fell victim to centralism and an urban focus oddly reminiscent of what had occurred earlier in U.S. radio. There were international artists as observers at this conference. One of them — the German documentary maker Peter von Braun, suggested I should look abroad if I intended to continue my career as a radio dramatist. For a time, I shelved his suggestion, feeling that the boisterous and rough-hewn experiment we made would revitalize and excite a national thirst for myth and irreverence. But the edge of innovation was gone, public affairs programing became more dramatically exciting than radio drama, and Esse Ljungh and I were not brought together again.

I relate this as a personal chronology by way of a metaphor for the demise of a time in Canadian broadcasting. We no longer can recreate the conditions which influenced those of us who wrote theatre for radio first. Our traditions in the field have been fragmented, thereby disrupting a continuity of experience.

Radio drama continues to be created, but its outreach and audience fall short of the expectations and excitement it once generated. We lost splendour and, like children growing up with indifferent parents, we had no one to look up to. The resilience and imaginative by-passes we once revealed in the face of budgetary hardships and bureaucratic stupidity have evaporated.

And I wonder if this is not a portent for Canadian theatre itself, with administrators and percentage-splitters from what was a vibrantly creative community moving in to shape or diminish the impossible dream — clipping and grooming it for a consensus that was never asked for, or given.

At such times I remember the advice of my German colleague, who probably rightfully read us out as exporters of primary produce — in cultural values as in other things. It is an uncomfortable and lonely thought.

George Ryga (1986)   Photo: Keith Ledbury

THE PLACE OF THE DRAMATIST IN SOCIETY TODAY

— U.N. Writers' Conference Bordeaux, 1983

After considering the topic of this address, I have serious misgivings as to whether the "place" of the dramatist in society has all that much importance. Surely a state of mind or a condition of heightened awareness might be more useful to examine.

I believe we have to address the question as to whether the dramatist is any more or less than a chronicler of human rituals. Certainly the question bears examination. Even if it blurs the distinction between the dramatist and the novelist. But it would be unwise to deny that confusion within current social realities drives the dramatist to reductive explorations. For above all else, the dramatist must work.

So examination of good and evil, of hope and cynicism, or survival and self-destruction — are more easily manageable when seen in terms of human rituals. The fact that this ground has been rather well covered in the past makes no difference. The allegories are updated. The current environment simply displaces settings of past ages. And overriding all this is fatalism about the human condition. King Lear never learned to drive an automobile, but that does not matter. We have learned nothing new in the passing centuries. Man is man, unchanging and unchangeable.

Forgotten in all this is the realization that much dramatic tragedy of the past resolved itself with the introduction of medication for tuberculosis, venereal disease and alcoholism. Which altered the framework of traditional ethics and the manners and methods of rituals. We emerged as different people, and the range of enquiry broadened to incorporate a materialist grasp on the levers of destiny. Families were no longer ordained as accidental manifestations of God and human sexuality. They were planned within the context of emotions and economics. Culturally nurtured fear and distrust — between man and woman — between one race and another — between generations — had to be critically evaluated and modified to avoid wholesale butchery. In all this, God either perished or took on recognizable human form and functions. More in the manner of a kindly judge with a flowing white beard than a vindictive and unforgiving presence who saw everything, everywhere and at all times. The new God was re-incorporated into ancient rituals, and the new person could, or should have, modified his or her relationship with earth, machines, and natural disasters, which were not the works of fate but understandable dynamics of the ever-changing planet and cosmos that is our home.

This succeeded in only a minor degree, and only in places where political evolution kept pace with human technical advances. Because the new changes possible were not universal, the dramatist in his society faced serious contradictions — particularly in the technically advanced societies, where his role as tragedian and explorer of the human spirit led to personal and social confusion. Using limited information, and labouring under the stress of needing to create, the dramatist narrowed his vision all too often. It became easier to reduce than to expand, to follow the trends of the popular media, which spoke in the language of banality, even as the local and national spirit hungered for dignity and for sensations, in image and language, of spiritual values larger than the mill floor or the commercial sales advertisement.

Political and social confrontations of will and spirit could be reduced to a cynical statement that all politics and social change were corrupting. In essence, this translated into a cliché: that human craving for perfectability was to be distrusted. In the shadows of earth-changing technology, there seemed fewer and smaller reasons why one must learn to struggle for the human right to thought, love and compassion.

And yet, that is only a personal response to high stress. There are other truths so overwhelming that they become less than self-evident because of familiarity. Great drama no longer is the exclusive domain of the dramatist and the theatre. When President Reagan announced last month a proposal for creating and launching laser weaponry into space to create a military machine unequalled in human experience, the great drama of our time was being created on an enormous stage with instant audiences embracing entire continents and nations in its audacity. The drama was tragic and comic when one analyzes the stature of its principal performer against the dark and majestic backdrop of universal annihilation. No play could be written and performed to match the impact of this dramatic production. No play can be written to equal the texture and sub-text of madness so crudely and exquisitely scripted by a man and his counsel skilled in the concept of total reduction of experience, both intellectual and moral. The unthinkable thought over the articulation of which dramatists laboured and tortured themselves over millenia, was simply and easily blurted out — the brute must prevail. Nothing else matters — not man, not art, not even the very Earth itself.

In the face of this, and other lesser hammer-blows racing across the newspapers and video screens of our time, the very definition of drama begins to wither and pale into near-extinction. As does the will of the less hardy. The message seems to be: "We know everything, and it is boring. Perhaps death, in the form of a thousand exploding stars, and ordered by the meanest and least feeling members of the species, will provide glamour and excitement for our one final moment?"

If only life were that simple! If only time stood still, and the dramatist, satiated by the heady sensation of finally being on the winning side, could surrender himself into exalting the demon in our nature. What a feast of exuberant degeneracy that would be! But life is not like that. We cannot sell our souls to the devil for a coin — if for no better reason than that the devil really has no use for us, even if we offer up our souls for a bargain. For we are part of the human experience, and nothing in heaven or on earth will change that.

Life is not simple in this or any other time. And time races on, oblivious to our dilemmas or debates. Nothing stops for our discussions about whether to write for this theatre or that one, or if this is the season to create farce or tragedy in our work. Or whether to write for a lucrative theatre of small but wealthy audiences, or whether to throw our lot in with the nameless millions who, more often than not, forget or cannot pay us royalties for the use of our writings. These are dilemmas of no consequence, for our place is not to ingratiate ourselves with either the brute or the brutalized. It is about all we can manage to give as honest as possible an assessment of the places we came from and the times we lived in.

But that is not a simple act of withdrawal. Quite the opposite. We must take positions, even if this invites danger. But we must also be prepared to leave and move on to new horizons if there is to be the promise of something worthy in that progression. Nothing can be reduced or left to chance. Human perfectability is not the domain of good people, or polite people, who reason carefully in frozen circles. Human perfectability can be found in prisons, on the front lines of the peace struggle, in the kitchen of the beaten housewife, in whose bruises and pain are the first stirrings of hatred which might eventually move to a larger love she never dreamed she possessed. All the brute lives with is the obsession that he must prevail. But the world is peopled in majority by those for whom a place in the sun, adequate food and medical care, and the right to raise families in their image would be paradise. Those of us fortunate enough to live in technically advanced societies must be sobered and stirred by what must seem such simple needs, and the great difficulty in achieving even a few of them in a lifetime. If this passes us, we do not deserve a "place" in society. Nor do we deserve a theatre, by whatever name.

Like an anthropologist, a dramatist or novelist must assume responsibility for his subject, his country of origin, and the people populating it. He must wish and will them to a larger life by translating that life into a spirit soaring above the commonplace. As he must oppose the death or oppression of that spirit. And because the process of a dramatist's work often implies the creation of characters that did not previously exist, with passion and pathos which are not commonplace, yet deeply understood, the dramatist must then come to terms with life not subject to ordinary mortality. What he or she has created will not age or be tempered by time. Will not suffer the ravages of illness or hunger on a daily basis. That process defies the understanding of the brute.

In these characters who never experienced birth lies the seed of optimism in the darkest or most indifferent times. For they are not the makers of a new technology of destruction. They are the record of humanity evolving ever so slowing in an instinctive move towards enlightenment and a state of grace beyond mere animal responses to their surroundings.

In his search for something greater than a fleeting moment of sound and light, the dramatist can endow his community and the wider world with a vision of its own potential for some fingerhold on immortality. This is not a "place" where any of us live. It is a state of being—of belonging to people in their desire to know and recognize what is of them and what is a manipulation of darkness and forces outside them.

THE FRANK SLIDE

HOST: At approximately ten minutes after four o'clock, on the morning of April 29th, 1903, the side of Turtle Mountain came crashing down on the mining town of Frank, Alberta. The scar in the mountain never healed — probably never will. Until the moment of the disaster, Frank had been a boom town — fed by the most productive coalmine in the world at the time. In less than two minutes, the valley under Turtle Mountain was buried under ninety million tons of mud and mountain boulder. The roar of the slide was heard over a hundred miles away. Those who survived were changed for the rest of their lives . . .

UP THEME: five-string banjo in spirited rendition of "Old Joe Clark."

EST. AND FADE UNDER AND OUT FOR: Working-class neighbourhood. Street sounds of passing pedestrians, car sounds, children playing, etc.

PONY: Sure . . . sure it was something to see in them days — the town of Frank. The damned town, with the damned mine under that mountain, and the damned people coming and going . . . going and coming.

Cross fade setting into memory of Frank. Est. Sounds of hammering from smithy. Horse-drawn wagons. Workers on the railway shouting in distance. Low sound of wind.

PONY: Nobody caring about yesterday or tomorrow. Not the storekeepers. Not the mine owners. Not even the miners themselves. I had no English in them days. All I could say was "hullo" and "goodbye." I didn't know how to buy a can of tobacco, so how could I tell anyone what I knew? You see, I was a miner. Not someone taking a job in the mine for a few months to make money for farming or prospecting. I was a miner. I worked with my father and grandfather in the mines of Silesia. The mine owners there *knew* all about mines, and they didn't want any disasters . . . or any coal they could get, left behind. And they wanted *miners* down in the pits, not village boys scared of the darkness. And they wanted all the work they could get from a man or boy for as little as they could pay! So I immigrated to Canada . . .

Fade under and up on street sounds of his residence.

PONY: And today I smoke my pipe on the back porch of my daughter's house . . . and I remember lots of things — some good, some bad. I live on an old man's pension . . . and I wait for death. Some people don't like that kind of talk, but to hell with them! If somebody asks about what I know, I tell them. If not . . . I keep quiet . . . My name is Zev, but they always called me Pony . . . even my daughter . . .

DAUGHTER: *(calling)* Pony — it's five o'clock! Time for your pill!

PONY: *(muttering)* Time for my pill. They give me pills for my heart. There's nothing wrong with my heart. It's my lungs where I got trouble — the same way most miners got trouble . . .

DAUGHTER: *(calling)* Pony!

PONY: But that sonofabitch doctor she got me doesn't want to say anything that would give a working man an excuse to sue those he once worked for. So I got a heart condition, he tells me. And he gives me pills I got to take at five o'clock. What he doesn't know is that I haven't swallowed one of his goddamn pills in over two years. I throw them down the toilet. There is nothing wrong with my heart, except that it's tired . . . same's me . . .

DAUGHTER: *(shouting)* Pony — come on, now!

PONY: *(irritable, shouting back)* Sure! Leave them on the table! *(muttering)* My daughter Sonja knows I throw them down the crapper. She doesn't care, as long as the bottle of fifty pills is empty in fifty days. She's a bookkeeper at the Hudson's Bay store . . . she thinks in numbers . . .

DAUGHTER: *(exasperated)* Pony!

PONY: *(shouting back)* I hear you . . . I'm not deaf! . . . *(muttering)* Goddamn, when you have to rely on younger women to keep you alive!

THEME — UP BRIEFLY. FADE UNDER AND OUT FOR: Sounds of a television set playing in another room.

PONY: Nothing to do . . . nothing . . . They all watch television . . . Sonja, the two kids who'll grow up to be monkeys if they don't learn to read soon . . . and Stewart, the second man . . . the boyfriend. Pete, her first man, took off when the twins were babies . . . I don't like that kind of business, but I don't talk about it . . .

Sounds of car chase and shooting on television.

PONY: Again they're doing it — somebody chasing some-body else with intent to kill or maim. I ask myself — why? And nobody answers . . .

Television sound is turned down.

PONY: On a night like this, when the moon sits like that over the city . . . a big yellow ball, leaking at the edges . . . I am sad . . . alone. Not alone without people. I could not live like that . . . there are always people . . . and kids . . . and all kinds of things for an old man to trip and fall over. It has been seventeen years since I spoke to another person from Czechos-lovakia. I don't think I know the language I was born with any-more. And as for here . . . today — what can I say? My name is Zev, but they call me Pony. When I die, they will bury a Pony, not a Zev . . . even my daughter will not see the differ-ence. *(chuckles)* That is democracy for you — I am equal to a horse . . . a small horse at that! *(thoughtfully)* Don't laugh at a horse — a man working with a horse in the coal mines has a friend. When I think of that, a lump chokes me here in the throat. Those days will never be again. The horses . . . and the men who worked with them under the earth are long ago gone . . . themselves under the earth, and their white bones in darkness forever . . . Except me . . . except me . . . .

THEME — *Faintly in b.g. Rising and fading away.*

PONY: I left a wife in the old country. I was going to bring her and my boy to Canada as soon as I earned enough for a place to live. After that catastrophe in Frank, I made up my mind to walk back to my family. I walked across Canada, right to the water's edge in Halifax. I wore out four pairs of boots and three pairs of pants on that walk. The pants wore out in the crotch from rubbing together as I walked. But the god-damned ocean stopped me. I had no money left for a ship back. So I sat down by the edge of the water and I cried . . . for them . . . for me. I cried that way again when the war came, and I heard they had both been killed by two armies fighting over the village where she and my son lived.

Sound of distant thunder.

PONY: You see, I'm an ordinary man. **They** were ordinary people. Being alive . . . or dying . . . doesn't count for all that much. Hurricanes, earthquakes . . . war . . . they have always been, like that thunder. That slide in Frank, Alberta . . . that was nothing. Life is cheap in war and disaster. A big building falling, or a coalmine caving in, costs money to fix. So if you're rich and have money in the business you worry more about that than about somebody's round-faced uncle getting buried under a thousand tons of rubble. The dead are dead. Nothing can be done for them. Disaster is what the living have, and that's for sure. That goddamned mountain falling in Frank has been on my shoulders an' in my skull for fifty years now. And nothing in heaven or on earth can change that . . . nothing!

Another sound of distant thunder.

CUT TO:

HOST: The Frank Slide was largely a man-made disaster. The rich coal veins inside of Turtle Mountain were mined brutally, and with little regard for human safety or the condition of the mountain. The mountain was unstable. Even local Indian legends made note of this. The mountain was made of limestone in its upper levels, and Cretaceous shales and sandstone at its base. Any disturbance within the mountain would destabilize it. Yet day and night, the coal-seams inside the mountain were dynamited willy-nilly and coal removed in volumes unprecedented in any coalmines in the world at the time, with little respect for proper safeguards or the warnings of seasoned miners who reported nightly phenomena of tunnel ruptures and shifts . . .

CUT TO: PONY's home — present time.

DAUGHTER: *(calling from inside of house)* Pony!

PONY: *(sharply)* Leave me alone!

DAUGHTER: *(shouting)* Where are you? . . . What are you doing?

PONY: *(irritated)* I'm thinking! I'm sittin' here . . . alone . . . and I'm thinking! *(to himself)* So mind you own business . . .

DAUGHTER: Shall I bring you a sweater?

PONY: I don't need the damned sweater!

DAUGHTER: You'll catch a cold . . .

PONY: Who cares? Leave me alone!

A thunderous explosion.

PONY: Just like that . . . underground! Like thunder, and the mine shaft went up and down, as if the mine was a small boat riding a wave. The prop timbers squealed and snapped. Old Charlie, the pit horse, coughed and neighed and ran to the men, he was that scared,

Sounds of secondary explosions and timbers breaking.

PONY: Sides of the mine shaft buckled and big pieces of coal dropped from the ceiling. Everywhere stones and dust fell or were blown out by trapped gas. We were working a coalface seven metres high. Each night, the twenty men I worked with on the shift would dynamite the seam, bringing it down for the day shift to remove. That night, the mountain did all the work . . .

Fade out sounds of explosions and disaster. Fade up sound of human cry reverberating in tunnelways.

PONY: There were twenty of us . . . twenty-one, but I was not counted, led by pit foreman Joe Chapman. Four men at the mine entrance died in the first seconds of the disaster. I was knocked down and pulled towards them by the air being sucked out of the mine. And then it stopped, and I knew the mine entrance was sealed . . .

Fade out sound of cry.

PONY: You see, I was a miner, and I knew even in the darkness and dust what was happening. A hole in the mountain has a language, too, and it speaks to men who can hear and understand. But many that night were not miners. They were workers in the mine . . . that's all . . . that's all they were . . .

Sounds of shouting over sharp tumult of timbers snapping and rumbling of falling coal and rock.

A MINER: *(screaming)* Help me!

ANOTHER MINER: Goddamnit!

THIRD MINER: Oh, God — no!

Voices shouting and screaming fade. Sustain mine collapsing sounds in low b.g.

PONY: There were some miners in the mine that night, but not all. I spoke no English, and Zev Brunovney was hard to spell, so I was hired and paid, but I had no name. The men

I worked with called me Pony, because I always knew which direction the tunnels went, like a pit pony knows. Because I spoke no English, I was not counted among the men on the shift that night . . . or any night. But I was a miner, as my father before me . . . and his father before him! I think that foreman Chapman was alright. I didn't understand what he said when he called the men around him. But I knew he had no idea what to do next. One of the men had a broken leg. The others came out of the tunnels and the dust, the lamps burning on their heads. They were scared . . .

Up sound of mine still collapsing.

MINER: Joe — we've got to get out!

CHAPMAN: Quiet! Everybody quiet! . . . Nothing to worry about now. Seems the worst is over. You okay, Bill? Can you walk?

WARRINGTON: Shit — I can't move. Leg's all busted . . .

CHAPMAN: Stay still, then. One of you go check the entrance . . . you, Halfpint!

HALFPINT: *(stammering)* I . . . I done that already. She's caved in way back . . . and . . . and . . .

CHAPMAN: And what? Speak up, man!

HALFPINT: It may be the way my light worked . . . but . . . there's water . . . comin' in under the rockfall!

CHAPMAN: Bullshit! The only water outside the mine is the river . . . and no goddamned river flows up the side of a mountain!

Fade down conversation growing more agitated.

PONY: I knew something more serious than this accident in the mine had happened. Outside, in the meadow by the river, there was a row of shacks. People who never wrote, or got a letter, lived there. In one of those shacks, I had left my friend, Tak . . . a little Japanese fellow who hardly came to my shoulder. A little guy whose back had been hit by a falling rock over a year ago. He had no family . . . no place to go . . .

Cut to sound of river. Birds in trees.

TAK: You have job, Pony. I no work . . . hurt all the time here. I cook for you . . . wash clothes . . . fix boots. I eat only a little bit . . . I small man. I sleep on floor . . . no trouble for you! Okay?

PONY: That wasn't how he said it . . . he said nothing . . . but I understood. As I understood how much it hurt him to lift water by bucket from the river and carry it to the shack for cooking, laundry, washing the floor. There wasn't much left of him . . . but who could let another man die because he had nothing?

TAK: *(anxiously)* You worry maybe I die, Pony? . . . Please don't worry . . . don't worry. Tak good like new soon!

PONY: He said it with his eyes . . . After a few months, he couldn't carry water no more. He could still cook, but he got smaller, thinner. At night, he would go outside not to bother me. One night, I heard him throw up, he was hurting that much. I was saving a little money to send to my family one day, but now I started spending it on more meat to fatten him up. And I bought him a woolen blanket. Having no language in common, we looked at each other a lot and spoke in languages we did know, using our hands like flails . . . telling jokes even! Describing our mothers and grandfathers . . . how they

375

walked. *(chuckles)* His people were all short, like him . . . it seems . . .

Fade in sound of TAK singing a Japanese folk-song. Over song:

PONY: To dream of what could never be — only in America! Only in America such dreams. No chance of that at home. You were a miner, or a bricklayer — forget the song playing in you head. I knew a boy when I was a boy. Young Peter was his name — and he said his hands were made by God to play music. He wore mittens in the wind . . . oiled them against the sun in summer . . . trimmed his nails. They were not a boy's hands . . . they were the hands of a wealthy woman. He never played music — never did much of anything. When we grew to be men, and I was about to leave for Canada, he was still caring for his hands. On Saturday mornings he would go to the marketplace to steal wallets from the back pockets of peasants selling chickens. They probably hung Peter long ago . . . **should've** hung him. But that is nothing. It was the **dream** he had of being something more important that made him special and not easy to forget. I never forget him . . .

Folk-song up for a full verse. Fade under for:

PONY: I never forget Tak. No hope for him, but I never forget. And them men who stopped by the shacks and put up tents for the night. Later . . . there was a story about how they didn't stay the night of the disaster . . . that they all went to another town. There were all kinds of men in them tents, all out of work. They made fires in front of our shacks. One of them came to ask for a pail to carry some water from the river for tea. He brought it back right away. He was a very young man — a boy with a little bit of beard on his chin. Soon, I could smell hot cakes fried on pans coated with lard . . . and boiling tea. Everywhere the smell of wood smoke . . . the men cooking their evening meal over open fires . . .

Fade out song and up sound of men in encampment.

PONY: Some had eaten and were singing . . . here and there a good voice, and some like braying oxen . . . some laughing . . . Others cursing their horses, or boots that didn't fit . . .

Sound of a short, noisy argument.

PONY: No women. Only men. And so poor you could smell their poverty — a sour smell of life without enough to eat. Even when they have washed their clothes and scrubbed their bodies, the smell is still on their breath. It was the town preacher . . . McPhail was his name . . . who said these men had packed their tents, because they were foreigners and superstitious, and gone to Blairmore the night the mountain broke in two . . . There was no Blairmore for them. There was a fast death . . .

Sharp crack of thunder and camp sounds of men turning thin and unreal:

PONY: The mountain falling through their torn cloth tents . . . through their thin, shivering bodies . . . made of their modes and flesh a thin layer of red mud at the bottom of the Old Man River. *(fiercely)* Men like McPhail got to learn respect for the dead! No more goddamn lies to make him sleep easier . . . no more!

CUT TO: Sounds of men trapped in the mine.

CHAPMAN: No goddamned river flows upwards and backwards!

HALFPINT: But if the river's backed up . . .

CHAPMAN: The whole river would have to be dammed from shore to shore! *(hesitating)* No . . . that's impossible!

HALFPINT: But what if . . .

CHAPMAN: *(angry, afraid)* Half the mountain would have to come down to fill in the valley. Nothing like that could happen . . . there's a town out there!

ANOTHER MINER: I got a family in town — we got to get out of here!

CHAPMAN: *(sharply)* No more of that talk! You hear? . . . As far as we know, we've had a cave-in . . . and we're alive. Now let's figure out what we do next . . .

MINER: We clear the main entrance. That's where they'll be digging from the outside to get us.

HALFPINT: I tell you it's impossible! The whole shaft is caved in, and water's risin' from somewhere!

Men begin to argue. Fade under for:

PONY: The air was getting sour. They tried not to show how scared they were. But we were ghosts in the darkness . . . In the light from our lamps each man seemed to have no legs, for our lower bodies were hidden by the dust that would not settle or blow away. The mountain still trembled . . . and there were explosions from somewhere deep inside the mine, like small dynamite charges going off. Coal and rock kept falling from the tunnel ceiling, and support timbers in the passages cracked and snapped like the telegraph keys of hell . . .

Men's voices rising, then subsiding.

CHAPMAN: Yes, the airshaft! Someone outside is bound to be at the airshaft by now! Halfpint — you're the smallest man here. You climb up the airshaft as far as you can . . . then holler to the diggers outside — tell'em we're safe, but Bill Warrington's gonna need a doctor, so they better dig in fast! Tell them the air's getting bad in here . . .

HALFPINT: But the shaft is too high. I need a ladder.

CHAPMAN: We'll boost you up. Let's go, men. We'll be out of here in no time!

Fade sounds into b.g.

PONY: He was worried. It was not a safe mine. It was being worked too hard, too fast. I worried every night I went on shift. The mine shafts were dug too wide and too high. Our explosives charges were too powerful. And on many nights, in the middle of our shift, the mountain moved. At first, the men were scared . . . stopped working as they listened to the distant thunder and watched the shivering passages for signs of cave-ins. Some timbers snapped, and coal broke free and fell. Then it would pass, and the men joked to hide their terror . . .

MINER: *(laughing)* Someone else we don't know about must be minin' coal below us!

ANOTHER MINER: Naw. It's only gas in Old Charlie's belly!

MINER: Yeah, you may be right. It smells that way now . . .

Fade down on laughter.

PONY: The mountain walked . . . by night, when the cold air on its outside skin made it shiver with pain from its insides. I had never seen this before, but old miners in my village spoke of such things . . . and how they left to work elsewhere, fearing great calamity if the mountain took a long step. Now I was trapped in the thing they feared, and the men who made it happen were doing what children might do . . . going for the airshaft, with water rising to their knees and the air dying. We should be digging and not wasting precious time. But I had no language they would understand . . .

Sounds of men in mine.

CHAPMAN: *(shouting)* How are you doing, Halfpint? See anything?

HALFPINT: *(muffled)* I can't climb any higher. The shaft is pinched.

CHAPMAN: Can you see any light?

HALFPINT: No . . .

CHAPMAN: Can you hear anything?

HALFPINT: No.

CHAPMAN: Start hollering. And see if anyone up there answers!

HALFPINT: *(shouting)* Help! . . . Help! *(desperately)* Help!

Sound of HALFPINT scrambling back and jumping to shaft floor. He is breathless and afraid.

HALFPINT: Jesus . . . nothing! I coulda been shouting from the bottom of my own grave! Hey . . . we're in trouble!

Sound of men turning restless, muttering darkly. Sound of mine tremors.

PONY: The foreman turned with his lamp, looking at the men around him. His light fell on me. He stopped and held it there.

CHAPMAN: Anyone know how to talk to this bohunk? I think he knows something . . .

PONY: I couldn't speak. But I understood everything, like Old Charlie the pit horse . . . who knew everything the men said. I pointed up with my lamp . . . with my pick . . . to where the coal-seam narrowed into the side of the mountain, away from the main seam. I motioned we should dig there. The men didn't need Chapman now to tell them what to do. Even as I pointed, they were moving tools and equipment to make a ramp from which to work.

Over sound of men digging:

CHAPMAN: *(loudly)* There'll be no resting! Those waiting their turns to dig make noise . . . shout, hit the iron rails . . . sing. If there's anyone outside, they better hear us!

Sound of harsh metallic banging and shouting. Through shouting, a chorus if men singing slowly:

MINERS SINGING:
    Onward Christian soldiers
    Marching as to war —
    With the cross of Jesus
    Going on before . . .

PONY: The Welsh miners sang like angels. Their voices filled the darkness with hope. We took turns cutting and removing the coal-seam, each group of men working for fifteen minutes, to be relieved by others. A man could not work longer in the dust and the dead air. When I had done my share of work I stumbled down the tunnel to find Old Charlie, still harnessed to his cart and standing in a side tunnel . . . hearing, but not seeing us. He was shivering when I touched him, and then swung his head to bring his face against my cheek. I stroked him and told him in my language not to worry. We would not leave him behind. Soon we would be free . . . soon we would be free . . . but I did not say aloud — who would find us? When? Old Charlie knew what I was thinking, because he whinnied softly, as if saying — ''don't worry, friend. I won't leave you, either . . . ''

Singing — muffled and distant now.

MINERS SINGING:
    Onward Christian soldiers
    Marching as to war . . .

PONY: We dug, dynamited, and clawed at the black rubble for thirteen hours. Towards the end, all hope turned to stubborness. It did not matter what the end would bring, so long as we kept working. To stop would be to surrender . . . and death. So we became one body, one mind. No one had to give orders or point the way. We broke out of the rock and the thin coal-seam . . . out of the mountainside . . . to find we had gone nowhere . . . that our way was blocked from the outside by a wall of huge stones, stinking of sulphur. Only one person cursed in the darkness . . .

MINER: *(in dismay)* Son of a bitch!

HALFPINT: *(singing fervently)*
    Onward Christian soldiers
    Marching as to war
    With the cross of Jesus . . .

PONY: We turned back to the first coal-seam going upwards. Here, we began to dig again. This time the coal was softer, falling easily. The movement of the mountain had stopped. No more singing . . . no sounds. There was not enough air left.

Braced against the sides of the steep cut we were making, we cut through thirty-six feet of coal. Suddenly . . . the remaining few feet of coal fell inward, over our shoulders, faces and hands . . . and there was light above us! How sweet the cold air tasted as it blew in around us, cooling the hot sickness in our faces . . . washing dust and despair from our bodies.

Sounds of panting and grunting, then a cheer.

The sudden exuberance dies abruptly.

Sound of a low wind, clatter of loose pebbles.

A MINER: *(gasping)* God — no!

PONY: The world we had left behind the evening before was no longer there. My shack was gone. Tak was gone . . . the meadow by the river was gone. The river was gone . . . and the mining horse stables . . . and the hay barn . . . all gone. Nothing was left. There had been a tree — a balsam poplar, where I had gone to sit in the shade on summer evenings to listen to the river and plan letters I would write to my family. It was gone.

The whole place . . . right into and across the river, was a great plain of broken stones piled high over homes we had lived in . . . over memories . . . over the faces of those we had cared for. A hundred feet deep, as if God made sure nothing we knew would ever be found.

A hundred feet deep, they later said — the ones who measure these things in feet. Two thoughts came to me as I stood there — that Tak was gone — not a hair of his head would ever be found. And my cast iron frying pan . . . the one that was made so good I could fry an egg over a candle with it . . . also gone. I started to cry and to laugh at the same time . . . laughing and crying like a small boy. Then this cold wind seemed to go through my clothes, into my skin . . . into my body. I was shaking all over, and fell to my knees . . . while the others walked and ran over and past me, stumbling through the field of rubble.

MINER: *(shouting)* My house was there! Ella!

ANOTHER MINER: Why am I living? Someone tell me — why them an'? . . . not me?

PONY: Behind me, Warrington, the miner with the broken leg, was carried out, tied to a plank. He turned his head towards the valley, and let out a cry I can still hear in my dreams. Then he twisted on the plank to look up at Turtle Mountain, split and ugly and crowned by a cloud of dirty grey fog . . . .

WARRINGTON screams in anguish.

CHAPMAN: It's alright, Bill. Hang in there, boy. We'll get you to a doctor real quick.

WARRINGTON: *(shouting)* My house and kids were over there . . . by that clothesline!

CHAPMAN: Easy, Bill . . . lie still.

WARRINGTON: My wife and children are gone! I got to go an' dig them out!

CHAPMAN: Someone else will dig, not you . . . Take it easy!

Shouting and sounds of people hurrying in the distance. Over sounds:

PONY: People from the town of Frank . . . who'd spent the day digging with their hands around the entrance to the mine, were running towards us. Some were shouting and waving their arms. Some approached with tears running down their cheeks. They had to tell us everything . . .

WOMAN: It was terrible . . . the earth shook and there was a sound of thunder . . . then a high whistle . . .

ANOTHER WOMAN: There was a tree still standing . . . and a clothesline with frozen diapers hanging on it. I ran away . . . I couldn't look anymore!

WOMAN: I ran to the window and looked towards the valley, but I could only see this dust in the darkness, and sparks flashing all the way up the mountain . . .

MAN: Everyone I seen or spoke to seemed like they rose from the grave . . . like ghosts, staring past me, saying little. I seen people today just walking away with their kids, leaving their homes and businesses behind, like it didn't matter anymore . . .

Fade voices down and out.

Sound of low wind rising in b.g.

PONY: The doctor came and took over getting Bill Warrington into town for treatment. People were crowding around Chapman, asking questions, pushing to hear every word he said. I remained kneeling, trembling with cold that had now reached into my heart . . .

CHAPMAN: I feel proud of my men. I wish the town had been as lucky as we. And I'm sorry about the loss of homes and lives . . . I really am . . .

PONY: Why was he saying this? What meaning did it have on this field of devastation? . . . One of the merchants talking to him stepped over me, knocking off my cap . . .

MERCHANT: What happened inside the mine, Joe?

CHAPMAN: Well, sir . . . I felt the concussion of the explosion very severe. The blast of hot air struck me and picked me up and threw me into the manway. But we didn't lose our heads, not for a moment. No sir. We just turned around and started digging ourselves out, we did.

MERCHANT: That's the spirit, Joe! Let's get the hell out of here and get ourselves a drink. Drinks are on me, Joe — you and the boys sure deserve it!

Sound of men hurrying away.

CHAPMAN: *(walking away)* The air was becoming foul, and I knew . . . twenty-four hours would fetch the seeping water into our tunnel from the backed up river.

MERCHANT: You knew . . . deep inside there, that the river was dammed?

CHAPMAN: *(fading)* Oh yes . . . so we decided we must make haste to do something . . . and together, we did . . .

PONY: There was a smell of hell in the air. It burned my nose, dried my throat and brought tears to my eyes. I still remember looking up into the cold sky and thinking of Tak, vanished among the stars like the memory of a summer day, when a man was a boy, and the day was forever long near a river where he fished . . . and fished . . . all of that long, long day without catching a goddamned thing, and it didn't matter . . .

CUT TO:

HOST: From the moment of the disaster, explanations, even official ones for what what happened and why, downplayed mining procedures and human carelessness. The superintendent of mines for the territory explained that the slide was due to a combination of causes — among them a weak mountain base, fissures, frost expansion, and even earthquake tremors. A similar disregard for an accurate casualty count was also evident. The dead were first reported to number 66 persons. That figure then became 70. Later it was acknowledged to be in excess of one hundred people killed or missing. A newspaper account of the time said some of those who might have died but were not counted were ''unknown immigrant Slavs and their concubines.''

CUT TO: PONY's present home. Television playing in b.g.

DAUGHTER: *(calling)* It's time for a cup of coffee — are you coming in?

PONY: *(startled)* What? . . . Ah, again she is calling — come to eat . . . come to drink. Come for your medicine . . . come to sleep.

DAUGHTER: *(calling)* Pony!

PONY: *(calling back)* Yah, I hear you! *(to himself)* One day she will call me in to die — come on, Pony, lie down now. Hold this flower like that. Be nice . . . *(chuckles)*

DAUGHTER: *(calling)* Pony — dad . . . what are you doing?

PONY: *(calling back)* I am thinking. Is there something wrong with thinking?

DAUGHTER: There's coffee and cake waiting, anytime you're ready, that's all . . .

PONY: Sure. Thank you.

Fade out b.g. sounds.

Up sound of wind rising.

PONY: It was a time and place of death. Those who perished were fortunate ones . . . to live was madness.

A distant clap of thunder, followed by sustained rumbling and whistling of compressed air in leading edge of slide.

PONY: On that great pile of broken rock, with a cold night coming quickly, I had the fear of a man staring into the unknown . . . the wilderness of hell itself! *(with rising passion)* The soul of my friend . . . flung to the stars along with all those other unfortunate souls . . . I never knew anything like it — even the old stories, of witches and stealers of small children, said nothing of this. Only the new world could teach me about such disasters that came and went like lightening, leaving ruins without colour or feeling. Even my tears were out of place now. Against the broken mountain, I was less than a speck. And the grief I felt was even less than that. The dust . . . the devastation . . . the end of all life in this poisonous field of ash — that was the first and last truth of working for better wages than I had ever earned . . . in the service of masters whose souls were like the rubble and ash I knelt on. No feeling for man or earth . . . fields wilted and burst into flame in their presence. Mountains groaned and collapsed, their bellies emptied with dynamite and shovels. Rivers boiled in rage, their waters blackened by the soot of a thousand man-made fires . . . There was still talk of God and love, but only if it did not interfere with conversations about business . . . new spur-lines . . . the buying and selling of all things. If ever there would be men capable of scorching the whole earth, they would have to rise from beginnings such as these . . .

CUT TO:

HOST: H.L. Frank bought the mining claim for thirty thousand dollars. A year later, it was yielding more coal per miner than any mine in operation anywhere. Frank gave a gala party at this time to inaugurate his town, which he dreamed would become another Pittsburgh. Three thousand guests were invited, with each guest required to pay his or her rail fare of from $1.40 to $2.25, depending on the distance travelled, to reach the town. All other expenses were assumed by Frank himself. These included meals prepared by a French chef, a tour of the mine in cars covered in white canvas, dancing in the ballroom of the new hotel to music by the best orchestras available as well as numerous other sports and outdoor events and entertainments. Two special trains were assigned by the CPR to bring in guests and dignitaries for the gala opening of the boom town.

Sounds of partying, music, laughter rising faintly in b.g.

PONY: It began two years before. A banker named Frank, from Montana, bought coal mining rights from a prospector named Gebo . . . whom he made mayor of the town he named after himself. To christen the town, Frank had the railway bring hundreds of guests from the East and the West. Speeches were made by important men from the government and the railway.

Sound of cheering. Distant speech. Musket fire. Drunken shouts.

PONY: The guests . . . mostly human rubbish in the service of the mighty . . . ate and drank . . . danced in the streets until they fell. Others fired muzzle-loaded rifles in the air . . . into trees . . . into the mountain — as if everything that could not run was there to be shot at! Some healthier guests ran races and were given medals. And all day long, lots were offered for sale in the new town. Even the poor were taken in — borrowing money from each other to make payments on land they could not afford. There were Indians, too. I watched a Blackfoot chief offer his wife to the premier of the territory as a present.

Sound of festivities coming to a stop.

PONY: That brought things to a stop for a little bit. The premier looked at the women who had come with the chief. *(chuckles)* I had to cover my face to keep from laughing. There was something in the premier's face that wanted to say . . .

PREMIER HAULTAIN: *(eagerly)* Yes . . . yes! I'll take two of them . . . That one there. And another you haven't used, you filthy, brown-faced toad, with your stupid hat and blanket!

PONY: That's what the civilized white man *wanted* to say. I read it in his eyes and the way his hands reached for something that wasn't there. But he was not a brave man, so what he said was . . .

PREMIER HAULTAIN: *(severely)* Now see here, my friend — polygamy is not a proper or civilized way to carry on. Whether you like it or not, laws are coming into place to end it . . . for people like you!

PONY: That Indian chief didn't understand a goddamned thing the white man was saying. He stepped forward . . . one leader to another. But a friend of the premier's jumped towards him and pushed him away. Everybody came to make money, one way or another. Everybody — the tavern-keepers, the railroad, the mining company, land speculators, pimps, provisioners. A wise man speaking his mind that day would have been shot, and his body used to prop open a bar room door.

Sounds of revelry, laughter, musket firing.

OFFICIAL: *(hoarse, loud)* On behalf of the railway, the coalmine company . . . and the town of Frank — let me say, this is a great day! Yes or no?

Cheers, shots, applause.

OFFICIAL: We came here to work, and the Frank Coal Company gives work! Let me hear it for the company!

More cheers, shots, applause.

OFFICIAL: That's better . . . and much appreciated, I'm sure. On a serious note, if I may . . . *(hooting, derision)* Now, now . . . there'll be more to eat and drink, I assure you . . . *(a lusty cheer)* Let it be known, I say . . . let it be known . . . that the railway . . . those two streaks of rust across the wilderness, as the saying goes . . . is the reason Frank will grow and flourish as a town! We must all, as one body, support the business of the railway. We will produce coal to go out on the trains. But the trains must not return empty, oh, no . . . We must see to it that all we need . . . comes to us on the railway! Our clothing . . . furniture . . . tools . . . even our food — must come in by rail to make this service profitable!

MAN IN CROWD: *(shouting)* You forgot the booze!

Laughter.

OFFICIAL: That, too. But let me say that perhaps a bit of temperance might be in order. *(booing)* You who boo remember — some of us have wives and children!

Laughter.

DRUNKARD: You who boo . . . eh? You who boo!

Phrase is picked up and repeated over:

OFFICIAL: *(loudly, irritably)* To assure the railway that we are all its most loyal customers and friends, I have this day put through a bylaw for the town of Frank . . . forbidding perambulating porkers being raised in the townsite! Which means that no pigs will be allowed to be grown for food here. I would advise you to refrain from keeping vegetable gardens, also. Whatever we need, the railway will bring in for us!

Sound of festivities dies. Sound of grumbling rises.

DRUNKARD: Some who you boo — shit . . .

OFFICIAL: *(nervously)* Will someone get that man out of here? . . . Come on, everybody . . . let's move on to some serious drinking! Let's go!

Sound of festivities renews in b.g.

PONY: We, the miners, lying on the hillside, watching the party, knew from what was said we were here to work for low wages . . . with open-flame lamps that would make explosions in gassy or dusty mine shafts. That we would mine coal in ways not permitted anywhere else in the world. And so the seeds of the great disaster to follow in two years were planted.

Sound of thunderous explosion — whistling winds and falling rubble.

MINERS SINGING: *(faintly in b.g.)*
    Onward Christian soldiers,
    Marching as to war,
    With the cross of Jesus
    Going on before . . .

Fade down. Up sounds of cold wind.

PONY: Rescued miners, and those who were above ground during the disaster and survived, became insane with grief for the dead and fear for their own lives . . . .

CUT TO: Sounds of tavern. Angry atmosphere.

BARTENDER: Pete! You've had enough, boy . . . Go for a walk!

MINER: Never mind that — fill the table, you sonofabitch!

BARTENDER: Okay, Pete — okay. You been drinking pretty good all night . . .

MINER: I'm gonna die! You're gonna die — we're **all** gonna die just like that! You know what's worse that that? Livin' — that's what's worse! So here's my money. Take it, and bring me whiskey!

BARTENDER: Pete, you've had enough.

Sound of glass being thrown. Then another, and another.

MINER: *(raging)* You get me booze, or I'll bust every god-damned glass an' bottle in this place, you slimey bastard!

BARTENDER: Alright — it's your damned life! Who cares?

MINER: You damned right it is — and who cares, indeed? All them houses in Suicide Row buried . . . Jim Graham gone like that . . . young McVeigh . . . Jack Dawe . . . and all those women an' sleeping babes. Gone . . . dead. *(begins weeping)* What makes me so special I should be around to remember how they looked . . . what they said?

BARTENDER: I'm not a religious man. But maybe it's something to do with the will of God . . .

MINER: Like hell you say! God didn't bring down Turtle Mountain. The Frank Coal Company did! . . . They made this town, an' in two years they killed it. Like some old time king who makes a kid with the kitchen maid, and when it's born, he has its head cut off!

BARTENDER: Keep your voice down, man — or the company will send you packing . . .

MINER: Four times I been blown out of a tunnel by a gas explosion set off by my lamp. Twice I been buried under an overmined coal-seam collapsing. But I went back in, thinkin' I was lucky to be working at all. Look out that window . . . there's your reward for what we all did. *(pleading)* Get me a drink, man . . . something's hurting inside of me so bad I want to run and scream until I fall down!

Fade out.

Up sounds of a street brawl.

FIRST MAN: You tell me you're sorry or I'll break you legs and arms!

SECOND MAN: Come on — try. I'm tired of waiting!

They fight, grunting and panting and urged on by observers.

FADE OUT FOR: Sound of wind.

PONY: Few of those buried were ever found. Women who survived stared at nothing. Men and older boys became drunks and fist fighters. At the funeral ceremony for the dead, the preacher said the disaster was a lesson to remind people of earthly futility. Miners and townspeople took that sermon to heart . . .

Sounds of partying.

WOMAN: You have to stop — please! There isn't a soul in town who can sleep through this . . .

MINER: To hell with them. The earthquake shows we won't be around much longer . . . so to hell with them!

ANOTHER MINER: I'll drink to that!

THIRD MINER: Me, too.

Laughter. Fade out.

Up sounds of wind.

PONY: The death count rose to a hundred. The fifty or more men who had no homes and had camped for the night in their tents in the path of the slide were not counted. The frenzy of drink began to pass, with the miners' money gone and the anger still sitting like a pain in the stomach no medicine would ever cure. The preacher McPhail tried to claim some honour for the town and the company by blaming the drinking on — who else? — foreigners like me, with no names, and no command of English to defend ourselves. He wrote to a Toronto newspaper . . .

"The foreign elements, more superstitious . . . have nearly all packed their belongings and gone to Blairmore. But dozens of finer spirits have been at work all day, rescuing all who could possibly be reached and lamenting over their fellow citizens who sleep the sleep that knows no waking . . ."

PONY: There were good people . . . doctors, workers in the hotel and on the railway, and the man they called Villan — who gave his own money and collected from his friends to help those who had lost everything. In such company, McPhail was a dwarf. He was holding on to nothing. It was rumoured that the man, Frank, was becoming sick with mental problems. The spirit of the people was broken, and hope for the mine was gone . . .

Up sound of song faintly in b.g.

MINERS SINGING:
> Onward Christian Soldiers,
> Marching as to war . . .

Fade out.

PONY: There were fears of further slides, and an evacuation ordered. Some left. I remained beside the tunnel we had dug to escape the mine. For two days and two icy nights I sat there. I felt invisible . . . people stumbled over the field of devastation . . . looked my way but did not see me sitting there, my head on my knees. My body and my soul seemed to separate. I felt no thirst or hunger. And the winds blowing down from the snowy mountains to the north no longer felt cold. When I shivered . . . and I shivered often . . . it was not from the cold. It was from sorrow. I wept much, and my tears fell to the broken stone beneath me, where they froze in drops as clear as glass. I wondered what providence would look after me now . . . what providence had brought me to this fate so far away from warmth and family. Did they exist? Did I exist? . . . Or had I died, and my spirit was here, among the ruins, with no place to go? I prayed to God for some sign that I mattered . . . that my life had not just come to this meaningless end among the ruins . . .

Sound of thunder and spattering of rocks falling down mountainside. Sounds of distant voices.

PONY: On the third night, I returned from the dead. Despair and longing for Tak . . . for my family . . . for all those who had been buried, fell away and I became cold and hungry. I went into town . . . into a restaurant . . . and remembered that my money had been left in the shack that was no more . . .

Sounds of restaurant.

WAITRESS: Come in an' close the door. It's cold outside.

PONY: Yes. I'm hungry . . . but no money pay you . . .

WAITRESS: You just sit yourself over there. I'll bring you some leftover soup and bread . . .

Over noises of restaurant:

PONY: She was a good woman. And the soup she brought me had pieces of meat so big I had to chew and chew before I could swallow. And bread this thick! . . . Covered with butter the way farmers butter their bread! Then a pot of tea and a bowl of sugar. I am ashamed to say, to this day, I sat there for over an hour, eating and drinking everything. I felt strong. And then I remembered Old Charlie, the horse . . . still inside the mine. He had nothing to eat, and there was no restaurant and good woman for him . . .

Fade down and out.

Sound of door being forced.

PONY: I walked through the town to the feed store. I found a three-foot bar in the shed behind the building, and with the bar I broke the lock on the door. I found a small sack with oats in it. I carried it out of town, over the rubble of the slide to where we had dug ourselves free. It was hard work, and I fell many times, spilling some of the oats. Near the opening we had made, I found my hat and lamp. I lit it, and with the sack tied to my belt, I started to climb down into the sealed mine. The air was sour only a few feet down, and I had to swallow to keep from vomitting up my dinner. I was afraid of firing gases with the open flame of my lamp. I started sweating with fear, my stomach knotted. But I could not go back. Now I was out of the narrow tunnel and sliding down the coal rubble we had dropped when we dug.

Sound of a horse whinnying, creating sepulchre-like echoes.

PONY: Old Charlie was alive! I moved carefully, not to stir up coal dust. Then I stepped into water — up to my knees. But below this was the firm floor of the mine shaft. Old Charlie ran towards me, his eyes two blue-white discs in the black tunnel . . .

Sound of horse trotting in water and whinnying.

PONY: *(joyfully)* Oh, he was so happy to see me! So happy! I swear I seen tears falling from his eyes as he put his face to mine and told me things so sad my heart ached just listening to him. I took the rigging off his head, pulled off his harness and held out the sack I brought. I had spilled so much of the oats there was only a little bit left. Charlie seemed to have trouble finding the open sack I held to him, and I realized he was going blind in the darkness where we left him. What could I do? I could not take him out through the narrow, steep tunnel we had made for our escape from this tomb. I scooped the oats with my hands and fed them to him. He was thin now, and his hair had turned grey. Even as he ate, he whinnied so pathetically. Charlie, Charlie . . . I said to him — they are digging at the main entrance from the outside. Soon they will reach you and you will come out. It is almost Spring

398

outside . . . the sun gets warmer every day and the grass will be greening. I will walk you to where fresh grass will be growing and there you will graze and run, and drink from the river. And I will sit under a tree, smoking my pipe. Together, we will celebrate freedom . . .

CUT TO: Sound of footsteps in PONY's home.

DAUGHTER: For God's sake, dad . . . what's got into you tonight? I see you walking past the window muttering to yourself . . . swinging your arms around. Then you disappear, and I think you've gone to bed. Next thing, you're walking back in the opposite direction . . .

PONY: I'm restless — I can't sit in one place. Maybe it's the moon . . . or something I ate . . .

DAUGHTER: *(startled)* Shit . . . I'd better see about getting you to see a psychiatrist . . .

PONY: Go to sleep . . . or watch some more stupid television. Can't you see I'm restless? Your mother tried to put me in an early grave with shouting at me . . . following me. And now you doing the same thing . . .

DAUGHTER: *(laughing)* Mom doing what? She died first — you outlived her!

PONY: *(distant, absentminded)* Yeah . . . yeah, I did. Sometimes I forget . . .

DAUGHTER: Hey — remember to take your medication before bedtime.

PONY: Sure . . . anything you say . . .

Sound of DAUGHTER walking away, closing door behind herself.

Suburban street sounds faintly in b.g.

PONY sighs wearily.

PONY: The years pass. How they pass! Her mother was alright, and I loved her, but she was not my first wife. This one was a North American — raised in Hamilton on popcorn and baloney. Ah, what sort of things am I thinking now? Why? . . . She was good to me — a lot better than I was for her. What did I do for her that I could be proud of now? Nothing, that's what . . . I didn't drink or gamble, and I always came home. But a young woman needed more than living with a man with a crushed soul. A miner still made a good living, but I couldn't go near a mine again. So I carried bricks and cement bags for construction companies. But when the coughing started, and I began spitting blood, I had to leave that and find work in city parks, raking leaves and cutting lawns with the old men. She worried about me, but she couldn't help me fight the devils I carried inside of me. Instead, she thought I might be happier and feel better if I immigrated back to where I came from. As if leaving one world for another was that simple . . .

FADE OUT FOR: Sound of baby crying in another room.

PONY: Why is she crying? Has your milk dried up?

WIFE: *(distressed)* No. I've got milk. She sucks a little, and then she cries like that . . .

PONY: *(muttering)* The old women knew what to do. They always knew something about these things.

WIFE: What old women?

PONY: The old women I knew . . . in the old country.

WIFE: *(angry)* That's stupid!

PONY: What do you know about them things? What do you know about anything? That kid is going to be like you if you keep talking to it without thinking!

WIFE: *(upset)* Oh, Pony — if only you would go back, just for the winter. See your friends . . . get better . . . .

Fade down and out.

PONY: There was a war, and then revolutions. Nothing remained as I knew it, but how could I tell her? She did not know about wars. Or pestilence. Or people wandering away, looking for food and never coming back. Besides, we had no money. I never told her about that. I was too proud for that. So I pretended we had some money in the bank. That was her problem — she believed in me and looked up to me, and by that time, I wasn't worth five cents!

Crash of thunder and faint sound of singing in b.g.

MINERS SINGING:
>Onward Christian soldiers,
>Marching as to war —
>With the cross of Jesus
>Going on before . . .

Sounds of horse stamping in water of mine and whinnying.

PONY: I had to leave. And soon, because everything was drawing me to madness — the rotten air, the fear of gas or coaldust exploding . . . this dumb, loving animal begging for

401

his freedom. And if not freedom, then for me to stay with him in this wet, cold, black tomb. I was halfway up the escape tunnel, the blood ringing in my ears, and he still called to me . . .

Echoing sound of horse whinnying in panic.

Sustain in fading b.g.

PONY: For so many nights I lost count, I stole sugar, oats cookies . . . anything he might eat . . . and carried it down into the pit. In the day, I watched the rescue workers digging out the entrance to the mine. Days became weeks . . . and once I went to argue for them to hurry up. Old Charlie was still inside . . .

Sounds of picking at mine entrance.

FOREMAN: Alright, men. We stop here and shore the roof. The damned thing doesn't look good . . .

PONY: How long? How long, eh? . . . How long this?

FOREMAN: How long what? . . . What in hell's he talking about?

PONY: I didn't know these men. I didn't have the words. I could not explain my friend was waiting inside, blind and dying of loneliness . . .

FOREMAN: What's he trying to say?

CREWMAN: Damned if I know . . .

FOREMAN: Anyone here know this bohunk's language? . . . No one?

PONY: He waved at me to leave, and once again I became invisible. I wasn't there — he'd waved me off this earth. All the men ignored me . . . looked through me like I was made of glass . . .

FOREMAN: Let's move — we're wasting time! And get those supports in before this goddamned thing comes down on us!

Fade under and out.

Sounds of wagons and muted b.g. conversations.

PONY: With the mine closed and people leaving, there was no work. I found some things to do while I took food to Old Charlie at nights . . . I got work digging a well for a merchant . . . and then I painted a house for a railroad man hoping to sell and move on, too. Then . . . on the twenty-ninth day after the disaster, a small opening was cleared into the mine. A few men squeezed through and went inside to check the passageways. Word got back they'd found Old Charlie. I put down the paintbrush and ran as fast as I could . . .

Sound of PONY running.

Sound of men's laughter and conversation in distance becoming louder.

Sound of PONY panting.

MINER: It was something to see alright. There was Old Charlie in the tunnel, thin as a rail and all grey. But was he happy to see us! He put his head right here, against my cheek, and made happy noises in his throat. We had to celebrate, so we gave Old Charlie a bit of oats and a good swig of brandy . . .

ANOTHER MINER: How in hell did he survive?

MINER: He must've et the bark off the mine supports . . . an' there's lots of seepage water in the main tunnel. Well, we turned to go . . . and suddenly Old Charlie sinks down to his knees . . . into the mud . . .

THIRD MINER: He must've learned to pray, being in there all alone . . .

Laughter from men.

MINER: We couldn't even try to get him out without widening the entrance first. So we left to get some blankets for him . . .

ANOTHER MINER: You bring him out yet?

MINER: No. Old Charlie's . . . dead.

Laughter and cheerfulness ends.

MINER: I don't know why . . . but as we were leaving, he threw up his head, swinging it from side to side, as if to see us . . . like he was blind. He gave this soft neigh . . . you could hardly hear it. And then he drops his head and dies. Just like that . . .

PONY: *(over b.g. conversation of men)* He died of a broken heart. I knew Old Charlie good. Without sight and men around him, he lived on hope. All by himself in that black cave, he lived on hope. When they came to him, and then began to leave, he thought they were forsaking him again. And that is more than a man or a horse could bear . . .

Fade out.

Up on sounds of PONY's home.

DAUGHTER: *(calling from another room)* Pony — your friend Stanley's on the phone!

PONY: *(loudly)* What does he want?

DAUGHTER: He says he can't sleep . . . . Wants to know if you want a game of cribbage tonight. What shall I tell him?

PONY: Tell him — no! Tomorrow maybe, but not tonight . . . not tonight. Tell him I got a headache. Tell him anything — but no cribbage!

DAUGHTER: Okay.

PONY: *(to himself)* I don't like that man. A retired police-man . . . Now with no teeth, his mouth all pooched. So when he speaks I don't understand half of what he is saying . . . and I want to reach for an umbrella. Why doesn't he buy himself teeth like other old men? Eh?

Faint sound of singing.

MINERS SINGING:

> Onward Christian soldiers
> Marching as to war . . .

PONY: That day . . . when I heard Old Charlie died, I knew that what I ran away from was waiting for me here. So I turned east and started to walk on the railway track . . . determined to walk back to my family. But there was an ocean between us . . . and already a war was in the making. The rest is history.

Sound of low wind rising and falling.

405

PONY: But sometimes . . . like tonight . . . I think of Old Charlie. And I think to myself — when the earth shakes, God rearranges everything . . . everything. Nothing is ever the same again. Maybe there is some kind of justice in that . . . but the years pass, and the young ask — who cares? The living go on living, and the dead don't vote or pay taxes anymore — so they don't count. As for the living dead . . . ah, that is another story! They are black angels walking past your window or through you dreams of good health and a long life . . . passing from darkness into darkness. Ghosts . . . every one of them . . . the errors we have made . . .

Distant crash of thunder.

CUT TO:

HOST: Despite efforts to revive the coal mine and the town of Frank on numerous occasions, the old townsite was abandoned for a new location out of fear for further devastating slides. The mine itself was re-opened but, with the discovery of new fissures in the old slide area, was sealed to further mining in 1911 — eight years after the disaster. The slide itself was mined by the Winnipeg Supply and Fuel Company until 1976, for limestone. Debris from the slide was used for road fill and railway grade in Alberta and British Columbia. In 1976, the Alberta government declared the slide a restricted development area. Local people had believed the slide area and connecting mountains belonged to the government. But in the summer of 1984, Winnipeg Supply and Fuel Company, who remained owners of the site, put the "Frank Slide Property" — as they called it — up for sale with a prominent Calgary realtor. The advertisement read: "This property of over 212 acres is a prime tourist area divided by the main No. 3 highway. Approximately 10 acres is flat building site with highway frontage and exposure. This is a tremendous opportunity to invest in this promotional property, which has proven to be an exciting tourist attraction. This could be an ideal way of advertising and promotion for any company. There are good flat building sites adjoining the slide on the eastern side that would be perfect for tourist related operations . . . such as an adventure land. Owners will sell or trade. Price — $1,400,000.00.''

Distant crash of thunder and theme in quickly to time.

The End

THE GREY LADY
OF RUPERT STREET

They entered her home with a minimum of civility, as unwelcome guests enter, lightly tapping on the door, glancing back to see if they were being observed, and then turning the doorknob without waiting for a response from within. The door was unlocked. They pushed it open forcefully and it slammed against the wall of the hallway. For a moment, they hesitated, their bulky bodies throwing a dark shadow over the linoleum covering the floor, now a non-descript grey colour from years of neglect.

The odour from the hallway was stale and sour, the odour of neglect. Of darkness and eye-watering sadness. They stood for a moment, squinting, unsure. Gone now was the crude, light-hearted banter in the car on their way to the house. Outside, a fresh fall of snow made the landscape glow with the holy light of late afternoon. Here, at the entry to the house covered in decaying shingles, with moss clinging to the eaves and the chimney showing no smoke or haze of heat, the light invaded the open door shamefully and fell quickly to the tattered floor.

"You sure this is the right place?" The taller of the two men asked. The other did not hear or would not answer. He entered, his opened galoshes tracking water and bits of snow. He struck the walls of the hallway first with one fist, then the other, as if to assure himself they were indeed walls made of some recognizable substance. His companion followed, stamping his feet loudly and snorting the contents of his nose.

"Boy, you sure don't have to work too many hours to pay the rent in this part of town," he said with mock joviality, then patted the side of his coat in the place where his service revolver rested in its holster against his ample belly. He turned again to look behind him into the street. His companion continued walking down the hallway, opening two doors — one on his left, the other on his right. One door opened on steps leading to the basement. The other into the kitchen of the house. He reached around the door frame and threw the switch of a light hanging from the ceiling.

"Jesus, will you look at this!" he said as he stepped into the room. It had been long abandoned. A film of dust covered a chipped stove. The refrigerator beside it was left with its door open. Inside, on one tray, a plastic bag still held a few slices of mould-covered bread. Beyond the refrigerator, the kitchen sink was filled with a haphazard stack of dirty dishes and cooking pots. The window opening onto the back garden had spider-web cracks radiating from its centre.

"Bullet damage?" the taller man asked. The other ran his finger over the damaged glass.

"Naw. Probably a pebble from a neighbour's lawnmower."

"Looks like a shot to me," the taller one persisted. His companion turned away from the window and faced him. His eyes were hard, dark pupils contracted in anger.

"I don't give a shit what it looks like to you, Bert. Someone phones in to complain about hanky-panky between a mother and her son. We're here to look into it. That's all I'm interested in. That, and getting the hell out of this place when we're done, right?" he spoke coldly, decisively.

"Yah, sure. No offence meant." The taller man took the reprimand badly, chewing on his lower lip, a blush of indignation rising in his cheeks. He detested humiliation at the hands of superiors, but what could he do? He only had a grade school education. He could not hold a family together. And all his life he had struggled without success against obesity. Someday he might even the score, when the secret organization he belonged to grew to sufficient numbers. But in the meantime, he had to cover his ass . . . hold his job. Do nothing to jeopardize his pension.

"Nothing here. Come on," said the older man brusquely.

They left the kitchen, neglecting to shut off the light. At the end of the hallway, in near darkness, were stairs leading to the second floor.

The senior officer reached the stairs first. Then he stopped and turned. He had a thin smile on his lips as he motioned to the taller man to go first. Bert was puzzled, hesitated.

"You first . . . just in case the person you thought shot out the window is up there waiting," the smaller man taunted Bert, and then broke into cackling laughter. His face was a waxen mask in the dim light. A mask bent and twisted into laughter without mirth or forgiveness. Bert slouched into his coat and brushed past his companion. The steps groaned and creaked under his weight, with the other man following. He wished for more light. Nat Satillo, Bert's superior, had a contempt for stupid people that he made little effort to disguise. It wasn't their stupidity really — it was the arrogance which went with it.

Gunshot at the window indeed . . . Bert's high points as a person and as a social animal were in the car, reciting jokes and slapping his knees gleefully as they drove about following through on complaints.

"Hey — you hear the one about the bank manager with the glass eye? It was the eye mortgage applicants looked at for a sign of human kindness!"

Nat enjoyed this part of Bert. It made the dull hours pass more quickly, as it had this morning. But there was stuff like his take on the shattered window in the kitchen. And the bastard voted. And always for the worst human scum running for office. Afterwards, he would not only defend his choices but would criticize others who voted differently. He voted like he ate, without any sense of proportion or discrimination. This personal habit had made him chronically fat. But Bert's politics annoyed Nat, like a dull headache that would not go away. Or music piped into apartment block elevators. He had come to the annoying realization that somehow he had always voted against Bert's choices to cancel the other's support for racists, fanatics and corner-store fascists.

"Why do you vote, if you marked your ballot as you say you did?" he once asked, peering at Bert over his reading glasses from behind a deskful of routine paper work that had to be done more as a factor of housekeeping than of valuable police activity.

"I do what I have to do," Bert responded in a dull voice, avoiding Nat's eyes.

"And I have to vote to cancel your ballot. The man you marked for mayor is a criminal — a lot of charges and no convictions. You know, and I know, why that is — but he's still a criminal." Nat paused, considered what he wished to say, then continued — "It takes me time to consider everything in the way I vote . . . the best interests of the community, my own interests — the future of generations to come. For you, it almost seems it's similar to visiting the crapper in the morning. And about as meaningful."

He regretted he had laughed when he said that. For Bert also laughed — longer and louder than he did. And then he jabbed at Nat with a thick finger, in a gesture of defiance.

"That's what democracy's all about, buddy! You worry about your vote, and I crap mine out — and we're both equal! If anything, I guess I feel better for it than you do. Yes sir, I feel better for it every time . . ."

Bert wished he hadn't said that. His organization stressed in their secret meetings to keep one's mouth shut. Laugh about everything. Never show anger. When the time comes, and there are enough of the right people recruited, then it will be different . . .

Nat, staring across the desk at him, suddenly entertained a cold contempt for giving the franchise to just anyone. Where was there a glimmer of human responsibility in giving this man such awesome rights? He sighed and silently wished for a rapid increase in Bert's weight.

In the drowsy afternoons of summer when flies clustered on the water-stained ceilings of their office building, they were apart from one another. Nat took prolonged holidays without pay due to declining health, while his big, heavy cohort logged overtime in other departments of the service as holiday replacement. Bert was a northern man, and, in the heat of summer, he could not sleep and his appetite diminished. But his weight remained constant and this gave him much to ponder. He consulted a surgeon with the mannerisms of a pimp about an operation to cut away a mass of fatty tissue from around his midriff. The surgeon promised a miracle, and Bert talked about it at work, to the sarcasm and frightening comments from Nat and the others.

"My cousin's friend had that done. Then she ate cabbage soup and got bloated with gas and the seam where they'd sewn her together tore open and her guts spilled out all around her."

"Naw . . . leave it alone, Bert. It gives me a feeling of class — having a man of substance on our team!"

From active work in law enforcement to mornings of follow-ups on complaints concerning family altercations, accidents, missing persons the weeks had led on into years. And the once ample cars in which they drove were now becoming smaller, shorter, more difficult to get in and out of — one man having to lift his knees with his hands against the deepening rigidity of arthritis, the other having to push his rotund belly and fold it around the dashboard, pressing ever closer on him with the passage of time. They no longer stopped to chase an escaping youth running out of a drug store with a shampoo bottle in his hand and a pursuing pharmacist close on his heels. They would both simply chuckle and silently wish a painful and debilitating mid-life illness for the thief.

Bert's wife had left with a younger man so many years ago the memory of her face and manners had become vague to him. He was a carpenter, who had come to the house to install some kitchen cupboards. A week later, he had left Bert with the new cupboards and taken off with his wife and small daughter. Bert remembered being shocked and saddened, for, in some way he could never explain to himself, the whole affair had trivialized his life — reduced his sexuality, love, home and family to the value of seven feet and nine inches of stained pine kitchen cupboards, which he painted over in yellow enamel.

Nat's wife died a lingering and painful death. His children, a grown daughter and son, had become estranged from him when, no longer able to tolerate her suffering, he had her committed to chronic care at the cancer ward of the general hospital and then stopped visiting her, because he knew he would lose his mind if he was to continue witnessing her decline, mentally and physically.

"No person should have to do that," he confided once in an unguarded moment, when his morning in the car was darkened with regret he could not keep to himself.

Bert had no idea what he was referring to, so he simply and agreeably said — "There's different jobs for different people, I guess . . ."

Neither man had seen his children in years, nor had the children made any effort to see them. They had become like aging bachelors — worried about health and embittered over real and imagined ingratitudes. Caged in ever-smaller cars on their way to wife beatings, window breakings, runaway children, boys in men's bodies threatening to end it all — all the scourings at the bottom of the human cauldron. No surprises and no victories. Only short glimpses of urban poverty and desolation of the spirit.

"I'm getting too old for this," Nat had complained only twenty minutes before. "I've heard of this gray-haired lady and her crazy son before. Nobody knows what they eat . . . or where they sleep. Their house never looks lived in. Harmless kooks, I guess. But people get suspicious, so every once in a while somebody calls in complaining."

"Shit, it's a job. I don't worry about such things. The world's full of kooks and crazies. I kind of see myself as caretaker of

413

the loony-bin!'' Bert replied, and laughed, his enormous stomach jiggling.

Caretaker of the loony-bin . . . Nat pondered, his brow furrowed in displeasure. This crap-sack considers himself superior in some way to what jumps in front of this car or runs down the street with stolen loot in its paws. What would happen if someday he got the upper hand? He can barely read, he can barely write, and what there is of his brain is stuffed with scatalogical jokes. If I asked him what he thought of the *Brandenburg Concertos*, it would remind him of some joke . . . and yet he considers himself a caretaker . . . of the human loony-bin!

The explosion at the top of the dark stairs was a crackling rupture in their order of time, duty, predictability. It all happened within a second — the door thrown open, its pale, flat panel illuminated by an unseen light. And on the panel, an enormous, grotesque painting of female genitals in lurid reds and purples with bristling dark pubic hairs painted in brush strokes thick as a mans' finger. Nat saw the thin youth step out on the landing, the shotgun clutched in one bony hand, his shirt out of his trousers and opened at the front. The grey woman, barefooted in a shapeless grey housecoat, came after him, her hands flailing for the shotgun. The youth pushed at her shoulder, pushed hard, and she fell backward into the room.

One step above Nat, Bert stopped and turned his head to see where his superior was on the stairs. Then he made a move — the last move of his life, throwing his massive body in front of Nat in the same split second as the shotgun thundered above them in the narrow stairway. Hurled backwards, Bert's head struck Nat in the mouth, spattering him with flecks of blood and sending him tumbling down in an agonizing, wrenching fall.

As in a dream that came and receded with the measured rhythm of waves on the seashore, he heard Bert somewhere in the darker edges struggling for gurgling breath, then sigh ''Shit . . .'' Then silence.

Raising his head, Nat peered through swollen eyes down the dim hallway, through the open door, into the snow outside and the small car parked in the street. The small car into which it was increasingly more painful for him to enter.

Diary Of A Small Person

With the American bombing of Libya, a disquietude settled over his life. He had a car, a comfortable apartment, a good wardrobe of clothes, the beginnings of a comfortable relationship with a girl he knew, a few close friends. His job with the customs office was secure and promising.

In his diary, he began to dwell on his malaise, wondering if perhaps it was all too much, resulting in a deepening unhappiness he had never experienced before. He resolved to rid himself of his car, as he seldom used it due to fuel and parking costs. He considered selling the car, but on a sudden, irresistible whim, he offered it as a gift to a friend. The friend refused at first but, under urging, finally accepted it.

He bought a bicycle. Then he assembled much of his clothing and took it as a donation to a thrift shop. He began to question his relationship with his girlfriend and would not join his friends for their end-of-week dinners and get-togethers. He then gave his bicycle to another friend and began first walking to his destinations, then running. He considered running better for his health.

He began to examine his dietary habits and began reducing the amount and variety of food he prepared and ate.

The nature of his friendships changed when he had his telephone disconnected and could not be reached easily. They came around, but finding he had covered the windows of his apartment with wrapping paper, their visits were darkened by suspicion and distance. They began asking him peculiar questions he heard but did not understand.

He began introducing paper into his diet. At first, he would moisten and nibble on a bit of typewriter paper. Soon, he was eating half and then whole sheets of shredded paper, while reducing the amount of vegetables and protein he ate. And it was then he began seeing angels and conversing with them. One of the angels was the daughter of Colonel Gadaffi, killed in the American air raid on Tripoli months earlier.

Obsessed with this vision, he began looking up his friends and telling them of his experience — what he had seen and heard. His friends now turned very distant. His girlfriend fled on foot down the street on the occasion of their last meeting.

He did not resign his post at work. He simply stopped going to work, until one day, the friend he had given his car to and the other who had received his bicycle came to his apartment in the company of two medical attendants. He did not resist as he was escorted to the waiting ambulance. Instead he talked warmly of the last entry in his diary, explaining how he now felt at peace with the world and with himself, having finally understood the explanations of the infant angel on the matter of how figs mature at odd times during the summer.

THE APARTMENT

"Over here we keep the grey rabbits. Soft as silk in the fur, and with meat that melts in your mouth!" He smacked his lips in the manner of one who knows of what he speaks, then he gently tapped the plywood door of the rabbit barn with the tips of his fingers. Turning, he grinned.

"We can't look in and disturb them today, they're busy making more little rabbits at this time of year," he said, and winked.

"They're busy doing that any time of the year. They're horny rabbits that we got," added his wife, and she giggled girlishly.

The bank loan officer blushed. He was a young man, the son of a shoe merchant, and not familiar with or appreciative of country humour. Nor of wide-buttocked women who bandied such reflections with such ease. He looked back at the grey house on the hill, with its shingled and weathered exterior — a rangy acacia tree beside it adding to rather than diminishing its gloom. His eyes wandered down to the hollow and the first of many outbuildings, the lean-to sheltering mowers and small garden equipment and tools. Then the first of many buildings with identical plywood doors held in place by utility hinges and clasps. The chicken barn, the feed barn, the pigeon barn, and this — the rabbit barn with its contingent of grey rabbits that could not be interrupted in their mating. What arrangements do they have, he wondered — are they paired for life? Or do they do it mother to son, sister to brother, father to daughter.

Suddenly, without warning, he began to laugh. The wide-hipped woman turned to him, smiling and nodding appreciatively, and the man reached over and slapped him on the shoulder.

"Yes sir, Eddy," he said. "In farming, even screwing can be profitable if you're on top of it, as we are . . ."

Eddy? He hadn't given him permission to call him by his first name. Even if he'd asked, permission would not have been given. Not on a first visit. Yet why was he laughing like a country bumpkin in these surroundings of manure stench, unpainted buildings and animal sex for profit? In one brief visit on behalf of the bank, he had become like the humping rabbits behind the plywood door, chortling with mouth open and nose running. Where was the dignity of his bank desk with the gold-lettered sign reading, "Edward F. Robinson, Loan Officer"? To be called Eddy by this toothless oaf standing in front of him and his nodding brood-mare of a wife? Nonsense. Permission to be called "Eddy" withheld.

But he couldn't stop laughing.

"Yeh, it's funny alright, Eddy. Those rabbits doing it in there and us standing outside like this. Kind of like waiting for the restaurant to open . . ."

He looked back to the house, turning his body away from them. He would leave and return another day to complete his assessment of their net worth. By then the rabbits would have whelped . . .

"You think we'll have any trouble getting overdraft privileges? Taxes are coming up, and we'll need some fresh feed for the laying hens . . ."

The words had a chilling effect, and his laughter subsided. He turned to the man and his wife, who now held a metal bucket in her hand. Both of them were staring at him quizzically.

It was then he noticed one remaining small building beyond the rabbit barn.

"What's in there?" he asked, pointing to the plywood door, identical to all the other barn and outbuilding doors.

"That . . . oh, that's the apartment. Liza's father lives in there. The old man had a stroke . . . couldn't hear or speak after that, so we figured it would be nothing to fix up a place for him with us . . ." The man scanned the sky, searching for further explanation, and then he added softly. "Next to the grey rabbits, with fur like silk . . ."

"But . . . that's a barn! In the barnyard!"

This time she spoke for the two of them, moving between him and her husband, switching the bucket from one hand to the other.

"You want to put people like him into an old folks' home? Is that what you want us to do with our folks? After they raised us good and took care of us? He's happy in there. He'd tell you so himself if he could speak! We couldn't take her as well because she smokes and might set the place on fire. But not him. He's no bother at all."

He moved away, walking backwards from them, his eyes fixed on the locked clasp of that last building. His mind conjuring images of a voiceless old man trapped in his own infirmity. Beyond reach, beyond help from anyone.

"Hey, Eddy! If you think the old fellow's another liability we can't afford, you're wrong." The farmer came towards him, his arms gesturing with assurance. "He came with money enough to keep him if he lived to be a hundred. He sold his house before he came here, and houses were priced pretty good four years ago."

The loans officer walked backwards almost to the house on the hill with the rangy acacia, its branches bare and dark in the late winter light. The two owners of the place followed him — she with her wide-buttocked waddle, bucket still in hand. And her husband, rangy as the acacia tree on the hill beside the house, his overalls and outsized boots stained with pale paint from seasons past.

"Eddy — let's go in the house and talk this over, okay? I don't want you to feel pissed off about anything. No need for that, okay?"

He tried to wave them back — away from him, with a motion of his hand. Nothing they said made sense to him. His eyes darted over and around that last barn. He saw no windows or chimney for a heating installation. The rabbit and the chicken barns had screened windows and metal chimney stacks to ventilate gas heaters inside. But the last barn had none.

Retreating uncertainly, he imagined himself back in town, in the bank. Explaining to the general manager of his branch his fears and reflections . . .

"They waited for me on arrival at their house. There was a scent of freshly baked bread. They left me . . . she left me . . . in the kitchen while she went to a back room for water for tea. Her husband was outside somewhere. On the table in the kitchen was a sleeping cat. The largest cat I've ever seen . . . the size of a small dog. There was a plate of cookies beside the cat. I reached for one, and the cat flicked its tail . . . and . . ."

"And what, Mr. Robinson? Get a hold of yourself, man. What did the cat do?"

"The cat farted, sir. A long I-don't-give-a-damn-fart. And then he raised his head and looked at me. I put the cookie back on that plate and left the house . . ."

"A loan officer in our branch — intimidated by a cat's fart? Did you all hear that?" And in his visions of anxiety, he saw the manager turn to the tellers and the accountant, his questions hanging like an anvil in the still cavernous hall of the bank. The tellers — those crafty bitches who always sided with management when one of their own was being ridiculed — cocked their eyebrows in surprise and clucked disapproval at his performance in the incident. The manager now turned to him, cold smile on his lips.

"And what, pray, was the state of their affairs — other than their possession of a cat with filthy habits?" he demanded.

"There is a man . . . an old man . . . in their possession," he blubbered, "He lives in a barn. He sold his home and gave them his money . . ."

"Okay — now we're cookin' with gas! Now we're talking money. Farm stock like cows, rabbits, horses, pigs can develop diseases and die. But money is something else, no matter what conditions it comes with. Money doesn't die. It merely changes hands, and that's what I want to hear about. Not about your farting cats and a goddamned cookie you never ate. Come into my office, Eddy . . ."

And in his gathering delirium, Eddy saw himself pore over notes and projections in the manager's office — all of it having to do with the mute old man he had never seen. And a resolution was reached to provide a loan to the man and his wife.

The same man and wife who followed him now, slack-jawed and worried, as he walked past their house with the rangy acacia tree and to the safety of his car on the far side of the farmyard.

DEAR YOUSEF

It was three o'clock in the morning, darkness outside my window and a cold rain drumming on the roof when you called. You had telephoned to speak to me of the commission exploring the possibility of war criminals residing in our country, and of that grotesque man they called Ivan the Terrible, who faces trial in Jerusalem as a war criminal from the death camp at Treblinka. Let us speak of these things in some order, for the voices of the living and the dead give me no greater peace than they give you, dear friend.

I am older than you by a considerable number of years. Yet the fears and passions which compelled you to call across a long distance in the dead of night cannot be dispelled, or lessened in their haunting pain, by anything I have learned or know about human nature. So in this way, I feel responsible for your pain and guilty for not being able to help you make sense of what remains senseless and beyond normal human comprehension. You and I are not evil men, and so the evil that lingers and bewilders, because it still goes largely unpunished, is beyond our understanding.

But there is a difference between you and me, and though you did not speak of it, I know it was paramount in your mind — perhaps the very reason you reached for the telephone and dialed my number on that cold, dark winter night. There are people now travelling about the country, raising money for the defence of the man they call Ivan the Terrible. They will not come to me. But they will go to you, and even though you are unemployed, you will contribute money in the amount they suggest, for your people were slaves, and mine were not . . .

You will contribute the money they demand, and you will remain helpless in your own absence of reason, compassion and rage. For none of these will exist for you in their presence, and in their argument that our race is threatened by events in Jerusalem, and the mutterings of some who know far more than they are willing to divulge. That you yourself reflected when you cried out to me on the telephone — ''They say in the commission report that only a few dozen are possibly guilty and enjoying refuge in Canada. They lie! They are still protecting the guilty ones, and I can do nothing about it!''

There is nothing *to* do that might ease the sufferings of the past. They will remain to the end of our days, and there is nothing we can do to change the silence of those who fell. Or the conditions of your origins, friend, born to a people swept away from familiar villages and fields by the fascist invaders to work as draught animals in their factories, mines and farms. And knowing the foreign fascist armies did not accomplish this alone, they were helped by native hirelings who had a new job to go to. Some of our countrymen were even given uniforms, to provide them with a visual distinction they could not attain among their own people in peaceful times. A few were given guns and increasing opportunities to shoot their countrymen in service of alien occupiers, attempting to reverse the course of history back to primitivism. They shot — often with indifferent aim, for which they compensated by increasing the volume of executions. These were carried out in the service of a mystical and romantic history that never existed — of a god and church few understood — of a master race in whose shadows hooligans felt warmth and acceptance.

Even though I am distanced by geography and birth from direct contact with the madness of those times and events, I too had a family member who became a morbid village gangster in service to the feudalists. So in these times, dear Yousef, I also wake in the dead of night and reach for my telephone. But I dial no one, for outside of yourself, I know nobody in that way. And I intend it should ever be so . . .

The long nights and short, cold days of slavery and feudalism have largely vanished from this earth. Yet *I*, and you, who cross continents in hours in jet aircraft, who create works of dignity in art using computer technology, who dress in the colours and fashions of our time on this planet, are haunted by recurring images from previous centuries. You were scarcely born, and I was a boy, when the last knights of darkness were hacking human flesh assunder in villages and towns where we might have lived. They were hacking and gouging that flesh and spirit in an effort to return history to a millenium long gone, when a democratic ideal meant death. When it was unthinkable to consider serfs capable of writing books, or bootmakers leading great armies of people into war against invading khans, sultans or führers.

The invader has always found his willing lackey — the morbid village gangster with such low self-esteem that only dominance, achieved through the death of others, gives his life misguided purpose and definition. Certainly, this is human scum scarce worthy of more than passing notice. But herein lies the danger. For given the opportunity to attach themselves to bigger forces than themselves — forces which provide ample support to all manner of local madness, prejudice and hatreds — this half-life takes on monstrous proportions from behind the barrel of an executioner's rifle or the lash of torturers who would reduce all human dialogue to moans and pleas without dignity and without redemption of the spirit.

Whether the one they call Ivan the Terrible really *is* now locked away in a Jerusalem prison, the person who committed the acts ascribed to him is a buffoon. And there *does* remain some doubt — a doubt which you ignore at peril of becoming the very thing you abhor. He is not the product of any single race or culture. He is little more than a handmaiden of fascism, who would, in time, have been slaughtered

425

by the same masters he served with such enthusiasm, for his usefulness was limited, even to them. He created nothing and he decided nothing, other than to choose whether he would wear a shirt or go shirtless into that hell where he greased some machinery and then entered the killing ground where he added to his new reputation — that of a mass murderer of imprisoned and helpless victims brought together for their final moments into the proximity of this shuffling, grinning caricature of a man, who could suddenly strike quickly and fatally, fuelled by some dark, strange energy.

He groans and turns in his prison cell, and you and I wake with a dim, distant premonition of horror. Somewhere deep in the recesses of our memory of night, a monster stirs but does not wake. His friends, awake in different countries and climates, fan out in search of money for the one they will not, cannot, abandon. We also stir, and reach for the telephone to call and speak to one another. But the gesture is frozen in mid-motion. It is impossible to transfer the nightmare to a conscious, waking act without creating further duress. The stirrings of the monster will in time bridge the nightmares and the wakeful awareness that something is wrong in the world we inhabit — that a long shadow chills the places where we stand, scanning the heavens for light and warmth.

A monster stirs but does not waken, and it no longer matters if Ivan the Terrible inhabits this obese, aging body or some other. Possibly he moves from this body to another and another — a hundred and a thousand times over and over, depressed and infuriated with the aging and diseased tissue he must now make his home, for the days of his jubilant evil are over. The earth which he turned into a graveyard, heaving and haemorrhaging with pools of blood, now sprouts fields of wheat and orchard trees that dim the memories of hell. Like all things on earth, the horrors age and fade into oblivion. Only the good is cherished and recalled, with a love and tenderness that ever resurrects and preserves what is worthy. The abhorrent remains to be punished where it can still be punished.

Otherwise, it is discarded among the pebbles of history, to be walked over as footpaths of small consequence.

For that which creates nothing is worth nothing.

In our people's earlier history, there was another, earlier Ivan the Terrible, who brutalized and maimed flesh and spirit. Yet he was also touched by a dark splendour, which gave life, through his artisans, to monuments of beauty which became the heritage of ordinary people. Because they were worthy, the monuments he initiated are cared for to this day, and much is forgiven of the violent excesses of the remainder of his nature.

But this monster, which wakes us in the dead of night, created nothing except death and horror, and this lingering wakefulness which haunts into a half-century after the events of the war, which enabled him to roam a once peaceful countryside hacking and burning willy-nilly. The death count at his hands mounted quickly into hundreds, thousands, tens of thousands — and, finally, millions — meeting and exceeding even the casualties of the great battles in that war. Death in conquered lands became a fascist industry, with its necessary call for transportation, housing, fuel — and funding for the processing of by-products such as human hair, dental gold, phosphate fertilizer. It is a chilling thing to consider that such activities could be carried on as ''normal'' work, with fixed hours of labour, time off from carnage for meals, rest breaks, business meetings, etc. Such labourers might conceivably even take advantage of the odd free telephone at the murder factory to place a call to their wives and families. And the operators of these factories walk out into the world with no sign on their faces or their bodies to tell of their undertakings. No stench, no smouldering flesh, no demons peering into sunlight from their eyes. They dress, converse, laugh and walk like ordinary men.

''They still protect the guilty ones, and I can do nothing about it!'' you say to me in a voice hoarse with fatigue.

''Then stop worrying about it,'' I try to comfort you. ''Let them lie. What is done is done. And the war criminals are no threat to you or to me.''

427

"But they are!" you counter with vehemence. "They threaten me by preying on my fears of what I do not understand. As you said — they will come to me for money I do not have to defend a war criminal. And I will give them money I do not have, for I am defenceless against their reason."

Indeed, you are. And again I lower my head in shame, for I should be able to protect you as a friend and fellow-artist. But I cannot. For the pain of the electric arc which throws lightening backward in time has speared you, as it speared and carried away your father and mother. I reach to take hold of you, but you slip out of my grasp, your hot flesh quivering with the humiliation of what it was to be a free man of the twentieth century stripped of all by Nazi thugs in grey and black, and reduced to slavery. No one returns from that experience intact. I know that, as do you . . .

But did the people in our government understand this outrage when they were asked, and agreed, to provide shelter to war criminals for the ugly business of gathering resources for the cold war to follow? The enemies of humankind in one season became the defenders of our moral values in the next. Former slaves and inmates of death camps saw faces on the street they could never erase from their wartime memory. Once more, the monsters lived and thrived, prowling the avenues of peaceful cities, their shadows clattering like iron wings over the bruised and tortured sensitivities of decent people.

"Where is the justice in all this?" cried your father. And when the killers turned to him, attracted by his protest, he cringed and drew back into his doorway, no longer certain there was a law to protect him, if it allowed the monsters the freedom of the streets, banks, and public institutions. A law which allowed freedom for monsters to charge him in the courts for defamation of their names. And as your father burned with self-contempt for cringing from them, they laughed the laugh he remembered from the camps — the laughter of last resort, falling into the abyss and pulling entire races and continents with them in a mystical dementia of power and destiny in the service of warlords and distant men of great wealth, of whom they knew nothing.

It is these men, dear friend, these distant monster-makers we must be on guard against. For it is they who make the Hitlers, the Maroses, the Pinochets, the Samozas, the Bothas of the days we knew and know. And they will not be called from the shadows to account for the harm they do to humankind, earth, forests, water, skies. For they are nameless, well-fortified behind barricades of legal paper that leads nowhere in the quest for responsibility. For they are the poverty-makers, the assasins of the spirit, violators of the nights that should be restful.

At three o'clock in the morning, with a cold rain drumming on my roof, you call me on the telephone. You call me, and the conversation we both know never happens. But it lingers in the space between us — your need — your plea for sanctuary in my home and life. For in slavery, they robbed you and yours of that most private core of human dignity, without which true life is not possible. A man whose spirit has been taken in this way by another, lesser man, must rise again through the flames and agony of hell for recovery and redemption. It is easier for the spirit to face death than that kind of humiliation. It would be easier, if there were time for choice. But there seldom is. The machines of war roll over the horizon, and under clouds of smoke, villages, fields and towns fall. In a very short time, collaborators are in place, pointing out people, houses, places of work and recreation which are surrounded and overwhelmed. Single people and families are led away. Those who resist or attempt flight are shot or beaten to death. In confusion and pain they reach for what is useless and leave behind all the best of life as they are led and pushed out into the frost and into the backs of trucks and other transport vehicles.

"I never praised the Soviets — my neighbour did!"

"Long live the Third Reich! . . . My uncle's wife was a German woman!" shouts another as he lurches to embrace the gestapo officer in the rear entrance of the truck. He is returned to his place with a blow from a rifle butt, which breaks off all his front teeth.

Nothing of value except life itself remains, and small groups reach and hold to each other for this warmth and comfort. "What will become of us? Where are we going? Why are our own people doing this to us? . . . The one who broke Osop's teeth and the one behind him are boys from the next village . . ."

The doors close into darkness and the vehicle shudders as it moves forward. When the doors open next, it will be on an altered world, for they will be slaves — owned body and soul as sub-humans — to dig in dangerous mines, clear collapsed sewers, and carry sacks of turnips and potatoes as draught animals when the transport system of the master race breaks down or is curtailed for lack of fuel. In the new order and this foreign landscape, slaves are less valuable than motor alcohol or gasoline.

A monster stirs but does not waken. He dreams of thirst, for his body has yet to adapt to the unaccustomed warmth and dryness of the country of his trial as a war criminal. He dreams of thirst and nothing more, for his life was never complicated. He executed the orders of his masters well, killed with vigour, and never allowed it to interfere with his appetite or digestion. He took some pride in sensing that his masters in some way feared him. He recalled some of them turning away or leaving rooms wherein he maimed women. They marked his travel documents with instructions he be shot if he deviated from travel routes to which he was assigned.

This made him aware they feared him, and this pleased him. For those who feared him were the thin-faced Nazi clerks he secretly detested. When had they last cracked a skull in fragments with a club? Or squeezed confessions of previous resistance to the armies which showed the Slavic peasants, Jews and Gypsies what war was all about! Confessions that sometimes required a bit of business with two fingers in the eye before they sang. And then they sang like meadowlarks, even the most hardened old bolsheviks who now tried to hide their pasts behind claims to another identity, another race. He, who did all the work that must be done, could smell out a Jew in the dark. Or point out a Gypsy in a crowd with his eyes tightly shut. As for those who turned against God and their betters, these were, sad to say — all the others. Even his mother, were she alive now, deserved to die . . .

The monster dreams of thirst. And fluttering past his dream are fragments of daytime conversations with his advisors saying he would be acquitted, and that he could make much money by writing a book on this sorry mess. This fragmentary thought of wealth makes him groan with pleasure, and he slowly turns in his bed, and he grins towards the ceiling in the darkness, his eyes shut.

At this moment there is a silence between you and me on the telephone. For the casualties of horror linger on, with victims frozen in a time of mental rearrangement. A misguided, foolish uncle of mine wandered through the forest, a Nazi rifle on his back and his mind fevered by a mad cultist's vision of his homeland governed not by people but by warlords emerging from the caves and swamps of the Carpathian mountains.

A Red Army patrol stumbled on him on a forest pathway. He moved quickly to loosen the Nazi rifle on his back, and the boy soldier facing him, who knew nothing of forest demons (for he was from the city) cut him in two at the stomach, with a burst from his machine-gun . . .

And in the same silence you recall a brother searching for his lost manhood, taken from him in a slave transport truck in childhood, searching for his loss in drink and fistfights. On a hunt beside a northern river, he leaves his sleeping companions and takes his life beside the icy water. A rifle shot echoing through the night, and his spirit is finally freed of the pain suffered at the hands of monsters long ago and far away . . .

Dear Yousef, these are the things we try to protect and spare our children from knowing too much about, for the wakefulness and dread must end with us. To tell about it once is important. To help history make the proper moves for justice and retribution is also important and an obligation to respect. But to dwell on horror in the gloomy chambers of our tormented memory brings no benefit except madness. And that would be a victory for fascism long after it was broken on the anvil of battles that touched us all and redirected human destiny for centuries to come.

These are dust-pan sweepings, Yousef — these remnants of war criminals who remain — that, and nothing more. I begrudge, as do you, money being spent on throwing light on them, even when that light is dim and inadequate for what we must consider. I begrudge their claim to pensions for the aged, after they have aborted life in its prime for millions who never lived to see old age. I begrudge them access to museums, highways and restaurants where normal folk rest and travel in their normal lives. I begrudge them food, for they can never replace what they struck from reaching hands or mouths of others worthier than they.

Most, I begrudge them the liberty of emerging now and then to throw outlandish lies into the face of history — shaking the black cloak of mysticism and slavery in your direction and in mine, and pooh-poohing with impunity the agony they once inflicted.

"There were no millions destroyed — that's a lie!"

"Me? . . . I never collaborated. Sure I wore the Nazi uniform . . . I had to. But all through the war I fought against them . . ."

"Ay, if we knew then what we know now . . . how different it would be . . ."

We both begrudge them much. But life is a process of learning to live with the best of all possibilities, even those out of reach. More so for you than me, for you were once a slave, and each day of light and music matters more to you.

So, dear friend — let us both remember we are in a time where fewer demons prowl. And the hard, cold rain of winter on my roof wets the earth for Spring. And plagues can be contained if we maintain good health in mind and body.

There is work to do, making songs and dances to celebrate

another conquest over hunger — another human like ourselves sailing into space to touch and probe the planets and the stars for life and truth — another cry from another unexpected place for love and peace upon this planet.

Norma and George Ryga (1985)   Photo: Claire Kujundzic

RESURRECTION

The long sleep ends in spinning shards of light
Arching through the sky like tracers
Fired from sacred armaments beyond horizons
Of this earth.
Such lovely colours now flare with bursts
Of red rage — of cool violets and blues —
The joy of gold and green lighting the canyons
And crevasses of stone. Lighting ribbons
Of moving steel which bind continents
In abundance of cereals and fruits,
Bunker oil and machines to further cut
And peel the granite layers of earth's skin . . .
Another distant crash and myriads of stars
Rise among the tracers, crystals of rare gems
In the finery of ribboned colours
Of the rainbow. And on a hill
Where dead men rest the long night
Of eternity, one rises to his elbow,
Then his knee. Dim eyes turn skywards
And parched lips quiver for a word
To greet the changing time. He sways
As rising cosmic winds with shrill sounds
Begin to bend and weave the coloured threads

Of heaven in an every-changing tapestry.
And in the restless play of image and of light
Momentary ghosts of time slip by
To vanish in a turning, pulsing sweep
Of fresh stars and streamers from the cold
And restless reservoirs of space.
He rises to his knees and sees
Faint tracings form and vanish of times
Gone or still to come — great horses
Pawing wind and cloud with faceless
Armoured warriors on their backs swallowed
By a wall of flame which vanishes with
The vanished horsemen. A cathedral in the sun
And chime of bells announcing harvest
Or approaching war — great northern rivers
Carrying ice to distant seas. Darkened fields
Of people running, stumbling from destruction,
Food and tools bundled on their backs.
Another wash of turning light and lovers
Can be seen beside a garden wall, transfixed
In time through chemistry and soul.
Children in a tree of children, pulling
Swollen plums from drooping limbs to nourish
Cries of laughter in the green and languid leaves.
A horse-drawn wagon with a load of summer hay
And a young boy sleeping in its shadow, straw hat
Covering his face and horses sleeping where they stand.
He points from his knees to the fading image
And hoarsely shouts — "That's me! That's me!
As I once was!"
Long forgotten tears now burn his eyes
And he drops his head, overcome by his own
Vision of a childhood spent with women gossips,
Men smelling of the barnyard and the field —
Of children like himself learning to cut wood,
Turn cereals to bread, mend shoes, mid-wife
Cows giving birth to calves in breach.

435

Love and death as constant as the changing seasons —
Enemies and friends alike worry for each other,
Share each other's triumphs and sad times;
Animals and poultry each with names like Susie,
John and Paul — cared for with tenderness
And only the most loved slaughtered gently
And then fed family guests for the most important
Dinner of the year. All faith is simple —
God is a garish painting in the country church —
God is water in the deep and icy well —
God is a patch of good dark soil or a stroke
of luck in the purchase of a needed horse.
God is a light of mystery and joy in the eyes
Of a girl retreating into womanhood, beckoning
For him to follow. God is darkness
Gathering light . . .
He lifts his face towards the firmament again
Refreshed and grateful for an end to lying prone
On the stony hill of those neglected
Dead — a human refuse heap that would not
Decompose or turn to dust. The fallen ones
Of whom no one spoke. Victims of unexpected turns
In history and ways of living.
These living dead, condemned with blighted hopes
And poverty to purgatory and despair
Which embittered everything — the food they ate,
The homes they could not pay for — bright flowers
In their window boxes which belied deep melancholia
Behind the windows of the house. Children
With half a chance at entry to the throbbing world
Of computer, commerce, politics and art —
Dulled by drugs, ignorance and fear of life
In the onrush of urbanized forests, fields
Beyond forgotten hamlets
Where the mayor and the village fool
Would meet as equals, for one could read —
The other shovelled snow in times of need.

He lifts his face towards the firmament again
To see volcanoes, storms, great fires mirrored
In the heavens, but only briefly, for the rolling
Lights and shadows gave further birth to images
Of times earth remembered. Beasts small and great —
Birds with jaws of dogs — reptiles and armoured fish —
And man, crouching at the roots of mighty trees,
Avoiding dangers of quick death for food. Content
With grubs and lizards, he avoids the fang and claw
Reaching for him. But he observes, and ponders.
He ponders and observes . . .
Rivers boil and rage and then subside. Huge fires
Flare as burning forests, pillaged cities, encampments
Of mighty armies of the centuries
Vanish in swirling vapours that cloud heaven
In forbidding darkness that chill him as he watches,
Wondering why it is his fortune to be witness
To the memories of earth.
He has not done enough to match the imagery
Of ancient horsemen in the clouds, their angry gazes
set on conquest of other lands and peoples —
Followed by the solemn priesthood of magnificent religions
Sowing deeper seeds in earth made fertile
With blood of war and ashes of scorched forests.
Groups of survivors pass in shadows, heads bowed
In weariness and hunger. Fiddlers and dancing players
Garish in their masks follow pain with lively
Pantomimes of triumph over darkness and despair,
Their throbbing sound of hope lift up his spirit
As he cranes his neck peering into clouds which have
Devoured their image and their memory.
He has not done enough — the words burn his lips
As he squints upwards, searching for the vanished
Spectres in the turbulence of a sky rebuilding order
Out of chaos and eternal revolution of the stars.
I have not done enough!
The cry now leaves his mouth

And in his inner eye he sees the reason
For his stricken state — his purgatory of the spirit
And dreadful fall from grace for which the fault
Was his — all his. Between the summer mowing of the hay
In boyhood and the climb up the hill to join the dead ones
So many seasons later, the world has fed and sheltered
His family and him. In return, this same earth asked
For his outrage at Hiroshima — incinerated
On a bright summer morning — Or a cry for Chile
Where the flames of freedom faltered
In a rush of bandits — The torment of Soweto
The fascist slaughter in Shatilla.
I have not done enough, he moans and staggers
To his feet. Frost now falls from the stilled
Heavens and he shudders in his rags.
Nearby, another body stirs, then falls face down
Into the earth. He is alone, chilling quickly
In the icy night of frozen stars and desolated earth
Whose memory now gives pause, waiting for a sign
Of recognition from these damaged gods who failed
In obligations for their lives of pain and splendour.
Then — drawing a fierce breath, his heart ignites
With a long-forgotten fire. Brighter and brighter
It flares, glowing through his skin and clothes.
He cries through parched lips — "Yes — I am free,
Free, free at last! I will go where I am needed.
Tend the sick and wounded — give courage to the fallen . . ."
Spirit now and weightless, he rises into the darkness
On wings he cannot see, hovers for a moment,
Relishing the icy chill washing at his fever,
Then turns and vanishes eastward, to meet
The rising sun. Racing now to meet the dawn —
To join the tragedies and triumphs to come.

BIBLIOGRAPHY OF MAIN WORKS
BY GEORGE RYGA

Song of My Hands, Edmonton, Alberta: Ryga, 1956

These Songs I Sing, Wales, U.K.: Publisher unknown, 1959

Hungry Hills, Toronto, Ontario: Longmans, 1963

Hungry Hills, London, England: Michael Joseph, 1965

Ballad of A Stone-Picker, Toronto, Ontario: MacMillan, 1966

Ballad of A Stone-Picker, London, England: Michael Joseph, 1966

Indian, Agincourt, Ontario: Book Society, 1968

The Ecstasy of Rita Joe, Vancouver, B.C.: Talonbooks, 1970

The Ecstasy of Rita Joe and Other Plays, Toronto, Ontario:
New Press, 1971

Captives of the Faceless Drummer, Vancouver, B.C.: Talonbooks,
1971

Sunrise on Sarah, Vancouver, B.C.: Talonbooks, 1973

Hungry Hills, Vancouver, B.C.: Talonbooks, 1974

Ballad of A Stonepicker, Vancouver, B.C.: Talonbooks, 1976

Night Desk, Vancouver, B.C.: Talonbooks, 1976

Seven Hours to Sundown, Vancouver, B.C.: Talonbooks, 1977

Ploughmen of the Glacier, Vancouver, B.C.: Talonbooks, 1977

Beyond the Crimson Morning, Garden City, N.Y.: Doubleday, 1979

Two Plays: Paracelsus and Prometheus Bound, Winnipeg, Man.:
Turnstone, 1982

A Portrait of Angelica/A Letter to My Son, Winnipeg, Man.:
Turnstone, 1984

In the Shadow of the Vulture, Vancouver, B.C.: Talonbooks, 1985

In the Shadow of the Vulture, Kiev, U.S.S.R.: *Vsesvit* Magazine, 1988

In the Shadow of the Vulture, Kiev, U.S.S.R.: Dnipro, 1988

Resurrection, Kiev, U.S.S.R.: *Vsesvit* Magazine, 1988

The Athabasca Ryga, Vancouver, B.C.: Talonbooks, 1990

Summerland, Vancouver, B.C.: Talonbooks, 1992

George Ryga (1985)   Photo: unknown